Copyright © Tom Field

Tom Field has asserted his right under the Copyright, Designs and Patents Act 1988 to be identified as the author of this work.

This is a work of fiction. Names, characters, businesses, places, events and incidents are either the products of the author's imagination or used in a fictitious manner. Any resemblance to actual persons, living or dead, or actual events is purely coincidental except in the case of historical facts.

Registered IP rights number 4928420270

This book is sold subject to the condition that it shall not, by way of trade or otherwise, be lent, re-sold, hired out or otherwise circulated in any form of binding or cover other than that in which it is published and without a similar condition including this condition being imposed on the subsequent purchaser.

Contact details for the author can be found on

www.therealtomfield.com

On Twitter @therealtomfield

Facebook: Real Tom Field

For Nicole Louise

For the pride you inspire in all you do

Part Two

Traffic

She was dragged into the room by her hair. She was no taller than five two and she was painfully thin. She had been stripped and violated by her transporters en route to the sprawling mansion which was situated in an exclusive part of Beverly Hills. She had entered through the obscenely grand gates, which were painted a rich gold colour, and driven slowly up the immaculately laid tarmac drive which led directly to the mansion doors. No mistakes had been made in completing the drive to the exact specification. The King would not tolerate mistakes; any deviation from specific instructions would result in punishment and the full wrath of his anger. He would view incompetence as a crime against him, and any crime against him would be punishable with the most sickening and unimaginable pain being inflicted. He enjoyed this part of being The King.

She had been pulled out of her room by three men just five and a half hours ago. It was a room that contained only five beds and one chest of drawers. She had begged for another chance as soon as they had burst through the door, her pleas met with a sharp slap to her face before the men laughed as they stripped her. All she could smell was vodka and cigarettes. It was a smell that reminded her of her uncle back home in Albania. She was afraid of him too.

She was shaking, not through cold, but through a fear that ran through every inch of her body. She felt sick and her voice had deserted her. Her tears were clouding her vision and she felt disorientated. The pain of her hair being pulled had long since subsided, and was now replaced by a pain in the pit of her stomach that was restricting her breathing.

The King was sat on his throne waiting.

Literally, it was a throne. He believed it impressed all who saw it. But it didn't impress the girl, as her tears thinned and her vision returned. It terrified her.

She saw the devil.

The eyes of twelve equally frightened and thin girls looked at the floor, refusing to look at her, as she was thrown down like a bag of garbage that had hung around for too long.

Her crime?

She had tried to escape.

Her name was Tatiana.

She was fourteen years old

ONE

Dublin - Ireland

Ryan Ward arrived in Dublin at 4:00pm, an hour before his scheduled meeting with Michael O'Leary. He strolled through the Temple Bar area of the city, casually walking past O'Leary's bar to carry out the standard recon work. The bar was called 'The Site'.

O'Leary was a gypsy. A gypsy who had amassed an eight million euro fortune over three years by trafficking young children from Eastern Europe into Ireland, and then across to the U.K. He had taken over a thousand of these children on the promise of a better life, and introduced them to a life of sexual slavery and misery. He ruled Dublin by fear and brutality, believing he was untouchable; and to a large extent he was, because he had the Garda and the immigration officers on his payroll.

But today Michael O'Leary was not untouchable.

Today Michael O'Leary was going to die, that was a certainty. As much of a certainty as Ward knew that right at that moment, the most deadly sniper in the world would be watching him.

The Optician lined him up in the dead centre of the crosshairs on his scope. He watched him casually walk past the bar and glance towards it without breaking stride. He was just another tourist to the three big guys standing as sentries outside the bar, and to the four men that were clearly visible inside, peering through the windows out onto the street. The bar had big wooden doors which were painted bright green, and three large sashed windows on either side. The whole building looked uncared for. There was an alleyway to the left hand side of the bar, and a cobbled access road which ran down the right, a road which was pretty much out of view from everyone. Ward smiled to himself. The bar could not have been in a better location if he had handpicked it himself. He continued walking for three hundred yards, turned the corner at the end of the street and took out his cell phone. He dialled The Optician's number. Three rings later it was answered;
"Can you believe how stupid this guy must be to have his base in a location like that?" The Optician asked without offering any greeting.

"He's confident no one is brave enough to pick a fight with him in his own backyard," Ward replied.
"That's what makes him stupid," The Optician stated, "How many guys did you count?"
"Seven in total, but I don't know if one of them is O'Leary or not, so let's assume five inside to be safe."
"How do you want to do this?"
"I'll get him outside down the access road and you take out everyone but him."
"And then you shoot him and we are done?"
"I'm going to talk to him first."
"Why bother?"
"Because he needs to understand why he is going to die," Ward said calmly, and then hung up the phone.

When he had asked Charlie 'Dunno' Dunham, his contact in London, to set up the meeting; Charlie had told him that O'Leary insisted on using a knife to inflict pain on people. He understood the psychology of this. Watching someone cut into someone's flesh and slice the life out of them until they were dead, is one of the most sickening sights a person could witness. Ward preferred using guns, mainly because they were a cleaner weapon of destruction. Stabbing someone through an artery was a messy thing, the blood will spray up to six feet at times, and it was impossible to have a knife fight without getting covered in blood.
No matter how much Hollywood had always portrayed it as a glamorous and clean act.
He called Eoin Cairns, who was his MI6 contact in Dublin;
"Hello?" Cairns answered.

"You have the clean-up crew on standby as I requested?"
"Yes," Cairns replied, "They are at the end of Temple Bar and ready to go."
"You have sufficient resources to move eight bodies?"
Silence on the end of the line for a moment.
"Eight?" Cairns eventually asked, almost in disbelief.
"Is that a problem?"
"No. I'll get another team here immediately."
"Make sure they are within grabbing distance of the cobbled access road by five past five at the latest, OK?"
"They will be."
He hung up the phone.

Three days ago he had been in New York hunting a terrorist. The subsequent events had left him feeling more agitated than he was used to feeling because he had held Sean Gilligan, his CIA contact in New York, in his arms while he had died. It was the first time that he had felt personal loss in his life, and it was a new feeling that he was struggling to make sense of. He didn't like this feeling. He thought it might cloud his judgement, or slow his reflexes, and the result of that would likely be his own demise and death. He breathed in deeply and thought about Eloisa Hammond, and he felt a warm rush run though his body. After all, he was here for her. He was here to kill Michael O'Leary because she had asked him to be there. He wasn't working under instruction or orders; even though he knew that his boss, Centrepoint, was plainly aware of what he was doing and who he was with. He was here simply because she wanted him to be there. To him, she was everything that was good in this rotten world. Her work for the United Nations in child

protection had saved thousands of young, innocent lives, and her unofficial requests to him to take out the world's bad guys, were always met with enthusiasm and brutal action. Today, Michael O'Leary would die, simply because that's what Eloisa wanted.
He felt the agitation lift; he was ready to go to work.

At 4:59pm, he was looking directly at O'Leary's three sentries as he approached the bar. They were no more than brawlers, that much was obvious. Probably the best bare knuckle fighters from the gypsy camps around Dublin, hand-picked by O'Leary, but that was all they were. They were smoking cigarettes and paying little attention to people walking past. There was no order to how they were standing, so it was difficult for him to establish who the main guy of the three was. They were dressed in grubby denim jeans, and all wore checked shirts, covering what were once white tee-shirts. Two of the guys had green checks and the other red. The guy in the red shirt was making a punching motion with his right hand, exaggerating his latest fight no doubt.
As he got about fifteen feet away, the guy in the red shirt stopped talking and turned to face him. The other two guys moved, one to the left, and the other to the right of the steps, and they immediately stood upright, pushing their chests out to make them look bigger. Not one of them was over six feet tall.
Now there was an order to them.
"The bar is closed fella," the guy in the red shirt said to him.
"I'm here to see Mr O'Leary," he replied.

All three of them studied him for a moment, his English accent making them curious.

"You have an appointment?" the red shirted guy enquired.

"Yes I do. Tell him Sean Gilligan is here."

"Wait here," the guy said, and turned and walked into the bar.

The other two guys in the green checks adjusted their feet and began staring at him, trying their best to intimidate him and make him feel uncomfortable. They failed miserably. He just smiled at them.

"We don't like English scum, you know that right?" the guy on the left said to him.

"I'm not English."

"You sound it to me. So what are you?"

"It's complicated," he replied with a shrug.

"Are you saying we are stupid? You think we are thick Paddies who don't understand? Is that what you are saying?" the guy on the right asked aggressively, as he started to step towards him.

The guy in the red shirt came back out through the doors and beckoned towards him, signalling for him to come in. He stepped between the two guys in the green shirts and walked up the steps and into the bar, leaving them to continue exaggerating their own latest fighting exploits outside.

The bar was much smarter inside than he had anticipated. There were tables dotted around the floor, with lots of space unused, so that people would not feel cramped sitting down. The walls were painted a nice clean beige colour and the wooden floorboards looked spotless. The bar itself was small, with only a few bar stools spaced out in front of it, and the inside was well lit. It was exactly the type of bar that he would happily take Eloisa to.

In the corner there was a large table. There were five men sitting around it.

Four of them were dressed in red checked shirts with a once white tee shirt underneath, and the other guy was wearing a crisp white shirt, which was unbuttoned half way down his chest, allowing him to display a large, thick gold chain with a cross on it.

This was Michael O'Leary.

O'Leary looked up at him and studied him for a few moments. He was a thick set guy; he had more than likely never lost a fist fight in his life. He had a large number of scars on his face that could only have been caused by the impact that a fist makes.

He looked nasty.

Even without the background that he had on him, he could tell that O'Leary gained great pleasure from inflicting pain on others. He had seen his type many times before.

"Sit down," O'Leary demanded, without making any gestures with his hand to indicate exactly where he should sit, and so he pulled out the chair nearest to him and sat at the table. The other four guys around the table stared at him intensely.

"So Mr Gilligan," O'Leary said, "What can I do for you?"

"It's more a question of what we can do for each other Mr O'Leary."

O'Leary studied him for a few moments once again.

"What can a man who spends most of his time in New York possibly offer me?" O'Leary asked suspiciously. Ward inwardly smiled. O'Leary had taken the bait. He had done his research and read through the electronic footprint that his digital experts, Nicole-Louise and Tackler, had laid out for him. He would know that this man sitting opposite him was someone who moved in the big time, and had amassed a personal fortune that dwarfed his own. O'Leary, like all criminals, would be greedy.
He began his sales pitch,
"I have a contact in Russia who has assured me that he has an unlimited supply of people, particularly children, which he can offer me as part payment for a debt. I'm a businessman Mr O'Leary, and I can see a good opportunity a mile off, so I'm looking for a partnership."
"I don't have partners," O'Leary replied.
"My involvement would simply be as a silent partner. This is an area I know very little about, but my people have told me that you are the king in this field, and as I have no other way of reclaiming the debt owed to me, I'm hoping that we can come to an agreement that suits us both."
"Keep talking," O'Leary demanded.
"I know that you have moved around twelve hundred children over the last three years. My people are very thorough in their checks, as I am sure are yours."
O'Leary smiled at him. It was a smile that indicated a silent agreement that they both understood each other.
"But here's the problem I have," Ward continued, "This part payment of my debt is a guarantee of one thousand Eastern European children within the next twelve

months, and I have too many other interests to be able to put my energies into turning them into hard cash."
O'Leary was now giving him his full attention.
"How many of these are girls?"
"I knew that would be your main concern," Ward replied with a smile, "Nine hundred and six of them."
He could see O'Leary getting excited at the prospect of increasing his fortune even further, so he continued to feed his greed.
"I am owed two million dollars," he said flippantly, "I would be prepared to take the payment in the form of the children for one million dollars of the debt only. If you can turn my one million into two million dollars, then you and I would have a beneficial arrangement for us both."
"That's it?" O'Leary said, "You realise how much money could be made out of nine hundred girls? It seems you aren't a very good businessman Mr Gilligan," he asked suspiciously.
"On the contrary Mr O'Leary, it makes me a very good businessman. You take all the risk, you plan getting them wherever you need to get them to, and in twelve months' time, I double my money for doing nothing but sitting at this table and talking to you."
It was obvious to him that O'Leary was completely sold on the proposition being offered. Now he had to move to the next part of the plan, and get everyone outside of the bar.
"But I have done my research and know that you are both ruthless and thorough," he quickly added, maintaining the momentum, "And I am well aware that

without seeing what I have to offer, then you are likely to run me out of Dublin for good."

"I think you need to understand that the cost of pissing me off runs a lot higher than being chased out of Dublin Mr Gilligan."

"Of course," he replied, "But as a show of trust, I have got three twelve year old girls here in Dublin with me for you to inspect the quality."

"Where are they?" O'Leary asked eagerly.

"They are in my hotel. I can make a call and get them brought to the bar right now if you want?"

"No. We will come to your hotel, I don't want them here."

He really is stupid.

"Where are you staying?" O'Leary enquired.

"At the Westin."

"Great, that's within walking distance, let's go now," O'Leary said as he stood up, "I'm ready for some action boys," he added, grabbing his groin in the process.

The four other guys at the table all stood up and mimicked O'Leary's groin grabbing motion and laughed loudly.

Animals, Ward thought to himself.

But animals with only about one minute left to live.

He headed to the door first and stepped outside; walking between the sentries, and turning to the left of the bar and stopping ten feet down the cobbled access road.

"Wrong way," O'Leary shouted.

"No, it's the right way."

"It's that way," O'Leary said, turning back towards the bar and pointing up the road.

As he turned, O'Leary watched in stunned disbelief, as two silent 7.62mm bullets crashed into each one of the three sentries standing at the steps of the bar. Each one a clean headshot, all omitting a fine spray of red mist out of the back of their heads, the bullets putting each guy on the floor within one second of impact.
The four guys with O'Leary all moved their hands to the back of their waistbands within a fraction of a second of each other, and pulled out identical eight inch knives. Ward was quietly impressed by this. It was like watching a synchronised swimming team in action. He noted in that split second that they were all right handed.
"Next one to move dies," he calmly said.
O'Leary and his men stood frozen to the spot. Five sets of eyes were darting up, around, across and along the street in both directions. Scanning, searching, for where the shots had come from.
"You won't see him," he said.
"You think that you can come into Dublin and frighten me?" O'Leary screamed back at him, "You won't muscle in on what we have here, there are too many of us."
"I'm not here to muscle in. I'm here to end your sick trade. Everything ends today."
"Who sent you?"
He pondered the question for a moment and then quietly said,
"The parents of over twelve hundred children."
He then pointed at the guy standing furthest to the left and a second later, the guy was falling back onto the floor, his face obliterated by The Optician's precise shot. The guy nearest to him lunged forward with his arm

fully extended, his knife gripped tightly in his hand, and he had only moved two strides, when his forward movement was suddenly stopped, by a bullet smashing into the centre of his chest; through his checked shirt and his once white tee-shirt, creating a large hole that was instantly visible, even to Ward ten feet away. The knife left his hand as soon as the bullet struck and shot forward, landing about two feet short of his feet. He bent down and picked it up.

"And then there were three," he said with a smile, staring into O'Leary's eyes as he said it.

He saw that O'Leary was showing no signs of fear and he understood why. His men were nothing to him and they could easily be replaced. He got the feeling that O'Leary genuinely didn't think he was going to die because he believed that he was too valuable, like the elders are off limits; maybe this was some kind of gypsy code, he thought to himself.

"You two," he said, looking at the other two guys, "Would you like to run away and leave me and him to it?"

They both looked at each other. O'Leary glared at them. Ward was enjoying this. It was plainly obvious that they wanted to run, but their fear of O'Leary prevented them from doing so.

"Last chance; put your knives on the floor if you want to live."

The guy nearest to O'Leary dropped his knife immediately. The other guy just stood there, afraid to move. O'Leary glared at them both with pure contempt. The Optician then shot them both through the centre of the forehead.

His work was done.
Ward spotted two blue vans stopping fifty feet away; the clean-up crews were here. Three guys in blue overalls got out of each van and headed towards the dead bodies. O'Leary was clearly finding the situation completely surreal, because he just stood still, opened mouthed.
"I'll give you a chance," he said, "What were you, a bare knuckle gypsy fighter?"
"Look at me you eejit, can't you see I'm not remotely scared of you?" O'Leary replied with a smile, which was then followed by a deep, throaty laugh.
It had always been important to him that when he killed animals like O'Leary, he explained clearly to them what their sins were. He always felt that he owed it to the poor children whose lives these people had destroyed to relay their messages of hate, and for him to see the fear in the eyes of their abusers before they died. But quite obviously, O'Leary had no fear. He was pure evil.
He pulled out his silenced Glock and pointed it at O'Leary's face.
Still no fear.
O'Leary just stared back at him with a genuine smile on his face.
So now it was time to lie,
"You have two sons, Robbie and Shay. What are they, eighteen and twenty two?" he asked, smiling back,
"They are already dead and laying in the back of those vans over there. Want to come and have a look?"
O'Leary's smile vanished and his whole demeanour changed.

"But you won't be able to recognise them," he said, emphasising his own smile even more, "Because I like shooting people in the face."

O'Leary clenched his fists and started to breathe in and out, deeply, slowly and loudly.

"So, your sons are dead because of you. What goes around comes around. Live with that for the next three seconds."

O'Leary let out a scream and lunged towards him. Ward pulled the trigger twice. The first shot hit O'Leary in the throat, stopping his forward momentum and jerking his head back; the second bullet smashed into his right eye, forcing his body back and he hit the floor, his head making a sickening crunching sound as it smashed against the cobbles.

He wasn't smiling now.

He put his Glock back into his waistband and turned around and walked away. Cairns walked towards him.

"Jesus," he said, "You are brutal."

He ignored him as he walked back past the bar, and continued walking up the street until he reached a precinct area full of people, all scurrying with urgency to wherever they were going. He pulled out his phone, wrote a text message to Eloisa and pressed send. It simply said, 'It's done'.

And then Ryan Ward melted into the crowds again and became what he always became.

A ghost.

TWO

Washington D.C.

Centrepoint sat in his sparse office in Washington D.C. with his hands cupped, resting against his chin, his stare fixed on one spot on the bare wall. Paul J McNair, as he was formally known, knew that he had to approach the next problem that he was faced with carefully. It was all very well being the man who controlled the ten best operatives that the CIA and MI6 could produce, The Deniables as they were known, but with that came big risks. The U.S. and U.K. governments had relied on him for over 20 years to carry out the illegal operations that their respective governments could never sanction. They were operations that would often require the elimination of natural born citizens of both countries, and operations that came with complete deniability and knowledge from those who were the public face of politics.
But today, they had given him one of the biggest problems that he had ever been faced with.

On top of that, he was concerned about Ryan Ward. Without question; Ward was the best operative that he had available to him, and he had only ever seen his equal once before, in a former agent who was now coming back to haunt him.

Three days ago, Ward had had been active in New York, on a mission which had earned Centrepoint even more kudos in the upper political echelons on Capitol Hill. In the process of his latest hunt, Ward believed that he had lost a CIA colleague, Sean Gilligan, during the operation. This had affected Ward in a way that he was concerned about and had been compounded by the fact that he had angered him through certain decisions that he had made. What Ward didn't know, was that Gilligan had just been taken off of a life support machine in a New York hospital, and was now stable. But he decided that he would keep that to himself for now.
More worryingly, Ward had told him that when he had confronted the bomber, he was told that his old CIA handler had his picture pinned to a wall, along with nine other people's photos. Someone knew who all of The Deniables were and appeared to be preparing a hunt of their own. But as he un-cupped his hands and leant back into his chair; he decided that part of the problem could wait. Getting Ward back onside and fully committed was crucial right now; he needed him back in The States and fast. The Optician had confirmed ten minutes ago that he was finished in Dublin and that they had completed the elimination of their target; an operation that he had not sanctioned, but had made the necessary resources, such as transport, clean-up crews, MI6 support and The

Optician available, as a way of keeping Ward firmly committed to the cause.

In Dublin, Ward had just sat down in a café and was in the process of ordering a coffee, when his phone vibrated. He finished his order and when the waitress had walked away, he pressed the answer button.
"I trust you have finished there?" Centrepoint said, without offering any kind of greeting.
"You know I have," he replied, "No doubt The Optician has informed you. He always follows your orders to the letter," he added flippantly.
"What does that mean?"
 "Maybe sometimes you get it wrong?"
"Maybe I do. But everything I do is for the bigger picture and to save a lot more lives than we lose."
Centrepoint always made reference to the bigger picture. Ward was smart, smarter than most people in the world; but sometimes, even he struggled to see the bigger picture through the haze of deceit that they lived and worked in.
"I know you are angry about Gilligan but we suffer casualties all of the time. Think of every life you save from now as a tribute to him, but for God's sake Ryan, let it go."
He knew he was right. He always was. He had always looked at Centrepoint as the father he never had, even referring to him as 'The Old Man', to everyone else in his team. He was plainly aware that Centrepoint made more allowances for his insubordination than any other operative, and that he valued him greater than anyone

else. The Optician was always there to protect him and most of the time he didn't even know.
The Old Man always made sure that he was safe.
Right then, Ward felt bad for taking it out on him.
"Yes," he replied, thinking back to the start of the conversation, "I'm done here."
"I need you back here as soon as possible," Centrepoint said, "There is a jet waiting for you right now."
"I'm busy at the moment; I thought I'd do some sightseeing."
"You are in a café drinking coffee. Cairns just called in. He's outside waiting to take you to the airport."
He didn't like it when his movements were planned for him, it made him feel less in control. He preferred dictating his own movements,
"Why the rush?"
"Because we have to stop someone from causing the biggest scandal that has hit the U.S. government for years."
"Who?"
"Have you heard of Andrea Yeschenko?"
Ward didn't recognise the name.
"Should I have?"
"He is the biggest brothel operator in the U.S."
"Russian?"
"Yes."
Ward hated the fact that the Russian mafia had so much control over the criminal activities in The States. He believed that America was becoming a weak nation, who let anyone settle on their soil under the name of asylum, but had in effect, opened the doors for a rise in crime and brutality; that was becoming increasingly out of control.

The way the movies portrayed the viciousness of the Eastern European crime bosses was one of the few things they got right.

"If he is that much of a problem, why don't we just take him out and destroy his empire. It wouldn't even be that difficult?" he asked.

"He has a house in every state and a loyal family of around 500 men," Centrepoint replied, "You know how complex their operations are, by the time we hit one of them, they would have disappeared."

"So, just cut off the snake's head."

"We can't. That's why I need you on it."

"Why can't we?"

"Because he is untouchable."

"Like certain others?" Ward said sarcastically, "Seems you have a growing list of friends you are trying to protect."

"Don't be so insulting," Centrepoint replied, "Our job is to clear up the messes that our governments make and no more than that."

"So you are going to let him live to continue his activities?"

"No. I want you to end his activities for good."

"So why not just get a team of Seals or Delta force to do it?"

"Because it's not that simple."

"It never is with you."

"I am getting a lot of pressure in Washington. There are a lot of worried people here."

"Because they were clients?"

"No," Centrepoint replied.

"Then why?"

"Because anyone with any political value was secretly filmed during their sexual activities."

"How much political value?" Ward asked.

"I'm not sure of that, but it must be Senators."

"How do you know that?"

"Because Yeschenko is threatening one of them."

"People get caught having sex all the time, they recover. There's more. What is it?"

"Yeschenko is not only the biggest brothel owner here he is also the biggest trafficker of young girls from Eastern Europe into The States," Centrepoint replied sullenly.

Ward fell silent. He knew Centrepoint was being smart. By giving him the opportunity to destroy one of the main players in the thing that he hated the most; he would have him well and truly back and focussed.

"And these activities were all with young girls?" he asked.

"Yes."

"I'm not that easy to manipulate. I'm insulted you think I am."

"It's not just a question of destroying Yeschenko and his operation. The key part is the retrieval of the video evidence."

"I would have thought the key part would be rescuing and protecting the girls who are forced into a life of misery?" Ward asked; fully aware that at that very moment, with that reply, he was agreeing to take the operation on.

"Of course it is," Centrepoint replied, suddenly sounding upbeat.

"I'll do it on one condition" he said, "You will let me do this my way."
"And I will agree to that condition with one of my own."
"Which is?"
"Once you have seized all copies of the evidence and have identified who the people are, you do not take any of them out without consultation. I mean it Ryan. I will sanction you to act but I need to make the necessary arrangements before you do anything," he replied, "Is that fair enough?"
Ward pondered this for a moment. He would say yes and do what he saw fit anyway, and so there was no harm in agreeing.
"OK. I'm in. Get me the information sent over immediately."
"Cairns has everything you need for you to read on your way back," Centrepoint replied, "The plane will take you to Los Angeles."
"OK," he said and hung up the phone.

He looked out of the window and saw Cairns parked in a grey Ford. He noticed him looking at him and put his thumb up. Ward smiled to himself. Cairns would be competent as a water boy but would never be a full blown operative capable of making his own decisions. While he was excited about the opportunity that Centrepoint had laid before him and he felt invigorated inside about ridding the world of scum like O'Leary, he still felt suspicious. It was a feeling he couldn't shake. He thought back to his picture being on the wall of a rogue CIA agents apartment, along with what he assumed were the rest of the Deniables, and how when

he had mentioned it, The Old Man seemed almost dismissive. He had always trusted him more than anyone he had ever known and this was the first time that he had any doubt in him.
He tried calling Eloisa but it went straight to voicemail. Another frustration he felt inside. He understood that she would be busy with her work at the UN, but she was as hard to contact as he was at times. He then felt a note of sympathy towards The Old Man and understood the frustration that he felt when he himself constantly ignored his calls.

He finished his coffee and walked out of the café and climbed into Cairns' car.
 "I was told to give you this," Cairns said as he handed him a thick manila file.
He took the file and opened it without speaking.
The first thing he saw was a large colour photo of Yeschenko. He studied it for a moment.
He always looked at the eyes first.
The eyes told him more than anything else about someone. Yeschenko's eyes had evil in them. He instantly knew that he was a guy who knew how to strike fear into anyone. They were dark, almost black, and they were sunk into his face. The next thing that he studied was the face. He always checked for scars, the best indication of someone's past. Yeschenko had no scars. This could mean one of two things. Either he kept himself out of harms reach and left the nasty stuff to the foot soldiers, or he was very, very good and extremely tough. Ward knew instantly it was the latter, as his own face had no scars on it; despite the number of close

combat battles he had taken part in. While the picture of Yeschenko didn't scare him, it made him cautious. He liked that feeling, it kept him focussed and alert and that was when he performed at his best. His focus was interrupted by Cairn's speaking.
"There is a plane waiting at the airport."
"I know," he replied, "Get going then."

It took just under twenty five minutes to get to the airport. Cairns drove straight through a back exit gate and pulled up about thirty feet from a shining, white Lear jet.
"Here you are boss," Cairns said.
Ward looked at him. Cairns was a really likeable guy, but not the sort that he would choose to cover his back. Still, he had been a big help in Dublin and he might need him again, and so he saw no harm in massaging his ego a little,
"As soon as I'm back I will report to the boss how efficient and helpful you were," he said.
Cairns' face lit up, he was visibly proud.
"Anytime you need me, anywhere, get them to inform me and I will be there," he replied with such joy that Ward was glad he had met him, even if his role had only been that of a glorified taxi driver.
"Don't worry, I will," he replied as he stepped out of the car, "And thanks for everything Cairns, you did well," he added, as he shut the car door and started to climb up the stairs to the jet. A young woman was waiting to meet him at the top of the stairs,
"Hello sir," she said in a soft Texan accent, "As soon as you are settled and fastened in, we will leave."

He smiled at her but didn't speak. Five minutes later they were airborne and he opened the file on Yeschenko and started to read.

THREE

Beverley Hills – Los Angeles

Andrea Yeschenko sat on his throne and looked out at the audience that he had assembled. He liked his throne. He had it positioned on an elevated platform, so when people stood before him, they had to look up to him. He was above them, like he was above most people, and they should never forget that in his presence. He looked down at the pathetic sight before him and he felt dismayed that something so insignificant could cause him so much trouble. He didn't like this disgusting creature one bit and he would enjoy what was going to happen next.

Tatiana Sielinski had lived on the outskirts of Tirana in Albania until six months ago. Her mother worked in a factory and her father was a violent drunk who never worked, but instead played the black market, to make a few Albanian Leke, which he would spend on alcohol and gambling. He was a vicious man who regularly beat Tatiana, her mother and three brothers. Eight months ago she had come home from school and her mother had told her that she had managed to get a loan from a man who had visited her factory to send her to America; where she would be looked after by the state and given an excellent education and a put in the care of a nice foster family.

She had left home three days after her fourteenth birthday. She had stayed in a hotel in Durres, on the Albanian coast, before being marched onto a boat which took her to the U.S. The journey had taken almost four weeks. She had been raped over thirty times by the time she was collected from the port of San Francisco and placed in a secure house just outside of Oakland. Her life was a cycle of having to satisfy disgusting men, clean and sleep. Any dissent was met with severe violence by both the paying customers and her managers. Three days ago, she had been in the kitchen; the back yard gate had been left open and so she had made a run for it. She made it to the main street and approached a police car with two cops inside. She explained in her poor English what had happened and was pulled into the sanctuary of the police vehicle.
Only to be immediately returned to her prison.

Yeschenko had received a call that afternoon from his Oakland manager saying the two cops were now demanding a payment of $4,000 a month, double their current rate, and if that was a problem, they couldn't guarantee that other cops wouldn't start snooping around. He reluctantly agreed, and then demanded that this girl who had dared to defy the rules of his house be brought to him for the appropriate punishment. He also demanded that one girl be brought along from the rest of his houses to witness what happens to those who dare to disobey him.

Tatiana lay on the floor crying. She was too scared to look up at the monster sitting on his throne. Yeschenko was an intimidating guy to the strongest of men. To a frail, tiny child he was a monster. He stood around six foot three and wore a sleeveless tee shirt which displayed his heavily tattooed, muscular arms. He had cropped dark hair that was as black as his eyes, and he had a thick neck, which was emblazoned with a hammer and sickle on the left hand side. He wore a thick, solid gold chain around his neck, and on his left hand, large gold signet rings on each finger. In his right hand, he held a large, jagged knife that had a red handle.
"Look at me," he demanded of the young girl. Tatiana kept her eyes fixed firmly on the floor, wrapping her arms around herself, trying to protect what little dignity she had left.
"LOOK AT ME!" Yeschenko screamed.
She looked up slowly.
"All of you LOOK AT ME!" he shouted to the other twelve girls, all of similar age, who he had forced to stand in a neatly formed circle around the centre of the room. Twelve sets of eyes immediately looked at him, joining the eyes of the thirteen men who were also in the room. Now he had everyone's full attention. That was how it had to be. He would accept nothing less.
"Arter, step forward," Yeschenko demanded. A guy who had been standing at the back of the room alone stepped forward. He was a lean looking guy who had virtually identical tattoos to the ones that Yeschenko proudly

displayed. He had cropped hair and a smaller gold necklace, which was clearly representative of where he sat in the organisations hierarchy. His hammer and sickle tattoo was on the right side of his neck.

"Explain to me how this pathetic thing managed to escape and how she almost destroyed my Oakland operation?" he demanded, "And how it is costing me more money to keep the police from my door?"

Arter looked up at his boss, the fear in his eyes now being reflected in the desperate stance that his body was taking.

Yeschenko knew that he was getting ready to plead for his life.

"I'm so sorry Andrea, it won't happen again. It was one of the men; they left the back gate unattended. I have punished him to within an inch of his life and for our failings; we will all make a payment to you every month."

"The money is nothing, we drink more vodka than that in a day," he replied. A comment that resulted in uniformed laughter from the other men in the room. Convincing The King that he was funny was something that they all accepted as part of their role. Yeschenko looked pleased with himself in response to the laughter, "Only to within an inch of his life?" he asked, "You have become weak. You should have killed him for such negligence."

"I will kill him when I get back," Arter replied, nodding his head in eagerness as he said it.

"No need, he's already dead," Yeschenko stated, "My concern is that I have a manager who I trusted, who has now failed me."

Arter looked at Yeschenko and said nothing.
The King stepped down from his throne, walked out to the centre of the floor and stopped next to Tatiana,
"Arter, kneel before me," he demanded.
Arter stepped forward and knelt on the floor.
"Your father was good to my father," he said, "He helped him when everyone else turned their back on him. Do you remember?"
"Yes Andrea, I remember. You have always told me that our fathers were more like brothers."
"So we are like brothers?"
"Yes we are."
"And your loyalty is to me alone?"
"Yes it is brother, you above anyone else."
Yeschenko pulled out a handgun from the back of his waistband and handed it to Arter.
"Blow her brains out and that will go some way to putting this right."
Tatiana froze, she didn't speak, and she just burst into loud cries and put her hands up to protect her face, leaving her bruised and beaten body fully exposed. Arter raised the gun until it was level with Tatiana's face and pulled the trigger.
Nothing happened.
No click, no loud bang, nothing.
Yeschenko laughed a deep, long laugh, which echoed around the room. He walked around behind Arter, bent down and began to speak in his ear,
"You have no trouble killing this vile little creature, but you are afraid to kill a grown man who nearly destroyed part of my operation?"
Arter looked confused.

"You are no brother of mine, you are a disgrace!" Yeschenko spat at him.

"I'm sorry, it will never happen again."

Without saying another word, Andrea Yeschenko lifted his knife and yanked Arter's head back violently by his hair. Without any hesitation, he slit his throat, the jagged teeth of the blade sawing through the gristle in his windpipe in one swift motion. Blood shot out immediately, it spurted forward and covered Tatiana's face and crumpled body, and she let out a deafening scream. It was a scream that was promptly echoed by twelve other high pitched screams.

There were thirteen girls in the room and all of them were crying loudly.

Yeschenko looked at the girl on the floor.

"That was your fault," he said to her, "I have known him my whole life and because of you, I have had to do that."

Tatiana thought back to the wonderful life she had left behind in Albania. How her life there was simplicity and bliss compared to the hell she had stepped in to. She missed her mother and her brothers. Right then, she even missed her father for the first time in her life. She missed her simple house, with no hot running water, and she missed her need to search for titbits of food, just to stave off the hunger. She missed the whole existence that she had once thought was miserable, and she wanted it back desperately. Chasing a new life had destroyed her. She had nothing left inside. She no longer cared what happened to her.

"But you have a value to me," Yeschenko continued, "What am I to do with you?"

"I don't care," she replied.

All of the girls in the room gasped, almost as one voice.
"What did you just say?" he demanded.
Tatiana said nothing.

Tatiana Sielinski never lived long enough to see her fifteenth birthday. Her life ended in humiliation and unimaginable agony. The events were witnessed by twelve other girls, one from each of Andrea Yeschenko's houses. They were then all instructed to return to their place of work and to relay clearly, and with great description, what happens to any girl who dares to attempt to escape from him. They all left the mansion with their escorts, without once looking back.

An hour later, Yeschenko was sitting back on his throne as though nothing had happened. To him, nothing had. Neither Arter nor the girl meant anything to him.
Nothing at all.
He had much more important things to worry about. Like how he was going to use what he had to make more money than he would ever need, and then he could use that to branch out into other areas. White collar crime was definitely the way to go, he thought to himself, and then he wouldn't have to rely on the Arter's' of the world. He picked up his phone and dialled the number in Washington.
No answer again.
He was becoming impatient and angry at the lack of respect being shown by the person he was calling. He would give him one more chance over the next few days and then he would destroy him.

Because Andrea Yeschenko had the ammunition to destroy a great number of people, and if he didn't get what he wanted, he would happily watch from the sidelines as the United States of America went into political and social meltdown.

FOUR

Santa Monica– Los Angeles

Ward stepped off the plane and took in the heat of the July evening at LAX airport. The 10 hour flight from Dublin, which included a refuelling stop in New York, had given him perfect preparation time for planning who he would need on board for this mission. He would contact his usual team members, Nicole-Louise and Tackler, who were his two computer experts, and Martin McDermott; an Ex-Navy Seal captain who had assembled the most effective team of warfare experts that he had ever known. They now operated as mercenaries and most of the time, as his private army. He was aware that he was going to need additional support on the ground and he couldn't think of anyone on the West Coast who he could rely on. He would need to make a call to The Old Man to get the right people allocated to him. But first he wanted to get home.
Ward had three homes; all purchased with money that he had stolen from a corrupt South African family. He had a cottage in London, an apartment in New York and a small bungalow just off the beach in Santa Monica. He had not stayed at the bungalow in Santa Monica for over nine months. He had a housekeeper, a Mexican lady called Mrs Rodriguez who visited weekly, stocked the

fridge up with fresh food and then replaced it with fresher food a week later.
Just in case.
He watched as a smart looking guy climbed out of a Ford Taurus and started walking towards him. Three feet away from him, he extended his right hand for him to shake,
"Hi," the guy said casually, "My name is Colin Buck, I'm your guy in L.A."
He liked Buck instantly. He reminded him of his old dentist that he used to visit growing up in England. He looked in his late forties, stood about five feet ten and had a reassuring look about him. He had greying hair and a moustache that didn't seem to be losing its colour as quickly as his hair. He was slightly built, but Ward knew just by looking at the way that his eyes narrowed, that he would not hesitate putting a bullet in someone if it was required.
"Just don't tell me to floss after every meal," he said as he took his hand and shook it.
Buck looked at him, a confused smile running across his face.
"Where am I taking you?" Buck asked.
"Santa Monica, Ocean Way," he replied as he headed towards Buck's car without breaking stride.
The twelve mile drive took just under half an hour. Enough time for Ward to discover that Buck had been working in Europe for the last six years, on undercover operations, but the Russian mafia had put a contract on him in Moscow and so he had returned home. He was familiar with how the Russian criminals worked and turned out to be an expert on Andrea Yeschenko.

Centrepoint always covered the bases. He stopped Buck a couple of hundred feet from his house. It was a habit that he never changed when he met new people.
"Here will do," he said.
Buck pulled the car to a stop.
"What do you want me to do now?"
"Do you have a family?"
"No, never found a woman who liked me," Buck replied with a smile.
He liked Buck's answer. He didn't want any more orphans in the world as a direct result of his actions.
"Then go home, get some sleep and be back here at 7:00am tomorrow," he said, as he climbed out of the car and headed in the opposite direction of his house. Buck nodded, put the car in gear and drove off.
Once he knew that Buck was out of sight, he turned around and started walking back to his bungalow.
It was situated on the corner of Ocean Way and overlooked the Pacific Highway; beyond that you could see the golden sands of Ocean Front Walk and then the deep, blue sea. The bungalow wasn't as grand as a lot of the other buildings. It had rendered walls that were painted a brilliant white, and a small, immaculate lawn, carefully cared for by the gardener who tended to next doors lawn, yet he had no idea who he was, or indeed, who the neighbours were. He had brought the bungalow for one reason only. He and Eloisa had sat on the beach and watched the sun set. As the sky turned to purple and orange before their very eyes, he knew that he wanted one day to be able to look out of his window every day and see that beautiful sight.

He found the key that he had hidden in a section at the base of the birdhouse fixed to the side wall of the bungalow, opened the door and stepped inside. The interior was as smart, fresh and as tidy as the outside. The entrance hall was spacious, the floor covered in terracotta brown tiles that were eighteen inches square. There were fresh flowers in a vase on a table, which sat under a long mirror on the right hand side of the hallway, courtesy of the housekeeper he never saw, Mrs Rodriguez; a three tier chest of draws made from oak and lightly varnished stood on the left hand side. The walls were brilliant white and the six doors that led into the various rooms in the bungalow were all a light oak colour. He inhaled deeply. He liked this place, but while he felt a semblance of normality whenever he stepped through the door, it still didn't feel like home to him. More like a familiar place. His homes in New York and London were what home really felt like to him.

He walked through to the kitchen and dropped his grab bag on the brown leather sofa that ran along the wall opposite the worktop. He stepped across to the sink and looked out of the window. It was getting dark now, and all he could see were the headlights of the cars driving along the Pacific Highway, the link between Los Angeles and San Francisco. He thought of Andrea Yeschenko for a moment and wondered how many poor, defenceless children he had transported along the highway; a thought that made him both sad and angry. His gaze was broken by his phone ringing. He pulled it from his pocket,

"Nice of you to give me a bit of settling in time," he said as he answered, without waiting to hear the voice on the end of the line.

"There isn't time for rest, we have about four days on this and then Yeschenko is going public," Centrepoint replied.

"Who is putting the pressure on you?" he asked, "I mean specifics like name, position and so on?"

"That doesn't matter. What matters is that you crush Yeschenko's operation and secure any evidence he has stored away."

"I'll find out anyway" Ward said, "I just thought it might make it quicker if we know what we are looking for."

"That's the problem; I don't know what you are looking for exactly, just that there are Senators who are worried."

He was in no doubt that The Old Man knew exactly what they were looking for, but understood why he was holding the information back from him. If he knew the names of the people he was looking for, he would more than likely miss someone who was equally or even more important. He consoled himself with the fact that he had complete faith in him to find out everything that there was to find out, without having to guide him.

Centrepoint spoke and broke his thought pattern,

"The file on his whole operation has been e-mailed to Nicole-Louise and Tackler already and they are working through the digital footprint of it as we speak. Your copy has been securely e-mailed to you as well. I suggest you read it all by the morning."

"What do we know about his operation?" Ward enquired.

"Everything," Centrepoint replied, "He has an 'Entertainment House' in forty five states. They are fundamentally on the East and West Coasts. Six in California, nine in New York, Washington and Boston and the rest scattered all across the country."

He stood still shaking his head. He couldn't fathom how they found it practical to invade a country to protect innocent people from harm, yet ignored it when it was happening on their own doorstep.

"And we just leave him to it so that we can protect a few politicians? Seems kind of wrong, don't you think?"

The Old Man ignored the question and continued talking,

"He has an army of about four hundred and fifty men Ryan; this isn't a small time operation."

He quickly did the math. Forty five houses and ten men allocated to each house. Assuming that they worked around the clock, that would leave five men at a time covering the girls that were living in misery. Ten men at a time would be no problem for the team that he was mentally building in his head as they spoke, and so five would not carry much of a risk at all. The only thing that was worrying him was the geography of the whole operation. America had a lot of space to cover.

"I need transport available at all times," he said, "A jet here and one in New York."

"Already done."

"I need money too, lots of it."

"Already done as well, I assumed that you would be using McDermott and his crew, so there is an initial three million deposited in the account already."

"And The Optician?"

"Where do you want him?"
"Where is he now?"
"He's in Los Angeles," Centrepoint replied.
"You need to get him to New York. I will need him to start ruffling a few feathers on the East Coast to send out a signal when we start this tomorrow."
"As soon as we end this call, I'll give him his orders."
Ward hung up the phone.
He now needed to call Martin McDermott, his most trusted comrade. He scrolled down his contacts and pressed the call button when he reached McDermott's name.
It had only been three days since he had last seen McDermott and his team in New York, but he found himself missing them. The team was made up of the best of the Navy Seals over the last ten years. They were now officially mercenaries working in the private sector, but in reality, they were his unofficial army and just another deniable to the governments.
McDermott was now in his early fifties and Ward dreaded the day that he would decide that he had done enough and wanted out; although that dread was balanced out by the fact that the team was in good hands when that day came. McDermott's son Paul was part of the team, and he was as thorough as his father. He was being given more and more responsibility lately and he was responding very impressively to the challenge. The rest of the team comprised of Lloyd Walsh, the team explosive expert, Danny Wallace, the telecoms guy, Wired, who was the team tough guy that would run head first into any deadly situation, Adam Fuller, who was the team joker and Fringe, who was the calm, thoughtful guy

that every team needs. Together, they were an unstoppable force; a phrase that he always used when referring to them. They were the closest thing to brothers that he had ever had.

"Are you stalking me?" McDermott asked as he answered without offering any greeting.

"I knew you would be missing me by now Martin and so thought I would read you a bedtime story."

"Your stories tend to be nightmares to most people," he said, "Fortunately, we like nightmares."

"Where are you now?"

"We are still in New York. The boys are having some rest and recuperation. What's wrong?"

McDermott listened carefully as he explained about Yeschenko; the politicians and how the retrieval of the video evidence was crucial, so they had to structure a plan of how they were going to get it, rather than go in with all guns blazing.

"Maybe we need to make it look like something else?" McDermott said when he had finished speaking.

"What do you have in mind?"

"Well, we can get our hands on some Kalashnikovs easily enough, so if we hit one of these houses on this side, I'll send a couple of the boys to Kansas or Colorado to do the same thing, and if you get your hands on some Kalashnikov's on your side and do the same, it will look like a Russian turf war. That will move Yeschenko's focus elsewhere and buy us a bit of time," McDermott replied.

He liked this idea instantly. Any distraction for Yeschenko would be a good thing for him and the others.

"I need a base in LA. Do you have one we can use?"
"We have a garage down in the marina. I'll send you the address."
"OK, I like all of it. I'm going to read the file now and I'll send it across to you shortly and you can plan tonight and confirm with me in the morning."
"I've already read it. It's just a question of Kansas or Colorado. I was waiting for you to decide before moving the boys," McDermott said without a hint of arrogance. Ward knew that Centrepoint was always one step ahead. Because of the urgency of the situation, he had provided the necessary intel to McDermott already.
"And has The Old Man agreed your half a million dollars a day?"
"Yes he has, and without moaning too."
"Shame," he replied, "I was going to push him to a million, and as he is so desperate on this one, he would have agreed."
McDermott laughed out loudly. A laugh that lasted a good five seconds,
"You still had to have the last word."
"I know" Ward replied, and he hung up the phone.

He turned on his laptop and opened the encrypted e-mail from Centrepoint. Forty five places meant a lot of ground had to be covered. The data was very comprehensive; addresses of the houses, approximate number of men stationed at each one, flow of customers and number of girls who lived there. It was very, very comprehensive.

He knew immediately that it was too comprehensive. Anything that was this good was normally this good for a reason.

After reading the file three times in two hours, he still had not changed his mind. He decided to get some sleep. He would call Nicole-Louise and Tackler in the morning and get them to verify the information that he had just read. He picked up his phone and dialled Eloisa's number. No answer again. He would call her first thing in the morning. He showered and climbed into his bed, the crisp, clean sheets caressing his body. Good old Mrs Rodriguez, he thought to himself, as he closed his eyes and imagined Eloisa lying next to him.

FIVE

Park Avenue– New York

He was on the phone to Nicole-Louise at 6:00am the following morning. He had slept exceptionally well and he felt refreshed, strong and focussed. Three things that Nicole-Louise most definitely wasn't as she answered her phone, still half asleep.
"Seriously, don't you ever sleep?" she asked as she answered with a clear frustration in her words.
"Not really," he replied, in the happiest tone that he could muster, "I need you to do something for me."
"You always do" she said, still sounding irritated, "How about let me sleep in now and again?"
Ward ignored the question, and her tone, and continued, "You've looked at the file on Yeschenko, yes?"
"Yes I have."
"What did you think of it?"
"I want you to do what you normally do to people like that. The guy sounds like an animal," she replied, her voice softening. It suddenly dawned on her that she sounded very selfish and spoilt compared to the plight of what those poor young girls in the files had to endure, day after day.

"I will, but I need you to verify everything in those files for me. It seems too good to be true."

"That means it normally is too good to be true."

"I want you to rip apart his whole organisation and find out how he gets the girls, who his contacts are, who transports them, and who his customers are."

Nicole-Louise was quiet; too quiet for her, it was unusual.

"What's wrong?" Ward asked.

"The Old Man says that we are to give him the client list and any video evidence we find and no one else, not even you," she replied, with clear awkwardness in her voice.

"And will you?"

"That depends on what you say."

"We will cross that bridge when we come to it," he replied softly, "But please just dig as deep as you can and keep me informed, OK?"

"OK."

"Say hello to Tackler for me."

"You are on loudspeaker and he has just stuck his finger up to you. I think something vexes him," she replied sarcastically.

"You deserve a more gracious man, Nicole-Louise."

Cunningham Park– New York

It was 6:10am and Erida Sufaj was in the bathroom scrubbing the floor of the house that had become her prison. Today was her sixteenth birthday and she was now the oldest girl who lived there. She had left Estonia

two years ago, and had been in this living hell for the past twenty months. The house was beautiful, the type of house she had always dreamed of living in whenever she watched American programmes on TV. It was situated in the more secluded part of New York, close to Cunningham Park. But she did not know that.
She had no idea where she was.
It could have been anywhere in the world for all it mattered. She was getting more worried and anxious with each passing day about what was going to happen to her. In the past twenty months she had seen a large number of girls reach their sixteenth birthday and then suddenly disappear. She was hopeful that she could still pass for much younger than sixteen as her body had not yet fully formed, and she looked no older than most of the girls who she assumed were around fourteen in the house. They were not meant to talk to each other, indeed, if they were found communicating, then they would be punished. All of the men who controlled the house were Russian, and insisted on being referred to as 'Мастер' which was the Russian for 'Master'. When Erida didn't have to do disgusting things with the old, fat, sweaty men whom she had to please, she would be clearing up after them. The vomit she was cleaning up right now was a result of her own 'Мастер', a man that the others called Alexei, drinking far too much vodka last night. After all of the clients had left, Alexei and the other men had been drinking vodka and smoking in the kitchen. She could hear the laughter getting louder as the night stretched into the early hours, and she knew that Alexei would soon be walking through her door demanding that she please him. She hoped it would be one of those nights

when he drank so much that he passed out. She sometimes got lucky like that. Last night, she didn't get lucky. Alexei had come into her room just after 2:00am and stripped naked. His overweight body and fading tattoos were a revolting sight to her, but she smiled and told him he was very handsome. If she failed to do that, he would hurt her internally so as not to mark her for the clients. He had lay upon her and started the act. She quietly prayed that the vodka had not dulled his senses too much and that it would be over soon. She looked up at his ugly face and the way he was breathing heavily and the stench of his breath almost made her want to vomit, but she smiled at him and tried to look completely lost in him to please him. As she always did. After he had finished violating her, he got dressed and said he felt sick. He walked out of her room and slammed the door. She had woken at 6:00am to Alexei telling her to get up and go and clean his mess up before making the breakfast, ready for him and the other men by 8:00am. She was holding her breath as she cleaned up his vile mess when he walked into the bathroom.
"Hurry up and finish cleaning that up," he demanded in a fierce tone. Erida nodded and forced a smile.
"It's your birthday today, isn't it?" he asked.
Erida nodded again.
"Answer me."
"Yes it is Мастер."
"Sixteen today?" he said with a sickening leer on his face, "That makes you legal in a lot of States."
She smiled at him, willing him to turn and walk away. The awful gloating look on his face was scaring her.
"But not in all?" she replied.

"The problem is, the moment you become legal you lose most of your value," he said, "So what do you think that means?" he added, before breaking into a sickening and frightening laugh.

Erida was now terrified. This wasn't the sixteenth birthday she had always dreamed of having. She had always imagined a coming of age party, where she would be fitted out in a ball gown and everybody would come to celebrate her. This birthday was her worst nightmare coming true. It had been compounded late last night when one of the other girls had returned, after being taken away in the early hours of the previous morning, and they were all called into the kitchen. The girl then went into graphic detail of how a girl from another house had tried to escape and she had been brought before a man called, 'The King'. She had explained how first the girls' 'Mactep' was killed by having his throat cut, and that it was The King's own brother he killed. The King had then turned his attention on the girl. At this point, the girl could not speak and she was visibly shaking with fear, but her own 'Mactep' slapped her hard around the face and demanded that she continued. She then explained how this poor girl had her genitals cut with a knife while she was still alive and then her breasts were then removed with the same knife. There were eleven other girls there as well who were all forced to watch this barbaric act. Erida had not been able to sleep all night.

"I don't know what it means," she replied, trying her best to say the right thing to him.

"It means that we will be moving you on."

"To where?"

"We will talk about that later. Clean up that mess and quickly."

Alexei walked downstairs to the kitchen. A strong, black coffee was in order to both wake him and sober him up. Another 'Мастер' was sitting at the table holding a steaming mug of coffee.

"It's still hot," he said to Alexei, who nodded his appreciation and went and poured himself a mug full. He then sat down at the table.

"Erida is sixteen today," he said nonchalantly.

"When are you removing her from the house?" the guy asked.

"About ten tonight." he replied, "The process plant are expecting her then."

"She's been here a while, it will almost be a shame to lose her. Her cleaning standards are better than most of the other girls."

"You are too soft my friend," Alexei replied, "These girls are nothing, they are dirt on my boot, they are just pieces of meat that we bring in and out."

"And tonight, she will become mincemeat," the guy replied, and they both let out a long, loud laugh.

Santa Monica

Ward called McDermott.

"Morning," he said as he answered.

"Morning," Ward replied, "I want you to hit the house near Cunningham Park and then the other........"

"The other is the one in Topeka, Kansas," McDermott interrupted.

"How did you know I was going to say that?"
"Paul and Wired are already there waiting. We can synchronise the time of the attacks and do them together. That will take away their ability to get the word out quickly," McDermott continued.
"The girls have to be kept safe and then handed over to the authorities immediately. Is that clear?"
"How do you want it done?"
"Call the cops as soon as you leave the house and tell them that there has been a gang shooting and they need to get there, that will ensure they will turn up en mass. Then just hide under cover until they arrive and then depart. Get Paul and Wired to do the same," he replied.
"Clear" McDermott said, "What time are you thinking?" he asked.
"8:00am my time," he said, "They wouldn't be expecting anything that early, their guard will be down."
"OK. I will communicate that to Paul and we will commence the attack at 8:00am your time, 11:00am my time, and 10:00am in Colorado, unless I hear any different," McDermott said precisely.
Ward hung up the phone.
It was now 6:30am.
He called Buck's number.
"Hello," he answered.
"I need you to get me something before you get here at 7:00am."
"I was just getting in my car, but what is it?" Buck asked.
"I need you to get hold of two Kalashnikov's for me and urgently. How quickly can you get them?"
"How quickly?"

"Yes."
"You are talking to a guy who has spent the last six years swimming in the waters of the Moscow underworld, so that is no problem."
"I asked how quickly?" he said, not in the mood for cryptic conversation.
"I'm looking at them right now in my trunk," Buck replied, "I always carry three of them. Best rifles in the world. I have two silenced Makarov's here too."
Ward smiled to himself. He liked Buck.
"See you at 7:00," he said, and hung up the phone.

He had one more call to make.
He hit Centrepoint's number.
"You must want something to be ringing this early," Centrepoint answered.
"I want The Optician to visit the small place in Union City and wipe the Russians out. I also want him to use a Kalashnikov."
"So Yeschenko thinks he has a gang war going on?" Centrepoint replied, "Smart move Ryan."
"It was McDermott's idea."
"Either way, it's smart. I like it."
"So can you have him wipe them out at 11:00am exactly? Guaranteed?"
"Yes I can guarantee it. Anything else?"
"One thing, one very important thing"
"Which is?"
"I'm making the safety of all the girls that we rescue your personal responsibility."
"Go on?" Centrepoint enquired.

"I want your word that you will use all of your powers to make sure that when the cops round them up, that there are social workers on hand immediately and that you make sure, no matter what it costs, that you get them all into good homes. You cut through all of the red tape and rush it through. They've been through enough already," Ward replied.

"You have my word that they will all be housed, granted refuge, and will have an educational plan in place within two weeks. Acceptable?"

"Thank you."

"Just get this one right. And tread carefully, we don't know who else we are up against here."

"Meaning?"

"Keep me informed Ryan, all the way through so that I don't come across any of your usual surprises at a later date. OK?"

"OK."

SIX

Santa Monica

At 6:55am, he left the bungalow and walked down the road to the point where Buck had dropped him off previously. He had looked at the list of targets that were included in the file and decided that he and Buck would hit the house in Thayer Avenue, Westwood. He chose that house for two reasons;
Firstly; it was only fifteen minutes away, straight up San Vicente Blvd and then onto Wilshire, and secondly; it made him feel sick to the stomach that these people were operating so close to a place that he called home. He had driven up both Boulevards countless times; totally oblivious to the misery that was going on behind the walls of the beautiful houses, and he had to breathe deeply to suppress his anger that these Russians had been welcomed into his country so easily. Not only did they create untold misery, but they also believed they were above the law.
Today they would discover that there was no law in his world.
Buck arrived at exactly 7:00am.

"Where to?" Buck asked.

"Thayer Avenue, Westwood, do you know it?"

"I know LA nearly as well as I know Moscow," Buck replied as he put the car in gear and started to move.

"The rifles are ready? Locked and loaded?"

"Yes. Plus I also have a couple of Makarov handguns for us to use. Locked and loaded too."

"So what's the plan?"

Ward had no plan for entering the house. He never did. He believed the problem with planning an assault is that you only need one variable to rear its head and the plan went south. He found it more comfortable and beneficial to think on his feet. It kept him more alert.

"No plan yet," he replied, "We will look at the house and then decide."

"No plan?" Buck asked, clearly surprised.

"According to the data, there are only ten guys who work out of that house. That means that there will only be six at the most awake. How much of a plan do you need?"

"It's just a different approach, that's all."

"I like different."

They drove the last ten minutes in silence; the silence only broken when Buck said,

"What number?"

"711."

They drove slowly along the street and passed number '711', Ward glancing at the house while Buck focussed on the road so as not arouse suspicion.

"Drive back up again so I can take one more look and then park the car about thirty yards back," he said.

Buck nodded.

They turned around and drove past the house again. It looked a nice place from the street. No hint as to the shameful acts that took place behind the walls. It was a Mediterranean type house, white with dark, terracotta tiles that adorned the roof. It was raised up about eight feet from street level and had a drive with a relatively step incline, which led around the back of the house to a parking area. It was secluded.

Once the vehicles were up the drive and around the back they would be out of sight from everyone. The front lawn was elevated from the road and immaculately manicured. To the outside world, this would be a perfect place to live. Buck drove past and parked thirty yards along the street as instructed.

"What do you think?"

"I think we will just knock on the door."

"No, seriously?" Buck asked, smiling as he said it. Ward didn't respond. Knocking on the door was the most effective way to get into a building in his experience. He looked at his watch. It was 7:45am. All they had to do now was wait.

Cunningham Park (New York)

Martin McDermott had got to the house on 197th Street, at 6:55am West Coast time. He liked to be thorough. The house was on a quiet street. Despite the fact that it was a large house, at least five bedrooms he guessed, there was

nothing grand or pretentious about it; built with plain red brick and a modest drive running along the side.
He had taken Fringe with him and carried out recon on the back yard, but there was nothing to be seen, as there was a large lean-to that had been erected; no doubt to protect the clients. He had decided that he and Fringe would take the back and Fuller and Wallace would take the front. The downstairs windows all had the blinds pulled, making it impossible to see inside, so establishing how many guys were in there was difficult. The file that Centrepoint had sent to him had said there was a crew of ten guys that managed the place. Even if they were all there; ten Russian guys against him and three of his guys would be a mismatch in his favour. He had no concerns. He looked at Fringe,
"What do you think?" he asked.
"I think that they haven't got a prayer."
"Just remember, keeping the girls safe and alive is the priority here, shoot the Russians to kill, we don't need to question them," McDermott reminded him.
"I love my job," Fringe replied, without a hint of a smile.
Martin McDermott looked at his watch. It was 7:45am West Coast time. All they had to do now was wait.

Topeka (Kansas)

Paul McDermott was starting to feel a little concerned. He had arrived at the house on SW MacVicar Avenue at 6:50am West Coast time accompanied by Wired. Like his father, he liked to be thorough. The avenue was

immaculately kept and was the picture book all American street. The houses were all adorned with wooden cladding, painted a brilliant white, and the Stars and Stripes was flying from poles erected proudly at the front of the lawns of at least half of the houses. It was the kind of street where if any of the neighbours let their house slip into disrepair, the rest of the street would probably be banging the door down, demanding a raise in standards. The house was an imposing building, set a good forty feet back from the road. It had a drive which led around to the back of the house, and when they had crept through three neighbour's gardens to carry out recon work on the rear of the building, they were surprised to see that a lean-to had been erected, which covered the whole of the back yard where the cars parked.
"What do you think?"
"I hope there are fifty of them in there, I hate Russians," Wired replied.
"Whatever you do, keep the girls safe and out of your line of fire. Kill as many Russians as you like but no collateral damage on this one. OK?"
"OK" Wired replied, "I love my job," he added, without a hint of a smile.
Paul looked at his watch. It was 7:45am West Coast time. All they had to do now was wait.

Park Avenue (New York) 7:45am

Nicole-Louise stared hard at the screen and then hurriedly said to Tackler,

"You had better come and look at this."
Nicole-Louise and Tackler were Ward's digital geniuses. Ward had always known that they were among the top ten best hackers in the world, although recently, he had decided that would now be in the top five. There was nothing that they couldn't find, anywhere in the world. If there was a digital record of it, they would find it.
Nicole-Louise and Tackler had created his digital life. They also stole money from those who had gained it by immoral means and re-distributed it as he instructed. But they had never taken any money for themselves. There was no need.
Centrepoint paid them a combined two million dollars a year to provide Ward with whatever information he needed, at any given time, and they always delivered. Tackler was in his late twenties, no more than five feet six and only weighed around one hundred and forty pounds.
Nicole-Louise was tall, over five feet nine, had long light brown hair and engaging blue eyes. She was naturally pretty but not stunning, yet after being in her company for just five minutes you would see that she was very attractive, strong and enticing, but you wouldn't be able to put your finger on why. She and Tackler made an odd couple. They didn't seem to fit. She was outgoing, confident, strong and vibrant and he never said much. But they were perfect for each other.
Their apartment was in Lennox Hill, a cosmopolitan area of New York, and they rarely ventured out into the real world. Their world was on their screens. The living room in the apartment was very cosy, cool and had a bohemian feel to it. Battered wooden furniture which had cost a

small fortune, and floral sofas from another age, were generously laid out all around the room. The only indication as to what they really did was in their workstations, each set up on opposite sides of the room on long, old oak desks, which looked like they had been hauled out of a skip; but in reality had cost over ten thousand dollars each. Matching leather swivel chairs were positioned directly in the centre of both desks. Each desk had four screens on them, touching together, side to side, and a keyboard positioned directly in front of the two screens, in the middle. The two outside screens were angled in about one hundred and ten degrees, and this gave a secluded feel to them both when they were at work.

Tackler leant over her shoulder, putting his arm around the back of her chair for support.

Nicole-Louise was never one to give the short version of events, so Tackler made sure he was comfortable before he spoke,

"What am I looking at?" he asked.

"These files that Ryan asked us to look through, they are too clean," she replied confidently.

"As in you think we were meant to find everything to verify the data in the file?"

"Exactly," she said, glad once again that he had tuned into her wavelength immediately, "So after ten minutes, I decided to forget what was in there and rely on my own instincts that something was wrong and approach it from a different angle," she added.

"I was thinking the same," he replied in genuine honesty, "And so I have started looking into how they get these girls here in the first place. Start at the beginning."

Nicole-Louise nodded in agreement and then continued, "So what I did was concentrate on Yeschenko, not his empire, not his finances but how he got here in the first place."

"And what did you find?"

"That's the problem. I didn't find anything. He isn't here. He is still a Russian national living in Moscow, look, here's his address and his income and his medical records," she replied, touching the screen to her right.

Tackler leant in closer to the screen and read for a minute.

"You hacked into the Russian system? I'm impressed you did that so quickly."

"Anyway," she said, rolling her eyes as she spoke, "I then looked at his relatives. I found his father, an unsavoury guy to say the least."

"And he has led you to Yeschenko over here?"

She shot him an annoyed look. Nicole-Louise liked to build things up when discussing her digital achievements.

Tackler cursed himself, he should have known better.

"That led me to Yeschenko over here," she continued, "And I have found three things that are interesting."

"Hit me with them?"

"Firstly, to save you wasting any more time, I have found that he launders his money through a shipping company called The Bahia Shipping Company; so I'm pretty sure that will be how they get here. If you look properly, I'm sure you can prove that."

Tackler cursed himself again. They always played this game, like a race, to see who could find the best information first.

"Secondly," she continued, "There are not forty five of these houses as the file says. The properties owned by The Bahia Shipping Company only total thirteen. Look, here are the addresses," she said, touching the screen directly in front of her left hand at the same time.
Tackler looked hard at the screen as he read the list. He was starting to get a bad feeling about this.
"And the third thing?"
"This address here," she said, using her curser to highlight an address in Beverly Hills, "It's an eight million dollar property, so I figured that if he was going to live anywhere, it would be there."
"So you hacked the IP address?"
She shot him yet another annoyed look. He cursed himself again.
"So I hacked the IP address, and then the e-mails, and three of them were sent to an address in Russia."
"And what was in the e-mails?" he asked, glad that he remembered to play along properly this time.
"There were three lists. No pictures or videos attached to the e-mail, just an attachment that contained a list of six people."
Tackler shot a glance at the other two screens that he had yet to look at. He couldn't see any lists.
"So I opened the other lists and there were names on them too, six on one and eight on the other, so twenty names in total."
"Who are they?" he asked.
"They are names that will create way too many problems, so I want us to get rid of them immediately. The Old Man said that as soon as we had any

information regarding names, we were to give it to him and not to Ryan, under any circumstances."

"I know that but is that wise?" Tackler asked, "Ryan is our friend, much more than The Old Man. What if he finds out?"

"It's to keep Ryan safe," she replied, "You know as well as I do that he doesn't care about the implications of eliminating people, no matter how much they deserve it. If he gets hold of that list, we both know that he will probably work his way through it until there is no one left. The Old Man was clear on that, we need to protect him."

"By lying to him? I don't like it. He's smart, you know he will work it out eventually."

"I've passed it on to The Old Man already," she replied.

"Who was on the list?" he asked again.

"I'm protecting you too," she replied, "Dig into The Bahia Shipping Company so that we have some information to give Ryan when he calls."

Tackler understood why she would do what she had done. Had he of discovered the information himself, he may well have done the same thing. He stood upright, leant down and kissed her on the cheek.

"Thank you," he said.

SEVEN

Westwood – Los Angeles 7:59am

"Let's knock on the door then," Ward said to Buck, as they walked up the elevated drive to the front of the house, pushing the silenced Makarov into his waistband as he spoke.
Buck was carrying a Kalashnikov, with little discretion, making no attempt to hide it at all.
"I thought you were joking," Buck replied, clearly not uncomfortable with the situation; a fact that reassured Ward a great deal.
They approached the large front door, which was painted brilliant white, and he noticed the CCTV camera pointing down with the red light flashing. He had spotted three at the back of the house as well, so he made a mental note to himself to get all the footage that he could retrieve, for inspection later.
He pulled the Makarov from his waistband and hid it behind his back.
He knocked on the door as his watch touched 8:00am. Three loud knocks.

One, two, three.
He waited eight seconds, counting each one in his head. And then the door opened.
A stocky guy answered the door. He was about five eight tall and equally as wide. He was wearing jeans and a white vest; his arms were like tree trunks, and were covered in tattoos. He had a shaved head and he had a hammer and sickle tattooed on the left side of his neck. He looked menacing.
Ward lifted up the Makarov and shot him in the face from three feet away.
His face exploded and his knees collapsed under his weight. He fell to the floor and his bulky frame blocked the whole of the doorway.
He wasn't dead. He was even tougher than he looked. His body was convulsing and his hands were moving up towards where his face once was.
He lowered the gun and shot him in the heart. He stopped moving immediately.
He stepped over the body and bent down to pull him into the house so that they could shut the door. Ward was strong, but he was having trouble moving him, he was that muscular and heavy.
"Some help would be good," he said, sounding annoyed.
Buck flung the Kalashnikov he was carrying on his shoulder and picked up the guys feet; moving him became easy with the two of them. They dragged him three feet into the hallway and shut the door quietly.
"You take the upstairs and I'll check down here," Ward said, fully aware that he expected to find whatever men were in the house, all gathered together in the kitchen. It's how Russian men were. They had no respect for

women and they generally only craved male company, vodka, cigarettes and women to abuse.

The staircase was directly to the left of them, and he watched as Buck moved forward without any hesitation, taking his rifle off of his shoulder and moving up the stairs.

He moved towards an open door directly in front of him, passing two doors on his right that were closed, and one on his left that was ajar. He peered through the one that was ajar and saw a computer and three monitors. He smiled to himself; he had sourced the video equipment. He continued moving forward until he reached the room at the end and looked inside. It was a big room. There were seven red leather chairs spotted throughout the room, the type you would expect to see in the private members clubs that were commonplace around Washington DC, each with a dark wooden table to the right hand side. There was a plush looking bar to the right hand side of the room, with a number of decanters lined up neatly behind it. He concluded this was the waiting room for the sick perverts who came here. He wished every chair was seating a client right now so that he could kill them.

Supply and demand.

If those sick people didn't want it, there would be no need to supply these poor children.

He moved back out to the hallway and reached the first door. He put his ear to it and could hear voices, deep voices. He quietly moved to the next door and listened. He could hear a TV playing and a crowd cheering. He knew by the sound of the crowd and the commentary, even though it sounded Russian, there were people in there watching soccer. It was the most specific sports sound in the world.

He now had the lay of the downstairs firmly fixed in his mind. He decided that the TV room would be the best room to take first; the sound of the soccer match blaring from the TV would hide any struggle. Any screams or groans could be interpreted as an ecstatic or frustrated fan engrossed in the game.

He counted to three in his head and swung the door open and stepped in.

And felt sick to the pit of his stomach as soon as he registered what he as seeing.

Three guys were sitting on the sofa watching the soccer match, drinking coffee and smoking cigarettes. They were all wearing jeans and had cut off tee shirts in different colours. They all had arms that were covered in tattoos and they all had a hammer and sickle tattoo on the left side of their necks.

Two of them had their feet up.

Below their feet were two young girls, no older than fifteen, and they were naked on their hands and knees, acting as footrests.

Rigid with fear.

He raised his gun and by the time the Russians had registered that he wasn't mean to be there, he had fired a bullet into all three of their chests. He didn't want to shoot them in the face; he wanted to avoid traumatising the girls any further as much as possible. All three guys slumped back and were dead immediately.

One of the girls let out a scream and they both scrambled to their feet. They looked pitiful. He looked around for something to cover them up and there was nothing.

He put his fingers to his lips in a 'Be quiet' gesture and they both nodded. He was initially alarmed at how calm they seemed to be and then remembered that they were probably immune to fear and shock, after the vile things they had been exposed to. He took off his jacket and handed it to the girl nearest to him, she gratefully accepted it. He then pulled off his white tee shirt and handed it to the other girl who took it from him with equal urgency. He was pleased to see that the items ran way past their knees. Their dignity had been restored. He pointed to the corner of the room with his finger and then raised his palm to indicate that they should wait there. They both hurried over and clung to each other. No tears, no screams and no fear. But he saw something else that lifted his spirits. He saw hope in their eyes. He nodded at them and smiled.

He walked out of the room, checking the hallway both ways before he stepped into it.

It was clear.

He approached the kitchen door and listened again. He could hear at least three different voices coming from inside. That would make at least seven men downstairs. He wondered how Buck was doing upstairs.

He opened the door and stepped in with his gun raised. There were three Russian guys sitting at a table eating. A quick scan confirmed there were no young girls in the room and without any hesitation; he shot all three of them in the centre of the head in less than three seconds. They all slumped back into their chairs, and bizarrely, all of their heads tilted to the right.

There was a fourth guy in the room leaning against the kitchen sink, drinking a coffee.

The fourth guy let out a scream and cowered back.
The fourth guy dropped his coffee mug and it smashed on the floor.
The fourth guy went to speak but nothing would come out.
The fourth guy was one of the best known actors in Hollywood.

Buck stood at the top of the stairs with his Kalashnikov pointing in front of him and looked along the hall. There were nine white doors, four on each side and one directly at the end, which had a sign saying 'Bathroom'. He smiled to himself and thought it would be a little too optimistic to hope to see a sign saying 'Bad guys in here'. He walked through to the end of the hall and tried the handle of the bathroom door. It was locked. He tapped on the door lightly. He heard a tap being turned off and then a lock being unlatched. The door opened and before him stood a gut wrenching sight. A small girl, her modesty covered by a towel, who was no older than thirteen, looked up at him and stepped back in fear when she saw the rifle in his hands. She had bruises all over her face and he could see clearly that she had numerous bite marks on her shoulders; the bite marks looked very deep. He put his finger to his lips and then whispered, "Do you speak English?"
The young girl nodded.
"How many men are in the house?"
The girl raised her hands and displayed seven digits.
"Where are they?" he asked softly.
The girl used the index finger on her right hand to point to the floor, indicating that they were all downstairs.

"How many girls are in the house?"
The girl raised all ten digits, then closed her hand and then raised them again.
"Twenty?"
The girl nodded.
"Where are the girls?"
The girl pointed to the doors on the right of the corridor. Buck looked at the doors.
"What are the doors on the left for?"
The girl raised her hand and pointed to the bruises on her face.
Buck understood. The girls were being crammed into rooms, five at a time and when the clients came, they were dragged across the hall to the other rooms.
"Come with me. When I open a door on this side," he said pointing to the doors on the left, "You open the one opposite and tell the girls to come out and follow me. Do you understand?"
The girl nodded.
He watched as the girl moved to the opposite side of the landing.
He opened the first door. The room was empty.
The girl opened the opposite door and beckoned to the girls inside to come out immediately. Buck did a quick headcount; there were now six girls opposite him.
He opened the second door. Empty. The girl did the same.
Now there were ten girls opposite.
He opened the third door. The room was empty.
Now fourteen girls were crammed on the landing.
He opened the last door. The room was empty.

Eighteen girls now huddled together, waiting for him to offer an instruction.
He turned around and looked at the girls and smiled.
"You will be safe now," he said.
Eighteen girls all at once started to cry in silence.
Something they had gotten used to doing through fear of punishment.
Buck walked down the stairs with the girls following him and glanced around. There was nothing to see but the dead guy who had opened the door, crumpled on the floor. He turned and put his hand up to indicate for the girls to stop.
"Clear," he shouted out.
"I'm in the kitchen."
"There are seven guys in the building," Buck shouted.
"Not anymore," Ward replied.
Buck walked towards the voice and beckoned for the girls to follow him, which they hurriedly did, seeing the dead guy on the floor had filled them all with hope.
"There are two girls missing," Buck said as he walked into the kitchen and then stopped dead in his tracks.
"They are safe next door," Ward replied.
"You're that actor, aren't you?" Buck said to the guy who had been standing in the kitchen, the guy looked terrified. The actor had pieced together what was happening, and he was coming to the conclusion, whatever angle he took viewing his situation, that his life was now in ruins. He might be able to use his money to hire the best lawyers, or even pay the girls hush money. That was it. He would buy his way out of it. He had hope.
"Finley Valence. That's your name," Buck added.

The girl that Buck had found in the bathroom ran forward and slapped Valence hard across the face, then stepped back and cowered behind the other girls.
"He did this to you?" Ward asked the girl, pointing at the bruises on her face. The girl nodded back at him.
"I'll put it right. I'll give her a million dollars as a way of saying sorry," Valence said urgently.
Ward lifted up his Makarov and smiled at Valence. He had seen some of his movies, although he wasn't a big modern cinematic fan. Valence played tough action heroes who always saved the world and got the girl, in the majority of his films. He didn't look very tough as he stood there and started to pee his pants.
He turned and looked at the girl and she nodded back at him.
He pulled the trigger and blew Valence's face apart. His head jerked back and he slumped to the floor. As he disappeared from sight, he noticed his blood and brains had sprayed through the back of his head and onto the window. Valence was just window dressing.
Literally.
He turned to the girls and not one of them looked shocked or scared. He couldn't start to imagine what they had been through, he didn't want to.
He couldn't.
If he had images in his mind of what these poor girls had experienced in this house, then he would be consumed with rage and hate. And that would destroy his focus. He pulled out his phone and called Centrepoint.
"I need the whole of the Santa Monica police force here in exactly six minutes," he said as soon as Centrepoint answered.

"You have the footage," Centrepoint asked.

"I'm getting it now, that's why I need a few minutes. But you have to make sure that any suggestion that we were ever here is dismissed as incorrect immediately."

"Don't worry. I will fix all of that side of things. Did you use Russian equipment to do whatever you have done?"

"Yes."

"Good. I can brief their chief about how this was the result of a Russian turf war and he will tell the news people that when I decide."

"Remember you gave me your word that the girls will be safe and given a good life here," he reminded him.

"Yes Ryan, you have my word," Centrepoint replied.

And Ward believed him.

"There is one small problem," he said.

"What?"

"There was someone else who took a bullet who wasn't Russian. He was probably a customer."

"Who was he?" Centrepoint asked.

"No idea," he replied, "I didn't recognise him."

"Then don't worry about it, I'll sort it."

Ward hung up the phone.

"Go and grab the computer and anything else you can find in that room," he said to Buck, "We have three minutes and then we have to leave."

Buck nodded and turned around and left the kitchen.

He looked at the girls.

"Have any of you met Andrea Yeschenko?" he asked softly.

All of the girls looked towards one of the girls standing to the side.

"Have you?"

"They call him the king. He sits on a throne," she replied.

"What happened when you met him?" he asked.

The girl spent two minutes explaining how she and eleven other girls had been forced to watch Yeschenko cut apart a young girl called Tatiana, who had tried to escape, and then instructed them all to go back to their houses and explain to the other girls what happens if they try to escape. He felt sick to the stomach and the anger started to wash through his veins.

"I've got it. We had better go," Buck said, as he stood in the doorway holding a computer hard drive and a duffel bag full of other equipment.

"The police will be here in three minutes," he said, "Lots of them. You are all safe now."

The girls stood still. A few of them smiled, a few of them cried but most of them showed no emotion whatsoever. They had probably forgotten how to feel or show anything after the horrors they had faced.

He stepped through them and walked out of the house without once looking back.

"Where now?" Buck asked.

"Marina Del Rey," he replied. "We have a base there."

EIGHT

Cunningham Park (New York) 7:59am

Martin McDermott and Fringe stepped carefully down the steep bank that led to the back door of the house. The blinds pulled down in the windows still made it impossible to know how many guys were inside. McDermott was now fifty two years old, but he moved like a twenty year old. He was a fraction over six feet tall and his face gave away very few clues about his real age. He had cropped hair which showed very little grey, and his square jaw and narrow eyes made him look like the lethal fighting machine he was. His senses were highly tuned beyond measure, and he knew, without a doubt, that no one was watching them as they reached the wall next to the back door. Fringe was the youngest of his team. He was just twenty six and he could easily have been McDermott's son. He had the same bone structure and eyes as his commander. Fringe was a Californian boy and he was obsessed with eighties music. He got his

nickname from the team because when he had first joined the unit, he had a floppy, eighties style fringe. McDermott tried the door handle. It was locked.
At the front of the house, Danny Wallace and Adam Fuller had already tried the handle on the front door and discovered that was locked too. Wallace was in his mid-thirties and was the team's telecoms expert. He looked like all the others. Around six feet tall, strong jaw, narrow eyes, cropped hair and carried a look that advised people not to mess with him. Fuller, while looking exactly like the rest of the team, was different to the rest of the team. He was a funny guy and he used his humour non-stop; sometimes to McDermott's annoyance. His favourite thing to do was to burst into rhyme when the team were in a pressurised situation. But it would be a mistake to let the humour fool you. Fuller was a lethal killing machine, specialising in close quarter combat. McDermott would back him against any of his team in a fist fight.
He nodded at Fringe as the display on his digital watch hit 8:00am, and Fringe used his silenced Makarov pistol to shoot the lock out. The wooden frame of the door splintered, and the force of the bullet opened the door about eighteen inches upon impact. Almost in perfect tandem, the front door was opening in exactly the same way as a result of the shot that Wallace had just fired. McDermott stepped into the kitchen with his gun raised vertically, in line with his eyes, and saw there were two guys sitting at a big, pine table, drinking coffee from large, yellow mugs. The guys had shaved heads and wore jeans and vests. Their arms were covered in tattoos and Fringe noticed that they both had hammer and sickle

tattoos on the left hand side of their necks. McDermott fired a shot immediately, and the bullet hit the guy sitting closest to him in the side of the neck. The force of the bullet knocked him off the chair and he was dead before he hit the floor.

"Who are you?" he said to the other guy who was sat motionless, frozen in fear, his eyes darting between McDermott and Fringe. Two mean looking guys with strong jaws and narrow eyes both pointing silenced pistols at him.

The guy said nothing.

And so McDermott shot him in the left thigh. The guy screamed and fell off the chair and onto the floor. McDermott walked over to him and kicked the chair out of the way and stood over him

"Last chance. Who are you?" he asked again.

"I am Alexei," the guy replied.

"How many men are in the house?" McDermott asked quietly.

"Four."

He pointed his gun at his other thigh and asked again, "How many guys are in the house?"

"Seven," Alexei replied, "Six now." he added, glancing at his dead friend on the floor.

"Make that five," he said, and shot Alexei in the centre of the chest, killing him instantly.

Adam Fuller and Danny Wallace had stepped into the hallway through the front of the house and walked straight into a young girl, who could have been no more than thirteen, mopping the floor. She gasped when she looked at the two men, who were dressed in combat trousers, black vests and bullet-proof jackets; one carrying a silenced handgun and the other a rifle that had a curved bullet magazine coming from the bottom. She had seen bad men back home carry those types of guns before.

The hallway was plush, filled with lots of elegant, mahogany style furniture which sat on an immaculately tiled, chequered floor that the girl was cleaning. Fuller put his finger to his lips to indicate to the girl to be quiet.

"Do you speak English?" he whispered.

The girl nodded.

"Where are the men?"

The girl pointed towards the stairs and to a door in the far corner of the hallway. As Fuller and Wallace looked at the door, it opened slightly. They both raised their guns and then lowered them when they saw Fringe peer out into the hallway. He stepped out followed by McDermott.

"Where are the cameras?" Wallace asked the girl.

She looked at him blankly.

He closed one eye, lifted both hands, made a square with his fingers and then made a clicking motion with his right index finger to indicate taking a picture.

The girl pointed to the door next to where McDermott was standing. He turned and opened the door and nodded at Wallace, using his thumb to command Wallace to move into the room to collect the equipment.

There was another door that was shut and so McDermott stood to the left hand side of it and turned the handle. The door opened and using the palm of his hand, he pushed it gently and the door quietly swung until it was fully open. It was dark in the room. McDermott peered

in and saw the room was empty. All he could see was lots of big leather chairs with small tables to the right hand side of them. It reminded him of the gentleman's clubs that he knew were commonplace around Washington D.C.
"How many men are in the house?" Fuller whispered to the girl.
She raised all of the digits on her right hand and two on her left.
"Two are down in the kitchen," McDermott said to Fuller.
"Where are the men?" McDermott asked.
"It is wash time. We have to wash them every morning in the bathroom," she said.
"Stay here with her," he said to Fuller, "Fringe, you come with me," he added, as he walked over to the stairs and started to climb them, carefully, one at a time, with his gun elevated to greet anyone who walked into his line of fire. Fringe was at his side by the time he had finished issuing his command.
They reached the top of the stairs.
There were four doors on either side of the landing and a door directly to the left that had a sign saying 'Bathroom' stuck to it.
He thought it would be too optimistic to hope to have a sign on the other doors saying, 'Bad guys in here.'
A door opened and a tiny girl stepped out carrying a pile of towels. She could have been no more than twelve. She stopped in her tracks, dropped the towels and put her hands to her mouth as she saw them. No scream, nothing. Something McDermott found odd but put it

down to the fact she was probably way beyond surprise anymore.

He put his finger to his lips and beckoned the girl over. She looked even younger when she was standing next to him.

"Where are the men?" he whispered.

The girl pointed to the door with 'Bathroom' on it.

"How many men are in there?"

The girl raised all of the digits on her left hand.

"Are there any other men up here apart from them?" he asked softly.

The girl shook her head.

"Are there any girls in there?" he asked.

"No, we do not enter there until five minutes after the eight," she replied in broken English.

"There are definitely no girls in there?" he asked again.

"No, all in rooms," she said, pointing over to the doors on the other side of the hallway.

"How many girls are here?"

"There is twenty."

McDermott looked at Fringe and their eyes met.

"Make it loud and make it messy," he said to him. Fringe immediately nodded his agreement, and his gratitude.

He stepped forward quietly to the bathroom door and stopped. McDermott walked over to the doors where the girl had said the others were and whispered,

"Stay in there until it goes quiet and then bring the other girls out here. You are safe now. No one can hurt you anymore," he said, and the girl responded by breaking out into the biggest smile he had ever seen. She walked into the first door and closed it. McDermott nodded at Fringe.

Fringe opened the door with his Kalashnikov raised at waist level directly in front of him.
Christmas had come early.
There were five guys sitting on a slated wooden bench opposite five showers, there was a Jacuzzi in the corner.
They all had cropped hair.
They were all naked.
They all had tattoos that covered their whole arms.
They all had a hammer and sickle tattoo on the left hand side of their necks.
They were all unarmed.
They were all dead.
He started firing, hitting the guy on the left in the centre of the chest first and then sweeping to the right; each guy taking a bullet in the chest, and then dipping the rifle slightly on the return sweep to catch them all in the stomach. He kept firing and swept left to right and back again three times until the magazine was empty. Thirty rounds fired, six bullets each, every one of them a direct hit in the centre of the body from five feet away. Three of them had fallen to the floor and two were slumped at contorted angles on the bench.
Either way, they were all dead.
There was blood all over the walls behind them and the floor in front of them was rapidly turning a deep crimson colour. He turned and walked out of the room.
"Done," he shouted across to McDermott.
McDermott knocked on the door and the girl he had given the instructions to, opened it and walked out, followed by four other girls.
"Get the others," he said to her.

She stepped to the next door and opened them, shouting "They have saved us," in Russian, something all three men standing on the landing understood, but pretended they didn't, so that they could remain detached and focussed. Less than one minute later, nineteen girls were standing on the landing. Fuller walked up the stairs with the other young girl, followed by Wallace who was carrying a rucksack which seemed to be bursting at the seams.
"You have everything?" McDermott asked him.
Wallace nodded to indicate that he did.
He looked at the girls, it was a heart-wrenching and pitiful sight, but they would be safe now.
"The police will be here within three minutes," he said as he watched Wallace make the call to the local law enforcement, "You will all be OK," he added abruptly, trying not to sound too emotional as it was not his thing; but inside, he was feeling every emotion possible.
The girls all started hugging each other and talking excitedly.
"Stay here on the landing and do not move."
He turned and nodded at the other three and they started to walk down the stairs.
"Wait," one of the girls shouted. They all stopped in their tracks.
She skipped over to them and put her arms around McDermott.
"My name is Erida," she said, "I'm sixteen today. They would have taken me away somewhere bad today, maybe kill me. You are my best ever birthday present." she added, gazing up at him with tear filled eyes.

McDermott nodded to her and walked down the stairs, out of the front door, down the driveway and across to their black Range Rover, and thirty seconds later, they were gone. Wallace could have sworn that he heard McDermott clearing his throat, but he wouldn't risk pointing it out.
He liked being alive.

Topeka (Kansas) 7:59am

Paul McDermott looked at the countdown on his digital watch and started to move. With Wired beside him, they covered the forty feet to the front door of the house in a few seconds. The house was still. He found this unusual, but assumed that whatever happened in the house would more than likely happen in the early hours of the morning to avoid prying eyes. They stood either side of the door, their breathing controlled and soft. They both drew their guns in perfect synchronisation and Wired leant in and tried the door handle. The handle moved and they heard the latch click. Paul raised an eyebrow and Wired just shrugged, before pushing the door open and stepping inside.
The house was still.
Too still.
They stepped into the hallway. There was no furniture apart from a wooden table and chair to the left hand side; like a welcoming post for anyone who walked in.
There were four doors that led from the hallway, two on the left and two on the right. Wired took the left hand side and Paul the right.

Wired pushed open the first door that he reached and stepped inside.
The room was empty apart from a worn wooden table and two uncomfortable looking chairs.
On the opposite side of the hallway, Paul turned the handle and peered inside the room. It was a big room, but all that was in there were two sofa's, big enough to seat four people each and two armchairs. An old bulky TV sat on a worn looking unit. But there was nothing else in the room.
Wired tried the next door and it was a kitchen.
It was empty.
There was a table in the centre of the room with four chairs and an empty breakfast bar, with a stool against the rear wall. He opened a cupboard.
The cupboard was empty.
Paul opened his second door and saw a bed. The bed was made up and had clearly not been slept in for a long time.
He walked out back into the hallway and watched as Wired stepped out of the kitchen looking confused. He walked across to Paul and whispered,
"There is something not right here."
He nodded towards the stairs and they slowly started to climb them. One on either side, Wired walking backwards to cover the rear while Paul covered the front.
They reached the top of the stairs. There were four doors on the left hand side of the top of the stairs and four on the right hand side.
He turned to the left and Wired went to the right.
Paul opened the first door and looked inside, all that was in there was a bed and a cupboard.

Wired opened his first door and looked inside, all that was in there was a bed and a cupboard.
They both stepped outside and looked across at each other.
He quickly opened the door to the other three rooms on his side of the landing.
Two of them only had a bed and a cupboard in them and the last one was a bathroom.
There were no soaps or towels in there. He ran his finger across the floor of the shower tray. It was bone dry.
He walked out of the bathroom and saw Wired stepping out of his last door.
"All that was in each of these rooms was a cupboard and a bed," he said, making no attempt to keep his voice quiet.
Paul became very worried.
"We need to get out of here and quick," he said and sprinted towards the stairs.
A few seconds later, they were running out of the front door, Paul breaking his stride to close the door behind them. He sprinted down the drive, Wired let him pass so he could lead the way, and he ran across the road, climbing through some thick shrubbery that occupied most of the front yard of the house opposite, and after falling to the floor, assumed a sniping position facing the house. Wired laid down next to him.
"What's wrong?" he asked.
"I know what that building is," Paul replied.
"What?"
Before he could reply, three black fords came screeching around the corner at over fifty miles per hour and stopped directly in front of the house. Three men in dark

suits climbed out of each car, and while one team went in through the front door, the other two teams took either side around to the back.

"What's going on?" Wired asked.

Paul ignored the question.

They sat there in silence for almost five minutes and watched as the nine guys walked out of the building and down the drive. They stood there surveying the neighbourhood and at least three of them fixed a long stare on the shrubbery where they were hiding, clearly contemplating having a more detailed look but eventually deciding against it. They watched as one of the guys put his right hand to his ear and covered his ear lobe with three fingers; the guy was clearly listening to a voice coming through a radio into his earpiece. He said something to the other guys and they all got back into their cars, taking one last look around before they stepped in, and exactly six minutes after arriving, the cars were driving off.

"What was that about?" Wired asked.

Paul McDermott was not sure what it was about but he knew what it was.

He knew that they had activated a pressure sensor that signalled an alarm when they had entered the house.

They had not hit one of Yeschenko's houses.

They had just hit a CIA safe house.

NINE

Beverley Hills – Los Angeles

Andrea Yeschenko had endured a horrific childhood growing up in the district of Voykovsky on the outskirts of Moscow.
His mother was an attractive woman, who was desired by all of the men in the district by the time she had reached her late teens. She had aspirations and dreams. She had planned to study to become a doctor and she was dedicated to making her future a successful one. And then she met Yeschenko's father.
He was a violent drunk who didn't work, but instead caught the train daily into Belorusskiy station, where he would rob tourists at knifepoint and then return back to Voykovsky, where he would drink in the seedy bars, fight with anyone who dared to look at him, and if he felt like it, rape women for his sick pleasure.
His father had a hypnotic way about him. He had met Yeschenko's mother when he was contemplating raping her, after another drink and violence fuelled evening

spending his daily, ill-gotten gains. He had changed his mind about assaulting her, and instead talked her into having supper with him. He was the first man that she had loved. They had married twelve months after meeting; much to the dismay and anger of her parents, and on their wedding night, he showed her the monster he had been so careful to hide from her for the first time. He offered four of his acquaintances the chance to sleep with his bride on her wedding night for one hundred rubles each. An offer they all accepted. She protested, and so he beat her until she agreed, and then he sat and watched, as he earned four hundred rubles by just drinking vodka, smoking and laughing.

Fourteen months later, Andrea Yeschenko was born. Every night, he would dread his father bringing home more people to have sex with his mother; her screams and the sound of his father's palm striking her face echoed around their disgusting and filthy apartment. By the time he was eight, his father would force him to watch these men violating his mother, and by the age of fourteen, he had raped his first victim; a girl who he had followed from the train station on her way home from school.

When he was sixteen his father killed his mother after she refused to have sex with eight men he had brought home. It was the first time she had refused. He claimed self-defence, saying that she had a knife and was trying to kill him; a claim he verified by showing the knife wounds which he had inflicted upon himself before the police had turned up at the apartment, and incredibly, he was acquitted. Everyone in the district knew what had really happened and he was shunned. He was refused entry into the bars he used to visit and he was evicted from his apartment. He was taken in by a friend of his, Marek, who provided food and shelter for him. Marek had a son called Arter and he and Andrea became close friends.

At eighteen, Yeschenko joined the Russian army. He was quickly despatched to their Special Forces unit after he demonstrated a unique ability and willingness to kill. He spent the next ten years killing Russian nationals under the orders of the Kremlin. When the new Russia was born ten years later, he left the army and joined everyone else in putting their hands into the pie to get what they could; he turned firstly to prostitution and then drugs. He built up a profitable business, employing ex Special Forces men to enforce his rules, but he started to resent the money that the people traffickers were making, so decided to take over their operation. Within three years he was trafficking over a thousand girls a year to the United States.

Using his contacts at the Kremlin, and a lot of bribery money, he was able to get a visa to work in The States and he now had the perfect life. He had been a resident in the U.S. for the past seven years and yet all records showed that he still lived in Russia. Some of his more high profile clients ensured that he was in America legally. At least life had been perfect, up until two minutes ago when he had received the phone calls.

He sat on his throne, elevated above his men, all of whom could tell by the look on his face that now was not the time to make eye contact with him. They all sat in their chairs looking at the floor.

To no one in particular, he said,
"Who would dare to challenge me?"
No one replied.
He stood up from his throne, stepped off of the platform and walked over to the line of eight men, who were seated to the left, all of whom were wearing jeans and vests, and had arms that were covered with tattoos, with a hammer and sickle tattooed on the left hand side of their necks, and asked again,
"Who would dare to challenge me?"
Still no one answered. And still no one made eye contact.
"Are you all cowards?" he spat at them, "Not one of you can look me in the eye?"
All eight of them looked up at once, not to demonstrate that they weren't cowards, because when it came to confronting Andrea Yeschenko, they were all cowards, but to show their loyalty to him.
"Who has dared to challenge you Andrea?" asked a guy who was sitting at the end of the line.
"Finally, the right question," Yeschenko replied.
He stood in front of the line and studied them all for a moment.
"Who here would ever deceive me?"
In one mumbled voice they all replied variants of 'Not me,' and he studied them all further, one by one.
"Our houses in Westwood and Cunningham Park have been attacked," he shouted, "Our keepers are all dead and the girls have all been taken in by the police. Every single one of them."

"Attacked by who?" the guy at the end of the line asked, by now presuming that he had become the unofficial spokesman for the group.

"That's what I want to know you fool. Who would dare to challenge me?" he replied; giving the guy at the end of the line the coldest and hardest of stares, so that he decided there and then that he would ask no more questions.

"I have just had a call that two hours ago they were both hit at exactly 8:00am" he continued, "Is there significance in that time? Does it mean something?"

None of the men said a word. They all knew that one wrong word now and they would be dead.

"I've just been told that ballistic tests have shown that the bullets were fired from Kalashnikov's and Makarov's. What do you think that means Mikhail?" he asked a guy sitting third in line from the left.

"That a Russian gang are trying to take over your business?" he asked, "But they will fail, we will kill them all," he quickly added, in the hope his answer would appease him.

"Is that what you all think?" he asked, looking along the line.

They all nodded as one. Two of them even stood up and clenched their fists, as if they were preparing for a fight.

"Sit down you idiots," he shouted at them.

They were sitting down and looking at the floor less than a second later.

"If you are all thinking that is what happened, then that is not what happened. But I want you Nikolay and Pavel to get over to Westwood and see what you can find out. There is a cop called Erikson who will give you all the

information that he has. Find him and then report back to me by this afternoon," he ordered, waving the back of his hand in the direction of the door as he spoke.
They stood up and left the room immediately.
"The rest of you," he said, looking at the other six guys, "Get on the phone to all of the keepers in the other houses and tell them to double their guard duties, and find them more men if you have to."

Two minutes later, Andrea Yeschenko was sitting in his private study. It was situated at the rear of the mansion, looking out over the immaculate lawns and the diamond shaped swimming pool he had built, symbols he knew showed real class. His desk was an expensive piece of art, deep mahogany and over eight feet in length, and had once belonged to Mikhail Gorbachev. He had it brought from a private auction in Sweden, at a cost of $150,000, and this made him feel like the powerful man he believed he was, and he also felt it kept him in touch with Mother Russia. On the opposite side of where he sat, there was a bookcase which ran the full length of the wall, from floor to ceiling. It was packed full of books, mainly historical, and all in Russian.
Not one of them had ever been opened.
He called the number in Washington and there was no answer, yet again. A beep on the end of the line indicated that a voice message could be left and so he paused for a few seconds and then said, as menacingly as he could,
"You have until 6:00pm tomorrow evening to get back to me with all of my demands met, or I will show the world what you are."

He then hung up the phone.
How dare they challenge me?, he thought to himself as he kissed his fingers and rubbed the hammer and sickle tattoo on the right hand side of his neck and smiled.
Mother Russia had always brought him luck

Marina Del Rey

Ward and Buck arrived at the warehouse close to Marina Del Rey. It was situated just off Lincoln Boulevard, opposite the FedEx shipping depot.
Martin McDermott had warehouses dotted all around the states, all of them displaying a sign saying 'A & B Auto's', and a local number stamped underneath. Anyone dialling the number, in any State, would be re-routed to a phone manned by Danny Wallace; who would politely inform the caller that they were fully booked and did not have room for any more customers.
All of the warehouses were immaculately kept and laid out in the same way. Entry into the warehouse was through a main door into what appeared to be a small reception area. Through the reception area and into the warehouse itself sat two black Range Rovers with tinted windows, ready to go, facing the roller shutter doors. Two long work benches, one for weapons and one for communication equipment, ran along either side of the warehouse and there was a dry wall at the rear of the building with another workbench against it, the bottom of which was hinged and once removed, gave entry into a secret room where every single type of weapon and

explosive was situated. There were enough guns, ammunition and explosives in there to start a small war. In the left hand corner there was a table, six chairs and an old battered armchair. The team's waiting area. There was often a lot of hanging around waiting for a call to move. Next to the armchair was a sink, an old refrigerator and a microwave. The warehouse was laid out identically in every state.

Martin McDermott liked order in his world.

Buck pulled the car to a stop and Ward stepped out of the car. He walked up to the reception door entrance and put the code into the numbered security entrance pad that McDermott always used.

0....9....2....1. McDermott's birthday.

The locking mechanism clicked open and he stepped in with Buck in close attendance.

They walked through to the warehouse and had a quick look around to confirm it was empty.

"Impressive," Buck said to himself rather than Ward.

For a moment, Ward felt as though he was in the exact same warehouse of McDermott's that he had been in recently in New York.

He pulled out his phone and called McDermott.

"Hey," McDermott answered.

"All done your end?" he asked.

"Yes."

"And the girls?"

"All safe and by now with the police," he replied. Ward noticed the relief in his voice, "But we have a massive problem," he added.

"Which is?"

"Paul contacted me. They couldn't get the girls from Kansas."

"What went wrong?" he demanded.

"Nothing went wrong, the house was empty."

"What do you mean empty?"

"There was no one there at all."

"Maybe the intel was a little out of date. Yeschenko has probably moved to another house, they tend to do that after a while."

"That isn't the problem," McDermott replied.

"So what is?"

"We sent him to a CIA safe house."

"Say that again?" he asked. Knowing that he had heard him correctly but he wanted him to repeat it.

"The house Paul and Wired hit in Topeka was a CIA Safe house. Nine agents turned up a few minutes after they had entered."

"Where are they now?"

"They are fine. Paul realised where they were and they got out just before the agents turned up."

Ward knew that they would not have made a mistake with the address, and there was only one person who could answer the questions that he now had running through his mind.

"I'll call The Old Man," he said and hung up the phone.

Washington D.C.

Sitting at his desk in Washington D.C, Centrepoint knew the call would be coming. When he saw Ward's name appear on his encrypted phone he breathed in deeply and prepared himself.

"Nice of you to check in," he said as he answered.

"I'm rapidly starting to lose faith in you," Ward said angrily.

"What's wrong now?"

"The file you provided us with was a load of bullshit. I want to know why?"

"You need to be more specific Ryan?"

"I sent Paul McDermott into a place in Kansas that was one of our safe houses. That was based on your information," he spat down the phone, "You can send me to wherever you like, but you don't ever put me in the position where I send other people into a trap."

"I don't like your tone," Centrepoint spat back down the line.

"And I don't like your bullshit."

"Tell me calmly what happened?" Centrepoint asked; his voice much calmer now.

Ward proceeded to relay the information that McDermott had just shared with him. Centrepoint listened quietly, his soft breathing the only thing that Ward could hear.

"Is that all of it?" Centrepoint asked.

"Yes. Now tell me why you would do that?"

"To know who we are up against."

"Don't tell me we are up against our own people?"

"They aren't our people."

"Stop bullshitting me," Ward shouted down the phone, "That was one of our houses."

"Yes, it was one of our houses."

"I'll trust Paul McDermott's eyes over the words you say any day of the week."

"They honestly weren't our people, but it is one of our houses."

"Explain?"

"They aren't CIA. They are Secret Service."

Ward went quiet for a few seconds. He started to piece it all together in his mind. He immediately decided to ask what had now become the most obvious question to ask, "How far does this go?"

"I think it may go above a couple of perverted senators."

"How far are we talking?" he asked, "Secretaries or the President?"

"That's the problem. I don't know. But some real big hitters in Washington know how far."

"Tell me about the file?" Ward asked.

"All of the information that you need is in there."

"But how much of it is inaccurate?"

"Most of it."

"Be specific or I'm out," Ward demanded.

"There are not forty five houses, there are only thirteen."

"So why the big lie?"

"Because the Secret Service and the NSA are chasing this evidence as well. No matter how good at hiding things we think we are, they are better at it. I suspected that they would have got copies of that file and I needed to know who it was we were up against."

"But two of the houses we hit were genuine?"

"You got lucky," Centrepoint said, " You had less than a thirty per cent chance of picking the right house and you picked two. Luck, or you had a feeling."

Ward knew it was luck.

"So how do you know they were Secret Service?" he asked.

"Because I've just had a call from their director telling me he will destroy me and my men in the field unless I give up the real addresses."

"Do you know them all?"

"Yes I do."

"Are you going to give them to me?"

"Of course I am," Centrepoint replied, "But you need to be very careful Ryan. This will get messy. You are fighting our own people and they will not hesitate to kill you and anyone who gets in their way."

"Good luck with that," Ward replied.

Centrepoint knew that he now had Ward back onside. He thought about telling him about Gilligan not being dead, but decided that it would be of better use a little later on.

"So," Ward continued, "We have eleven houses left. Where are they?"

"Where have you had a successful hit so far?" Centrepoint asked.

"Cunningham Park in New York and Westwood."

"Then the ones left are the two in Washington, the three in New York, the one in Texas, the one in Arkansas and the four that are left in California."

"And how many people know that?" Ward asked.

"Only me, you and Yeschenko."

"They are going to be on their guard now. We are too thinly spread," Ward replied, "I need help," he added.

Centrepoint knew another argument was coming after he said what was coming next.

"The video evidence that you collected from the two houses that you hit, where is it?"

Ward remembered that the equipment that Buck had gathered was still in the car.

"It's safe," he replied, knowing that McDermott would have his evidence securely stored.

"I need it given to me; no one else is to look at it."

Ward ignored him.

"What help can you give me?" he asked.

"I have two men that I can trust completely. They will be landing at LAX in an hour," he replied.

"Who are they?"

"Peacock and Murray. They are good men. If I had the room for them then they would be Deniables already," he replied, "I'll send you their pictures after this call ends."

The Old Man's statement reassured Ward that they would be perfect for what he would need.

"That still leaves me with a lot of houses to hit. Eleven is no small number," Ward said.

"It's six," Centrepoint replied, "In twenty five minutes time, The Optician is going to lead a team into the most likely house to have the footage in New York and I have pulled in all the other Deniables to take out the second and third houses there too."

Then he waited.

"Why are you calling the shots?" Ward demanded angrily, aware that The Old Man's math was out.

"Because we have to move on this quickly and as you said, you are too thinly spread," he replied, "You can now call McDermott to California and I will take care of Texas and Arkansas. Then you have everything you need to support you with the four on the West Coast."

"And Washington? The two there?" Ward asked,

"I'm hoping you have everything before Washington," Centrepoint replied.

"Why?"

"Because you running around in my backyard will cause serious problems Ryan, but, if you haven't found it in California and I haven't found it in New York, Arkansas or Texas then I will have to let you run riot here because I will have no choice."

Ward knew this made sense, and so did Centrepoint's math. He just didn't like him assuming control over his operations, when he was the one in the field risking his life.

"So where is the video evidence you have collected so far now?" Centrepoint asked.

Ward hung up the phone.

Buck heard every word and looked at Ward.

"That sounds ominous," he said.

"We aren't just fighting the Russians here, the Secret Service are hunting the same evidence as we are and they will kill us without hesitation,"

"Good luck with that," Buck replied.

"We need to be at LAX in an hour to meet two guys who will be helping us."

"I hope they are proper operatives," Buck said, without a hint of sarcasm.

TEN

Los Angeles

Ward called McDermott and he agreed; it made perfect sense to get him and his team to California as quickly as possible to provide support. He got the feeling that he didn't like having his team too thinly spread either. McDermott said he would ring The Old Man to get the jet sorted, stop in Kansas on the way across to L.A. to collect Paul and Wired, and then he would meet him at the Warehouse in Marina Del Rey by nightfall. He had no doubt that he would be talking to McDermott face to face long before nightfall.

"Let's get to the airport," he said to Buck, as he studied the two pictures that Centrepoint had sent through of Peacock and Murray.

They drove into the airport, passing the large L.A.X letters that signified to the tourists where they were. He always felt that they were just unnecessary letters stuck on the ground which had an appeal that he couldn't fathom out, just like the 'Hollywood' sign up in the hills. They pulled up outside the arrivals door, and Buck put the car in park.
"If you leave the car here it will get towed away," he said.
"I wasn't planning on coming inside," Buck replied, "The Old Man told me you were 'The Man', so I didn't think you would need me to hold your hand."
Ward smiled; he got out of the car and walked through the doors into Terminal seven where he had been told they would be arriving.
He didn't normally see the inside of airports like this. He usually entered through a back entrance and got straight onto a jet, by-passing passport control, not that he carried a passport, and there was never any trace of him on passenger lists or flight manifestos.
He approached the arrival gate where Peacock and Murray would be walking out, and stood and watched the people coming and going for a few minutes. He watched as people came through the doors and ran straight into the arms of family and loved ones, and he heard the words 'Welcome home' at least twelve times in three minutes. He watched as a young boy of about eight dipped under the barrier and ran into the arms of a man who he presumed was his father, and the young boys smile seemed to light up the whole airport. This was a happy sight and he took it in for a few seconds longer than perhaps he should have. He walked a little

further and stepped into a small eatery, ordering a coffee to go. As he was waiting, he looked up at the large TV screen on the wall and saw a headline scrolling across the bottom which read,
"BREAKING NEWS……..USBC SOURCES……..HOLYWOOD STAR FINLEY VALENCE HAS COMMITTED SUICIDE……. MORE TO FOLLOW"
He pulled his phone out of his pocket, checked the screen and saw there were three missed calls from Centrepoint. He knew he would be furious with him for killing the actor, but he would deal with that later. Perhaps The Old Man was right about being the newsmaker after all.
He walked back out of the eatery to the arrival gate, and stood drinking his coffee, watching reunion after reunion; the happy smiles occasionally broken up by the tourists walking through the doors looking completely lost, yet trying their hardest to look like they knew exactly where they were going.
He saw Peacock and Murray walk through the doors and studied them for a good minute.
David Peacock was a wiry man, in his early forties he estimated, judging by the grey flecks of hair that were starting to break through on the side of his head. He was a fraction under six feet tall and he wore silver rimmed glasses. He walked like a man with authority and direction, like he was focussed on where he was heading, and he wore a smart and well cut expensive suit.
Taylor Murray was the complete opposite. He looked late twenties, stood around six foot two, had black hair which was shoulder length, and for now, had been put

into a ponytail. He was a well-built guy, big arms and shoulders and Ward could not decide if it was his natural physique, or had been earned by devoting lots of torturous hours to the weights in a gym. He had dark eyes which gave away nothing, and Ward's initial impression, was that regardless of Centrepoint's claim that they would be Deniables already if there was room, he was happy that they were on board.

He waited until they had walked out into the main hallway and approached them from the left hand side.

"Peacock and Murray I presume?" he said, extending his hand.

They both took his hand and shook it; Murray squeezing his hand harder than he needed to, which he took as a good sign. He was eager to prove himself and make a good impression.

"You've both been briefed?" he asked, fixing a stare on them as he asked the question.

"Comprehensively," Peacock replied.

Murray nodded.

"What were you told?" he asked Murray.

"That we are to follow your lead and that you are hunting some very important evidence. The Old Man said you would tell us all we need to know," Murray replied.

"And to try and limit the number of people you kill as well," Peacock added with a smile.

"He said that?" Ward asked, unsure if Peacock was joking or not.

"Yes he did. He also said that we are to call him and keep him informed of your movements at all times and the moment you are out of our sight, we are to tell him what you know so far."

"But we figure that you are the one on the ground, and so we aren't going to come into your team and start telling tales behind your back, so you tell us what and when you want him to know," Murray added.

Ward liked these two immediately.

Outside, they saw Buck leaning against the car in deep discussion with an airport cop. It looked like a friendly conversation and they reached the car and climbed in without speaking or acknowledging either of them; Ward in the front passenger seat and Peacock and Murray climbing into the back. Buck stepped in a few moments later.

"He let you wait there?" Ward asked quizzically, knowing how petty and pedantic the airport cops were about parked vehicles.

"I used my charm," Buck replied, "Nice to meet you two," he added, looking in the rear view mirror at Peacock and Murray as he said it.

"What did you say?" Ward asked.

"I told him what any cop would understand," he replied.

"Which is?"

"I'm almost twenty years on the job and I've just found out that my wife has been sleeping with my partner and my brother has popped inside to try and smooth things over."

"Why would you want your wife back?" Murray asked.

"I want my partner back!" Buck replied and they all laughed out loudly.

Westwood – Los Angeles

The two men that Andrea Yeschenko had sent to Westwood, Nikolay and Pavel, arrived at the scene and were dismayed to see there were at least forty officers, paramedics, cops, crime scene people and suited guys milling around. They stood looking at the people walking in and out of the house and both felt afraid of having to be the one who had to break the news to Yeschenko about what they had seen.
"You can't stand here," a cop said as he walked over to them, eyeing them up and down suspiciously.
"We need to see Erikson," Pavel said, "It's about the burglary in Hollywood he is working on and we have some information for him."
The cop eyed them up and down once more before finally saying,
"Wait here."
They waited for over five minutes. Not speaking, just watching people swarming in and out of the house and around the gardens. Then a flustered looking cop with ginger hair and sergeant stripes walked over to them looking very irate.
"You shouldn't be here," he said as he approached them. He took out his notebook and pretended that he was starting to take notes.
"The King wants to know what is happening," Pavel said.
"What does it look like?"
"I mean with the girls, when can he get them back?"
Erikson looked at them, stunned.

"You think they will let the girls go back?" he asked in disbelief, "What planet are you on?"
"The planet where you are paid good money to keep the girls and the house secure," Nikolay replied.
"Then perhaps you should get your own house in order first," Erikson said.
"What do you mean?" Pavel asked.
"Ballistics confirmed that the bullets came from a Makarov handgun. That's a Russian gun. Someone is picking a turf war with you," Erikson replied. He looked afraid. This had escalated from turning a blind eye to Yeschenko's operation to a Russian mafia war and he wanted no part of it.
"Where are the girls?" Nikolay demanded.
"You don't understand this. It's over here. The cops are sifting through a pile of dead bodies that all dress and display the same tattoos as you two, and the girls will now vanish and be put into the social care system. I couldn't find them if I tried," Erikson replied. "You should leave now."
"You belong to us. You do not give us the orders" Pavel said threateningly.
"You see those guys over there," Erikson said, pointing to three guys huddled together talking.
Nikolay and Pavel both nodded.
"Look at their earpieces. Look at their suits. They came into this crime scene and walked over anyone with any jurisdiction. That means they are big hitters. More than FBI, although I don't know exactly who they are, but I'm out of this."
"You are out when we say you are out," Pavel said.

"Officer," Erikson said to a rookie cop standing twenty feet away, "Can you remove these men from the crime scene please and arrest them if they come back," he added, and then he turned and walked away.
The cop walked over, puffing his chest out en route and said,
"Beat it."
Pavel and Nikolay turned and walked away without speaking. Both trying to establish how they could convince the other that they would have to be the one to tell The King what they had just seen and heard.

Ward, Buck, Murray and Peacock arrived back at the warehouse in Marina Del Rey twenty five minutes after leaving the airport. They entered through the key code system and stepped through into the main warehouse.
"Make yourselves comfortable," Ward said to them all, pointing to the battered table and chairs, "I need to make a call."
He stepped back into the reception area and closed the door.
He dialled Eloisa's number, not really expecting her to answer.
"Hello stranger," she said as she answered.
"You answered!" he said in mock surprise, "I was starting to wonder if you were a figment of my imagination."
"I'm so, so sorry," Eloisa replied, "It has been manic here. I got your message about O'Leary and tried ringing back but it went to your voicemail."
"You could have left a message," he replied, realising just how disappointed he was that she didn't do so.

"I don't like doing that Ryan, you know that. I would rather hear your sexy voice."

Every time, every single time he thought to himself. He only had to hear her voice and he was captivated once more.

"I miss you. I want you to come over to California for a few days. I could do with some downtime and I want that time to be with you."

"I can't spare three days Ryan. But I can probably push to tomorrow night if I come over for a few hours and get the red eye back."

Ward felt his heart sink.

"They are putting more and more on me. They have hinted that I might be in line for a promotion and that means an even higher access level for me. Think of the good we could do."

As much as he loved Eloisa, he sometimes got the smallest feeling that she was using him. Her job in the child protection arm of the U.N. was an admirable job and was one of the reasons that he admired her so much, but the use of the word 'We' sometimes sounded hollow. Eloisa would feed him targets and he would risk life and limb by taking them out. It didn't seem so much of a 'We' when he analysed it like that. But he didn't want to argue or say anything negative about his perception of 'We' and so he let it slide.

"Tomorrow night then, the night together in Santa Monica?" he asked, pretending to forget about her saying she would catch the red eye flight back.

"Four hours Ryan," she replied, "I will spend double that travelling but you are worth it. I am desperate to see you too."

Ward smiled to himself, his spirits immediately lifted.
"There is something else" he said.
"What is it?" she asked.
"What do you know about a guy called Yeschenko?"
"Andrea Yeschenko?"
"Yes. You've heard of him?" he asked, surprised she knew his first name.
"Yes I have" she replied, "His name has come up a few times in high level meetings that I have attended."
"What do you know about him?"
"I know that he traffics young girls into The States. I know that he has an exclusive client list, and I know that you need to be very careful if you are working on anything that involves him right now Ryan. Are you?" she asked, genuine concern in her voice.
"I'm always careful" he replied. "What else do you know about him?"
"I also know that he is untouchable" she said, "There is a reason why he is off limits. What that reason is, I don't know, but I know that the executive committee have pulled back from investigating him whenever his name is brought up, so you need to be very careful."
"I'm always careful," he repeated.
"I meant on whose toes you tread on Ryan."
He felt calm. She had confirmed the information that Centrepoint had given him and now he knew definitively that he was up against the political elite of Washington. They would be the only ones with the power to stop the U.N. investigating Yeschenko.
"I love you," he said down the phone, "Promise to get here by tomorrow evening?"

"If you promise to give me a massage with your fingertips," she replied.
"We have a deal."

ELEVEN

Park Avenue – New York

"What have you got on The Bahia Shipping Company?" Nicole-Louise asked Tackler.
"Yeschenko launders his money through the company but he doesn't own it," he replied.
"So who does?"
"Two guys called Taft Yeshelvin and Saburo Pavlechenko," he said, "I think they are supplying the children."
"Why?"
"Look at their accounts and see what you think," he answered, knowing full well he was laying down a challenge to Nicole-Louise, to see who could solve the puzzle first.
She turned and started tapping furiously on her keyboard. Within ten seconds she had the same set of accounts on her screen that Tackler had spent the last hour digesting.

"Can you see the payments that have been made over the last four years?" he asked, knowing that giving her an indication of where to start looking would piss her off.

"I have good eyesight Tackler, I don't need you to point out the obvious," she curtly replied.

"Only trying to help you catch up."

He felt a pencil hit him on the shoulder but chose not to turn around or respond.

"There's over four million dollars been paid into their personal accounts. The account numbers don't match the company registered accounts, so where is that coming from?" she asked him.

Tackler said nothing, simply because he hadn't noticed it. He stared at his screen and saw what she was saying immediately.

It was now a race to discover where the money had come from. For the next ten minutes, they both tapped away at their keyboards with renewed vigour. Neither of them spoke until Nicole-Louise finally broke the silence by screaming,

"Beat you!"

It made Tackler jump. And then he cursed under his breath.

"The money is coming from an account in the Bahamas under the name of 'Red Star Progressions' and no doubt if we dig deep enough, it will then lead back to Yeschenko," she proclaimed, leaning back in her chair and putting her hands behind her head as she did so. Tackler conceded defeat and started looking into the accounts himself.

"They are based in the L.A. docks. I think we should call Ryan and tell him what we have found," Nicole-Louise said, "Do you want the honour, make you feel like you helped?" she added, with a big smile which reminded him why she was so perfect.

"OK. I will bow to your greater ability and call him," he replied.

"But do not tell him I found the list of names in the e-mails," she demanded.

Marina Del Rey

Ward's phone vibrated and he saw Tackler's name on the screen.

"What have you got for me?"

"Yes, I'm very well thanks Ryan, nice of you to ask," Tackler replied.

Ward ignored him and waited for him to continue.

"The short version is that Yeschenko is using a company called The Bahia Shipping Company to launder his money and move the children. His ill-gotten gains, we believe, are stored in the Bahamas in the accounts of a company called Red Star Progressions, but we need to confirm that."

"Well done. So you now know how the money is moving, but what else have you got for me?" Ward asked.

Tackler was clearly aware that he was asking whose names he had to give to him, so he could no doubt go and speak to them.

"Taft Yeshelvin and Saburo Pavlechenko," Tackler replied, "Both Russian nationals with extended visas," he added.

Ward could hear Nicole-Louise speaking in a muffled voice to Tackler in the background but he couldn't work out what she was saying.

"That's interesting," Tackler said. Ward was unsure whether he was talking to him or Nicole-Louise and so he stayed quiet.

"Nicole-Louise has just checked all of the shipping manifestos of the company and they take a standard route every time," he said.

"What is the route?"

"They start in Kaliningrad, Russia and spend ten days sailing to Durres in Albania, where I think they are collecting the children."

"And how do they get here?"

"Four weeks on a boat to Los Angeles."

"Have you any idea how many children have been moved?"

"No. But judging by the amount of money they are generating, a lot."

"They have offices in California?"

"Better than that," Tackler replied, "They have their headquarters there. Their only registered depot."

"Where?"

"In the Port of Los Angeles."

"How much money do they have between them?" Ward enquired.

"Cash and assets?"

"Just cash?"

"Four million dollars between them," Tackler replied.

"Steal it and hold it."

"All of it? Why?"

"Because they won't be needing it."

"OK," Tackler replied
"Send me the address and pictures of them right now," he instructed, "We will go and pay them a visit."
Ward hung up the phone.

Buck, Peacock and Murray looked at Ward quizzically. All of them heard his end of the conversation.
"Who are we going to pay a visit to?" Buck asked.
"There are two guys who are based in the docks called Yeshelvin and Pavlechenko. They are the guys bringing the girls here. They own a shipping company called Bahia and we need to go and find out what they know."
"And then what?" Murray asked.
"Do you know what these people do? Did The Old Man brief you on their operation?" he asked
"Yes he did," Murray replied.
"So what do you think we should do?"
"Well I was hoping you would say that we can kill them at our leisure."
"You have my permission, all three of you," he said, "But only after we have questioned Yeshelvin and Pavlechenko and got what we need."
All three of them nodded their understanding.
His phone vibrated and he saw he had received a message from Tackler. He opened it up and saw two pictures attached. He studied Yeshelvin and Pavlechenko for a moment and then made a note of the address underneath.
"Do you know the Port of Los Angeles at all?" he asked Buck.
"I know it very well."
"Slip number five, on Canal Street?"

"Yep, I know it."

"That's where we will be heading."

Buck nodded.

He passed his phone to Murray, who looked at the two pictures and handed it to Peacock, who stared long and hard at the screen and then passed the phone to Buck, who did the same.

"Now you know what the two people we need to question look like, make sure they are alive so we can actually get to ask them," he said.

"How much trouble are you anticipating?" Buck asked, "Supporting numbers that they might have for example?"

"No idea" he replied, "I figured we would know that when we got there and did a little recon work."

"A plan?" Peacock asked.

"Sure, we just knock on the door," Buck replied.

Port of Los Angeles – Canal Street

They turned into Canal Street from Nissan Way, Buck feeling the need to comment that Nissan's were "Shit cars," as he drove past the giant car park which had brand new models parked neatly as far as the eye could see. They drove past a building that displayed a worn and dirty looking sign that said, 'The Bahia Shipping Company', and parked at the end of the road.

The building was effectively just a warehouse with a two-storey brick building erected on the left hand side of it. It didn't look right; Ward thought to himself, it looked

like it had just been stuck on the side of the building in a rush.
There was a door at the front of the building and a sign above saying 'Visitors'. There were three windows either side of the door and the same on the first floor above.
He checked the magazine of the Makarov handgun that Buck had given him and tightened the silencer.
"You have any more of these?" he asked, waving the gun in Buck's direction as he said it.
"Three more in the trunk," Buck replied.
"Give one each to these two," he said, using his thumb to point over his left shoulder.
"We have our own," Peacock said.
"Are they Makarov's?"
"No, Glock's."
"Then you haven't got a gun. Take one from Buck and use that. Any bullets fired have to look like they came from Russians."
"OK. I get it now," Peacock replied.
Buck opened the trunk and handed Peacock and Murray a Makarov with a silencer attached.
"These won't fail on us?" Murray asked.
"I guarantee it," Buck replied, "I fire and clean them weekly. When you get to my age, you learn that being thorough is what has gets you here."
All four of them tucked their guns into the back of their waistbands and started walking towards the building, Ward out front.
"Seriously, what is our plan?" Peacock asked.
"Seriously? We just knock on the door and see how it plays out," Ward replied.

"Are you for real?" Peacock asked. Ward ignored him. They reached the building.

"Buck, you take Peacock and check the back to make sure that no one tries running off, and Murray and me will take the front," he said.

Buck nodded. Peacock still looked confused, like the knocking on the door plan was a joke that he didn't get. They both peeled off to the side and left Ward and Murray approaching the visitor's entrance.

They tried the door and it was locked. Ward peered through the dirty glass and could see that there was a reception desk in the hallway but no receptionist. That was a good sign. He looked to the left of the door and saw an intercom box. He pressed the call button.

"Follow my lead," he said as they waited for an answer. He scanned the exterior of the building and could not see any CCTV cameras; this made him feel that Yeshelvin and Pavlechenko were sloppy and not expecting any trouble.

Still no answer so he pressed the intercom again.

A moment later, a voice rang out through the speaker, "What?" a male voice, thick in Eastern European accent asked.

"I'm here to see Mr Yeshelvin and Mr Pavlechenko."

"Not here," the guy replied.

Ward looked at Murray and smiled,

"So rude these people at times," he said.

He pressed the button again.

"I said they are not here. Go away."

"Listen up you. I'm with the Port Authority and you have one minute to open this door, or I will have every

single officer down here with me smashing your door down. You have one minute," he said assertively.
They waited thirty seconds and then a figure appeared the other side of the dirty window, but neither of them could make it out clearly.
The figure opened the door.
Before them stood a thick set guy, early thirties, wearing jeans and a vest and his arms were covered in tattoos. Ward also noticed the hammer and sickle tattoo on the guy's neck, on the left hand side.
"You don't look like Port Authority" the guy said, looking at Murray and deciding his ponytail looked too much out of place.
"You don't look like Yeshelvin or Pavlechenko so that makes us even," Ward replied, "Where are they?"
"What do you want with them?" the guy asked.
"That's official business, not for your ears I'm afraid."
"What are you, Port Police?"
"I can't divulge that either," Ward replied, "I need to see them both now, it's urgent."
"Why is a British guy working for the Port Police?" the guy asked.
Ward rolled his eyes; he was now bored with the conversation,
"I'm not British dipshit," he said, and as he did so, he stepped forward with lightning speed and jabbed the guy full force directly into his Adam's apple, and the guy lurched back, his hands desperately clutching at his throat. He stepped through the door and then delivered another quick blow to the bridge of the guy's nose, the bone shattering as soon as it made contact with his fist. The guy fell to the floor, straight onto his back and he

was instantly struggling to get any air into his lungs to breathe. Murray stepped in behind Ward and closed the door.

Ward bent over the guy on the floor and quietly said, "Where are they?"

It was a pointless question. The guy wasn't going to be able to talk, he was barely conscious. He estimated that it would take him at least half an hour before he would be able to breathe properly, and then he would need to go straight to the hospital to have his throat and nose tended to.

But he was conscious all the same and a conscious guy can get back up and hurt you, so he pulled out his Makarov, swung his arm back and smashed it into the guy's temple full force. The guy lost consciousness immediately. Or he was dead. Either way, it didn't matter; he wouldn't be getting back up.

TWELVE

He stepped over the guy and walked forward to the bottom of the stairs and peered upwards. All was quiet. The reception area was neither warm nor inviting and he doubted that anyone had manned the worn desk that was facing the door for at least five years. The stairway was grubby, the white walls had long lost their colour, and there were hand marks and grime above the handrail that ran along the wall. The first set of stairs led onto a flat landing, running about six feet, before turning 90° right into another set of stairs. He climbed the first set and peered around the landing upwards.
All was quiet.
He turned and looked at Murray who had now drawn his gun and was three steps behind him. He nodded at him to let him know he had his back.
They moved forward up the second set of stairs and reached the landing of the first floor.
Still all was quiet.

There was an open plan office in front of them and it was completely empty; a worn beige carpet covering the floor, but not one piece of furniture to be seen. To the left there were two doors which led into an office with windows in partition walls. Ward peered inside the windows. They were both empty.
Still all was quiet.
At the far end of the open plan room there was another door which was closed. It was an oak door with varnish peeling off of it. He quietly moved towards the door, making sure to distribute the weight of his feet evenly so that the floor would not creak. He reached the door and put his ear against it to listen.
He heard voices.
Lots of them.
He estimated that he could hear at least five different voices or more specifically, five different types of laughter.
He beckoned Murray to come over and listen. Murray put his ear to the door for ten seconds and then stepped back and raised all of the digits on his left hand.
Ward nodded his agreement.
Five guys in there. Two would be Yeshelvin and Pavlechenko, and so that meant there were three who had no use to him.
He leant into Murray and whispered,
"You take the right, I'll take the left."
Murray nodded.
He put his hand on the door handle and mouthed 'On three,' followed by, "One….Two….Three."
He pushed open the door and stepped in four steps, leaving room enough for Murray to come in behind him.

He had his gun pointing to the left and Murray covered the right hand side of the room.

There were five guys sitting at a table on the right hand side of the room, drinking vodka and smoking. He noticed Yeshelvin and Pavlechenko immediately and saw that there were no weapons within reach on the table.

"Hands where I can see them," Murray shouted and the five guys raised their hands, open palmed, and then as one, lowered them on the table.

Ward stood still. No movement, no words, nothing.

He was just holding a cold stare straight ahead.

Murray looked at him and felt uneasy.

He was not moving and Murray had no idea why.

He stepped sideways to nudge him and then he saw it.

Crumpled up on the left hand side of the room, in a heap, next to some filing cabinets, was a girl.

She was naked.

She was no more than sixteen.

She was dead.

Murray caught a glimpse of Ward's eyes and then he understood. He was trying to contain his anger and calm himself down enough to refocus.

Murray kept his gun pointing at the guys and then after what seemed like an eternity, Ward spoke.

"How old is she?" he asked quietly

None of the guys replied.

Ward studied the guys for a moment. Yeshelvin and Pavlechenko he knew, but the other three looked like clones of the guys he had killed in Westwood and the guy who had opened the door to him earlier.

"You," he said, pointing his gun in the face of the nearest guy to him, "Why do you all have tattoos of a hammer and sickle on the left hand side of your neck?"
The guy said nothing. He just snorted and threw Ward a look of utter contempt.
Ward pulled the trigger and blew the side of the guy's head clean away. The bullet smashed into his skull and obliterated it. Blood and brain matter exploded across the table, over his hand and over the guy next to him. The guy slipped from the chair and was dead before he hit the floor.
He swung his gun around to the guy sitting to his right.
"How old is she?" he asked, still in a soft voice.
"Sixteen," the guy replied.
"Why is she here?"
"Because they gave her to us?"
"Why?"
"Because she is sixteen and they have no use for her anymore."
"What do you mean no use?"
"The customers don't want them once they are sixteen so they give them to us."
"Who gives them to you?"
"The King," the guy replied.
"Who is The King?"
"You have no idea what or who you are messing with," Yeshelvin spat across the table.
"Who is the king? Yeschenko?" he asked.
They all looked at him surprised. If he knew who the King was he was either crazy or well supported to attempt to take him on.

"You," Ward said to the guy who had given him answers so far, "Why do you have a hammer and sickle on the left hand side of your neck?"

"Because we belong to Mother Russia."

Ward thought back to the picture he had seen of Yeschenko and he knew that his tattoo was on the right side of his neck.

"Who killed the girl?" he demanded.

The guy said nothing but looked across at Pavlechenko.

"Who do you work for?" he asked the other guy, who was clearly one of Yeschenko's men.

"The King."

He lowered his gun and shot him straight between the legs. The guy let out a sickening scream and the other guy turned in his chair to lunge at him.

So he shot him in the chest, the guy's chest exploding and the blood started to pump out even before he hit the floor.

The guy who had taken the bullet between the legs was screaming in agony and writhing around the floor.

"Why did you do that?" Pavlechenko asked, fear etched across his face.

"They have crap dress sense, all of them," he replied, "It's a crime against fashion and we are the fashion police," he added; a comment that had Murray quietly laughing.

He bent down on one knee and stood over the guy who was desperately clutching his groin.

"It hurts, doesn't it?" he asked softly, "It probably hurt that poor girl just as much, so now you know how it feels you animal."

Yeshelvin and Pavlechenko were now frozen in fear. Their eyes were darting between the guy on the floor and Ward.

"How long before he dies?" Murray asked.

"Thirty minutes. Leave him, he deserves it," he replied as he pulled out a chair and sat himself down at the table. "I'm going to ask you two questions. If you tell me the truth you will remain unharmed, but if you lie once, I will kill you. Is that clear?" he calmly asked them.

They both eagerly nodded.

"Now I know how your boats sail from Kaliningrad to Durres to collect young children and then bring them here to the port and Yeschenko collects them," he said, "So are you clear on what I mean by I know you will be lying to me?"

They both nodded again.

"So to make this easy, I will ask you some questions, some of which I know the answer to and some I don't. So you have to decide if you want to gamble or tell the truth. OK?"

Yeshelvin and Pavlechenko both nodded again.

"I'm going to need a bit more than you two just nodding. Is that clear?"

"Yes," Pavlechenko said.

"OK," said Yeshelvin.

Ward studied them for a moment. He smiled at them. He knew that they were going to tell the truth no matter what. Their eyes told him that.

"How do you get through the port police and customs guys?"

"Hank White," Pavlechenko replied.

"Tell me about Hank?"

"He is the Harbour Master for our slip," Yeshelvin said.
"Slip number five?"
They both nodded. Ward raised an eyebrow to ask for verbal verification and they both said,
"Yes!"
"Hank is on Yeschenko's payroll?"
"Yes," Yeshelvin said.
"What else do you transport apart from poor, innocent children?"
"Timber and minerals," Pavlechenko replied.
"So that gives your company a legitimate foundation?" he said, more to himself than the other two, "How do you launder Yeschenko's money?"
"He pays us way over the odds for the materials that we import," Yeshelvin said, "And then we buy it back at a massive reduction under the market value and we pocket the difference."
"Then you make a big profit, transfer it to your accounts in the Bahamas, syphon some off to your personal accounts and then put it back into the system through operating costs and then you are legitimate again?" Ward asked.
"Pretty much so," Pavlechenko replied.
"How much does he pay you for the girls?"
"Nothing, we have no choice. We have to do it," Yeshelvin replied.
"What do you mean you have no choice?"
"The King will kill us if we don't help. It's easier to do what he says and take a cut than disobey him."
"Hank can't be the only one who would want to check your cargo. What about the customs people?" Ward asked.

"Yeschenko deals with it," Pavlechenko said, "Someone in Washington makes sure we have no unwelcome inspections."
"Who deals with it?"
"We don't know, we just collect the cargo from Albania, bring it here and it is taken away."
"Red Star Progressions. What is it?" Ward asked.
"It's Yeschenko's front," Pavlechenko replied.
Ward studied them both for a few moments. They had told the truth, he knew that. Now he knew exactly how Yeschenko got the girls here, cleaned his money and how he never got caught. Hank White would be the next one that he visited.
"So really, you are innocent in this?" he asked them.
They both nodded eagerly.
"Who were the four guys committing crimes against fashion?" he asked, pointing at the guy on the floor who he had shot in the groin, noticing for the first time that he was now unconscious. Or maybe he was dead. He didn't care either way.
"Yeschenko keeps four men here at all times, more when a shipment is arriving," Pavlechenko replied.
"When is the next shipment arriving?"
"In two days' time," Yeshelvin replied.
"How many children are on board?"
"One hundred and eight."
Ward felt sick to the pit of his stomach. He did not want to imagine the hell those young children were going through.
"How many are girls?"
"All of them," Pavlechenko replied.
"How old, youngest to oldest?" he asked.

"Nine to thirteen," Yeshelvin replied, looking down at the table as he said it.

No good showing or feeling shame now you sick bastard, Ward thought to himself.

He looked at Murray and said to him,

"What do you think we should do?"

"I think we should find out who killed that poor kid," Murray replied.

"It was Yeschenko's men," Pavlechenko replied.

"It honestly was," Yeshelvin added.

Murray stepped forward and stood right next to Yeshelvin. Without warning, he unleashed a thunderous right hook which caught him square on the jaw. The crack of his jaw breaking echoed around the room. Yeshelvin rocked on his chair and fell to the side, clutching his jaw.

"I hope that hurt," Murray said, "That's how it would have felt to that poor kid," he added as he walked over to where he was rolling around on the floor and raised his leg so his knee was at a 90° angle and stamped it down hard onto Yeshelvin's head. Not once, but four times until he was unconscious. Ward noted the hate that was in Murray's face and he wondered if he had the ability to be able to control his emotions when it mattered most. Maybe Centrepoint thought the same and that was the real reason he was not a Deniable.

Murray looked at Ward, almost apologetically.

"He's still alive," he said.

Murray looked at him quizzically.

"The girl isn't alive."

Murray nodded, moved over to Yeshelvin, pulled out his Makarov and pumped three bullets into him. He wasn't alive now.
Ward looked at Murray and nodded.
He then looked across the table at Pavlechenko.
"What is the name of the boat that will arrive in two days' time?"
"The Siberian Storm," he replied.
He raised his gun and shot Pavlechenko three times in the chest and watched as he slumped to the floor. Then he walked around the table and put two more bullets in him.
"Let's go" he said to Murray.
They walked out of the building and into the L.A. sun without speaking.
"You nearly lost control in there," Ward eventually said to Murray, "Don't let it happen again."
"I have a little sister who is sixteen."
"Don't let it happen again," he repeated.
Buck came walking around the corner with Peacock in close attendance.
"No one came out the back," he said with a big smile on his face.
"Make the call to the police," he said to Buck, "Tell them that you have seen some men, with vests and tattoos, dragging a kid into the building."
"I'm on it," Buck replied.

On the drive back to Marina Del Ray Ward turned and looked at Peacock,
"The Old Man says you are good Peacock, very good."
"I am," he replied.

"I believe you," Ward replied, "So I want you to do something for me after you have dropped me back at the warehouse."

Peacock shuffled in his seat and looked focussed, finally glad to be given something specific to do,

"What is it?" he asked.

"I want you to find someone for me and have him brought to the warehouse in less than three hours from now," Ward said, "And you can take these two with you for support.

"Who?" Peacock asked.

"A guy called Hank White."

THIRTEEN

Washington D.C.

Centrepoint scrolled through the lists that had been hurriedly prepared by his tech team. They had been compiled from the video evidence that had been collected in the hits on the three houses in New York and the singular Texas and Arkansas houses. There were some impressive names on there, some he expected, some had surprised him, but the two names that he was looking for were not there.

That meant that they were either customers in California, or in, God forbid, Washington. Having Ward running around the streets of the nation's capital was the last thing that he wanted.

He had sent The Optician, and the small team he had assigned to him, to what he considered was the most likely house that the two names would have visited, but he had come back empty handed. There were a few minor political players on the list he was now looking at, but nothing that could have an effect on the amount of influence that he held. The bulk of the list was made up of minor celebrities and sports stars.

The other two hits in New York by the rest of his team had been similarly fruitful, but it was still a long way away from what he was after.

Nicole-Louise and Tackler had managed to provide him with the most important information that he was holding right now. They had managed to provide him with the names of the three serving U.S. Senators, but he still didn't know what to do next. Nicole-Louise had informed him that she had got their names directly from Yeschenko by hacking into his e-mails but he would be way too smart to send any evidence electronically so Centrepoint had concluded weeks ago, when he first received the call asking for help, that Yeschenko would have the hard copies close to him. He was now slightly concerned that they were running out of places to find it. But names on a list meant nothing. He needed proof.

There was a knock on his door and he shouted, "Enter!"

A flustered looking tech guy walked in holding some sheets of paper,

"The lists from Texas and Arkansas sir," he said without making any eye contact at all and placing the papers on his desk.

"Any names on there that I should worry about?" Centrepoint asked as he picked up the paper and scrolled down the list himself.

"The CEO of Anson Oil, but that is the only major player sir. The rest are celebrities and small public eye figures," the tech guy replied.

"OK. File a summary report on everyone and everything you have, and do it quickly," he demanded, without looking at the guy, "And encrypt it in the usual way so that only I can read it," he added.

"Yes Sir," the guy replied and walked out of his office, closing the door quietly behind him so he wouldn't irritate The Old Man further. The guy had seen that look on his face many times before and he knew he would take it out on the foot soldiers who were available, rather than the operatives out in the field.

Centrepoint now had two very important calls to make but he could not decide which one to make first.

The decision was made for him when his private line rang and he recognised the screened number as a Washington number,

"Yes," he answered.

"What have you got for me?" the voice demanded rather than asked, in a tone which annoyed him immediately.

"You've had the three names that matter so far, the rest you don't need to concern yourself with," Centrepoint replied.

"People are getting nervous already, I've had Senator Calvinson call me at least six times today, have you seen the news?"

"Hiding the discovery of numerous dead Russian mafia and lots of young girls is not an easy thing to do. I think under the circumstances, I have managed it extremely well."

"It doesn't look like it from my viewpoint," the voice said, "I need the two key bits of evidence that you promised me and I need them quickly."

"I will find them. I have my best people on it."

"These tech people in New York who got you this information, how do you know they will keep quiet?" the voice asked.

Centrepoint thought about Nicole-Louise and Tackler and the secrets they knew; particularly the secrets they held about Ward's activities, and he had no worry that these secrets would stay safe with them. What he was extremely concerned about, was how the voice knew they had discovered the information.

"How do you know my people in New York found it?" he asked.

"You think you are the only person in Washington who has people working for him in every department?" the voice asked, a contemptuous tone ringing through his voice, "Two criminals who now work for you aren't hard to find."

Centrepoint didn't like being threatened. He had done it himself to people hundreds of times over the years but rarely had anyone in power made such a blatant attempt to throw threats his way. He decided the best way to play it was to ignore the threat and stay cool.

"We will find it and the tech wizards in New York will never reveal what they found. They know bigger secrets than what you are looking for," he replied in a calm voice.

"I doubt that very much," the voice said, "Your man leading this hunt, who is he?"

"Does it matter?"

"It matters to me. So who is he?"

"He's my best man. That's all you need to know."

"Well I suggest you get your best man to resolve this and find what I want quickly, or our deal is off," the voice replied.
"I will ensure everything will be resolved."
"Keep me informed McNair," the voice said.
"Goodbye Senator Reid," he said as he hung up the phone.
Centrepoint sat back in his chair and breathed in deeply and then exhaled loudly and slowly. Senator Madison Reid was an idiot and an irritant, but he sat on a high number of Senate Committees that rubber stamped finances and control his way, and he was too important to make an enemy of. He was fully aware that Reid was after the evidence in question for his own political progress, but he would be an important friend in the future. The bigger picture was always more important than the here and now he reminded himself. It was an ethos that had served him exceptionally well throughout his entire career and he would stick to it.

The next call he needed to make was to Ward. He doubted very much if he would answer, he never did but he picked up his handset and pressed the quick dial number more in hope rather than expectation anyway.
"Where are we?" Ward answered, the fact he heard Ward's voice threw him momentarily.
"Not a lot further than we were," he replied.
"Meaning?" Ward asked.
"Meaning that we have taken out the three houses in New York and the ones in Texas and Arkansas and we still haven't found what we are looking for," Centrepoint replied.

"What are we looking for exactly?"
Centrepoint knew that he was going to have to tell him they were looking for something important, but he could not tell him what,
"You are looking for all of the evidence that you can find in the houses. That's it."
"Why do you think it is here in California?" Ward asked, "I mean, if this was just political then it would be in Washington so there is much more to this than you are telling me."
"I don't know what we are looking for," Centrepoint lied, "Only that we have to have it before any damage is done with it. You will know what it is before I do."
"I don't like it," Ward replied, "It seems back to front."
"You have four more places in California. Did you get my comprehensive list?"
"Yes I did. I will concentrate on them now. But I need two things from you and quickly."
"Shoot?"
"Firstly, I want you to put The Optician on Nicole-Louise and Tackler to keep them safe. We have enough people here now, McDermott is on his way and they could be in danger, I know how departments work," Ward said.
Centrepoint smiled to himself. That was why he rated Ward so highly, the second best ever after an operative called Gill Whymark, who had gone rogue. Ward was always one step ahead; almost as though he had heard the conversation that he had just finished with Senator Madison Reid.
"OK. And the second thing?" he asked.

"There is a harbour master here in Los Angeles who is ensuring that these children get through undetected. Someone in Washington is sorting the paperwork and it has to be someone important. I want you to find out who it is."
"What's the Harbour Master's name?"
"It doesn't matter. He'll be here shortly; I will get everything out of him that I need. You just do those two things for me. OK?"
"OK" Centrepoint replied and the line went dead.

Marina Del Rey

Ward had been waiting patiently at McDermott's warehouse for the last two hours. Now he was becoming impatient. He took out his cell phone and called Buck's number,
"Hello?" Buck answered.
"Where are you? It shouldn't take three of you that long to get one guy."
"He was down at the port investigating why a shitload of Russians and a young girl have turned up dead," Buck replied.
"So where are you now?"
"We are just pulling up outside."
He walked out into the reception area and opened the front door and stood in the doorway watching. Murray and Peacock stepped out of the rear of the car and Peacock beckoned with his gun into the back seat and Hank White stepped out.

Hank White was not what he expected him to be. Simply based on his name, he had assumed him to be portly and old; after all, Hank was a fat man's name he had told himself, so it was a fair expectation. But this guy wasn't portly or old. He was in his mid-thirties, looked very trim and well presented in a smart suit, and he looked handsome and respectable. He had short, neat hair and when he stood up, he was well over six feet tall. He looked like a ladies man.
Peacock kept his gun on White and ushered him towards the warehouse reception entrance. Ward turned when they were about six feet away and walked through to the main warehouse and took one of the chairs from the table in the corner and sat it in the middle of the floor, with a good twenty feet of space on either side. Peacock, Murray and Buck all walked in behind White and Ward said,
"Sit him there," pointing to the chair.
Peacock sat him down and he threw Murray a bunch of cable ties,
"Secure him," he said and then watched as Murray cable tied White's hands and ankles tightly to the chair.
He studied White for a moment. He didn't look frightened which indicated that he was either completely unaware of the seriousness of his predicament, or he was a nasty guy. He decided to find out which one it was.
"Have you any idea why we have brought you here Mr White?"
"No. Whatever it is for, you have made a massive mistake, I'm a federal employee and most of the LAPD and LAPP will be looking for me right now. So you are in serious trouble," he replied.

"Well, if you help us and answer a few questions then we can have you back before anyone notices you are gone," he replied.

White studied Ward for a moment, so he played along, smiling at him as he stared back.

"You were investigating an incident at the offices of The Bahia Shipping Company. What was it about?" he asked.

White still looked at him, an unsure look on his face.

"What's it got to do with a Brit?" he asked.

"I'm not British," he sighed.

This seemed to confuse White. He sure as hell knew what a British accent sounded like and he knew this guy looking down at him, with a smile on his face, had one. Ward knew exactly what White was thinking and so he thought he may as well use it to his advantage,

"I'm Russian. I was educated for ten years in London, which is why I have the accent," he said.

Now White didn't appear to look so comfortable. He wasn't afraid of the Americans who kidnapped him or the British guy who initially spoke to him but after the lie he had just told, it was clear that he was afraid of the Russians.

"So I will ask again. What happened at the offices of The Bahia Shipping Company?"

"It's LAPP business, I can't divulge that," he replied.

Ward stepped closer to him,

"My guess is that you have found six dead Russian guys and a young child dead there and you are doing all you can to cover it up," he said.

The whole demeanour of White changed.

"I also think that Yeshelvin and Pavlechenko gave you up to us because they knew they would die if they didn't.

But I didn't like them anyway so I killed them," Ward said, "And at this moment in time, I don't like you either, so you are in a really shitty position."

He looked into White's eyes and saw the fear that was creeping into them. He wasn't tough and nasty; he was stupid and totally unaware of the seriousness of his predicament.

"So, if you tell me what I need to know, I might start to like you and then we can forget about this. Do you understand?"

"Yes. I won't lie," White replied.

"Good," Ward said, "I will know if you are lying. We gave Yeshelvin and Pavlechenko every opportunity to tell the truth, but they lied and so that is why they are now dead."

"I promise I won't lie" White repeated.

And Ward knew that he wouldn't.

"We know about the children coming in on The Siberian Storm and where they go, so tell me how you oversee the transfer of the children from the boat to the vehicles that take them away?" he asked.

"Prior to the boat docking I fax some documents over to a number I have been given," White replied.

"What type of documents?"

"Applications for collection notes and access passes."

"Who does the fax number belong to?"

"I don't know that."

"Who raises the collection notes and access passes?"

"They are done above my head," White replied.

"By who?"

"Someone at State who agrees the shipping route at the start of the journey. Anything moving from Russia has to get approved by State before it leaves for here," he replied.

"So what is your part in it?"

"I draw up the rota for all ships that dock in slip number five and I make sure that the unregistered cargo is moved before I send a team on board for the statutory checks that have to take place. There is no getting away from them, so I make sure the boat has nothing on it that it shouldn't before letting my team on board," he replied.

"They aren't cargo, they are children," Ward replied, "How much do they pay you for that?"

"Nothing," he replied.

"Nothing?"

"I have gambling debts, big debts that I owe to the Russians. It wasn't my fault, they kept offering me credit, more and more of it and eventually they called it in and I couldn't pay it."

"You really are stupid," Ward said, "It didn't occur to you that they targeted you for what you can give them and gave you the credit so you would have no choice but to do what they say?"

"It didn't at the time but I guess you are right," White replied.

"How much is a big debt?"

"Three hundred thousand dollars."

"How many boats have you let come in unchecked?" Ward asked.

"Nineteen so far," he replied.

"That's almost two thousand children," Ward said, struggling to control his own anger, "You've knowingly let them bring in two thousand children knowing what they do with them?"

"It was that or they will kill me."
"Have you been instructed by anyone to cover up what happened down in the docks this morning?" Ward asked.
"Yes I have," he replied.
"By who?"
"The Secret Service," he replied.
Ward looked at him carefully. He was telling the truth. He knew that without a doubt.
"Do you have children of your own?" he asked.
White looked shamefully at the table and didn't speak, but his body language answered for him.
"Why would the Secret Service tell you to cover it up?"
"Because they said what happened could have political ramifications between Russia and the U.S."
Ward wanted to get his gun out and shoot White in the face. But right now he needed him and so he made the call, against his own urges, for the sake of the bigger picture and said,
"Do you want me to clear your debt forever?"
White looked up at him, slightly confused.
"What do you mean?" he asked.
"I mean, do you want me to erase your debt forever so you can go back to having a normal life?"
"Of course I do."
"I'm not interested in you, only the Russians. The next delivery can lead me to their main man and I am going to destroy him and everyone close to him. Help me do that and your debt has gone," Ward said.
"What do you want me to do?" he replied.
"In two days' time The Siberian Storm is going to dock. I want you to make the area as clear as you can and we will be waiting to board ourselves. Can you do that?"

"No," White replied.

The answer surprised Ward,

"What?"

"It's not docking in two days' time, it's docking tonight," White replied.

"What time?"

"Midnight."

Yeshelvin and Pavlechenko had lied. But why? Maybe there was something else on that ship that needed hiding too, Ward thought to himself.

"These two will take you back now," he said pointing to Peacock and Murray, "They will give you my number and you will contact me and keep in touch throughout the day. Is that clear?"

"Yes, I promise. I want this to end," White replied.

He nodded at Murray to cut the cable ties and release him from the chair. White stood up and shuffled on his feet and then looked at him,

"I know it was bad what I did and I am sorry," he said.

"You are apologising to the wrong person," Ward replied.

"I was scared, real scared and these Russians are ruthless, actually, beyond ruthless, they are evil."

"Do what I have asked you to do and that will go some way to putting things right and then you can have your life back. Maybe invest your time and efforts into charity work, you know, helping abused children."

"I will. I promise."

Murray beckoned for White to follow him and Ward watched him walk out of the warehouse with shoulders slumped.

He had no sympathy for Hank White. Any decent human being would rather have died than subjected those poor children to the hell they had been exposed to, he thought to himself.

He decided right then that Hank White would die within the next twenty four hours.

He didn't like Hank White.

FOURTEEN

Park Avenue – New York

Nicole-Louise stared at her screen and scrolled down the numbers that were the most frequently called over the past three weeks from Andrea Yeschenko's cell phone. One number jumped out at her, not for the frequency of the calls, but for the duration. There were over thirty calls that had lasted exactly ten seconds, and it was obvious that someone was not answering his calls and that the phone was going to the numbers voicemail box. It was a non-existent number according to the phone company records, so she went in through a back door that she had discovered phone companies keep for numbers they want to hide, and found the call history of the phone in question. There were three numbers that jumped out at her, numbers that had been constantly used over the past twenty four hours and she then checked who they belonged to.

And then she pulled her hands away from her keyboard and stopped what she was doing immediately.
She had now found the two missing names that Ward was hunting.
She looked over her shoulder and Tackler was tapping away on his keyboard, oblivious to what she was doing. She closed all of the windows on her screen and stood up,
"I need to get some fresh air, she said, do you fancy a bagel from the deli?" she asked.
"Not giving up already are you?" he replied, "I'm making real progress with Yeschenko's money trail and within the hour I will be ready to steal it all if that's what Ryan wants," he added smugly.
Nicole-Louise feigned a smile and said,
"I'm giving you a chance to catch up."
"I'll have my usual, and a passion fruit smoothie," he said with a wink, "I know how you love it when I am full of passion," he added, a big smile breaking out on his face as he spoke.
But passion was the last thing that Nicole-Louise could think about, she felt sick to the pit of her stomach and very frightened.
She was not meant to find what she had found, she knew that. She also knew that the likelihood of her setting off a trigger when she accessed the records of the people she had just discovered was very high.
She had made a big mistake and she didn't know what to do.
She grabbed her denim jacket from the sofa, collected her keys and walked out of the apartment.

Hart Senate Office Building – Washington D.C.

The Uniformed officer of The United States Capitol Police stood guard outside the door of the Senator, and nodded to the guy in the dark suit, with his ear piece clearly visible, as he approached the door. The guy in the suit knocked three times, just below the gold name plate that said 'Senator Madison Reid'.
"Come!" the voice bellowed out from inside.
The guy in the suit walked in and closed the door.
"You have a problem," he said.
Senator Madison Reid seemed to have nothing but problems these last few weeks, ever since the blackmail threat had been brought to his attention. Reid was an overweight guy in his mid-fifties, whose face was always bright red. He also sweated a lot, and even with the air conditioning at full throttle, he was sat at his desk, his face covered in beads of sweat, as though he had just completed a five mile run.
"What now?" he asked, without even looking up at the guy in the suit.
"Someone has just hacked into your private phone records. We got a flag that someone was digging around and so we bounced them around but they were pretty smart and got in all the same. You know what that means?"
"Do we know who it was?" Reid asked.
"It's a New York address, probably those same kids who sent that stuff over to McNair."
"Do you know what they found?"

"Everything I'm assuming," the guy said, "If they are smart enough to get into our system, they are smart enough to find out who you were calling."

"This gets worse."

"So you now have a much bigger problem. Get it sorted," the guy in the suit said before walking out without saying another word.

Marina Del Rey

Ward was still trying to decide why Pavlechenko and Yeshelvin had lied to him. Maybe there wasn't a reason apart from protecting themselves from the wrath of Yeschenko.

"Why do you think they would lie about the ship arriving tonight?" he asked Buck.

"Maybe there is more on the ship than children?" he replied, "Whatever it is, we now know when it is coming in, so we can find whatever it is and stop it from ever reaching its destination. And kill every single Russian that we come across."

Ward nodded his agreement.

The quiet of the warehouse was broken by the noise of the motor which opened the warehouse doors kicking in, and they both jumped to their feet, guns drawn.

As the doors rose at a much quicker speed than they should have, they revealed a smiling Martin McDermott standing there, dressed all in black, and behind him two black Range Rovers.

"The cavalry is here," he shouted to Ward.

"You're late," he shouted back.

"I said nightfall." McDermott replied as he walked into the warehouse with the two black Range Rovers creeping in behind him.

"And I took nightfall to mean 3:00pm. It's ten past," Ward replied looking at his watch.

The two Range Rovers came to a stop inside and the doors opened and Fuller and Fringe stepped out of the first one, joined almost in tandem by Paul McDermott, Walsh, Wallace and Wired.

The best fighting team in the world were now here. They all stepped forward and hugged Ward. He introduced Buck to everyone and they all shook his hand. Then they instantly walked over to the table and assumed their positions, McDermott sitting in the old, tattered armchair and Fringe scooping up the chair that Hank White had been sitting on twenty minutes previously and bringing it over to the table on the way.

"I guess we stand," Buck said with a smile.

"So, The Old Man called me again which is highly unusual; what is this about?" McDermott asked.

"We hit some offices down at the docks this morning and the Secret Service were sniffing around after. So what does that tell you?"

"The President has been a bad boy and someone is trying to cover it up?"

"That's what I thought," Ward said, "But really, with what you know about him, can you see it?"

"All politicians are liars so I wouldn't trust any of them," Paul McDermott interrupted.

"I can't see it," McDermott said, "So perhaps the Secret Service aren't protecting one of ours?"

"Meaning?" Ward queried.

"Meaning that The Old Man said that we have to do whatever we have to do, to help you find the evidence you are looking for. The Secret Service protects the President and Vice President only," McDermott said.
"And also any Senator who has been first lady," Wallace said, thinking about the recent Secretary of State.
"But they also look after foreign heads of state and their attaché's. We can't risk having one of them killed on our soil and we don't trust their own security," McDermott said.
"I didn't know that."
"No one does," McDermott said, "So what I want to know is what we have so far?"
"I had better call him and ask him then," Ward replied and he walked out of the room, into the warehouse reception area and dialled Centrepoint's number.
"You are getting better at checking in," Centrepoint said sarcastically as he answered.
"I need to ask you a couple of questions and you have to give me the truth. OK?"
"If I can," he replied.
"From the evidence that we have all collected already, what have you got?"
Centrepoint paused for a few seconds and then said, "I have evidence of three U.S. Senators engaged in sexual acts with children under sixteen."
"Three? And there's more?" Ward was starting to feel sick inside, "Was that on the computers that we found?"
"No. Nicole-Louise and Tackler hacked into Yeschenko's information and found them."
"Are they serving Senators?"

"Two of them not anymore, but one of them is," he replied.
"Do you have The Optician protecting Nicole-Louise and Tackler as I asked?"
"Yes I do."
"Swear that to me."
"I swear," Centrepoint replied. "There are two more people. High ranking government people who we believe are involved," he added.
"Who are they?"
"I don't know. That's the problem," he lied.
"So what do you know?"
"I know that people on Capitol Hill are trying to threaten me and push me away from it."
"Do you think the President is involved?" Ward asked.
"No, it doesn't go that high."
"Secret Service involvement suggests it does."
"They are often used to sort messes out. The Chief of Staff allocates them where he sees fit. I wouldn't get too hung up on that part of it. Just don't kill any of them," Centrepoint replied, "That will cause huge problems that I can't protect you from."
"What did you find out about who is clearing the ships down at the docks?"
"I'm still waiting for the information on that. You will have it as soon as I do."
"OK. I have some things to do."
Ward hung up the phone.
He walked back into the warehouse; eight pairs of eyes followed him in.
"What did you get?" McDermott asked.

"Three Senators, one still sitting on the Senate, have been abusing the children that Yeschenko supplied, but there are still two more people that we have to identify."

"So what do you think this is about?" Buck asked.

Ward smiled; he now had a clearer idea of what was happening.

"This is about good, old fashioned blackmail," he replied, "That is why we have a free hand to obliterate Yeschenko and his operation completely. They will use us to bury whatever evidence there is and they can carry on as though nothing has happened."

"And will we?" Buck asked.

McDermott and his team all laughed out loud as one voice. Buck looked at them in confusion.

"What?" he asked McDermott.

"Your first time working with him is it?" he said, pointing at Ward, "He has his own way of getting justice," he added.

"OK," Ward said, trying to bring focus back into the room, "We need to be in two places at midnight tonight."

"Where?" McDermott asked.

"We need to be hitting a ship down at the L.A docks and entering a house in Oakland up in San Francisco at the same time."

"Then let's start planning," McDermott said.

Ward nodded and walked over to the table to join them.

"How is your young lady?" McDermott asked.

"Shit!" Ward said, he had forgotten Eloisa was meant to be arriving tonight, "I need to make a call," he added and walked out into the reception area.

He dialled her number and was surprised yet again to hear her voice say,

"Hello?"

"You are getting good at answering."

"I'm learning" she replied and laughed, "I'll be heading to the airport in an hour or so," she added.

"Can we take a rain check on that? Something important has come up," he said, clear dejection in his voice.

"I was looking forward to it," she replied, sounding equally dejected.

"It's this Yeschenko thing, it's taken a new turn, and we have to move on it tonight."

"I looked into him out of curiosity" she said, "And I didn't like what I found."

"What do you mean?"

"Every time he gets highlighted, the files get shut down. That only happens when people in powerful positions want it to go no further."

"I think I've established that much."

"You need to be very careful Ryan. I have a bad feeling about this."

"You always have a bad feeling"

"That's because I love you," she replied.

"Look. This shouldn't take long and in a couple of days I'll be back in New York and then we can spend every night together. Deal?"

"Deal. Just make sure that you stay safe. I love you."

"I love you too."

Then the line went dead.

Hart Senate Office Building – Washington D.C.

Senator Madison Reid picked up the phone and dialled the number.

"Hello?" the voice answered.
"You've opened a can of worms McNair. I told you to keep those computer kids away from this," he spat down the phone.
"What's your point Senator?" Centrepoint asked.
"They hacked into my records and they will have pieced everything together; what they now know has just signed their own death warrants."
"I would consider that very carefully before you go down that route," Centrepoint replied.
"Are you threatening me?" Reid asked.
"No, I'm advising you to consider it very carefully."
"I've got your funding and secrets cleared through countless committees and so that means I own you. I am advising you not to pick a war with me."
"I'm not picking any war with you. You just need to think of the consequences of your actions."
"Nothing you say or do can influence me. You should have pulled them off. You were given clear instructions on what you had to do. You should have stuck to them."
"Again Senator, I advise you against doing any harm to either of them."
"You don't scare me McNair."
"I know Senator, but the person who will come after you if you harm them should. You should be very, very afraid of him."
The line went dead.

FIFTEEN

Park Avenue – New York

Nicole-Louise walked back into the apartment with the bagel and smoothie for Tackler. She took off her coat, handed them to him and went and sat back at her workstation. He didn't take his eyes off of his screen once; he was too engrossed in winning the race to find the exact flow of Yeschenko's money.
"Are you not eating?" he asked as he bit into his bagel.
"I'm not hungry," she replied, without turning around and looking at him.
"You are always hungry."
"Not today. I'm hungry to whip your ass and beat you but that's all," she replied still without turning around.
"Bring it on," Tackler said and got back to tapping on his keyboard.
But Nicole-Louise didn't take up the challenge. She frantically started tapping on her keyboard to try and erase any trace of where she had been looking and deleting any evidence of her ever having been there.

She started silently praying to God that she wasn't too late.

Washington D.C.

Centrepoint wasn't looking forward to making the call to Ward. He was fully aware that any threat against Nicole-Louise and Tackler would result in him making this whole thing personal, and that was when he was at his most lethal. But he had no choice but to tell him. Nicole-Louise and Tackler were crucial to everything that Ward did and without them, his ability to find the correct information would be greatly diminished. He decided that now was the time to tell Ward what he had been holding back.
He dialled his number.
For the second time that day, he was surprised to hear him answer.
"Yes?" Ward said.
"Are you alone?" Centrepoint asked.
Ward surveyed the room. He looked at McDermott and his team and saw seven of the most efficient killing machines in the world and Buck, a guy who was more than adequate.
"Yes. I'm alone," he replied.
"We have a big problem."
"What is it?"
"Nicole-Louise and Tackler have done something they shouldn't have."
"They did what I asked them to do so if anyone is in the wrong, it's me," Ward replied, a defensive tone in his voice.

"I know that but no one knows you exist and they have put themselves in a lot of danger by digging where they shouldn't have gone."

"Tell me you have The Optician protecting them, or I will be on the plane to New York before you can hang up," Ward said aggressively.

"It's OK. He's watching them and he has a couple of men on the ground with him, so for now they are safe," Centrepoint replied.

"For now?"

"You need to get the evidence quickly so we can close this."

"What do you think I have been doing?" Ward asked sarcastically, "It would help if I knew what I was looking for."

"I told you, I don't know," Centrepoint lied, "But I'm getting threats too from Capitol Hill, so you must be getting close."

"From who?"

"I don't know," Centrepoint lied again.

"There is a ship coming in tonight with over a hundred children on it, we will be there to welcome them," Ward said.

"And the houses Yeschenko operates?"

"We will be hitting another one at the same time that the ship docks."

"Where?"

"In Oakland."

"You think the evidence could be there?"

"I don't know," Ward replied, "But it's the furthest one away from us, so if we cross that one off of the list, we then have a neat little group of three more house around L.A. so we won't be stretched," he added.

"OK. Get the evidence and have Peacock or Murray race it over to me but don't look at it."

"I won't," Ward lied, "But you keep Nicole-Louise and Tackler safe or I will be coming for you. I mean it. They are my friends."

"There is one other thing," Centrepoint said, surprise in his voice from the threat that Ward had just made.

"There always is."

Centrepoint paused. He was gambling on the reaction he was going to get. Ward was always unpredictable.

"Gilligan," he said.

"What about him?"

"He's alive."

Ward almost dropped his cell phone.

"Say that again?"

"I have just found out that the paramedics managed to get a pulse and he was in a coma for three days, but came out of it yesterday. He's alive, Ryan. Critical but alive," Centrepoint said.

Ward felt a complete wave of emotion consume his body. He had been feeling such an intense anger over Gilligan's death that he questioned everything he did. Now he was being told that he was alive.

"Where is he?" he asked.

Centrepoint smiled to himself. The gamble had worked. Ward would now do anything for him and he decided now was the time to put the icing on the cake.

"He's in hospital in new York. We have the best surgeons working on him, and we have round the clock protection set up. I will make sure he pulls through."

"Thank you," Ward replied, still feeling confusion over what he had just heard.

"So you concentrate on finishing this quickly over there and I will make sure that Nicole-Louise, Tackler and Gilligan are safe and no harm will come to them," Centrepoint said.

Ward felt a warm, all-consuming rush of gratitude and faith for The Old Man at that moment.

"I will. I guarantee it," Ward replied.

Centrepoint hung up the phone.

Marina Del Rey

Martin McDermott looked at Ward. He knew him better than most and he could see something different in him. He saw a look that he had never seen before.

"What's wrong?" he asked.

His whole team turned their heads around and looked at Ward.

"It's Gilligan," Ward said, a frown on his face, "He's alive."

"What?" Paul McDermott said.

Ward went on to explain the conversation that he had just had with Centrepoint. Seven lethal killing machines all smiled as he spoke.

"That's me off the team then," Buck interjected.

Ward smiled.

"Can we trust them to protect Nicole-Louise and Tackler?" McDermott asked.

"For now, yes, The Optician is looking after them." McDermott nodded. He knew they would be safe.

A bell rang, indicating that someone was at the reception door.

"That will be Peacock and Murray," Ward said looking at Buck, "Let them in and then we can start to plan the attacks for this evening."

Buck returned thirty seconds later with Peacock and Murray. Ward introduced them to McDermott and his team and Ward allowed the statutory handshaking to take place and then said,

"What I don't get is how Yeschenko rose to prominence so quickly; coming into one of our cities as a virtual unknown and then a few years later becoming untouchable."

"Maybe I can help you with that," Peacock said

"How?"

"Have you heard of Gianfranco Deluca?" Peacock asked.

"The Mafia guy?" Buck said.

Ward nodded.

"Yes," Peacock replied, "Well he is out in Redondo Beach and he will be able to tell us why. He is the number one in L.A."

"And I'm sure if we just turn up he will welcome us with open arms," Ward said sarcastically.

"He will actually," Peacock said, "He's one of our informants and we use him to hide people we need to be kept hidden."

Ward sighed, dismayed that Peacock hadn't thought of mentioning that earlier.

"Sort a meeting with him," he said.

"For when?" Peacock asked.

"Now."

Peacock nodded at Murray and they both left the main warehouse to set up the meeting with Deluca.
McDermott looked at Ward and once Ward's eyes had set on his, he nodded towards the far corner of the warehouse and stood up. Ward followed him over to the corner,
"What's wrong?" Ward asked.
"These three guys you have here with you. What do you think of them?"
"The Old Man has vouched for them."
"And your feeling?"
"They seem competent," he replied, "And Buck is definitely old school."
"The other two?"
"Why do you ask?" Ward said.
"I don't know, I'm just getting a feeling about the other two. We are dealing with big hitters here, these people on Capitol Hill have a lot of power, and I guess I would feel more comfortable with just our usual team. But if you vouch for them, that's good enough for me," McDermott replied.
Ward studied McDermott for a moment. Along with Eloisa, Nicole-Louise and Tackler, Gilligan, Mike Lawson and The Optician, he trusted McDermott and his team more than anyone else in the world. If McDermott had a bad feeling about Peacock and Murray, he would trust that.
"I'll go with the two of them to meet Deluca. I'll see what I can find out about them while we are gone and try and dig to see if anything comes up."

"OK, I'm sure it's nothing more than the fact that they are new to the team, but being thorough has saved our lives on a number of occasions," McDermott replied. Ward nodded.

"Can you plan the hit on the Ship and the house in Oakland while we are gone?"

"I already have in my head," McDermott replied, "I'll send Wallace and Fringe down to the docks now to carry out the recon work and me and Paul will head up to Oakland to check out the house."

Ward's phone rang. He didn't recognise the number. He pressed answer but didn't speak.

"Hello?" the voice said.

"Who's this?" Ward asked.

"Hank White."

"What have you got for me?"

"I've got the paperwork from Washington and I just received a call."

"From who?"

"I don't know," White replied, "I never know, they are just voices."

"What did they say?"

"That I am to keep the area out of bounds to everyone when the ship docks."

"You told me they always do that?"

"They do," White replied, "But they don't usually tell me to prepare an extra fifteen passes for their people to access the area."

"OK Hank. You are doing well so far. Continue keeping me in the loop and all of your problems will go away," Ward said and hung up the phone.

"Trouble?" McDermott asked.

"That was the harbour master. He has just told me that he has been told to issue fifteen more access passes than usual for Yeschenko's men when the ship docks."

"He's nervous," McDermott replied, "Probably protecting his cargo."

Ward didn't respond. He just stood there staring into space. McDermott watched him thinking for well over a minute and then said,

"What is it?"

"I think I know what is happening."

"Are you going to share?" McDermott asked.

"No. Because I really hope I am wrong."

This was not an unusual reaction from Ward. McDermott had seen it many times before. Ward would work things out in his mind and keep it firmly to himself. He always did this. McDermott understood why. If Ward highlighted his suspicions, then the team would be less focussed on the task at hand, and that is when mistakes were made. He knew that Ward would tell him when he was ready, or when he knew definitively that he was right.

Like he usually was.

The fact that Ward was hoping that he was wrong, made McDermott a little edgy.

"OK. When you are ready," he said to Ward, "I have two hits to plan," he added and turned and walked back across to the table where his team were sitting.

Murray and Peacock walked back into the warehouse and for a moment didn't spot Ward in the corner and looked confused. Murray caught sight of him and nudged Peacock. They walked across to Ward and Peacock said,

"He'll see us in an hour"
"Let's go now," Ward said.
Peacock frowned.
"He's a bit strict with rules and meetings."
"He's a criminal. A rich one at that and I don't know how you two are used to working, but no scumbag dictates to me what I do and when I do it."
Peacock and Murray looked uncomfortable with Ward's sudden change of attitude.
"So let's go," he said and headed towards the reception area.
"Do you want me to come with you?" Buck asked.
"No," Ward replied, "McDermott has something for you," he added as he disappeared out of the warehouse with Peacock and Murray in close attendance.
"You two take the front, I'll have the back" Ward said as they reached the car, "I want to stretch my legs," he added.
If Martin McDermott said he had a bad feeling, he sure as hell wanted to find out why.

SIXTEEN

Redondo Beach – California

The drive down to Redondo Beach took half an hour. Ward did not speak all the way down.
Both Peacock and Murray had tried to instigate a conversation with him, but he simply didn't respond.
He did this to unnerve them. If they did have anything to hide, they would start to think that he was onto them and they would make a mistake very soon.
They turned up from the main beach and cut across a number of streets, all of them lined with sprawling mansions. It was an impressive area, one that Ward had never been to, and the whole place oozed with money. They turned into an Avenue, Ward noted it was called Avenue C, and they drove to the end. It actually wasn't an avenue at all; it was a cul de sac. They had almost reached the end when a guy stepped out into the road and started to flag the car down, by waving his right arm in the air. Peacock slowly pulled to a stop.

The guy was thick set and wearing a heavy, dark blue suit, in spite of the late afternoon sun still burning.
"No entry from this point sir," he said.
Ward noticed the bulge on the right side of his suit jacket, clearly a gun. But this guy was also clearly stupid Ward thought to himself, he could lower his window and shoot him in the face, before the idiot even had a chance to unbutton his jacket. These Mafia types always made him smile. They liked playing the tough guys but were never the smartest.
"We have an appointment with Mr Deluca," Peacock said.
"Who are you?"
"Mr Hastings," Peacock replied.
Ward wondered where Peacock had come up with that name and made a mental note to ask him later.
The guy pulled a cell phone out of his pocket and called up to the house.
"Hastings," he said down the phone.
The guy then nodded and said, "OK," and put the cell phone back in his pocket.
"When you get up to the house…" the guy started to say,
"We've been here before," Peacock said, "We know the routine."
The guy nodded and stepped back from the car, a sign that gave Peacock permission to continue.
They drove another three hundred yards and reached the end of the cul de sac. In front of them was a set of large iron gates, they were painted black and led onto an immaculate drive. To the right of the iron gates was a wooden gate, just wide enough for one person to walk through, painted brilliant white. Two guys were

stationed outside the iron gates; both in the same dark suits and both with bulges inside their jackets. One of them raised his right arm and opened his palm for Peacock to stop, which he was already starting to do.
"We need to get out of the car here," Peacock said over his shoulder to Ward.
All three of them stepped out of the car. The guy who had raised his arm to stop them walked over to them and said,
"If you have weapons, leave them in the car."
Ward watched as Peacock and Murray took out their guns and spare magazines and put them back into the car.
"What about you?" the guy asked Ward.
Ward ignored him.
"You had better leave it in the car if you want to talk to Deluca," Peacock said, "We have to go through the scanners next."
Ward shrugged and took out his Glock and his spare magazine, opened the back door of the car and tossed them onto the back seat.
"Anything else?" the guy asked.
Peacock and Murray shook their heads, Ward ignored him.
The wooden gates opened and another guy said, "Walk through."
Ward followed Peacock and Murray through the gates, as the Guy stood two feet inside holding it open for them.
As they stepped through the gate they walked straight under a giant metal detector, identical to the ones that were used at all international airports throughout the

world, and six feet beyond that were three more guys, all suited with the obvious bulges under their jackets. Ward smiled to himself. He imagined them all lining up on parade in the morning, so that their uniform could be approved as suitable for the day's tasks.
Ward hated Mafia criminals.
He had seen the misery that they caused, generally to innocent people, through their racketeering, trafficking, drugs, prostitution and intimidation, and then pretended that family was everything to them, regardless of the fact they had destroyed millions of families over the years. Close up though, these guys were nothing. They found safety and strength in numbers, like all bullies do, and right now, they were here to help him, not out of public duty, but for their own advantage and he would just have to suck it up and accommodate them.
They passed through the metal detector without any alarm sounding and stopped in front of the three guys.
"Raise your arms," the guy in the centre said.
They all raised their arms, almost as one, and the guys proceeded to frisk them roughly and thoroughly.
The first of the guys to do something properly Ward thought to himself.
"Clean," the guy in the centre said, "Follow me," he added, as he turned and walked away from the gates.
The two other guys followed behind them as they were led up a path which was shielded by thick greenery to the side and branches that hung overhead.
They reached the end of the path and came out into the glorious sunshine and the full view of the grounds and building of the Deluca residence.
Ward was instantly impressed.

The drive twisted like a snake from the gates up to the house. Either side there were immaculate green lawns, with flower beds that must have had a plant representing every colour of the rainbow, firmly embedded in the soil. The house itself was huge.
It was a Mediterranean style property with white, rendered walls and the sun was bouncing off of the walls, meaning he had to squint slightly. The whole house was covered in orange terracotta tiles and he counted twenty two windows at the front of the house alone.
They followed the guy up to the front doors, big double doors, which were big enough to fit four doors, and they were varnished in a deep oak colour. The doors opened as they reached them and they were led into an entrance hall.
There were six guys sitting on chairs randomly laid out, one either side of the sprawling staircase, one against the right hand side of the hall, one to the left and one either side twenty feet beyond the staircase.
They all wore the same suits.
But these guys were the smart guys; they all sat there with their guns in their hands.
An old guy in his late fifties came out and said,
"Mr Hastings, good to see you."
He had a thick New York accent and he certainly didn't look like the Mafia Godfathers that the movies liked to portray. He was about five feet six, heavily overweight and was completely bald. He was wearing a bright pink jumper with green and yellow diamonds across the front and beige coloured slacks with white Nike trainers.
Ward felt a massive smirk spread across his face. An

action that the guy took as a 'pleased to meet you' look and he smiled back at him.
"I'm good thank you Mr Deluca. How are you?" Peacock asked.
"Things are good. Who are your friends?"
"We aren't the fashion police," Ward said, "So you are safe in our company," he added, without a hint of sarcasm.
"He is the one that needs your help," Peacock replied, nervously pointing at Ward.
"Well come through," Deluca said, and led them into an office, the door opened by another of the suits as they reached it. Inside there was a big desk and Deluca went and sat down behind it and leant back in his big, leather executive chair and looked at Ward,
"So what do you want to know?" he asked.
"Andrea Yeschenko," he said, "Tell me what you know about him, right from the start?"
"I know that if you plan to pick a fight with him then you should reconsider your plans," Deluca replied, "My advice would be to walk away now. It's a fight that you can't win."
"Why do you say that?"
"Let me explain from the beginning?" Deluca said.
Ward nodded at him.
"Four years ago, word got back to me that there was this new kid on the block, a Russian guy," Deluca started, "Naturally, we can't have people setting up on their own so we put an end to it."
Ward frowned,
"You put an end to it?" he asked. "I don't understand?"

"We did just that. He had opened up a shop without our permission and so we hit it, took care of his guys and burnt the house to the ground."

"But you never put an end to it?"

"These Russians think they are tough, little value on human life, but they were so out of their league against us that they just upped and ran," Deluca replied.

"And then what happened?"

"We heard nothing for three months. He was just another punk that we had smacked down and put in his place, as far as we were concerned."

"And then?"

"We got a whisper that the punk had not only opened up another shop but three others around L.A."

"And what did you do then?"

"I pulled in some guys from New York and we decided to obliterate his whole operation."

"And did you?" Ward asked.

"The punk deals in kids. Do you know that?" Deluca asked.

Ward nodded.

"For all the bad things we do, children are a no-go. It was as much what he was doing to those poor kids, as the fact that he thought he could muscle in on our action that infuriated me and my colleagues so much," Deluca replied.

"So what happened?"

"We picked a place that he ran over in San Francisco and we sent twenty guys there to close it down."

"And did you?"

"Comprehensively," Deluca replied.

"And then?"

"And then we planned to take out the others in the same way. We put a half million dollar contract on Yeschenko's head."

"So something changed," Ward queried, "What was it?"

"They hit us," Deluca replied.

"The Russians hit the Mafia and you lost?"

"You are jumping too far ahead my friend; let me explain," Deluca replied, "We had a place down in Inglewood. Not a shop, a place where the families meet and discuss business opportunities and who has what slice of the cake. But no kids, ever. You understand that?" he added.

Ward nodded once more.

"They hit the place, an army of at least forty men. They wiped half of the bosses and their men out. Sure, we took down our fair share but these guys were good, too good to beat," Deluca said, sighing as he said the words, and for a moment, it looked as though he was remembering the friends that he had lost.

"So why didn't you call in reinforcements?" Ward asked.

"Obviously that is exactly what we did."

"And?"

"Their places started getting hit too, from Boston to Washington. But someone picked a fight with us that we could not possibly win," Deluca said, an air of defeat clearly audible in his words.

"The Russian Mafia swarmed into the country en masse?"

"I'll get to that."

Ward nodded.

"We hit a place in Westwood that he had."

"I've been there," Ward interrupted.
"We hit it hard, forty five guys and we managed to capture some of his guys and take them, so we could get a clear picture of how his operation worked, but we still could not take the shop down. They were too good."
Ward thought of Deluca's guys in their suits, with their guns completely out of reach and he wasn't surprised that a team of Russian fighters were too good for them.
"Maybe you should have hired some more efficient people?" Ward asked in all seriousness.
"That's the point my friend. We did. We hired ex marines, soldiers, anyone who we could find."
He studied Deluca for a second and right at that moment, he understood exactly what had happened. He understood why Deluca was resigned to keeping far away from Andrea Yeschenko and there was only one more thing that he needed to find out, although he was sure that he already knew the answer.
He looked at Peacock and Murray.
"Give us a minute alone," he said to them.
Peacock and Murray looked confused. Murray looked at Deluca,
"It's fine Mr Hastings. I like your friend," Deluca said.
They both got up from their chairs and walked out of the office. As soon as they had shut the door, Ward looked at Deluca and said,
"I have three questions Mr Deluca. Can you answer them honestly and accurately? What you tell me will stay with me."
Deluca nodded.
"Do you trust Mr Hastings?"
"He's a government agent. No I don't," Deluca replied.

"Who warned you off of Yeschenko and said that he was out of bounds?"

"The Don. The top boss in the whole of the U.S."

Ward nodded. He already knew the answer to the next question that he was going to ask, but needed to hear it straight from the horse's mouth.

"The guys you captured. You interrogated them effectively and got them to talk?"

Deluca nodded.

"They weren't Russian were they?"

Deluca shook his head.

"I need you to tell me exactly who they were?" Ward asked.

Deluca looked at Ward and studied him. Ward knew that he was weighing up if he could trust him or not and so he gave him a little nudge to help him make his mind up, "You need to tell your guys to step their game up. I could have killed every single one of them outside of the house on my way in and you would never have heard me, so whatever you tell me now, it is something that I can deal with and address in any way I see fit," he said.

"There is something about you I like my friend, so ask your question again," Deluca replied.

"Who were the guys that were fighting Yeschenko's war for him?" Ward asked, "The guys you captured, who were they?"

"They were American. They were government operatives. Two of them were CIA and two of them Delta force," Deluca said quietly.

"And the one thing you are holding back from telling me. I need to hear that too?" Ward said.

Deluca studied Ward. It was now decision time. Deluca made up his mind to tell him.

"The other three were serving Secret Service agents," he said quietly.

"Thank you for your help Mr Deluca" Ward said, as he stood up and walked out of the office without looking back.

He didn't speak until the three of them were back in the car,

"Get back to the warehouse as quick as you can, we need to review what we are going to do."

"Problem?" Peacock asked.

Ward ignored him.

SEVENTEEN

Park Avenue – New York

The Optician looked through his scope at the two guys that Centrepoint had provided him with on the street. They looked more than capable and they were blending in well, so he was confident that for now Nicole-Louise and Tackler were safe. He scanned up to their apartment window and saw that they were busy working away on their keyboards, back to back, totally oblivious to the fact that they were being watched.
He was good at that.
Watching people, undetected.
His mind wandered back to other occasions when he had been watching people. He remembered the time that he was in Dallas, a mission that ended with him eliminating the entire board of a pharmaceutical company, who were injecting a virus into unsuspecting people in bars and nightclubs, in a cruel plan to increase their profits. He had many, many stories to tell but he knew that the world would never hear them.

Inside the apartment, Nicole-Louise had done as much as she could do to cover her tracks. She hoped she had been quick enough before anyone traced it back to them. Oddly, she thought to herself, she was more worried about Tackler's safety than her own. She knew that she would never be able to live with herself if any harm came to him through her actions.

Tackler subconsciously knew she had stopped working by the lack of tapping on her keyboard and so he said to her,

"I've found all of the money, well almost all of it."

She turned around and threw a playful smile at him,

"But not all of it," she replied, "I'm right behind you."

"You seem very slow today, maybe you need a rest," he said and winked.

"It aint over 'til the fat lady sings," Nicole-Louise replied and started tapping aimlessly on her keyboard.

"I feel you," Tackler said and got back to work.

But Nicole-Louise didn't feel herself, or Tackler. All she felt was sick to the pit of her stomach and afraid. She would ring Ward and tell him what she knew and hope that he would know what to do. But she would give it a few hours and wait for him to call. All she could do now was keep looking at the digital time display in the bottom right hand corner of her screen and she found herself wishing that she as somewhere else, in fact, anywhere but in front of her screens.

But she was safe, even though she didn't feel it. The most deadly sniper in the world was across the street in another building, protecting them from harm

Marina Del Rey

They arrived back at the warehouse and saw McDermott and the team loading up the Range Rovers as they walked into the main area. Buck was standing at the workbench on the far side, loading a number of Makarovs; checking them for balance and ensuring that the firing mechanisms worked. He was inspecting each one of them very thoroughly.
McDermott saw Ward come in and walked over to him. "Can you two see if Buck wants a hand," he said to Peacock and Murray, and they both nodded and walked over to where Buck was standing.
"What do you think of them?" McDermott asked.
"I think they are good operatives, they are in The Old Man's pocket and they didn't get edgy when I was off with them and so I think we can rely on them," Ward replied.
"Good enough for me," McDermott said, "Now, do you want to agree the plans that we have come up with?" Ward nodded.
"Paul, Fringe, Wallace and Buck will head off to Oakland in a couple of minutes," he said, "That leaves you, me, Wired, Walsh, Fuller and the two new guys to handle the ship."
"Fifteen additional guys and the standard six that Yeschenko always sends, makes twenty one guys against seven of us?"
"Which is only three kills each," McDermott said with a smile.
"I fancy our chances," Ward replied, matching McDermott's smile in the process.

Paul McDermott walked over and said,
"We are ready. Synchronise?"
His father looked down at his watch and said,
"Now," and they both pressed a button on their watches.
"Be careful," McDermott said to his son,
"Always," Paul replied.
Buck loaded the last of the Makarovs into a hold all and walked over to Ward,
"They've just been telling me stories of your missions," he said, "Very impressive. I'd love to meet this Optician guy."
"No," Ward replied, "You really wouldn't."
Buck nodded and walked over to the Range Rover and climbed inside. Paul, Fringe and Wallace joined him, and the four doors shut with the clunking sound that solid, new vehicles always make when the doors are closed. The rollers shutter doors raised, much quicker than they should have, and within thirty seconds, the Range Rover was gone and the roller shutter doors were closed once again.
"Now we need to get ready," McDermott said to Ward.
"We have to get this right," he said, "We need to find if there is anything else on that ship apart from the children."
"We will be thorough as always."
"Good," he replied, "Now run your plan past me in every detail."

Oakland – California (11:30pm)

Paul arrived at the house in Oakland at 10:00pm. It was just off of Grand Avenue on Linda Avenue. The house itself was similar to the CIA house that he had been to the day before in Kansas.

Almost exactly the same.

The house was set a good forty feet back from the road. It had a drive which led around to the back of the house and their recon work had taken them to the rear of the building, where they saw that the same kind of lean-to had been erected to cover the whole of the back yard, where the cars parked so that no one could see who came in and who went out.

As the team had crept around the house they had counted twelve men. Clearly Yeschenko was taking the threats against him very seriously.

Paul and Fringe were to take the front of the house and Buck and Wallace the back. They were all sitting in the Range Rover while Paul went over it for the third time to make sure that everyone was completely clear on what they were doing. Like his father, Paul McDermott liked to plan, plan and plan again, covering every single eventuality that he could think of.

"Remember, the kids are the priority and then you get the digital stuff," he said to Wallace, who nodded his understanding, "And Buck. We shoot to kill and don't ask questions, is that clear?"

"It's fine with me," Buck replied, "I'm not the talkative type anyway."

All they had to do now was get into position and wait.

Port of Los Angeles – Canal Street (11:30pm)

Ward stood in the shadows of the giant shipping containers, pulled out his cell phone and called Hank White.

"Hello?" White replied.

"Have you issued the passes out yet?" he asked.

"Yes I have, they came here fifteen minutes ago."

"Describe them to me?"

"They were Russian. All wearing those tee-shirts and with those tattoos everywhere."

That was not the answer he was expecting. Now he felt slightly confused.

"Are you sure?"

"Of course I'm sure," White replied, "I've just processed them."

"How many of them?" he asked.

"I told you earlier, fifteen," White replied defensively.

"OK. Where are they now?"

"They will be down in slip five waiting for it to dock. It is on time, I have spoken to the captain and given him permission to bring her in."

"So fifteen guys, that's all?"

"Yes."

"OK. Good work, this will soon be over," he said and hung up the phone.

"Everything OK?" McDermott whispered.

"Hank White just lied to me," Ward replied, "He told me earlier that he had been told to issue an additional fifteen passes, now he is saying that he issued only fifteen passes."

"So he's hoping that we get caught on the hop and get hit by the other six guys they have down here?" McDermott asked.

"Exactly that."

"What should we do?"

"We will do what we have spent the last three hours planning to do," he replied, "And after we have done that, I am going to kill Hank White," he added.

Beverley Hills – Los Angeles

Andrea Yeschenko sat on his throne and decided that this would be the last time that he dialled the number in Washington. He took out his cell phone and dialled the number.

It went straight to voicemail.

He threw his phone hard at the floor and it smashed immediately,

"Fix it!" he shouted out to the foot soldier sitting nearest to him. The guy stood up from his chair and walked over to where the phone had shattered and got on his hands and knees, sweeping around the floor with the palm of his hand like a blind man trying to find something.

The King was now angry.

Very angry.

He had given the people in Washington plenty of chances and now they would pay the price.

But first he had to ensure that his new shipment had come in without a hitch and he had made sure that he had allocated plenty of men to collect it. Tomorrow, he would start putting the wheels in motion to carry out the threat that he had made to the people in Washington.

The shipments had never given him concern before now. The people in Washington and the idiotic gambler Hank White had always ensured an easy passage for his merchandise, but the people in Washington were now shunning him.

He knew that the access passes onto the ship had been granted by Washington and that Hank White had issued them, because he had received a call a few minutes ago confirming that to him.

Once the shipment was safe he would relax. He had even instructed his men to bring three of the merchandise back to his palace for him to test, after they had cleaned them up of course.

He liked the new ones.

He liked the look of fear in their eyes when they saw him.

He knew that whenever they were in his presence that he became his father. That evil, sick part of him was all that he had left of his father and he did not want to ever let it go.

The people in Washington have made a very big mistake.

He was the King.

He was untouchable.

He was Andrea Yeschenko.

He muttered these three things to himself over and over again for a long minute.

"I have cleared it up Andrea," the guy who was picking up the broken cell phone pieces said.

Yeschenko looked at him with contempt.

He was pathetic, picking up his rubbish and being so afraid. Yeschenko pulled out his handgun and shot the guy three times in the chest in front of the others.

Just because he could.

EIGHTEEN

Oakland – California (11:59pm)

Paul McDermott and Fringe approached the front door of the house slowly. Fringe crouched down and picked the lock, using a device that looked similar to a corkscrew handle to do so. There was a gentle click as the door unlocked. They waited for ten seconds.
No one came.
Paul looked at his watch and when the display hit twelve, he nodded at Fringe who put his hand on the door handle and turned it. The door cracked open an inch.
No one came.

At the back of the house, Wallace and Buck had reached the back door and peered through the window to see five guys in the kitchen, huddled around a table, drinking out of small coffee cups and smoking cigarettes.

They all wore jeans and vests, had arms covered in tattoos and a hammer and sickle on the left hand side of their necks.
"You take right and centre and I will take left and rear," Wallace whispered to Buck.
Buck nodded his understanding.

Paul stepped into the hallway with his gun pointed level with his chest. The first thing that he noticed was the similarity in the layout of the house to the one in Kansas. The staircase in the centre, the four doors, all of which were closed, two on either side of the staircase and the chairs positioned in the same place. If Kansas was a CIA safe house, it was more than a coincidence that this house was laid out in exactly the same way. Fringe stepped in behind Paul and quietly closed the door.
No one came.
He pointed to the right of the staircase, indicating for Fringe to move across to the opposite side and he stepped to the left. If he was right, the first door on his side would be the CCTV room. He slowly crossed the floor, keeping his gun on the staircase, and reached the door; he put his ear against it and listened. He could hear voices inside.
Fringe reached the first door on his side and put his ear against it and listened carefully. He could hear voices inside.
No one came.

Wallace put his hand on the door handle and assumed the position of an athlete starting a long distance running race, raised his silenced Makarov and mouthed, "On three," to Buck who nodded his understanding in return. "One, two, three," Wallace whispered and threw the door back.

The five guys at the table had no time to react.

Wallace stepped in four small steps, leaving enough room for Buck to come in behind him. The first shot that Buck fired hit the guy directly in front of him and the bullet smashed into his chest, he then swung his gun around to the right and fired four shots in quick succession, two in the upper body of the guy sitting furthest away, and two into the guy closest to him; the second bullet hitting the guy on the side of the face and blowing a gaping hole in his upper cheekbone. All three guys that he had hit fell off their chairs and smashed hard against the floor.

To his left, Wallace fired on the guy furthest away who was on his feet moving towards the sink, one shot in the centre of his back made the guys knees crumble below him and as he was on the way down to the floor, Wallace swung his arm around slightly to the left and shot the guy nearest to him twice in the chest, the force of the bullets sending him sideways off of the chair. Wallace then walked around the guy and put an extra bullet in the guy he had shot in the back to make sure.

Buck did the same to all three of the guys he had shot, even though he was sure they were dead. They then looked at each other and almost in perfect tandem, ejected their magazines and reloaded fresh ones without speaking.

Paul and Fringe heard the shots clearly from the hallway, despite the silencers.

And then everyone came.

The first door to open was the one where Paul was standing.

A guy in a tee shirt and jeans pulled the door sharply open and stood no more than a foot away from him holding a gun in his hand. Paul shot him twice in the face and the guy's head jerked back and his body twisted unnaturally to the right as the force of the bullets pushed him down to the floor. He stepped into the room and fired two shots into the chest of another guy who was reaching for the gun he had on the desk next to him. Blood sprayed out of the bullet holes and he slumped over the desk, covering the two hard drives which were sitting to the right of two screens. He had found the CCTV hard drives they were looking for.

Fringe watched as the handle started to turn slowly of the door he was facing, and he stepped back and crouched down with his gun pointing straight. He saw a head appear around the door. This guy was definitely not Russian; he had thick grey hair and wore spectacles. Fringe stood up and kicked the door hard with the sole of his boot and it smacked into the face of the guy who was standing behind it. He heard a groan and stepped into the room. It was a very large living room with a lot of comfortable chairs laid out sporadically. It looked like three rooms had been knocked into one. Obviously Yeschenko thought making his customers comfortable was a priority. Inside there were three men, all respectable looking, all in their fifties and all obviously waiting for their turn to violate the poor children who were probably waiting in fear upstairs. He looked at them, they looked petrified. He pointed his gun at them and reached into his jacket and pulled out a bunch of cable ties. The guy who had been standing behind the door was holding his face, his nose bloodied from the impact of the door smashing into him. Fringe waved them over towards the radiator that he spotted under the large window and all three of them stepped over towards it. He said,

"Sit," and they all leant against it. He then cable tied the one nearest to him to the radiator and worked his way along the line until they were all secure, making sure he pulled the cable ties more tightly than he needed to, enjoying watching them wince in pain as he did so. He then turned and walked out of the room and stopped by the door and nodded across the hallway at Paul who had his gun pointing up the staircase.

The door to Fringe's right opened and he swung around and raised his gun but lowered it as soon as he saw Wallace step out with his gun raised, followed by Buck just two feet behind.

Wallace raised all of the digits on his right hand and then pointed down to indicate 'Five down,' and Paul nodded and then raised two fingers and down to indicate his body count. Fringe shook his head and used his hands to mimic that he was playing a cello to indicate the signing for 'captured' and then raised three fingers. Paul moved down to the next door on his side, with Buck following, and listened carefully, as Fringe and Wallace stepped around to the bottom of the stairs. He could hear nothing and so he swung open the door for Buck to step in with his gun raised.

The room was empty.
"Downstairs is clear but only seven guys down so let's plan for at least fifteen," Paul whispered to the other three, as he and Buck joined them at the bottom of the stairs, aware of the fact that his father had told him there would probably be a maximum of ten guys to face.
"And remember," he added, "There will be twenty girls up there; their safety is the main priority so no stray shots."
All three of them nodded their understanding.
He took the lead and started to slowly climb the stairs first, one at a time, pointing his gun to the left of the top of the stairs. Fringe skipped up two steps and got into the same sequence of movement as Paul, pointing his gun to cover the right hand side of the stairs. Buck and Wallace came up two steps behind them, walking backwards to cover the rear.
They reached the top of the stairs. There was one door directly in front of them with a sign saying 'Bathroom' on a brass plate attached to it, and four other doors on either side of the hallway.
Paul walked directly ahead to the bathroom and put his ear against the door. He could hear noises coming from inside. It sounded like whimpering. Fringe and Wallace covered the hallways and Buck joined Paul at the door, standing to the right. Paul nodded to the handle, indicating for Buck to try it, which he promptly did.
It was locked.
Paul stepped back five feet and took three giant strides forward, lifted his right foot and smashed the sole of his boot just below the door handle. The wood splintered and the door flew open. In the same movement and

without breaking stride, he took two strides into the bathroom with his gun raised.

And then he stopped and felt sick to the stomach.

An old man, easily in his late fifties, was naked and had the head of a slight, tiny young child pushed into a basin full of water while he was standing behind her violating her. The old guy let go of the young girl and stepped back and raised his hands.

"You sick bastard," Paul said and pulled the trigger of his gun three times and shot him in the chest, the bullets ripping through his saggy, old skin, and tearing it apart. He was dead before he hit the floor.

The young girl screamed and Paul raised his fingers to his lips. Buck stepped in, realised what was happening and threw the girl a towel.

"You need to be very quiet, OK?" Paul whispered to her.

The frail, little thing nodded.

"We have come to get you all out of here. Do you understand?" he asked her softly.

The girl nodded again.

"How many men are there here?"

The girl shrugged.

"You don't understand?" he asked.

"No, I don't know," she replied.

Can you step outside and tell me who is where and in what rooms?"

The girl nodded.

Paul looked at her and noticed that the dead guy wasn't unsettling her at all. She had probably stopped being afraid a long time ago, he thought to himself.

Buck turned and stepped out first and instantly noticed the handle on the door to his left start to move down.

"Who's in there?" he turned and asked the girl.
"I don't know, it's one of the pleasure rooms," she replied, "All the rooms on this side are the pleasure rooms."
"How big is the tallest girl here?" he softly asked the girl.
She used her hands to indicate about four inches above her head which would make the tallest girl about five feet tall Buck estimated.
He moved to the front of the door and could still see the handle moving down slightly. He raised his gun, estimated five foot five and pulled the trigger three times and three bullets smashed through the door. The handle sprung back up and he heard a scream from inside, He pushed open the door but it stopped opening after six inches when it hit a dead weight behind it. He pushed hard and managed to open it another six inches and peered inside. He saw a big guy on the floor wearing a tee shirt and jeans, and the top of his chest had been obliterated.
He pushed again and the door moved another eight inches.
"Take my hand," he said to the two girls inside, the need for silence had vanished from the moment Paul had kicked the door in.
A small and slight hand clasped into his, and he pulled a young girl out. She could not have been more than ten years old. The next girl who held his hand and stepped through only appeared to be slightly older.
"Into the bathroom, now," he said assertively and the girls joined their friend in the bathroom, walking past Paul on the way in.

"Cover yourselves up with towels," Paul said, looking at the neat pile of towels on the shelves.
"Where are the other men?" he asked the biggest of the two girls who had just stepped inside.
"In the end pleasure room," she replied.
"How many?"
"Marco and Sergei," she replied.
"With who?" he asked.
"Elena. She is sixteen today. All girls disappear on their sixteenth birthday," she softly replied, looking at the floor as she said so.
Paul knew that he had found the last two Russian guys in the house.
He looked across to Wallace and Fringe,
"Go slowly down the corridor on your side and get all of the girls together," he said, "But keep away from the end of the hallway until I give you the all clear," he added.
They both nodded at him and Fringe opened the door to the first room and stepped in, while Wallace guarded the hallway.
Paul and Buck carefully stepped down to the door at the end of the hallway. Paul put his ear against the door. He could hear laughing and the noise of skin striking skin with force and a barely audible muffled scream.
He realised that the two guys in there had no idea what was happening, in spite of the noise they had made in smashing the door down.
The laughing got louder as he listened.
The screams got a little clearer.
He had heard enough.
He tried the handle slowly and it went all the way down. The door was not locked.

He counted to three in his head and then flung the door open and stepped in.
Marco and Sergei were striking a naked child with their fists.
Marco and Sergei were both naked.
Marco and Sergei were unarmed.
They spun around and looked at Paul and he shot them both in the face, less than half a second apart and their heads exploded.
Marco and Sergei were dead.
He looked at the girl and her eyes were swollen and he could see blood running down her legs.
He felt sick.
The girl was trying to see what was happening but her eyes were so swollen she was unable to see clearly. Paul stepped forward and said,
"Elena, you are safe now."
She opened her arms, willing him to hold her and protect her. He moved forward and wrapped his arms around her.
"Buck!" he shouted, "Come here quick."

It took no more than three minutes to get all of the girls out of the rooms and assemble them together. Wallace had gone downstairs to the CCTV room and returned to the top of the stairs with the hard drives.
"There are only nineteen girls here?" Paul said.
"Tatiana never came back," one girl replied.
"Back from where?"
"The devils house," she replied and then promptly burst into tears.
"Make the call," Paul ordered Fringe.

"The guys tied to the radiator downstairs?" Fringe asked. Paul had forgotten about them.

"Let's leave it to the girls," he replied, "Bring them down," he added and he headed down the stairs to the living room.

Walking in, he saw a pathetic sight. Three grown men, all of them in tears. They disgusted him.

A minute later, nineteen girls were in the room.

He faced the girls who were all looking at the three sick, evil men with pure hatred.

"If any of you want to kill these men, step forward now," he said.

Seven girls stepped forward.

The men started to beg and cry; pleading and explaining how they were sorry and that they had children at home. But no one cared.

The three men were dead within a minute. Each one of them with seven bullets implanted deep within their bodies.

"Now make the call," Paul said to Fringe.

"Do not call the police," one girl pleaded, "They are bad too, and they come here all the time," she added.

"You will be safe now. I promise," Paul replied.

The girls started taking in Russian and Paul thought he saw at least five of them smile.

Fringe walked back over to them after finishing his call and said,

"The Old Man says we have about four minutes to disappear."

Paul nodded.

"The people who will keep you safe will be here in four minutes," he said to the girls, "I promise that they won't

hurt you," he added as he walked past them and out of the house.
They reached their Range Rover and all climbed in.
"We will wait until we know they are safe," he said to the three of them.
They all nodded their agreement.

Twenty minutes later, after they had watched social services, the police, paramedics and finally the F.B.I. turn up; Paul McDermott started the engine of the Range Rover and they gently pulled away, in the opposite direction away from the house.
They knew that the girls were now safe.
The Old Man had been true to his word.

NINETEEN

Port of Los Angeles – Canal Street (11:59pm)

Ward had watched the ship come into the slip at 10:45pm and they had seen Yeschenko's men gather on the quayside just twenty minutes ago. He had counted fifteen men waiting to board the ship. He had also counted six vans, and had noticed that in every one of them, a guy sat in the front passenger seat undisturbed; apart from occasionally one of the guys on the quayside walking up to the vans and communicating something to them.
Hank White had lied to him.
Hank White would die tonight as well.
He had used the last hour to piece together in his mind what was happening and what was on the ship; if there was anything, apart from the children, he had come to a definite conclusion of what it was. He hoped he was right about things but he also hoped he was wrong.
If he was right, then things would have to move quickly and the danger for the rest of the team was going to increase tenfold.

McDermott had laid out the plan of attack back at the warehouse and everyone was clear on what they had to do. McDermott had been smart in the tasks that he had allocated to Peacock and Murray. He had given them the first part of the plan, which was to let Yeschenko's trusted guys go onto the ship first and then, along with Walsh and Fuller, they would take out the guys left on the quayside. If they failed to do their part effectively, it would not affect the overall operation; Walsh and Fuller would take out the men on the quayside on their own from their vantage positions on top of the shipping containers, which were already stacked, and then if Peacock and Murray joined in, all was good.
That left Ward, McDermott and Wired to board the boat. They were comfortable with those odds.
McDermott was standing next to Ward, under cover of the shadows, no more than a hundred feet away from the gangway that led from the pier onto the ship.
"Hank lied I see," McDermott said.
"Did you expect anything less?" Ward asked.
"One hundred and eight poor little kids on that ship, God knows what they have had to endure on the way here," McDermott said, not really to Ward or himself.
Ward ignored him.
He was almost positive that there were not one hundred and eight victims of Yeschenko's vile trade on that ship. The doors opened to all six vans and the guys who had been sitting in the passengers seats all got out. They had been instructed to start moving by the lieutenants, who were all wearing jeans and black shirts. One step up the ladder was represented by losing the tee shirts; easily pleased these Russians, Ward thought to himself. They

headed towards the gangway and reached it in a neat, single line, and started to cross over the water onto the ship and ten seconds later, they were out of sight.
Ward glanced at McDermott.
Now was the moment of truth for Peacock and Murray. They watched as fifteen men on the quayside, all wearing jeans and tee shirts, with arms covered in tattoos and a hammer and sickle tattoo on the left hand side of their necks, were all dropped to the floor in no more than eight seconds. Both Ward and McDermott noticed the four different nozzle flashes coming from the elevated positions at the same time.
Fifteen Russians, shot by CIA and Navy Seal trained snipers from less than one hundred feet away, with a non-existent wind.
They never had a chance.
"We were wrong about them," Ward said.
"It wasn't we, it was me," McDermott replied, "You just followed my doubts."
"That's because I trust you completely," he replied sincerely, "Plus, I was wrong once, at least I think I might have been, so it happens to the best of us," he added with a smile.
They stepped out of the shadows and Wired joined them from the other side of the container.
"Insurance payment," McDermott said to Wired, who nodded and when they reached the group of dead Russians on the floor, Wired put a single shot in the heads of every single one of them, to ensure that they were dead and then he reloaded.

They walked up the gangway and onto the ship. There was no one on the deck and everything seemed quiet. Just how they were expecting it to be.

When McDermott had checked the crew manifesto he had discovered that it only took thirteen men to sail this giant ship, due simply to the technology and automation that ships had, and Ward agreed with him that they would offer no resistance. They were just sailors.

Ward looked towards the quayside and saw Walsh, Fuller, Peacock and Murray walking purposefully towards them. Thirty seconds later the whole team was standing on the deck of the ship. They carried out a quick check on their radios and ear pieces and they all confirmed that they were working.

"Wired, you come with me," McDermott said, "Walsh, you take Peacock to the stern side and Fuller, you and Murray know what you have to do," he added.

All four of them nodded and peeled off in the direction of their allocated target areas.

In the centre of the boat was a building. It literally looked like someone had picked up a square white building and dropped it in the middle of the boat. It was where the bridge, living quarters and the access to the lower deck and engine rooms would be. The children had to be in there somewhere.

"Clear the way then my friend," Ward said to McDermott and watched as he headed towards the centre of the boat with Wired, both scanning the area with their machine guns as they moved.

He waited for two whole minutes.

He wanted to be alone when he found what he was looking for.

McDermott and Wired reached the centre of the ship and stepped into the giant metal building. The corridor was narrow and there were no doors or stairs feeding off of it; which meant no one coming behind them apart from Ward, and they were pretty sure that he wasn't going to shoot them in the back. They moved along thirty feet and came to a landing area. There were stairs directly in front of them which went down, and to the right of them, another set of stairs that went up.
A voice came over the radio,
"I think we have found where they are," Fuller said, "Three guys in black shirts are standing next to a container on the East side with torches."
"Can you confirm?" McDermott replied.
"No visual yet."
"Take them out anyway," Ward's voice interrupted over the airwaves, "Three less to worry about even if you are wrong."
"Understood," Fuller replied and the airwaves went quiet.
McDermott nodded to the stairs that led up. It made sense to clear the top decks first and work their way down, so that no one could come behind them and surprise them. They started to climb the stairs and reached the first landing which ran ninety degrees to the right; then the stairs turned and went up in the opposite direction. When they reached the top of the second set a maze appeared. The landing was huge and there were five corridors which fed off of it and still another flight of stairs to go up.
Decision time.

Fuller and Murray were lying flat on top of a container fifty yards away from three guys that were standing beside one specific container. It was big, easily big enough to hold one hundred tiny children inside.
"I have a sister who is no older than those kids," Murray said to Fuller.
Fuller ignored him.
"How do these people live with themselves?" he asked.
"We are here to get those kids out, so focus," Fuller replied.
He looked back into the scope of his silenced rifle and lined up the two guys to the left of the container.
"Take the one on the right, on my three." Fuller said.
Murray nodded.
"One, two, three."
Three silent shots hit their targets in the dead centre of their chests. Ten seconds later three more shots were fired into the lifeless bodies on the floor for insurance. Ten seconds after that, a voice echoed over the radio which said.
"The three by the container are down."
No one replied.

McDermott pointed upwards. The radio controls would be on the bridge and so he wanted to secure that first. As they started to move up the stairs, a guy walked out of the first corridor almost right into them.
He was dressed in overalls.
He was a sailor.
Wired spun around and hit him with the butt of his gun full in the face and the guy went down, clutching his

nose. He then pulled out his silenced handgun and shot the guy twice in the back of the neck.
McDermott shot him a disapproving look. Killing innocent people was something that the team never did. McDermott covered his radio microphone and said, "What the hell are you playing at?"
Wired said nothing.
"You know the rules, no innocents," McDermott said.
"I read the file you had boss. Every one of those kids is fair game for these scumbags. They know they are on this ship and they know what they are being brought here for. There are no innocents on this ship," Wired replied.
McDermott knew that Wired was right, there were no innocents. He moved his hand from over the microphone and said,
"Walsh, you and Peacock clear the deck and then come inside. Fuller and Murray, stay with eyes on that container. All of you shoot to kill, no questions, crew and all."
Echoes of 'Understood' came back through the airwaves. They started to move up the stairs towards the bridge. They got halfway up and a guy came walking down towards them; he looked startled and stopped immediately in his tracks.
McDermott pulled the trigger on his gun and fired four shots into the guy's stomach. He doubled over and fell, his body weight tipping him forward, and he fell through the air towards him. McDermott put up his right arm to deflect the guy's body and he managed to divert him against the railings and the guys face smashed down hard into the metal stairs about a foot in front of Wired. He was wearing a black shirt.

McDermott continued moving forward up the stairs with more urgency and Wired skipped up behind him; two steps at a time, treading on the dead guy in the black shirt as he followed.

They reached the top of the stairs and saw an opening in front of them, about the size of standard double doors, and McDermott pointed to the right of the opening as he headed towards the left hand side. They stopped behind the wall for a moment and listened.

There were a number of different voices and laughter coming from inside.

McDermott covered his microphone and whispered, "Black shirts go down first."

Wired nodded.

He raised his left hand and lifted a single finger, then a second and then a third. They both spun around into the opening, exactly at the same time and assessed the room in less than a second.

McDermott fired first, sending a shot into the head of a guy in a black shirt who was standing no more than five feet away from him; blood and brain matter spraying from his head and covering the three guys who were standing beside him. They were all dressed in black trousers and white shirts, all three of them doubling over and raising their arms above their heads to protect them from what they hadn't yet computed.

Wired fired three shots a split second after McDermott and hit a guy in a black shirt in the centre of his back. The guy had been standing twenty feet away, looking out of the window across the countless containers.

There were three other guys in the room, as well as the ones in the white shirts and slacks and they were all wearing overalls.
They were all unarmed.
"Who is the captain?" McDermott asked.
A guy in his fifties, with blood splattered across his face said in very poor English,
"I am. Who are you? We haven't done anything wrong,"
"How many crew do you have?" McDermott demanded.
"Thirteen," he replied.
McDermott knew he was telling the truth and that the rest of what they had to do would be a walk in the park. He then spoke into his microphone,
"Walsh, Peacock. Get to the bridge now. There are two bodies on the stairs on your way up. Bring them with you," he said. He didn't want the crew startled by dead bodies on the stairs, when they made their way up. He then looked into the captain's eyes.
"Call them all to the bridge now," he demanded.
"They are winding the engines down."
Wired lifted his gun and shot a guy in a white shirt standing to his left twice in the chest and his body shot backwards, landing against a control panel with force.
"Last chance," McDermott said.
The captain turned to his right and said something in Russian into a microphone.
"Sit on the floor over there on your hands," McDermott said pointing to the far side of the room, and they all moved instantly.
Exactly eight minutes later, eleven crew members were all sitting on their hands in the control room of the ship, frightened and in silence. The only respite from total

focus for McDermott was when he smiled, watching Walsh and Peacock struggle with the two dead bodies that they had moved.

Fuller and Murray had confirmed that the ship was secure and that no one else had been near to the container.

McDermott spoke into his microphone,

"All clear and secure, the ship is yours," he said to Ward.

"The crew?" Ward asked.

"Eleven alive here."

"I want you to get them to take you to the container and get the children out," Ward said.

"And then what do you want done with them?"

"Have a vote on it."

"Are you not coming to the container?"

"No," Ward replied, "I am looking for something else."

McDermott looked at the captain with distain.

"There are over a hundred young girls on this boat. I will ask you just once where they are, if you don't tell me, and then take me to them. I will kill you. Where are they?" he demanded.

"In container 4652."

"What colour is it?"

"Red," the captain replied.

McDermott spoke into his mic.

"Fuller, what number and colour is the container you are looking at?"

"4652, red."

"Can you open it?" McDermott asked the captain.

"Yes."

McDermott leant down and pulled him to his feet,

"Take me there now and open it. Murray, you stay here and guard the rest of these, if any of them move, kill them. You two come with me," he said to Wired and Walsh as he pushed the captain towards the double doors.

Three minutes later, McDermott, Walsh, Fuller, Peacock and Wired were watching the captain undo three padlocks and remove the chains from container 4652. When the last of them had been removed, he pulled on the handle and the latch unlocked. Fuller and Walsh stepped in to open the doors, one on each side. When the doors were fully opened they exposed a harrowing sight. The young children, some of them looking no more than ten years old, all cowered and moved to the back of the container. But there were not one hundred and eight girls in there. There were one hundred and seven. The one hundred and eighth was laying naked at the front of the container, her legs covered in blood and her lifeless body discarded like trash.

There were empty water containers and dried food sachets littered everywhere. The container stank of urine and excrement.

"Who did that to her?" McDermott softly asked.

"It must have been before the container was loaded," the captain said, looking down at the floor.

To his right, McDermott caught a glimpse of flashing lights out of the corner of his eye coming from the bridge. It went on for five seconds.

"Murray," he said into his microphone, "What's happening?"

There was a pause for a few seconds and then the voice came back over the radio,

"They tried to attack me; I've had to shoot them."
"All of them?"
"Yes," Murray replied.
McDermott pulled his handgun from the holster on his right hip, raised it and shot the captain in the face from three feet away. As his body fell to the floor, he fired three more into his back. He was dead before he hit the ground.
"Make the call to the number The Old Man gave us," he said to Walsh, who promptly took out his phone and dialled the number.
"We have them," he said down the radio to Ward.
"I'm taking your Range Rover, you'll have to make your own way back," Ward replied.
"Where are you going?" McDermott asked.
"I'll meet you back at the warehouse in a couple of hours," he said, "And I want you to stop in the Harbour house on your way out and kill Hank White, OK?"
"With pleasure," McDermott replied.
"They will be here in five minutes," Walsh said to McDermott, as Murray ran down to join them, took one look inside the container and turned away; a combination of disgust and the stench.
McDermott stepped into the container and one hundred and seven painfully thin and filthy girls all cowered as far back as they could against the rear of the container, the ones at the front turning their backs, so that eye contact would not be made.
"Can anyone speak English?" he called out, his voice echoing inside the container walls, "You are safe now."
A girl on the right hand side of the container said, "Me."

She was no more than twelve and she looked like she had just crawled through a sewer.

"The police and people who can help you will be here soon and they will look after you and make you safe. No one will hurt you anymore. Do you understand?" he asked loudly.

A few girls started mumbling and it got louder and louder, as the message was translated to each girl and the tone almost sounded excited. A number of girls burst into tears.

"We have to go now because we have killed all the people who hurt you, but I promise, if you stay here for a few more minutes, you will be safe," McDermott reiterated.

He turned and walked out. He felt awful for leaving them there, petrified and confused, but he had to. There were still a lot more children to save from Andrea Yeschenko.

TWENTY

Santa Monica

Ward had found what he was looking for the moment that he came across the landing with five corridors feeding off of it, in the ships main building. He knew that the evidence he was looking for would be down one of those corridors and he knew that it would more than likely be down the centre corridor, where the captain's quarters would be. Yeschenko would not trust it to just anyone. He walked halfway down the corridor until he came to a door which had the word 'Kapitan' written on a name plate. He opened the door and stepped inside, closing it behind him. It was a plush room, much more elegant than he would have expected. There was an oversized plasma TV screen on the wall, the floor was covered with a plush, beige carpet and it was furnished with dark mahogany sideboards and tables. There were two doors that lead out from the main living quarters. He opened the first door and looked inside and saw a sparkling bathroom which had a vanity sink, shower, toilet and a full length mirror on one wall.
He stepped out of the bathroom and closed the door. If he was right, what he was looking for would be in the

next room; by the lack of a bed in the main living quarters, the other room had to be a bedroom. If he was right, the evidence that he wanted would be in there.
He turned the handle, pulled the door open and stepped inside.
He was right.
He carefully picked up the evidence and walked out of the main quarters and back into the corridor. He walked down to the landing, where he heard over a dozen shots ring out from a silenced firearm above him, but he ignored the shots, and continued down the next set of stairs, out of the building, along the deck, down the gangway, past the group of Yeschenko's dead guys in their jeans and tee shirts, their tattoos on their arms, and the hammer and sickle tattoos on the left hand side of their necks, across the quayside and climbed into McDermott's Range Rover, securing the evidence safely on the passenger seat so he could keep it close.
McDermott radioed him and told him that they had found the children and he told him that he was taking his vehicle and that he would meet him back at the warehouse in a couple of hours.
He didn't want this evidence being seen by anyone apart from those he trusted with his life and that meant Murray, Peacock, and as much as he liked him, Buck too, would never get to see it. So even before he had found what he was looking for, he had decided to take it back to his place in Santa Monica and keep it there until it needed to be used. He knew full well that Centrepoint would exploit the evidence to the full, and he wasn't going to give it up until he knew for sure what his plans were for it.

The drive from the docks to Santa Monica took forty minutes, and with each passing mile he doubted that many people knew this evidence even existed. He knew for sure that Centrepoint didn't, or he would have had it in his possession a long time ago.

He arrived at his bungalow and put the car in park. He stepped out of the car and walked around to the other side and opened the passenger door, lifted out the evidence, which was much lighter than it looked, and walked into the bungalow and closed the door.

An hour and a half later, he stepped out of his bungalow and climbed back into the car.

The evidence was safe and no one would find it. He was thinking to himself that if he was smart enough to work out what was happening, why had no one else. Or perhaps they were, he said to himself, and he was simply one small step ahead of them.

He knew for sure now that no one would find it, and he started to think to himself that perhaps no one should ever find it. But keeping it safe was his top priority and he was happy that he had done that.

For now.

Because now he held all the cards.

Thinking of safety made him think back to Nicole-Louise and Tackler. The Optician was watching them so they wouldn't be harmed but where exactly did they go that they shouldn't have gone, he asked himself.

He would call them, Centrepoint and Eloisa when he got back to the warehouse.

He now knew everything that was happening and why.

Beverley Hills

Andrea Yeschenko didn't feel like a king right now. In fact, he felt like a man who was on the verge of losing everything that he had worked for.

He had received a call from Hank White saying that there were police and F.B.I. storming the docks and that not only were every one of the twenty one men he had sent down there dead, the girls were all free. The call was ended when Yeschenko heard the sound of gunfire and Hank White stopped talking.

The termination of White's call was immediately followed by a call from a cop in Oakland, saying that his house had been hit by a team of government assassins, probably C.I.A., and that there was nothing more they could do to help him and the line went dead.

The girls he could live with losing, there were thousands more where they came from; even the house wasn't a problem, he could set up another one, but the evidence that he had lost seriously weakened the hand that he was playing. He only had part of the evidence now but he was no longer convinced that it would be enough to enable him to follow through with his plan, to get what he believed he rightfully deserved.

He knew that the evidence he had e-mailed to Russia was safe, no one would be able to find it, so he decided to call Washington and take back control of the situation. He climbed down from his throne and walked across the floor to the giant sash windows and gazed out into the darkness.

He dialled the number in Washington.

Finally, the voice answered.

"Yes?"

"You have made the wrong choice," Yeschenko said.
"What are you talking about?"
"You thought you could destroy me? You have done the opposite, we are now stronger than ever," Yeschenko said, quietly but threateningly down the phone.
"I really have no idea what you are talking about. Explain it to me?"
"Don't you dare insult me by trying to plead ignorance," he spat back.
"If you don't tell me what the hell you are talking about I will end this call," the voice spat back, equally as threatening.
"You had your people hit one of my deliveries and kill my men," Yeschenko replied.
The voice went quiet for a few moments and then said, "Tell me there was nothing taken that could be used against us?"
"Do not play games with me, I know it was you."
"It wasn't me, but I have a real bad feeling I know who it was," the voice replied.
"If it wasn't you, then who was it?" Yeschenko demanded, "I will hunt them down and kill them."
"No you won't," the voice replied, "If it is who I think it was, they will already be hunting you."
"You Americans don't scare me."
"These ones should," the voice replied, "Now tell me, to reassure me, that there was nothing on that boat that could be used against us?"
"There was nothing," Yeschenko lied.
"You got greedy Yeschenko," the voice continued, "Everything was rosy for you and then you started to blackmail us and now look where you are," he added.

"No!" Yeschenko screamed down the phone, "Look where you are. You will either find these people who are doing this and eliminate them by tomorrow evening or in two days' time, the world will see what you and your friends are."

"I'll make some calls and see what I can find out. Believe me; we have some of our best people hunting them. The only ones we know for sure who might know what is happening are a couple of kids in New York, who hacked into some records. We will get them to talk."

"Then for your sake," Yeschenko said, his voice calm and in control once more, "Do it quick," and he hung up the phone.

Marina Del Rey – 03:00am

Ward arrived back at the warehouse and parked the Range Rover in front of the roller shutter doors. Inside the warehouse, he noticed Paul was back. McDermott's entire team were asleep on the floor in sleeping bags, Peacock and Murray were asleep in Paul's Range Rover and McDermott was napping in his chair. He looked up, instinctively gripping his handgun, when Ward walked over to his chair.

"Where's Buck?" he asked.

"Outside in his car," McDermott replied.

"Why?"

"Because he snores like a pig and Wired said that he was going to shoot him if he didn't get out of the warehouse."

"What did he say to that?"

"He said your mom never complained," McDermott replied.
Ward smiled.
He liked Buck.
"OK," he said, "Let everyone get some sleep and we will go again tomorrow morning at 07:00am."
"Where did you go?" McDermott asked.
"I'll tell you in the morning," he replied and turned to walk out of the warehouse.
"Where are you going now?" McDermott asked.
"Back into the Range Rover, it's much more comfortable than the floor," he replied with a smile, a comment that had McDermott rolling his eyes.
Outside, he dialled Eloisa's number in New York.
For the third time running, and much to his surprise, she answered.
"Hello."
"Did I wake you?" he asked.
"It's 6:00am Ryan, I was just getting up," she replied, "What's wrong?"
"This thing I am working on with Yeschenko, I need your help on it."
"I've already told you all that I found on it, but if I can help, I will. What do you need?"
"I need you to find out definitively, who has been protecting him and why?"
"OK. I can't promise but I have a friend who works in the communications department at the office, I'll see what he can find out."
"Thanks."
"I miss you," she said, "It seems ages since we have spent any decent time together."

Every time he thought to himself. Every single time she said something like that, he felt cleansed. He felt normal, like he lived a normal life.

"I always miss you Eloisa," he replied.

His tone sounded flat, she knew when something was wrong with him, her ears and senses had by now been trained to tune in to what he was feeling.

"So what else is it?" she asked.

"It's me. It's us. It's what I do."

"What do you mean?".

"When I'm running around, doing what I do, I never have time to think about anything but what I am doing. When that stops, like now, and we speak, I just want a normal life, a life with you. You know, a family, love, normal jobs," he replied.

"We spoke about this the other day Ryan," she replied, thinking back to the conversation they had when they were together in New York last week, "We will have that, and more."

"I know. I'm sorry. You must get fed up with hearing me mention it."

"Never. There isn't a woman in the world who wouldn't want to hear the man she loves say that he wants to build his life with her and he thinks about doing it all the time," she replied.

He instantly felt better, re-energized and strong.

"And as we said last week," she continued, "In a few years' time we will have all of that. I know it and you know it. But for now, just for a short period of our lives, we have thousands of innocent children to protect and give them the chance of having the life we are going to build together."

He paused for a few moments. Eloisa stayed silent on the other end, just listening to his soft breathing.
"And that is why I love you so much," he eventually said, "You always put everything right."
"It works both ways Ryan. There is no 'I' in team."
"Thank you Eloisa. Just for being you."
"You inspire me to be me, so thank yourself," she replied, "Now, are you going to let me get up and get ready for work?" she asked with a giggle.
"Go for it."
"I'll ring you if I find anything out about Yeschenko."
"Thank you. I love you," he replied.
"I love you too."
The line went dead.
He leant back into the soft leather chair of the Range Rover and reclined it fully. It was comfortable and he exhaled a long sigh. Eloisa had recharged him once again, just be simply listening to him. He set the alarm on his phone for 06:45am. Three and a half hours sleep would be enough. He would shower in the morning, when he went back to Santa Monica to verify the evidence, he said to himself. He knew where he was going with this, exactly where he was going with it, and once again, right then, he knew that he was going to win.

TWENTY ONE

Park Avenue – New York 08:00am

The Optician had not slept all night. He didn't like sleeping. It had been that way since he was fourteen years old. Going to sleep had always left him unable to defend himself, and left him vulnerable to the predators that prowl the night. It transpired that his fear of sleeping became his greatest weapon, and it was this curse that had made him the most feared sniper in the world. It wasn't an exaggerated claim made by him or others who knew him; it was a claim made out of fact, by the number of kills that he had chalked up and equally in the extreme conditions that he had overcome to complete them. Everyone who moved in the secret world of clandestine operations had heard of him, from the Russians to the Chinese, and had he of chosen to step into the field of private assassination; he would be sitting on a fortune of well over $100 million by now.

But he had never once been tempted by the offers of unimaginable wealth that he knew were there for the taking. His life was a lonely one but he had finally found his family the day that Ryan Ward had spoken to him for the first time. He considered him to be the brother that he had lost, just as he considered Centrepoint to be the father he had always craved.
Yet he had never met Ryan Ward.
Well actually, that wasn't quite true. He had been within six feet of Ward at least thirty times.
But Ward never knew it was him.
On three separate occasions, Ward had spoken to him. But Ward never knew it was him.
The first time was when Ward asked him to take a bag from him as he climbed into a helicopter in Vienna. Ward had been on a mission to eliminate a group of Koreans who were trying to buy plutonium, and he had taken nine of them out while protecting Ward. He had simply disguised himself as an average soldier on the chopper when the extraction took place.
But Ward never knew it was him.
The second time had been at a New York Mets baseball game, when Ward stood up to cheer a home run and turned around and high fived him and said, "What a hit." But Ward never knew it was him.
The third and last time was eighteen months ago when Ward was in a coffee shop with Eloisa in New York and he was sitting at the table behind him, for no reason other than he enjoyed the fact that Ward had no idea who he was. Eloisa had received a call from her bosses at the U.N. and stood up and left immediately, leaving Ward at

the table alone. He turned and looked at him and said, "Women eh?" and smiled.
But Ward never knew it was him.
All of the other occasions had been when Ward had stepped onto the private jet that The Old Man provided for transport, and Ward had glanced at the back of his head as he sat in the co-pilots seat. He knew that Ward would one day question how he managed to get to wherever he was at exactly the same time.
He rarely slept but he had the ability to go into a trance-like state when he was peering through his scope. It was like his body and mind slept but his eyes remained alert. Any movement or sudden change in the environment and he was completely focussed and alert within a second.

This morning, his trance had been broken by a dark blue Sedan pulling up right outside Nicole-Louise and Tackler's apartment building. It was, without doubt, a government car.
He adjusted his lens slightly to get a better view of the driver, but from his vantage point above the apartment building opposite, he could not make out their faces.
The two guys that Centrepoint had put on the ground for him were nowhere to be seen and he pressed redial on his phone,
"Where are you?" he said to one of the guys who should have been guarding the apartment.
"We are having breakfast, the kids won't be awake yet, these hacker types don't rise out of bed until gone noon," the guy replied.
"Where are you having breakfast?" The Optician asked.
"We are on East 117th. Why?"

"Did you drive?"

"No, we walked."

"That's ten minutes away," he said, "Five if you run," he added.

"So?" the guy said.

"So, if the two guys going into the apartment hurt either of them, I will hunt you down and kill you," he said calmly and then hung up the phone.

He now had a dilemma. Did he risk running down the stairs from his vantage point and losing them from his sight for three to four minutes or stay where he was and hope that he could get a shot at the two guys through their apartment window.

Right then, the decision was made for him.

The two guys stepped out of their car.

He still couldn't see their faces, only the back of their heads and he considered taking them out there and then, but he had no idea if Ward had sent them so he watched as they walked into the building.

He dialled Tackler's number; it rang but went to voicemail.

He dialled Nicole-Louise's number; it rang but went to voicemail.

Panicking wasn't in his nature but he was concerned. Everything was about timing to him and he knew that time was on his side.

If the two guys who had just entered the building were there to try and get information from Nicole-Louise or Tackler then they would have to spend a few minutes trying to find it.

What concerned him was the fact that if he was one of the guys, he would walk in and shoot either Nicole-

Louise or Tackler immediately, that tends to get the information given up a lot quicker.

But then everyone wasn't him.

He decided to wait it out and hopefully the two breakfast guys would get there in time.

He watched to see if any lights came on in the apartment but nothing happened. He could not see inside the bedroom as the blinds were down.

He watched carefully.

After a minute, the blinds had still not opened and there was no movement through the window that looked into the living area.

He watched carefully.

Two minutes passed and still no movement. The breakfast guys would no doubt be running back, or maybe they had the brains to call a cab, but it was doubtful that they would be able to hail one at the start of the rush hour.

He watched carefully.

Then he saw movement in the living area through the window. He saw Nicole-Louise move over to her workstation and pick up a laptop and a square box which looked like an external hard drive and then she threw a coat on and headed out of view towards the apartment door.

He watched carefully.

He knew they would be coming out of the building, probably before the breakfast guys got back. And right then, he smiled to himself.

They were going to come straight back out to him.

Into his terrain.

Into his world.

Into his scope.

He waited and he watched carefully, he anticipated that they would be walking out in front of him in exactly twenty six seconds if they were taking the stairs, which he knew they would be if they were bad guys, it would be longer if they took the elevator and good guys would choose the elevator as it was less threatening.

He started counting down in his head silently, when he got to the last five seconds he started silently mouthing out the words,

"Five, four, three, two, o…."

For a fraction of a second, what he saw threw him.

He recognised the two guys.

But that's all it was. A fraction of a second, no more than a tenth of a second to a normal person and then he was back focussed, his finger on the trigger.

Nicole-Louise and Tackler were walking out of the apartment building with one of the guys on either side of them. He could clearly see the handguns that were drawn and digging into the side of them both. He could see Tackler carrying a laptop as well. He slowed everything down in his mind. And pressed number three on his cell phone, his speed dial to the breakfast guys.

The first 7.62mm bullet hit the guy who had his hand on Tackler's neck and it hit him exactly in the centre of the forehead and his body capitulated backwards. Just as the second guy who had a firm grip on Nicole-Louise's arm, turned his head slightly, as his brain started to process some movement to his right, the second bullet smashed into the right side of his forehead and his whole body spun around through the force of the bullet and he flipped to the floor.

The Optician could see Nicole-Louise open her mouth to scream and Tackler ducked down and put his arms over his head to protect himself.

"We're just there now… holy shit…." The breakfast guy's breathless voice came over the loudspeaker of the cell phone.

"Tell them Ward sent you and that you have to take them somewhere safe immediately and get them out of the city; then wait for me to call," The Optician said, "And if one hair on their heads is damaged, I will find you and kill you and everyone you have ever spoken to. Are you understanding me?"

"Yes… yes…" the breakfast guy said breathlessly.

The Optician hung up.

He watched as the two guys spoke to Nicole-Louise and Tackler and one of them sprinted off and returned less than a minute later with the car. He watched as Nicole-Louise and Tackler climbed into it and drove off. A small crowd had gathered, but he would call The Old Man to sort the two bodies out later, it was too late now, people were already on their cell phones and a guy in a suit was looking at the car that was speeding off as he was talking; no doubt trying to give the vehicle registration to whoever was on the end of the line.

The Old Man has sorted out much bigger messes than this before.

This was the first time in a long time that The Optician felt something other than nothing about killing someone. Killing to him was a way of life, a job and a way of ridding the world of bad people.

But what had just happened was different, Very different.

He had to decide whether to call The Old Man first and tell him what had happened, or to phone Ward.
His father or his brother?
He decided that the head of the family should take priority and so he dialled Centrepoint's number but it went straight to voicemail.
Fate had decided.
Nothing was about luck or chance to him.
So he called Ward.

Marina Del Rey – 05:15am

Ward's phone vibrated and for a moment he thought it was his alarm going off. He had fallen into a deep sleep; the seat of the Range Rover was even more comfortable than it looked.
He scooped up his phone and saw it was The Optician.
"Do you ever sleep?" he said as he answered.
"Sleeping is for girls."
"What's wrong?" Ward asked.
"I've had to move Nicole-Louise and Tackler."
Ward shot upright, using his left hand on the steering wheel to pull himself up,
"Why? What happened? Are they OK?" he asked, a sense of dread rushing over him.
"They are fine."
"Where are they?" he demanded.
"I don't know. I've just got two guys to move them out of the city and said I will call when I know what to do with them," The Optician replied.
"You are talking in riddles. Are they safe and where are they?" he asked aggressively.

"Calm down. Nothing will happen to them, they are safe. I've called you to find out what you want me to do with them?" The Optician said.
"I'm sorry. I got a really bad feeling then."
"You know I will keep them safe, have I ever let you down?"
"No. So tell me what happened?"
"Two guys turned up and went into the building and came out with them a few minutes later with their guns on them."
"So where were the guys you had with you?"
"Can you believe it, they went for breakfast."
"Are you being serious?"
"Yes."
"So what happened?"
"I dropped them as they came out of the building."
"And Nicole-Louise and Tackler?"
"The breakfast guys came back just as the guys hit the floor and so I told them to take them both out of the city and wait for me to call them."
"OK," he said, "Can you keep them safe for six hours? It will take the jet five hours to get there."
"You know I can. You tell me where and when and I will have them there."
"I need you here with me now as well."
"I'll make my own way there once they are safe. You know I don't let anyone see me."
"I'm sure you can make an exception now."
"I'm sure I can't," The Optician replied.
Ward smiled to himself.
"Thank you my friend, I'll let you know what time, I'll send a couple of McDermott's team to collect them."

"Wait," The Optician said before he had a chance to hang up.
This took him by surprise. He was so used to most of his calls ending abruptly that it had become second nature.
"Problem?"
"A big problem," The Optician replied.
Ward instantly felt uneasy with the tone of The Optician's voice. He had never heard this tone in his voice before.
"What is it?"
"The two guys that I dropped, they weren't just any old government types."
"Secret Service?"
"No. Much worse."
The reply took him totally off guard and he didn't like it.
"The two guys, I knew them," The Optician said.
"Who were they?"
"Dan Leany and Paul Morgan."
"Ex Seals?"
"No idea."
"How did you know them?"
"Well, I didn't know them personally, but I know who they are."
"How?"
"Because I covered their asses at least twenty times."
"I don't get what you are saying," Ward said to him, genuine confusion in his voice.
The Optician was quiet for a moment and then he said, "They used to be Deniables."

TWENTY TWO

Marina Del Rey

Ward sat in the Range Rover in stunned silence for ten minutes, trying to piece together what he had just found out with what he already knew.
He concluded that he was the only person who had established what this whole operation was about, and that he had the upper hand because he had the key part of it in his possession.
Had Centrepoint sold out Nicole-Louise and Tackler? He asked himself that question four times before deciding to ask him directly.
He looked at his cell phone which was still held tightly in his hand and scrolled down his contacts and called him.
The Old Man answered on the third ring,
"Was that mess at the docks really necessary, twenty two bodies? That's a massacre," he answered without offering a greeting.

"Dan Leany and Paul Morgan, why?" Ward demanded, completely ignoring Centrepoint's opening question.
There was silence for a few seconds; his question had clearly caught The Old Man off-guard.
"Why would you ask about them?"
"I want to know why you sent them."
"Sent them where? Los Angeles?" Centrepoint asked, genuinely sounding confused.
He decided not to play his hand too soon in case The Old Man was bluffing, so he tried another approach.
"I want you to tell me about them. No cryptic clues, the meat on the bones," he demanded.
Centrepoint paused and then said,
"Tell me why you want to know about them first?"
"Because they have just tried taking out Nicole-Louise and Tackler."
"Are they OK? Tell me The Optician was there?" Centrepoint replied with genuine concern in his voice.
"You didn't know, did you?"
"Of course I didn't know. I would have had the whole of the NYPD over there guarding them by now if I did. I'll get some people sent to their apartment immediately."
"No need," he interrupted, "They aren't there."
"Where are they?"
"The Optician has them safe and out of harm's way."
"You need to get them over to you. The jet is still at LAX so get it to New York now."
"It's OK. I'm going to talk to McDermott in a couple of minutes and get a couple of his team down to the airport and over to New York immediately."
Centrepoint was quiet for a few seconds; Ward could almost hear the cogs in his brain turning.

"Tell me about Leany and Morgan?" he enquired again.
"They were good solid operatives. Nothing spectacular," Centrepoint replied, "Used mainly on home soil and the occasional jaunt to London, but not involved in the real deep missions," he added, recalling their files back through his mind as he spoke.
"So what happened to them?"
"I dispensed with their services. They dropped back into the C.I.A."
"Why did you drop them?"
"Because they stole money and didn't have that edge," he replied.
Ward thought of the money that he had taken from the corrupt South African family to buy the houses that he lived in, and was deciding if he should mention it, but Centrepoint beat him to it.
"It's different to the money you took Ryan," The Old Man said.
"You know about that?" he asked, trying to sound surprised.
"Of course I know about it. You had Nicole-Louise and Tackler put it there for me to find for God's sake," he replied, "I've just never bothered looking for anything else you might have taken because if you have, I trust that you have a good reason for it. These two took it for a different reason," he added flippantly, not in the mood to play along with pretending not to know about the money anymore.
He took the tone of The Old Man's voice on board and dropped any intention of ignorance regarding the money immediately.
"So why did they take it?" he asked.

"They stole over $7 million from an oil billionaire and then brought pure cocaine down in Columbia and attempted to bring it into The States for sale."
"To treble their money?"
"To at least quadruple it," Centrepoint replied, "But we hit the boat and destroyed it. Then they moved back to the C.I.A."
"So who has the power to send the C.I.A. to kill Nicole-Louise and Tackler? I thought you controlled them?" Ward asked.
"I do. And I can tell you now that they were most definitely not working for the C.I.A. They have either gone rogue or they are being paid."
"Well it won't do them much good. The Optician killed them."
"Then they have got what they deserve. I promised to keep Nicole-Louise and Tackler safe and I will, but I would be happier if you had them with you so that you can watch over them."
"That's the plan," Ward replied, "But I have one question," he added.
"I have many more than one, but sure, go ahead?"
"Who are we up against?"
"I still don't know, but I will by the end of the day, no matter what it takes," he replied.
Ward believed him.
"Make the arrangements for take-off and landing between JFK and LAX please so that we can get them out of there. OK?" he asked.
"I'm on it now," The Old Man replied, "I'll call The Optician and tell him what is happening and make sure

he will have them waiting for the jet at JFK," he added, and the line went dead.

He got out of the Range Rover and headed into the warehouse.
He wanted to establish who the evidence he had in his possession was going to be used against, but right now, his only concern was getting Nicole-Louise and Tackler safely back to him. He walked into the warehouse and McDermott and his team were all awake. Peacock and Murray were still sleeping. Buck was probably snoring loudly, alone in the vehicle outside.
McDermott looked at him and noticed the concerned look on his face and so he got up from his chair and walked across the floor to him.
"What's wrong?" McDermott asked.
"They tried taking out Nicole-Louise and Tackler" he replied, "The jet is waiting, I need you to send some people to collect them from New York and bring them here."
"Are they OK?" he asked.
"Unharmed but knowing them, petrified."
"Paul!" McDermott shouted to his son, "Over here."
Paul stood up from his chair at the table and walked over to them carrying the stained coffee mug he was drinking out of.
"What is it?" he asked, as he nodded his welcome to Ward.
"Any problems in Oakland?" Ward asked him.
"No, pretty straightforward, we watched as the police, feds and social care guys turned up. Why? Something wrong with it?" he asked Ward, looking concerned.

"No. We have a different problem," he said, "Someone tried taking out Nicole-Louise and Tackler."

"Are they OK?" Paul asked with urgency.

Ward smiled. Everyone knew how important Nicole-Louise and Tackler were, to everything that they did, and every single one of these men had real and genuine affection for them both.

"They are fine, but I need a couple of you to get down to LAX and get on the jet to New York right now, so that we can collect them and bring them back here. The Optician will have them waiting for you."

Paul spun around and said,

"Wired, Fuller, Fringe, with me, now!"

Hart Senate Office Building – Washington D.C.

Senator Madison Reid picked up the phone on the third ring. He was really hoping that whoever was on the end of the line had some good news for him, he needed it.

"Yes?"

"Did I not advise you against going after the hackers?" Centrepoint asked.

"I don't know McNair, I wasn't listening," he replied sarcastically.

"Well you should have been. What happens now will be as a direct result of your actions and I can't control the outcome on this one."

"Your job is to control it. I decide what the select committee passes for your murky little practices, and if you can't control a simple little situation over a couple of kids, then we are wasting our money on you. Control it, or your funding stops being approved without question. Take those as my actions," Reid spat down the phone, "Find what I told you to find and find it quickly. If the Secret Service gets it before you then I won't ever be able to use it, they will bury it," he added.

"It would help if you told me exactly what we are looking for, we have been searching and nothing has turned up yet?" Centrepoint replied, letting Reid think he was the one with the power once more.

"I don't know. All I know is that Yeschenko has said that he has proof of certain people's activities and we both know the activities that he provides, even if some of us got trapped into it without realising," Reid replied.

"You didn't realise you were having sex with a minor?" Centrepoint asked, trying to sound as innocent as he could.

"I never said I was involved. Just find the evidence and quickly, or you will discover that your funding stops very abruptly," Reid spat down the phone again, "I want Yeschenko squashed like the insect he is," and the line went dead.

That damned, greedy Russian, Reid thought to himself. They are all the same. He couldn't just be satisfied with the level of wealth that most people can only dream of, he had to want more. Well, he will soon discover that picking a fight with him was the worst thing a Russian could do.

Beverley Hills

Andrea Yeschenko was awake already. He hadn't really slept. Senator Madison Reid had let this whole situation get out of control. All he had to do was pay the money for him to keep quiet and none of this mess would have happened.

He had lost most of his men, his loyal soldiers, and now here he was in his throne room with his six trusted lieutenants no longer alive to make him feel important. All he had left were the three houses in Los Angeles and the two in Washington, and the ones in Washington were never frequented by powerful people, because they were too close to home. He didn't even have anyone left to take his anger out on. There was a rage that had been building up inside him for the last two days and he really had to take it out on someone. Maybe he would go and visit the house in Malibu and take it out on some of those vile little animals that had caused all of this. It was always their fault. It was always a woman's fault, no matter how young or old they were. His mother was no different. He hated women, they served one purpose only.

He was becoming increasingly agitated and annoyed. His trump card, the evidence on the ship, was taken, and he had no idea where it was. If Senator Reid had it already then he would not have answered the call last night and so he didn't have it, he concluded. So where was it, he asked himself over and over. He would find it. That's what he would do. He would do what he does best. He would get out in the street and find it. Whoever you are, he thought, I'm coming for you.

Marina Del Rey

Ward watched the roller shutter doors close and said to McDermott,
"I've got an idea."
"Does it hurt?" McDermott asked with a smile.
"Yeschenko has three houses left, right?"
"Yes. In Brentwood, Malibu and Ladera Heights. Why?"
"Can you hit one this morning, do you need time to plan?"
"Look at this," McDermott said, as he walked over to the workbench at the side of the warehouse and opened a large file,
"Here are all of the houses and the plan is already prepared. Just needs some on site recon and we are good to go. Why?" he asked.
"Because I want Yeschenko's focus somewhere else other than on what he's lost."
"And what has he lost?"
"I'm not sure yet," Ward replied.
"You know," McDermott said, "Maybe if you shared what you know sometimes, we might be able to help?"
"If I do that, you won't look so hard."
"So what we need has to be in one of those houses. If it isn't, it has to be in Washington?" McDermott asked.
"Or we might already have it and we don't know we have it yet?"
"What do you mean?"
"Why do you think it was so important to them that Nicole-Louise and Tackler were eliminated? The more I think about it, the more I think they stumbled upon something and they didn't realise it."

"It's video evidence we are looking for, we know that much," McDermott said, "But they would be able to trace money and payments and who exactly it is that we are trying to protect."

"I think so. But if so many people are hunting it, it can't be that simple."

"OK. What house do you want us to hit?" McDermott asked.

"You have enough men?"

"Wallace, Walsh, Me, Buck, Peacock and Murray. What do you think?"

"I think they haven't got a chance," Ward replied, "Can I leave that in your capable hands?"

"I'm on it," McDermott said and he walked back across the warehouse, nudging Peacock and Murray, who were asleep on the floor, with his boot as he passed them.

Ward walked out of the warehouse and approached Buck's car and tapped on the window. He woke instantly. Ward opened the door.

"I need this car for a few hours," he said.

"Sure," Buck replied as he started bringing the seat back up, "Anything I can do?" he asked.

"McDermott will brief you inside. You have another house to visit."

"Good. I like Killing Russians," Buck replied.

TWENTY THREE

New York

The Optician ended the call that he had made to the breakfast guy. He had told him to be at JFK in exactly two hours' time, where the jet would be waiting. He would be at the airport twenty minutes before the breakfast guy turned up and he would take his place in the co-pilot seat even though he could not fly. No one ever took notice of the pilots. Then he would arrive in Los Angeles at the same time and be ready for Ward's call.

The breakfast guy had said that he was near the airport now and that he had spent the last four hours driving around with the two computer kids in the car and he couldn't see the point. The Optician had simply responded by telling him that if he failed to follow one simple instruction, he would kill him. The breakfast guy

said that wouldn't be necessary and he would drive exactly an hour north and then come back.
And he would kill him if he had to.
He had lost count of the number of people that he had killed over the last eight years. But he knew they were all bad people. He knew that he was fighting back for the people who couldn't fight back, and that was all he needed to justify what he did.
There was a time when he needed someone to fight back for him and no one was there.
His phone rang.
It was Ward.
"They are safe," he answered.
"I'm sure they are my friend. I need you to get to Los Angeles as quickly as you can. I'm going to need you here."
The Optician was always one step ahead of Ward. He had to be. It was his job to keep him safe.
The truth is; he had pretty much lived Ryan Ward's life with him for the last three years. Even when they weren't on The Old Man's missions, or running an errand for the woman in his life, Eloisa, he was watching him. He had no life other than protecting Ward and he couldn't switch off.
"I'll be there," he replied.
"Tell me something" Ward said, "How did you feel about killing Leany and Morgan?"
The Optician didn't need to think about this answer, so he just said it straight,
"I didn't feel anything."
Ward paused on the line for a moment and then said,

"And what if the Old Man tells you one day that you have to kill me?"

"Are you a bad man Ryan?"

"You tell me. You know everything I do. What do you think?"

The Optician did know everything Ward did, it was true, and he knew that Ward was a good person to the core, however ruthless and fearful his reputation was.

"I think you always make the choices you make with the best intentions. If that makes you a good man then you are certainly that," he replied.

"Have you spoken to The Old Man?"

"Yes, a couple of hours ago. He told me about the flight and to make sure that I get them to the airport safely."

"I want you to guard them when you get here. I'll find a motel for them and if you can watch them, it will be a weight off my mind."

"Don't worry, The Old Man said as much to me. He wants you focussed on this."

"What do you make of all of this?"

"This Yeschenko thing?" he asked.

"Yes."

"I'm not here to think, that's your speciality. I'm here to follow orders and to protect you. No one ever expects me to think."

"I'm asking you to. You are the best and most extraordinary guy I have ever known, or rather never known, because we've never met, so I value what you think," Ward said.

The Optician thought about this for a moment. He knew that the Secret Service and C.I.A were hunting for whatever he was looking for, but Ward would be one step ahead of them and so he delivered his answer carefully.

"I think that The Old Man needs you to find whatever this evidence is before anyone else because, judging by the agencies that are also involved in trying to find it, it is going to mess up some seriously powerful people on Capitol Hill," he replied.

"And that's it?"

"No," he replied.

"What else?"

"Knowing you as I know you, I think you either already have it, or you know where it is."

Ward was quiet for a moment.

"And have you told The Old Man that?" he eventually asked.

"I don't go telling tales out of school. You know that. But if I think it, I'm pretty sure that he does. I have seen all of your missions first hand. I know how good you are. I see how he lets you get away with doing pretty much what you want and he tolerates it. No other Deniable has that freedom," The Optician replied and he meant every word.

"Do you know who all of The Deniables are?" Ward asked.

"Yes?"

"Want to share?"

"No."

Ward laughed down the line and then said,

"This is the longest conversation we have ever had outside of talking about baseball, yet I still don't know anything about you."

"Why would you want to know anything about me?" The Optician asked.

"Because as much as we both probably hate it, you are the closest thing to a brother I have ever had," Ward replied.

The comment that Ward had just made hit The Optician hard. He had felt that towards Ward for a long time and that is why protecting him was equally as important to him as following The Old Man's orders.

He felt something apart from nothing for the first time in a long, long time.

He knew for sure that Ward had never broken his word and tried to find out who he really was, any access to his secret file would have been flagged up and he had been close to Ward so many times, that if he did know who he was, his eyes would have given him away.

He actually felt, for the first time since they first put a rifle in his hands, that he belonged somewhere.

"Are you going soft on me?" he asked Ward, unsure of how to deal with the emotions he was feeling inside.

"No. I'm just tired of knowing nothing about the person that I trust more than anyone in the world," Ward replied.

"OK," The Optician said, "As we have a couple of hours to waste, I will offer you something?"

"Sounds ominous."

"You want it or not?"

"I'm listening."

"You can ask me three questions. I will answer them honestly," he said.

"For real?"

"As long as it isn't my name or where I come from, anything is open."

"Your name is The Optician and you come from wherever I happen to be so I know that one anyway."

"Use them well my friend," The Optician said.

"OK," Ward replied, "Seal or Delta Force? I have to know, it's been bugging me from the beginning," he added.

The Optician laughed and then said,

"I was Delta Force…."

"I knew it!" Ward interrupted.

"But I had my skills fine-tuned somewhere else," The Optician finished.

"Where?"

"I spent eighteen months on secondment to the S.A.S in Britain."

"Holy shit," Ward said, "I didn't see that coming," he added,

"Last question?" The Optician asked.

"I've only had one question," Ward said.

"No, you had two. What was I in and where? That is two."

"No, it's part of the same one," Ward replied, starting to sound like a kid in a schoolyard.

"One more or I hang up," The Optician said, completely unaware of the fact that he was now sounding equally juvenile.

"OK," Ward said, "Last one………"

The Optician waited.

And then he heard the question that he hadn't anticipated when Ward said,

"Why do you enjoy killing bad people so much?"

There were a number of ways he decided that he could answer that, but the comment Ward had made about him feeling like they were brothers had left him with an urge to help Ward to understand him, accept him for all he was and so, for the first time since he was fourteen years old, he dropped his guard.

"The truth?" Ward said, as he was still deep in thought. The Optician paused for a good ten seconds, took a deep breath and then spoke out loud the words that he had never spoken,

"When I was a kid growing up, I wasn't the biggest and the other kids used to pick on me because I didn't like to fight back. I was an easy target," he said.

"They wouldn't pick on you now," Ward replied instantly, sounding reassuring enough for him to continue.

"My dad ran off with a woman from the bar at the end of our block and left my mum to raise five of us, with no money and a shitty apartment that the welfare services supplied us with," he said.

"I had no father to raise me either so I can relate to that feeling. You didn't think anyone was there to protect you?"

"I didn't want him there. He was a loser, a bum, the kind of guy who would come home drunk, if he bothered to come home, and take his frustration over his pathetic life out on my mum," The Optician continued.

"I'm sorry, I won't interrupt again," Ward said.

"Good," The Optician said, "My poor mom got sick of me coming home from school every day in tears and with my clothes torn to shreds, where the neighbourhood bullies had attacked me. She couldn't afford to keep buying clothes, so she sent me to the local boxing club to toughen me up."

"And did it?" Ward enquired.

"Initially, yes. I started to fight back and the stronger I got, fewer and fewer kids started on me, because as you know, bullies only attack the weak."

"Initially?"

"I was just fourteen and I started to feel confident for the first time in my life and starting to believe in myself. The trainer at the gym, a guy called Fat Phil was good to me. He brought me gloves and used to bring me food in that his wife had cooked, to take home to feed my brothers and sisters. He was the first man to seem to give a shit about me," The Optician softly said.

"So what happened?" Ward asked.

"After training one night, he asked me to go back to his house to move some boxes into his garage and……" The Optician tailed off.

"If you don't want to say anymore, you don't have to," Ward said down the line.

"When I got there," The Optician continued, completely ignoring Ward's offer, "He had two old guys with him and it was all a trap. They did things to me, sick things, and afterwards they blamed me and said if I told anyone they would say I was lying and no one would believe a kid from a deadbeat family over them. So they threw me out of the door like some unwanted trash and I never went back," he added.

"I'm so sorry my friend, I really am," Ward said down the line, emotion clearly audible in his wavering voice.

"So I went into my shell again," The Optician continued, "I stopped going to school, the bullies reappeared and I didn't have the strength to fight back and then it got worse," he added.

"How much worse?" Ward asked.

"I told my mum what had happened. It was the straw that broke the camel's back as you say, twenty four hours later, she overdosed on her anti-depressants and killed herself."

"There is nothing I can say my friend, apart from the fact that the admiration and respect that I had for you before, is nothing compared to what I have now," Ward said.

"So me, my brothers and sisters all got put into foster homes and we never saw each other again. The foster family I went to were good people, they raised me well, put me in the junior cadets, got me through high school and then I joined the forces. The rest is history."

"You've never tried to find your brothers and sisters?" Ward asked.

"No."

"Why not?"

"Because they blamed me for mom killing herself," he replied.

"That can't be your fault, you know it as well as I do," Ward said firmly.

"So every single bad person I kill, I see the face of Fat Phil and his friends. So why do I enjoy killing the people who do those evil things to kids? Because I'm standing up for them when they have no one else to do it, and that is the very reason Ryan, why I devote my life to keeping you safe. You stand up for them, not for payback or because you were wronged against, just because you want to," The Optician said, "I'll have them on the plane and be with you this evening," he added and hung up the phone.

Santa Monica

Ward felt a very large lump in his throat that he couldn't seem to clear. He had been back to the bungalow, showered, changed his clothes and checked the evidence one more time before leaving.
He had got into the car and decided to make a quick call to The Optician on the drive there. He could never have anticipated the conversation that they had just had.
Now he understood why The Optician liked to live in the shadows. His whole life had been about feeling shame, and Ward knew that none of it was his fault; everything that churned away and ate at his insides was as a consequence of someone else's actions. He had probably felt alone his whole life.
He sees everything but no one sees him, was the handle that went with his legend, Now he understood why, he was tortured by guilt and shame.
Ward immediately decided that he would do two things. Firstly, he would make sure that he spoke to The Optician regularly, about normal, everyday things, so he felt that Ward saw more than just a killing machine and that he actually cared about his life outside of killing people.
Secondly, he was going to risk breaking a promise. Ward breathed in deeply and exhaled, pushing The Optician's turmoil to the back of his mind.
It was now time to finish Yeschenko off.

TWENTY FOUR

Brentwood – Los Angeles

McDermott had decided on hitting Yeschenko's house in Brentwood because it was only twenty minutes away and likely to be the least busy of the three that were left in operation.
Brentwood is an affluent area, very few of the houses sell for less than five million dollars.
That was another reason why McDermott chose it. The simple shame for the arrogant neighbours, with their 'I'm better than you' attitude, in discovering that such a disgusting place was thriving in their own neighbourhood, would hopefully make them realise that money alone cannot buy you class.
McDermott hated those who thought that wealth set them apart from others. Even more so because of the fact that he had more money than most of them could ever

dream of and it meant nothing to him. Doing the right thing came before anything else. His career in the Navy Seals had been nothing short of sensational. He had quickly moved through the ranks, from a seal to a planner and selector. He was a natural leader in every sense of the word and commanded respect through his actions, not his words. He had no time for those text book managers, who worked for manufacturing or white collar companies and pretended they were born to lead, or at least told each other that frequently. He would always look at people like that with contempt, and he had come across them often enough on his travels.

The houses were simply stunning, at least what could be seen of them from the road through the lush greenery, high walls and grand wrought iron gates was.

The house in Brentwood was just off of Sunset Boulevard on North Carmelina Avenue, on the corner of Helena Drive. It was a large property with brightly painted magnolia walls and dark brown tiles on the roof, which tried, but failed, to give the house a Mediterranean look. Off colour yellow brick walls tried to give the property a secure look.

This house was different to the rest of Yeschenko's, but McDermott concluded this was because of the fact that the gardens were so big, and the walls that offered privacy to the owners were so high, that prying eyes would not be an issue.

Access into the house was through a wooden gate situated at the end of the wall that ran along the front of the house. There was an intercom system by the gate and CCTV cameras pointing down towards the point of entry.

He had had taken Wallace, Walsh, Buck, Peacock and Murray with him to the house. In spite of Peacock and Murray proving their commitment to the cause at the docks, the fact that he had initial doubts about them still played on his mind slightly, and so he told them that they would watch the outside of the house while he attacked it with Wallace, Walsh and Buck.

The recon work had only taken an hour. He had parked their black Range Rover thirty feet up from the house and decided that the best way to attack would be to send two guys over the back yard wall and enter the house through the back door. He and one other would come in through the front. The plan had worked very well so far in every house that they had hit.

"Wallace, Walsh," he said, without looking at the two of them, as all six of them crouched behind the thick shrubbery of the garden opposite Yeschenko's place, "You two take the back door. Buck, you are with me," he added.

"And us?" Peacock asked.

"You two watch the road and if any of Yeschenko's men turn up once we are inside, you shoot to kill. Clear?"

"With pleasure," Murray replied enthusiastically.

Maybe I was wrong after all, McDermott thought to himself.

"Go," he said to Walsh and Wallace, and he watched as they stepped out from behind the thick bushes and into the road, sprinting across to the other side, running twenty yards up the road that was adjacent to the garden and then jumping up to grab the top of the wall, before pulling themselves up and out of view.

They were out of sight in less than seven seconds from the moment that they had stepped out from the bushes.
"You two stay here," McDermott said to Murray, "Let's go Buck."
"Don't tell me you are just going to knock on the door too?" Buck asked as he scurried to catch up with McDermott.
"I don't know yet."
"What is it with you guys?" Buck replied, genuine dismay in his voice, as he looked up and down at McDermott, who was wearing black combat trousers, black tee shirt, a black flak jacket, and carrying a silenced Glock in his right hand, "You lot aren't fans of complex entry, are you?"
McDermott lead the way up the grand concrete steps that led to the solid oak front doors that had no windows. The CCTV camera pointed down at them, so he reached up, and used the tip of his gun to push the camera around so that it faced down onto the street.
And then he knocked on the door.

Wallace and Walsh smiled at each other as they crouched behind the small garden shed ten feet away from the back door of the house.
They smiled because right in front of them, sitting at a table on the decking outside the back door, drinking coffee and smoking, were six guys, all dressed in jeans and vests, with tattoos covering their arms and hammer and sickle tattoos on the left hand side of their necks. There were two young girls there, both no older than fourteen, one ferrying more coffee out to the table in miniature white cups, and the other standing to the side,

looking as though she was waiting for instructions to be barked at her. They both looked frail and frightened.

"Which ones do you want to kill?" Walsh asked.

"The guy in the white top with the bleached blonde hair," Wallace replied, "He's committing numerous crimes against fashion and hair styling," he added.

"OK," Walsh said, "You take him and the two guys to the right and I will take the other three."

"That's not fair," Wallace said.

"Why?"

"Because you get to see their faces when you kill them, and all I get to see is the side of two guys' heads and the back of the other's head. How is that fair?"

"So what do you suggest?" Walsh asked.

"Rock, paper, scissors? The winner choses," Wallace replied.

"OK."

Walsh put his gun on the floor and said,

"On three," and started to move his clenched right hand forward and then back three times.

On the third count, Walsh stuck out two fingers and Wallace opened his hand flat.

"Shit!" Wallace said.

Walsh smiled.

"Best of three?" Wallace asked, completely seriously.

"Just take the three I said, the boss will probably be inside by now," Walsh said abruptly, as he took aim with his gun. Six seconds and six shots later, the six guys were all dead, every one of them with holes in their heads where the bullets had hit from close range.

The young girl carrying the coffee cups shrieked and dropped the cups on the floor and the other young girl, who had been waiting for her instructions, just stood still, motionless, no reaction at all.

They both stepped out from behind the garden shed and approached the table.

"It's OK," Walsh said to the girl who had been holding the cups, "We are here to help."

The girl nodded back to him,

"How many men are in the house?" Wallace asked the other girl.

She just stood there motionless and said nothing. He looked over at Walsh,

"How many men are in the house?" Walsh asked the coffee cup girl,

"Just two more," she replied.

"Are you OK?" Wallace asked the motionless girl.

"She won't talk," the coffee cup girl replied.

"Why not?" Walsh asked.

"Because she complained about what the old men who come to visit were doing to her and so they cut out her tongue."

Wallace looked at the poor, innocent young thing,

"Which one of those did it?" he asked.

"None," the coffee cup girl replied, "He is inside the house."

Wired and Wallace nodded at each other,

"Stay here," Wallace said and they both headed into the house through the back door.

McDermott delivered the last of his four knocks on the solid door with his knuckles and waited. Five seconds passed and no one had answered it, so he knocked again, four times. Five seconds passed and no one opened it. He was about to lift his hand to knock for a third time when the door started to open.

As the door reached six inches open, he raised his Glock. A foot and he started to squeeze the trigger gently. Eighteen inches and a guy with a shaved head started to appear through the opening.

McDermott shot him in the face from two feet away. The guys' whole face exploded and the force of the bullet pushed him back, with his hand still on the door handle. His fall fully opened the door for him. He stepped in, the guy's body was still jerking on the floor and so he fired another bullet into him without looking down.

His eyes were focussed on the staircase.

Buck stepped in behind him and closed the door.

"Subtle," he whispered.

To the right, he saw a door starting to open, he raised his gun and then saw Walsh peer around the corner and then move his head back in.

Walsh looked again, saw his boss and then stepped out into the hallway with Wallace close behind him.

McDermott stepped forward to the bottom of the stairs and Walsh approached him and looked at the dead Russian guy on the floor behind him.

"There is only one more guy in the house. We have six down in the garden and there were two more in the house, but I see one of them has met you already," he said.

"Go and get the video evidence," McDermott said, I'm sure that we can take the last one and get the girls out."

"Can you do something for me boss?" Walsh asked.

McDermott raised an eyebrow.

"Don't kill him, capture him alive and then bring him out to the garden."

McDermott nodded. He knew Walsh would have good reason to make such a request.

Wallace came and stood to his left and they started to climb the stairs, Buck walking up backwards behind them, while Walsh went to find the CCTV footage.

They reached the top of the stairs and there were eight doors leading off of the giant landing. One of them had a brass plate on the door with 'Bathroom' written on it and the rest of the doors were all painted a clean, brilliant white colour.

"These houses are all laid out the same," Wallace said, "The girls will be in those rooms there," he added, pointing to the doors on the right.

"Buck, get the girls together, and quietly," McDermott said.

He walked up to the bathroom door and knocked gently.

"Ukhodi," a gruff voice shouted out

McDermott looked at Wallace quizzically.

"It means go away," Wallace said.

McDermott reached out for the door handle and turned it.

It opened.

He stepped in quickly and urgently with his gun pointing out straight, with Wallace beside him, and they stopped immediately.

The guy was sitting on the toilet with his pants around his ankles reading a magazine.

"An appropriate place to be considering what you are feeling right now," Wallace quipped.

"Trousers on now!" McDermott demanded.

The guy stood up and reached for the toilet paper and McDermott said,
"Now!"
The guy reached down and pulled his pants up.
"Out!" McDermott barked.
The guy walked out of the bathroom with Wallace right behind him.
On the landing, they could see that Buck was now entering the last of the four doors. There were already thirteen girls on the landing; another five came out of the last room a few moments later.
"That's all of them," Buck said, "Apparently there are two more on kitchen duty," he added.
"Bring them down to the back yard," Wallace said as he dug his gun into the Russian guys back to push him forward towards the stairs.
Walsh got halfway up the stairs with a duffel bag bulging at the seams and then stopped,
"I have everything," he said to McDermott who nodded his approval.
Wallace then nudged the guy down the stairs, into the hallway and said,
"Kitchen."
The guy turned left and headed towards the kitchen. He reached the door and opened it,
"Backyard!" Wallace barked, and the guy walked through, followed by Walsh, McDermott and eighteen painfully thin and confused children who were all staring at the dead guy lying by the front door. Buck tucked in at the back of the line.

They all followed the guy out into the backyard and when they were all outside in the brilliant sunshine, Walsh said,
"Stop!"
The girls all looked at the six dead bodies lying around the garden table and a couple of them started talking hurriedly and excitedly in Russian.
The coffee cup girl, and the girl who couldn't speak, came out from behind the garden shed, where they had taken up sanctuary.
Walsh raised his gun and hit the Russian guy hard across the back of his skull.
He fell to the floor.
"Do you all talk English?" he asked the group of girls.
They all nodded as one.
McDermott concluded that the customers probably insisted upon it so they could understand their desperate words when the sick bastards were hurting them.
"In five minutes, you will be safe. The police, feds and social services will be here to look after you. Do you all understand that?" Walsh asked.
There was a chorus of "Yes!" and a lot of head nodding and clinging to each other, amidst the most warming smiles imaginable.
"Come here please," Walsh said, beckoning to the girl who couldn't speak, smiling as he said it.
The girl walked across the lawn to him.
"Is this the guy who cut out your tongue?" he asked softly.
The girl nodded.
The Russian looked petrified.
"I want you to decide what we should do to him."

He heard a murmur from the group behind him.
"Ubey yego!" two of the girls shouted out.
"Sokratit yego yazyk!" one girl screamed at the top of her voice.
McDermott looked at Walsh,
"It means kill him and cut his tongue out," Buck said.
The girl extended her arm and offered her hand towards Walsh.
"What?" he asked, forgetting that she couldn't speak and instantly feeling stupid.
She pointed to his right hand.
The hand that was holding his gun.
He looked at McDermott.
McDermott nodded.
The guy on his knees started speaking in Russian, too quickly for Buck to understand; he was looking up at the girl who couldn't speak and so Walsh hit the back of his head again so he would not have any eye contact with her.
The girl reached him and he moved around behind her. He lifted his gun with his left hand and leant around the girls shoulder and used his right hand to put her hand on the trigger.
The guy curled over into a ball and put his hands over his head.
The girl who had been carrying the coffee cups came over to them and said,
"Eto dlya vsekh nas."
The girl who couldn't speak pulled the trigger and blew the back of the Russian guys' head apart. And then fired the last eight shots in the magazine into his back to make sure he was gone forever.

"We have to go now," McDermott said.
Walsh gently released the girl's rigid grip from the gun and pulled away from her.
Every single girl in the group walked over to her and embraced her.
"Wallace," McDermott said, "Make the call."
Wallace promptly took out his cell phone and made the call.
"Stay here. You are all safe now, the police will soon be here," McDermott said, "Now, all of you, let's go," he added.
They all ran back into the house, through the kitchen and the hallway, and out of the front door.
Murray and Peacock stepped out of the bushes, about thirty feet apart.
"We are done," McDermott said to Murray, "Back to the warehouse."
Murray and Peacock jumped into their car which was parked just behind the Range Rover and five seconds later, both vehicles were moving.
Just as a government Sudan, five police cars with sirens blazing, three unmarked cars and an ambulance turned into North Carmelina Avenue, going in the opposite direction to them.
McDermott smiled to himself.
I wonder what the neighbours will make of that he thought.

TWENTY FIVE

Beverley Hills

Andrea Yeschenko knew that he was out of options and hope.
Now his plan would change dramatically.
It was no longer about getting more; it was now about salvaging what little he had left.
He had been told about the house in Brentwood a few minutes ago by a cop on his payroll.
All eight of his men were dead. He would have had more men there if it wasn't for the massacre at the docks, and what few good men he had left he needed to keep in his mansion, the houses would have to make do with the less capable of his men.
The warrior in him accepted that whoever was behind this on the ground was good. Very good in fact, and he hoped that he would get to meet this man face to face.
He wasn't afraid of him. He had never been afraid of anyone in his life and he wasn't going to start letting fear rule him now.
He called the number in Washington.

The voice answered immediately,
"I was expecting you to call."
"You have fought a good fight so far. So now we talk," Yeschenko replied.
The voice laughed out loud,
"And you picked the wrong fight," he said, "The only talking that will take place now is me talking and you listening."
"Then talk," Yeschenko said.
"You made a mistake in getting greedy. I protected you and made sure that you were left to your own devices and you had built up a reasonable business. Now my understanding is that it has been obliterated."
The word, 'Understanding' echoed around Yeschenko's brain. Surely the voice knew how it was, not just understood what had happened?
He then decided that listening was actually the best thing that he could do.
"I want the evidence and I want it now, even if you have to drive it across to Washington yourself," the voice demanded.
"And you will continue to protect the businesses that I have left?"
"Yes I will. I give you my word on that."
The guy's word meant nothing to Yeschenko. People who did what he did for a living were born to lie. He had seen it over and over back home in Russia.
"OK," Yeschenko replied, "I'll get the footage across to you by tomorrow. One of my men will deliver it personally," he added.
"And the rest of the evidence?" the voice asked.

Yeschenko was confused. The voice should have the rest of the evidence already in his possession after it was taken from the ship. Rather than ask outright why he didn't have it yet, he decided to dig a little deeper to see what he could learn.

"And your men that have done this to me, you will call them off?" he asked.

"I will make the call immediately after I have everything you tried to use against me," the voice replied.

"You are a devious man," Yeschenko said, "You want the evidence against you so that you can destroy it and the evidence against the other two men you want to use to destroy them."

"It's the way of the world," the voice replied, "Winners and losers. Everything comes down to that."

"The men that you sent, they are good, very good. Who are they?"

"They are my personal army."

"And you have control over them?" Yeschenko asked.

"Complete control."

Yeschenko laughed.

"What's funny?" the voice asked.

"Your men have the rest of the evidence already, I only have the intimate video footage," Yeschenko replied, "So maybe your control isn't as absolute as you think."

The voice was quiet for a few moments and then said, "Then you are really out of luck. You picked the wrong fight," he reiterated again.

Yeschenko laughed,

"So it seems did you," he replied.

"You had better hope you find it before me because if I do, I will finish you completely," the voice replied

"Goodbye Senator Reid," Yeschenko said and hung up the phone.

Hart Senate Office Building – Washington D.C.

Senator Madison Reid slammed his phone down hard on his desk. Yeschenko had just signed his own death warrant. But that could wait.
Right now he was more concerned with who exactly had the evidence that he was desperate to obtain. Even worse, he thought to himself, he hoped to God that it still wasn't on the ship.
He called Centrepoint.
"Yes?" he answered.
"You have a big, big problem McNair."
"I'm not sure I'm the only one," he replied, a more confident and smug tone to his voice than in their previous conversations.
"What does that mean?"
"It means that you went after the hackers in New York. I advised you against it."
"I don't think getting worked up over a couple of grungy kids is worth losing my approval for your covert operations and your funding, do you?"
"I'm not worked up about it, but you made a mistake going against my better judgement," Centrepoint stated.
"I want you to call your men off now. The mission is over."
"Yeschenko is still alive and some of my team are pissed at you."
"Well they will get over it. You will make sure of that."

"I'll do what I can but I can't guarantee it."
"And also," Reid continued, completely ignoring Centrepoint's threat, "I want you to hand over everything they have. All of the evidence from the houses and the boats and everything those snotty kids stole with their hacking tricks."
"I'll get that together as quick as I can."
"And no copies of anything are to be made. Is that clear?"
"Very," Centrepoint replied, "But now it is time for my conditions," he added.
"Shoot."
"You pass all requests for funding without exception. You no longer ask for specific breakdowns of the black ops that we carry out."
"That's a big ask."
"I'm keeping a very, very big secret…"
"OK. That seems like a fair exchange. You get all of the evidence to me by tomorrow and you will have your conditions met."
"Thank you," Centrepoint replied. "So it seems that we have reached a plan that suits both of us."
"Get it done and quickly," Reid said and hung up the phone.

Marina Del Rey- 7:00pm

Ward arrived back at the warehouse and walked inside. McDermott was there with Wallace, Walsh, Buck, Murray and Peacock.

He had spent most of the afternoon coming up with a plan for securing the evidence so that no one would ever be able to find it.

He knew that Nicole-Louise and Tackler would be arriving within the next ten minutes, as The Optician had called and said they landed twenty minutes ago. He had run through his instructions with The Optician and he noticed after he had ended the call that he felt different talking to him now, somehow a lot closer.

McDermott looked up as he walked into the main warehouse.

"Paul will be here with Nicole-Louise and Tackler within fifteen minutes," he said to Ward.

"Excellent," Ward replied, "Brentwood went OK I take it?"

"Almost too easy."

"Meaning?"

"The guys he had at the house," McDermott said, "They were poor, I mean really poor and there was only eight of them. My guess is that he is running out of men and he has no one left to defend the last two houses."

"You got the evidence?" Ward enquired.

"It's all over there," McDermott replied, pointing to a row of computers and laptops which were laid out in a line on the workbench at the far side of the warehouse.

"Good. Nicole-Louise and Tackler will be bringing what they have so they can now piece it all together for us when they get here."

"Next time we raid somewhere; can I knock on the door?" Buck suddenly asked, trying to lighten the mood and making Ward smile in the process.

The moment was interrupted by the roller shutter doors of the warehouse starting to rise. Within four seconds, the front of a black Range Rover was completely visible and started rolling forward.

Paul McDermott drove into the warehouse, the doors shutting just as quickly as they had opened behind him. The car rolled to a stop and the rear doors opened. Nicole-Louise stepped out and she looked exhausted. She saw Ward and moved towards him. As she reached him, he put his arms around her and held her tight and felt the urge to protect her, like a big brother would want to protect his little sister, and then Tackler slid out of the rear door, looking haggard and frightened. McDermott, who had sensed how vulnerable Tackler was feeling, stood up and walked over to him, shook his hand and then put a friendly arm around his shoulder, simply to reassure him that he was safe.

Ward held Nicole-Louise for a long minute and then said,

"I need to talk to you two alone," and led Nicole-Louise off towards the reception area, with Tackler following behind. They reached the reception area and after Tackler had stepped inside, Ward closed the door.

"First things first," he said, "No one will ever get that close to hurting you again. I'm so sorry you had to go through that."

"It was horrible," Tackler said, his eyes watering, "I thought we were going to die."

"We aren't cut out for that side of things Ryan," Nicole-Louise said, anger in her voice, "It is your job to keep us protected from that and you didn't do that," she added.

He knew that she was right and he was furious with himself that he hadn't anticipated the danger that they would be in.

He knew what the next question that he had to ask was. In fact, he already knew the answer but he had to hear it from the two of them.

"You know why that happened, don't you?" he asked them both.

"Of course we don't," Tackler replied loudly and angrily, "We were just checking company accounts, how does us nearly getting killed come from that?" he asked.

He could see by the look in Tackler's eyes that he was telling him the truth. In one respect, that was a good thing because he knew that Tackler never held anything back from him. Unfortunately, it meant Nicole-Louise had been hiding things from Tackler and Ward knew that he really wasn't going to be happy about that.

He took a deep breath and said,

"You have to tell us both what you found Nicole-Louise."

Tackler looked at her blankly and then shot a confused look in Ward's direction.

Nicole-Louise said nothing.

"She's been through enough, don't put any more crap on her," he shouted at Ward.

The three of them knew that Tackler was petrified of Ward and yet here he was standing toe to toe with him, bawling at him in defence of the girl that he loved.

Ward envied what they had.

"Nicole-Louise, you need to tell us so I can fix it," he said again.

"I've told you, she doesn't know what the hell you are talking about," Tackler said, as he tried to position his body in between Ward and Nicole-Louise.

"Yes I do," she softly said.

Tackler turned and looked at her.

"What?"

"I know why they came for us. I tried to cover my tracks after I had found it but I couldn't have been quick enough," she said, looking at the floor.

"I don't understand," Tackler said softly as he glanced at Ward, suddenly aware that he had been shouting at one of the most ruthless killers on the planet and remembering the fear that he felt towards him.

"I have just one question," Ward said softly.

"What is it?" she asked.

"Can you prove it definitively, not just names but visually?"

"By the time I have gone through the stuff you got from the houses and the data I found, I will be able to."

"How do you know all of this and I know nothing about it?" Tackler enquired.

"Easy," Ward replied, "I have the missing piece of the puzzle hidden away."

"I'll leave you to explain to Tackler what you know and then I will get Paul to take you to a motel for the night where you can freshen up and sleep. He has money for clothes and anything else you need," Ward said, as he turned and walked out of the reception area and back into the warehouse.

He approached the table where Paul was sitting. Buck, Murray and Peacock were on the sofa next to him telling him about the events in Brentwood.

"Paul," Ward said, "I need you to take Nicole-Louise and Tackler to the Ramada motel on West Washington Boulevard," he added.

"You want me to do it right now?" Paul asked.

"Yes. They need to freshen up and rest," he replied, "When you drop them off, go and buy them whatever they need and throw them a few bucks and then tell them you will be back for them at 7:00am in the morning."

Paul nodded and got to his feet straight away.

"You three," he said looking at Buck, Peacock and Murray, "You stink so I suggest you go wherever it is you go, get cleaned, changed and be back here in the morning at 7:00 am ready to go again," he added.

"Finally, a break," Buck said and Murray and Peacock laughed.

"Thanks boss," Murray said as he stood up and followed Buck and Peacock out of the door into the reception area.

He watched them all leave and he hoped more than anything that he was completely wrong about what the three of them had planned next.

TWENTY SIX

**Ramada Motel – West Washington Boulevard
9:00pm**

"I can't believe that you never told me about it when you found it," Tackler said to Nicole-Louise, "It hurts that you would hold anything back from me if I'm honest."
"I didn't want to put you in any danger," she replied apologetically.
Tackler was making every effort to stay calm and be supportive of her. He was fully aware of how strong Nicole-Louise was, and he wanted to be strong for her too, to show her that he could be a man like Ryan Ward and Paul McDermott. He hated the fact that the moment Paul had met them at the airport, her shoulders relaxed for the first time, and seeing her in Ward's arms for reassurance and protection in the form of a hug had really upset him. Tackler readily accepted that he was a geek, a smart guy who could outthink most people, but for the first time since the day he had met her, he felt inadequate.

Tackler had met Nicole-Louise at Columbia University in New York, where they were both studying advanced computer science. She was originally from Newark, he was from Brooklyn. They hit it off immediately.

He was drawn to her quirky ways. She loved all things British, he was a massive fan of the Punk music that had swept the U.K. in the late seventies and he loved the Sex Pistols.

They would talk about their plans to visit London, to look at the Houses of Parliament, Big Ben and the hidden clubs and music halls of Carnaby Street and the city's West End.

Their friendship had turned into love. A love bound together by their similar likes and dislikes and their staggering ability to make the most complicated things on a computer, seem easy. They were so far ahead in terms of ability and understanding of programming and network systems, that their tutor told them not to bother coming to lectures for a whole term so that the other students could catch up.

They used that time off to set each other a challenge of being the first to hack into the F.B.I. secure database and after they found that too easy, they had turned their attentions to the C.I.A servers.

And then they got caught.

They were facing twenty years in jail and then a mysterious old guy appeared when they were awaiting trial and offered them a way out by working for him.

An offer that they both readily accepted and they were set up with an apartment on Park Avenue in New York. They had been working for Centrepoint, more specifically for Ward, for a number of years now and this was the first time that anything so dangerous had ever happened to them.

"But that is exactly what you did do," Tackler replied, "Put us in danger by keeping quiet."

She didn't say anything.

"And what if The Optician hadn't been there?" he asked softly.

"But he was there," she replied, "Ryan would never leave us alone if we were at risk, you know that."

"This evidence that you found, where is it now?" Tackler asked.

"It's safe. When I left the apartment to get the bagels yesterday, I stopped at the Internet Café and sent it to our secure e-mail address."

"And it was just lists?"

"No," Nicole-Louise replied, "An encrypted file that has one half of it missing."

"And you can only decrypt it when you have the other half. So where is it?"

"Hopefully on the hardware that Ryan has collected so far. This guy was smart, breaking one file into two. However, I think that the other half was never moved electronically. It has to be in his possession."

"Just promise me one thing?" Tackler asked.

"Anything, I'm so sorry."

"Never, ever do that again. It's my job to protect you. I know you are the strong one and I might not be as tough as Ryan, or as scary as The Optician, but it is my job to protect you. I would have worked out a way to do it. No matter what it took," Tackler said.

She looked at him with her big blue eyes and she felt such love for him. This one hundred and forty pound geek standing before her was her rock, her colossus and her soul mate.

For the first time, she saw how strong he was.

"I promise. I love you so much Tackler."

"I love you too," he replied, and he leant in and kissed her.

"Now," he added, "Can we have some of that sex stuff that happens in the movies?" he said, and winked at her as she pulled him towards her and kissed him,

"Yes we can. But only if you say I am better at finding hidden shit than you," she said.

"Nicole-Louise, you're the best," he replied, his tee shirt removed before the last syllable of the sentence had finished.

The moment was shattered by the door to the room swinging open and two guys bursting through it, closing it behind them.

One of the guys was massive, the other older. They were both holding guns in their hands.

"Which one of you is the girl?" the big guy asked, looking at Tacklers skinny, shirtless frame. The other guy laughed.

"You two have caused a lot of trouble, you know that?" the old guy asked.

Nicole-Louise clung to Tackler. She instinctively turned her body in front of him to shield him.

"Sit down skinny," the big guy said, "Piss me off too much and I will break you in half," he added.

Tackler glared at him. Strangely, he stopped feeling frightened; his only concern was to let Nicole-Louise know that he would die defending her.

The big guy stepped forward and shoved Tackler hard in the chest. The force of the push knocked him into her and they both fell onto the bed, with him landing on top of her.

The big guy pulled the chair out that was placed under the mirror on the wall beside them, swung it around so it was three feet away from where they had just pulled themselves upright on the bed, and sat down on it.

"Now listen to me carefully," he said, "I'm going to explain how this will work," he added.

Nicole-Louise glared at him.

"OK?" the big guy repeated.

"OK," Tackler replied.

"You have something that you shouldn't have. I need it and I need it quickly. You are going to give it to me. You understand that?"

Tackler knew exactly what they wanted but figured that playing dumb would buy them some time.

"I don't know what you are on about?" he replied, trying to look as confused as he possibly could.

"For someone who is meant to be smart you are acting incredibly dumb," the older guy said.

"Maybe if I rape your pretty little girlfriend and force you to watch, it might jog your memory," the big guy said, grabbing his groin as he said it for added effect.

"Don't you dare lay a finger on her," Tackler screamed and stood up from the bed quickly, his upright body no more than eighteen inches away from his tormentor.

The big guy lunged forward and jabbed Tackler hard, right in the centre of the stomach. He doubled over, the air escaping from his lungs, leaving him unable to breathe. As he doubled over, the big guy clamped the same hand on the top of his head and pushed him back onto the bed. He landed flat on his back next to Nicole-Louise and then promptly shot forward, desperate to get some air back into his lungs.

The old guy laughed loudly and said,

"Jesus, you are pathetic."

Nicole-Louise put her arm around Tacklers shoulders. He had tried defending her and she loved him so much for that.

"You have a list. It is a very important list that you stole from someone very important. I need it now," the big guy said.

"We don't have it," Nicole-Louise spat at him without looking, she was more concerned with Tackler getting his breath back.

"Now come on, I'm not going to ask again. I haven't had sex for a week. I like it rough. Lots of punching and broken bones; so if you want to avoid that, you had better tell me right now where it is," he replied.

Tackler got his breath back and thought hard, he was panicking and then he took a deep breath and told himself he had to think like Ryan Ward. What would Ryan do he asked himself.

And then a moment of clarity washed over his whole mind.

He knew exactly what Ryan would do. Therefore he knew exactly what Ryan Ward would want him to do right now.

He would put all of his trust and faith in Ward and prayed to God that the words of praise that he had always heaped upon him were genuine, and his promise that he would always protect them, was a promise that he would never break.

If Ward was the man that they both thought he was, they were both going to live. If he was engrossed in his own progress and mission, they were going to die very soon.

"It's two blocks away," Tackler said, "We aren't stupid enough to have it here," he added.

"Then let's go and get it skinny," the big guy said, "And put your shirt on, the dogs might think you are a bone," he added and the old guy laughed out loud.

Tackler stood up and offered his hand to Nicole-Louise, who took it, and he pulled her to her feet. He put on his tee-shirt and the old guy turned and opened the door. He peered out, looked left and right and then turned and nodded at the big guy.

"Let's go. And if you are bullshitting me, I will make you watch me beat that bitch to death before I rip your limbs from your sockets," the big guy said to him threateningly.

Tackler walked out of the door, holding Nicole-Louise's hand tightly.

'I need you Ryan Ward. I need you to be all the things I believe you to be, and I need you to keep the promise you made to us both that you would always keep us safe' he said to himself.

He needed Ward to be everything he thought he was.

As it turned out, Ward was most definitely everything that Tackler needed him to be.

As Tackler and Nicole-Louise were being led out of the motel room by an old guy carrying a gun and a big, bulky guy coming out behind them, The Optician lined all four of them up in his scope.

Five minutes earlier, he had called Ward.
"There are two guys who have just turned up at the motel. One old, the other one looks like a steroid user with a ponytail, so you were right, this Murray and Peacock are bad apples. Their guns are drawn," he had said.
"The third guy I told you about, Buck?" Ward asked.
"Nowhere to be seen."
"Good," Ward had replied, "I like Buck."
"You want me to take them? I don't have a shot but I can be in the room in thirty seconds," The Optician asked.
"Give it a few minutes. Tackler will work out a way to bring them out to you. Paul is on his way now."
"Are you sure?"
"Yes I'm sure," Ward had replied and hung up the phone.

The Optician had watched over Nicole-Louise and Tackler a number of times, for both Ward and Centrepoint and he had grown very fond of them. He had been in close proximity to them a number of times and when they flew to L.A. that morning, he listened to them teasing each other on the plane and they made him smile. He was envious of the relationship they had and the way that they seemed so innocent and yet so content with what they had. They were good people. The world needed more good people like Nicole-Louise and Tackler he thought to himself.
He liked them.
They were his friends even though they didn't know it. Peacock and Murray were trying to hurt his friends.

And for that, they were now two seconds away from dying.

The night was still and there was no wind. They were perfect conditions for an average shooter.

For The Optician elevated fifty feet away, lying on a dumpster under the cover of the shadows of the motel building, it was a double kill he could make with his eyes shut.

He lined Murray's head up in the dead centre of his crosshairs. Always take the one at the back out first was a golden rule of his. The one at the front will have no time to use Nicole-Louise or Tackler as a human shield. He squeezed the trigger softly and watched through the scope as Murray's head jerked back as the 7.62mm bullet hit him directly in the centre of the forehead and embedded in his brain. His head shattered and a fine spray of mist floated into the air, as his knees stopped receiving a signal from his brain and his bulky body collapsed to the floor.

At the front, Peacock did not even have time to register what was happening before he received delivery of his own bullet. It hit on the left hand side of his forehead, The Optician making sure it did, so that Nicole-Louise and Tackler would not get covered in blood standing behind him and he lurched forward and hit the floor face first.

Nicole-Louise put her hands over her mouth and let out a silent scream and then something happened that completely surprised The Optician. Tackler looked up, his eyes burning straight into his scope and mouthed the words, 'Thank you.' The Optician smiled and lowered his gun, just as a black Range Rover came speeding around the corner.

Wired jumped out of the passenger seat before the car had even come to a stop and sprinted towards them. Paul spun the car around so that the rear doors were facing them just six feet away.
"Let's go," Paul said through the window.
Nicole-Louise and Tackler jumped into the car and Wired approached the two dead bodies.
He stood over them and fired three shots into their lifeless bodies. Not to make sure they were dead, he knew that The Optician always killed with a single shot. And not because he was genuinely psychotic either and he liked playing on it.
Wired fired three shots into the bodies of Peacock and Murray because he had a secret.
The great love of his life was a young computer hacker called Nicole-Louise. He had never told anyone that. But he thought about her, every day, and he spent bored days hanging around imagining being with her and all of the exciting things that they would do. It was his way of protecting her.
In the car, Nicole-Louise and Tackler watched.
Nicole-Louise shuddered and said to Tackler,
"That guy gives me the creeps, he's psychotic."

TWENTY SEVEN

Marina Del Rey

Ward called Centrepoint immediately after he had hung up the phone to The Optician.
"Hello?"
"McDermott felt that Murray and Peacock were wrong from the word go. So how come you didn't?" Ward demanded, "Or maybe you did?"
"What do you mean wrong, in what way?" Centrepoint asked.
Ward listened to Centrepoint's reply carefully. He knew him well, he trusted him and he could tell that The Old Man had no idea what he was talking about.
"They've just tried to kill Nicole-Louise and Tackler," Ward furiously spat down the line.
"WHAT?!"

It was the first time in the four years that he had known him that he had heard him raise his voice.

"You told me they were good enough to be Deniables," he said, "So how can you get it so dramatically wrong?"

Centrepoint was quiet for over ten seconds and then calmly said,

"Firstly, are Nicole-Louise and Tackler OK?"

"Yes."

"Tell me exactly what happened?" Centrepoint asked.

He spent a few minutes explaining what had happened and how McDermott's doubts about the two of them had been niggling away at him, and so he had made a point of letting them and Buck know where Nicole-Louise and Tackler were staying, as they all sat on a sofa listening to a conversation that he was having with McDermott. He had then sent The Optician to watch over them and given them a description of Murray, Peacock and Buck.

"Buck I can personally vouch for," Centrepoint interrupted.

"I know. I had no concerns about him," Ward replied.

"So, the question is, who were they working for? Centrepoint asked.

"You need to tell me everything you know, right from the beginning."

"There are a committee of Senators in Washington who approve our funding and our operations," Centrepoint said, "The chair of that committee contacted me last week, saying that Yeschenko was blackmailing them with evidence of members of the committee engaged in sexual activities with the minors that worked for him."

"How does a Senator get away with doing that?"

"Anyway," Centrepoint continued, "As far as I was concerned, it was a pretty straightforward op. You would wipe out Yeschenko, get the evidence, the Senator would give us a free hand to do what we have to do without question, and that was it."

"Who was the Senator?" Ward asked.

"The who doesn't matter. What does concern me is how whoever is hunting the same evidence got to Peacock and Murray. They were good men."

"Not good enough and not anymore."

"And I still don't know who the other people hunting the evidence are. We assumed Secret Service, but that doesn't fit. I'm starting to think they are people masquerading as Secret Service," Centrepoint said.

"I thought you knew who everyone was and had all the power in our world?"

"So did I," Centrepoint replied, "That is what worries me."

"Who is the Senator?" Ward asked again.

"Anyone who can work without my knowledge and above me must have some powerful friends. Extremely powerful; so I want you to finish this and get the evidence now," Centrepoint said, completely ignoring Ward's question.

"It would help if we knew who we were up against"

"You need to keep Nicole-Louise and Tackler safe. Have you got a plan for that?" Centrepoint asked.

"Of course I have. But I will keep that to myself, just like you with the name of the Senator," Ward said sarcastically.

"That's fine, I trust you impeccably," Centrepoint replied.

Ward's concentration was broken by the roller shutter doors starting to raise, Paul McDermott's black Range Rover almost fully visible within five seconds.

"I have to go," he said and hung up the phone.

Paul rolled the Range Rover into the warehouse and stopped about six feet away from him.

Tackler climbed out of the rear door first and then Nicole-Louise followed him.

Nicole-Louise approached him,

"Tell me that is the last time anything like that will happen," she angrily said.

"I'm so sorry," he replied.

"Well thankfully, Tackler was amazing," she said, hugging his arm and pulling his small frame into hers, "He stood up for me and would have died for me. It was his plan to get us outside," she added.

"I'm sorry to you too," he said to Tackler.

Tackler approached him. Ward knew that he was imagining it but Tackler looked different, somehow less frail and bigger.

"Give us a minute," he said to Nicole-Louise.

She frowned and then walked over to the workbench where all the computers and laptops were laid out.

Ward was totally unsure of what Tackler was going to say but he had a real fear that he was going to tell him that he and Nicole-Louise were finished with helping him.

But he never said that.

What he said, took him totally by surprise.

"I trusted you not just with my life, but more importantly with Nicole-Louise's," he said.

Ward just looked at him with no emotion, waiting for the hammer blow.

"I trusted that your promise of always keeping us safe was not just a bunch of words, but a desire that you had to protect us," he continued, "I convinced those two guys to walk out of that motel door because I had total belief in your word Ryan. I knew you would have someone there protecting us. I believed it with all I am," he added.

"I've told you before that you and Nicole-Louise are…."

Tackler put up his hand to stop Ward in mid-sentence.

"And apart from Nicole-Louise, I don't trust anyone. But you, you have always convinced me that you would look after us and you never let me down. And you didn't. You had everything in place, or rather The Optician, and not once, but twice, because you did the same in New York."

"I've told you before, take you two away and I won't be any good at what I do," Ward replied, getting a feel for the gratitude that Tackler was feeling.

"I just wanted you to know. I trusted you and knew you wouldn't let me down. That's a new and incredible feeling for me so thank you," he said.

"No thank you needed," Ward said. Then he looked across at McDermott and his team talking around the table and said,

"You lot, as bad as this is for me, are my family. Brothers, sisters and the grandfather," he said looking at McDermott and smiling.

"Someone tried hurting my Nicole-Louise," Tackler said, "Now we will hunt them down and find them for you and you will kill them."

Ward nodded,

"Whatever it takes?" he said to Tackler.
"Whatever it takes," he replied, as he turned and walked towards the workbench where Nicole-Louise was.
He was pleased that Tackler would do whatever it took, because he now had a clear plan. Tomorrow they would destroy Yeschenko's empire and find what everyone was looking for and then he would move Nicole-Louise and Tackler out of harm's way until the whole mission was completed and he could guarantee their safety. He just knew that Tackler was not going to like what he had in store for them.

He called McDermott over.
"Tomorrow I want us to all hit Yeschenko's home," he said as McDermott reached him.
"You are talking about his house in Beverley Hills?"
"Yes. What we are looking for will be there."
"What about the last two houses he runs?" McDermott asked.
"After we have taken care of him, the police, feds and social services can deal with them."
"You want to tell me what is going on yet?"
"Tell me something, why did you have such a bad feeling about Peacock and Murray and yet I missed it. What gave it away?" Ward asked quizzically.
"They listened too hard," McDermott replied.
"What do you mean?"
"Watch my team," McDermott explained, "They pay no attention to anything I say or do when we are not on the ground working. Look at them now," he added.
Ward turned and looked at them. Not one of them was looking in their direction.

"Peacock and Murray followed you around like a hawk with their eyes, straining to hear what you were saying. At first I thought they knew who you were and they were trying to understand what set you apart in The Old Man's eyes, but after a while, it just gave me a bad feeling."

"Good job I trust you then," Ward said with a smile, "Buck?" he then asked.

"He's a solid, old school type, no worries there." McDermott replied.

"Yeschenko's place, can you plan it?"

"I'll start now."

"Just one thing, I want to be the one who kills him," Ward said.

"Then you had better get there quicker than the rest of us," McDermott replied, without a hint of a smile.

"I need to take the Range Rover, I'm going to go back to my place for a few hours; I'll be back at 07:00am for the start. We will hit him early in the morning, about 08:00am?"

"You read my mind," McDermott replied and turned and walked over to the table where the team all stopped talking as one and looked up at him, ready for their instructions.

It was time to check the evidence again.

Hart Senate Office Building – Washington D.C.

Centrepoint dialled Senator Madison Reid's number.

"Yes?" Reid answered.

"Two of my men, Murray and Peacock, how did you manage to get turn them?" he asked.

"Everyone has a price, or the ability to turn for a promise of something they want," Reid replied.

"You know they are dead?"

"I do and so what?" Reid asked flippantly.

"I told you the hackers were off limits. They would have handed everything over to me and I would have passed it on to you," Centrepoint replied.

"Like I am going to trust you McNair" Reid spat down the phone, "Your files are probably full of murky little secrets on all of us on The Hill. No way would I give you that ammunition over me."

"But now, you are relying on me to get it so you are where you didn't want to be anyway."

"You can't blame a man for trying. And I still have a few hands to play yet. If I get what I want before you, then all will be fine. You will get your funding and your approvals from the committee and we both win."

"And if I get it first?" Centrepoint asked.

"Then you will give it to me anyway, but I will be open to blackmail from you, so that makes you the new enemy," Reid replied.

"You want to pick a war with me?"

"No. But I will if I have to."

"Who are the people you have working for you?" Centrepoint asked.

"That doesn't matter. But they are good, very good."

"I'm sure they are," Centrepoint replied, "But I can almost guarantee you, mine are better, and you have seriously pissed them off now by going after the hackers again. Once I probably could have controlled, but twice, they tend to take that personally."

"You are way too sensitive," Reid replied.

"I have a question?"

"What?"

"So as we are more likely to find it, what exactly is the evidence that we are looking for?" Centrepoint asked.

"What do you think?"

"Well, whatever it is, it is electronic. That's why getting the computer hard drives and video footage is the end game on this mission," Centrepoint replied.

"Yes it is," Reid said, "And I know that your hackers have half of it already. As do I. It is the missing half that we are looking for. One without the other is no use."

"OK. As soon as we get everything, I will pass it on to you as discussed, but I want this to be done amicably. I want your word that the hackers are off-limits from now."

"I can do that McNair," Reid replied, "We will make a politician out of you yet. You win some, you lose some. The secret is to know when to lose. This is your turn. Don't take it so personally."

"So, I have your word that the hackers are now completely off-limits?"

"You have my word," Reid lied.

Centrepoint hung up the phone.

Madison Reid leant back in his chair and exhaled loudly. He felt a lot better after the conversation he had just had with McNair.

He clearly had no idea what the evidence that he needed actually was and that meant that he didn't have it in his possession and more than likely, he would not recognise it even if he walked right into it.

This was all starting to fall into place rather well for him. Yes McNair was a tough nut to crack and he was aware that after this he would have to do some ass-kissing to get back in his good books, but he could live with doing that.

Once he had the evidence in his possession, his political career would go through the roof. There would be no limit to the control and power that would be awarded to him, simply upon his request. The big money he wanted was in the gun committees and the oil and farming industries. That's where the big companies would pay millions and millions of dollars to him to earn their favours, legislations being passed, and concessions.

Yes, he thought to himself, McNair's men have been a nuisance, but he still had control of him. The hackers would die, unfortunately they would have to. He knew that would piss McNair off, but he would soon get over it. The Old Man was losing his edge and his influence in comparison to where he himself was heading, and he didn't feel one little bit of sympathy for him.

Yes, everything was looking rosy for Senator Madison Reid.

TWENTY EIGHT

Marina Del Rey – 07:00am

Ward arrived at the warehouse and was pleased to see that everything and everyone was prepared.
McDermott's team were kitted out and ready to go. As he stepped out of the Range Rover, Walsh and Fuller opened the trunk and started loading equipment into it. He saw Buck sitting on the sofa, looking remarkably relaxed.
"You know about Murray and Peacock?" he asked him, as he walked across the warehouse floor to where Nicole-Louise and Tackler were standing by the workbench with the laptops.
"Never trust a guy with a ponytail," Buck replied without looking up.
Ward smiled.

"Have you two found anything?" he asked Nicole-Louise and Tackler.

They looked at each other and never spoke. Ward noticed it immediately.

"You had better tell me before we hit Yeschenko's house."

Nicole-Louise firmly explained what she had found, who was on the list and specifically what they were looking for. She looked at Ward waiting for a surprised reaction and saw nothing.

"Oh my God!" Tackler exclaimed, "You knew, didn't you?"

Ward said nothing but just nodded.

"So the other half of this encrypted file is not on any of these hard drives and so I'm hoping you find it at his house," Tackler added.

"So am I," Ward replied.

"Time to go," McDermott shouted across to Ward, as his team and Buck all began heading towards the Range Rovers.

Ward turned to walk away and Nicole-Louise grabbed his arm,

"I want you to find that file and then I want you to kill Yeschenko and after that I want you to hunt down the person who tried killing us and I want you to kill him too," she said, "You owe us that."

"I will," Ward replied, "The moment they tried harming you, they signed their own death warrant."

He climbed in to the front passenger seat of the nearest Range Rover, next to McDermott behind the wheel. He looked across at Nicole-Louise and Tackler as the engine started. He would protect them until this was over, and he would protect the evidence too. And he knew exactly where he was going to send them to keep them safe.

Beverley Hills 07:59am

"That is some house," McDermott said, as Buck became the last of the team to drop over the high garden wall into the lush grounds of Andrea Yeschenko's mansion. It had taken just twenty minutes to get to the house on North Rexford Drive. It really was palatial. It had an eight foot wall which ran all the way around the grounds. Big wrought iron gates, at least fifteen feet wide each, painted a ghastly gold colour, with an immaculate drive leading right up to the front of the house. Rows of softly swaying trees and high bushes obscured a clear view of the house from the road. They had driven around the back of the mansion and all climbed over the back wall and grouped together behind the thick evergreen bushes that lined the border. They crouched looking at rest of the impressive rear of the house. There were grand, granite steps that splayed in from either side into the centre of the house and they lead to a decking area where there were tables, chairs, sun loungers and parasols laid out in a straight line next to a diamond shaped pool. The decking area was laid out in front of four large, full glass doors. They were all shut.
"Everyone clear on their point of entry?" McDermott asked.
All of his team nodded.

"I'm not happy though, I was looking forward to knocking on the front door this time," Buck said with a deadpan expression on his face.

"Walsh, all hard drives are your priority. I don't expect there to be any children in the house, so this is a simple fight. We shoot to kill, except Yeschenko, he's mine. Is everyone clear?" Ward asked assertively.

They all nodded again.

"Clear the way then please," he said to McDermott.

McDermott, Wired, Fuller and Walsh sprinted forward along the right hand side of the garden, reached the bottom of the steps and ducked behind the excessively large retaining wall. Ward counted for ten seconds in his head.

No one came out of the house.

Then it all started.

Wired stood up, pointed his FN SCAR machine gun at the four large glass doors and opened fire.

The glass shattered and the noise was deafening.

McDermott, Fuller and Walsh stood upright with their own guns pointing at the huge opening that now sat in the centre of the giant building.

No one came out of the house.

Ward, Paul, Wallace, Fringe and Buck all ran forward on the left hand side of the steps and took cover behind the giant wall, with guns pointing at the opening.

Still no one came out of the house.

So now it was time for them all to enter the house as uninvited guests.

McDermott nodded at Paul and instantly, Paul stood up and sprinted up the steps, closely followed by Wallace, Fringe and Buck, and moved around to the left hand side

of the house, crawling below the window ledges until they reached the end of the building where there was a door into the kitchen. Fringe stood up briefly and peered through the window and then ducked back under the cover of the wall. Wallace then stood upright, swung around in front of the door and fired three shots from his machine gun into the frame of the door. The door flew open and he stepped in, followed by the other three two seconds later.
They were now in the building.
No one came out of the house.
McDermott, Wallace, Fringe and Buck, came out from the cover of the wall and skipped up the steps to the opening where the large glass panels once were, and walked through with their guns pointing straight ahead.
Now they were all in the house and out of sight.
Ward waited. He kept checking the windows that ran all along the rear of the house for movement, but he saw nothing. This was not the response that he was expecting.
He spoke into his radio,
"McDermott, any signs of resistance?"
"All clear," came back the reply.
He stepped forward, walked up the steps and approached the opening.
And then all hell broke loose.
The first thing he heard was the sound of a machine gun being fired from the left hand side of the house where Paul had entered, the exchange of gunfire was relentless and lasted for a good thirty seconds. Almost on cue, as soon as the gunfire had stopped to the left, there was an explosion of noise from directly in front of him. He

recognise the sound of the FN SCAR machine guns that McDermott's team used but could not make out what weapons were making the sound of the return fire.

He stepped into the house and saw three guys, all with shaved heads, all wearing jeans and vests, arms covered in tattoos and a hammer and sickle tattoo on the left hand side of their necks, lying on the floor with bullet holes punched through their bodies. One of the guys had taken at least twenty shots to his midriff and there were intestines starting to unwind from the holes.

Wired is getting excited yet again, he thought to himself.

"Everyone OK?" McDermott's voice crackled over the radio.

"All good here," Paul replied, "We have four of them down and Wallace and Buck have secured the data room. There are some big servers in here," he added.

Another burst of gunfire echoed out and Ward ran across the vast floor of the room he was in and reached the door that led even deeper into the house. He peered around the corner to see Fuller heading up the stairs behind Wired.

There were four more dead Russian guys on the floor at the bottom of the grand stairs, which would not have looked out of place in the most stately of homes back in the U.K. All four wearing jeans and vests, arms covered in tattoos and a hammer and sickle tattoo on the left hand side of their necks. All of the doors were thick, dark mahogany and looked solid. There were seven single doors that lead out of the hallway and one big set of double doors in the centre of the hallway, directly behind and below the grand staircase.

Another burst of gunfire from the left rang out instantly, this time there was no exchange fire, and Paul declared over the radio,
"Two more down."
Ward moved forward into the giant hallway and passed the stairs. He saw Buck standing in the doorway of a room with his gun pointing out.
Buck flashed him a big smile.
McDermott came out of a room to the left, looked at Ward and shrugged his shoulders to indicate that the room was empty.
McDermott then entered the single door behind him, looked inside and stepped back out. The last two single doors were ajar, one directly to Ward's left, and so he moved silently towards it and peered through the crack in the door. It was a plush sitting room, each individual piece of furniture looked like it cost more than most people make in a month.
But it was empty.
"Fuller's voice came over the radio,
"Upstairs is secured. No resistance."
McDermott walked across to Ward.
"Are you thinking what I am thinking?" he asked him.
Ward nodded,
"Through those double doors," he said.
Paul stepped across the room with Fringe,
"Every room is clear apart from that one," he said pointing at the big double doors.
Not knowing exactly what was behind a door unnerves most people. There are a million and one scenarios that can be played out in a person's mind, but Ward had always believed that it was pointless trying to picture

what was behind a door when you could just ask to be invited in.
So he stepped forward and knocked on the door.
And promptly got invited in.
"Come!" a voice bellowed out from inside the room.
He turned the handle and walked cautiously into the room.
He walked straight into a situation that would never have been one of the one million scenarios that he could have pictured in his head.

The room was a big open room, like a ballroom and there were a number of expensive looking chairs dotted against the walls on three sides. Directly opposite him, was what looked like stage, elevated about eighteen inches above the floor. The stage was covered in a thick red carpet and in the centre of the stage there was a throne. Not a plush seat or an expensive chair, but a throne, one that looked exactly like the one that Queen Elizabeth sits on.
Andrea Yeschenko sat on the throne. He had a shaved head, wore jeans and a vest; he had thick, strong arms that were completely covered in tattoos and a hammer and sickle tattoo on the right side of his neck. There were two young, frightened girls, who were so dirty and thin that they looked like street urchins, either side of him. Their wrists were tied to the legs of the throne with cable ties.
Andrea Yeschenko had a gun pointing at each of them. McDermott, Paul and Fringe stepped in behind Ward and pointed their guns directly at Yeschenko and started to move slowly around to the side of him.

"I would stop there if I was you or these two bits of dirt will be dead if you take another step," Yeschenko said, in clear English and in a soft tone.

Ward nodded at McDermott who stopped instantly. Yeschenko knew that he was going to die anyway and he had clearly decided that he was OK with it, and Ward could tell by the look on his face that if his final act on earth would be to kill two poor innocent children, he was content with how his life ended.

He was pure evil.

Ward's best weapon was how he understood bad people, so in an instant, he made the decision on how he would approach this.

Keeping the girls safe was his priority.

"What were you?" he asked Yeschenko, "Russian Special Forces?"

"Among others. You?" Yeschenko replied.

Ward started to feel in control, he had a dialogue going.

"I was never that good," he replied, "Plus I was too smart."

Yeschenko let out a long laugh. It was genuine.

"Are you the one?" Yeschenko asked, the smile disappearing from his face instantly.

"Who?"

"Tore everything down that I had built up."

"Yes I am."

"What are you, Secret Service, CIA, what?" Yeschenko said, more out of curiosity than a real need to know.

"What do you think I am?"

"Not Secret Service, you wouldn't look right in a suit and shades, yet not CIA either, you are something different," he replied, studying Ward carefully, "I'm really curious to know."

His only concern was the two frightened young girls and so he made a decision, there and then, which was a massive gamble but for them, it was worth it.

He put his gun on the floor and then pulled out his spare Glock from the rear of his waistband and laid it next to it.

"You know that you are going to die soon, don't you?" Ward said to him.

Yeschenko smiled at Ward,

"Yes I do. I have made my peace and I accept my fate."

"So listen, no guns, just two warriors together. Let the girls go, I'll send my men out of the room and you and me can talk. I'll give you the answers that you want and you can maybe fill in the missing pieces for me," Ward said calmly.

"Why would I do that?" Yeschenko asked.

"Because after that you can fight me, man to man, fist to fist. If you win, you will die, they will kill you," he said pointing at McDermott, "But you will die with the satisfaction of knowing you beat to death the man who tore your empire down."

It was now or never. Ward was sure that he had read Yeschenko right. A warrior, after all the wealth, splendour and spoils, was still just that.

A warrior.

A warrior that Ward had read correctly.

"Take them," Yeschenko said.

McDermott instantly stepped forward, pulled out his knife and cut the cable ties as Yeschenko kept his guns pointing directly at the girls. They were free within five seconds and McDermott picked one of them up in each arm and turned to walk out of the room, Yeschenko's guns now pointing firmly at the unarmed Ward.

It was gamble time for Ward again.

"Out you go," he said to Paul and Fringe.

They both looked confused so he repeated himself.

"Out you go and close the door."

They both slowly walked out of the room and shut the door.

Yeschenko studied Ward for a moment.

"I still have my guns," he said eventually.

"You won't need them."

Yeschenko raised an eyebrow, "Why?"

"Because you won't shoot me, you aren't a coward."

"Believe me; I put no value on life at all."

"Then you are stupid," Ward replied, "I'm the most valuable life to you right now."

Yeschenko laughed loudly again.

"I'm the one holding the guns, how can I be the stupid one."

"Simple," said Ward, "The people who gave me the orders to bring you down, will walk away from this without punishment if you kill me. I'm the only one who cares enough to take them out for what they have done. They are no better than you."

"You have no idea why any of this is happening, do you?" Yeschenko asked.

It was gamble time again for Ward. Was it truth or lie time?

He chose truth.

"I know exactly why. And to prove that, I will tell you something that no one knows, not even my men who have just walked out," he said.

"Which is?" Yeschenko asked curiously.

"I have the evidence from the ship. I have it safe."

"If that's true, tell me what the evidence is?" Yeschenko demanded.

Gamble time again.

Truth or lie.

Ward chose truth.

"The evidence is Yana Podskalnaya. She is sixteen years old."

Yeschenko lowered his guns.

"I still don't know who they are protecting though," Ward said, "You know that we need the other half of the encrypted file, that's why we are here," he added.

Yeschenko looked at Ward carefully.

Ward knew he was making his mind up right then.

So Ward helped him make it up.

Truth or lie time.

Ward chose lie.

"If you give me the file, I will hunt them down and kill them. All of this is because of them. I hate what you do but without them, you would never be in business. We are simple soldiers, we follow orders but I give you my word as a soldier that if you give me the file, I will hunt them down and kill them and I will kill you quickly and mercifully," Ward said, with real sincerity in his voice.

Yeschenko stood up and put his guns on his throne.

The king was abdicating.

He put his hand into his pocket and pulled out a flash drive and tossed it at Ward.

Ward caught it and quickly put it in his pocket. Yeschenko stepped down from his elevated platform and moved towards Ward. He stopped two feet away and knelt on the floor below him, picked up Ward's guns and handed them to him.
"I'm happy to die at your hand," he said and closed his eyes.
Ward used the gun in his right hand to smash hard into Yeschenko's left temple.

Andrea Yeschenko never lived long enough to see his next birthday. His life ended in humiliation and unimaginable agony. The events were witnessed by Ward, Buck and all of McDermott's team. After Ward had beaten Yeschenko so badly that his face was unrecognisable, he told Wired he could finish him off. Every one of them stood and watched in silence.
Yeschenko cried, begged and prayed out loud for the pain to end.
Just like the poor innocent children had that he had administered the same punishment to.
When he finally died, Ward stepped over to his lifeless body and pumped three bullets into his head.
Not a single one of the men in the room felt any remorse for their actions.
"We best get going now," McDermott said.
"I have the hard drives," Wallace interrupted.
"Then let's go," he replied.
The king was well and truly dead.

TWENTY NINE

Marina Del Rey

Nicole-Louise looked very uncomfortable as she took the flash drive from Ward.
"Load it and get into the file so we can see what is on it," he said softly.
She nodded. Ward believed that she already knew what was on it.
"I need to talk to you quickly," he said to Tackler.
They walked out of the warehouse and into the reception area.
"Is he dead?" Tackler asked.
"Comprehensively," Ward replied, "But there's something I am now going to ask you, no tell you, to do and you will not like it," he added.
"What is it?"
"As soon as you have broken into that file and we have seen what's on it, I want you and Nicole-Louise gone until this is over."

"You said he was dead. It is over," Tackler replied.
"No. It's only just starting," Ward replied.
"I don't understand."
"When you open that file and we see what is on there, you will."
Their privacy was interrupted by McDermott walking into the reception area.
"Buck did well today," he said.
"You think he is one hundred per cent trustworthy?" Ward asked.
"Without a doubt," McDermott replied, "Why?"
"Because what he is going to see as soon as Nicole-Louise has decrypted that file, cannot leave this warehouse."
Paul then appeared,
"You'd better come in, Nicole-Louise says she is ready," he said.
Ward looked at Tackler surprised.
"Well we aren't likely to just sit here doing nothing, are we? We worked out how to break into the file while you were off doing your man shit!" he said without a hint of a smile.
The four of them turned and walked back into the main warehouse.
Buck was sitting on the sofa again and Walsh, Wallace, Wired, Fuller and Fringe were at the table.
"All of you, I want you to see this," Ward said as he headed towards Nicole-Louise who was stood at the workbench in front of a laptop facing them.
"You have all of the data and lists?" he asked her.
"No," she replied.
Ward looked confused.

"Why not?"
"Because it is not data and lists," she replied.
"Then what is it?"
"Watch, I'll show you."
Nicole-Louise turned and moved the curser on the screen to a folder marked 'Oplata' and clicked it.
"Oplata?" Ward asked.
"It means payment," Buck said.
The file opened and there were three smaller icons with a picture of a small video camera on each of them.
"They are videos," Nicole-Louise said, "They are numbered one to three."
"Open number one," Tackler said
She moved the curser onto the file marked number one. The file opened and a small video screen opened up, she moved the curser to expand the box for the whole screen. In crystal clear clarity, a child who could have been no older than thirteen was being forced into a degrading sexual act by a man who was well into his fifties. The young child was crying, as the beast of a man was pulling her hair.
Wired turned and walked away and at least two others looked down to the floor away from the screen.
"Turn it off," Ward said, equally unable to look at the screen.
Nicole-Louise closed the video box on the screen.
"He looks familiar," Fuller said.
"He's Senator Clint Calvinson," Tackler said, "Florida's chosen man," he added.
"That explains the Secret Service," Paul said.
"Play file two," Ward said to Nicole-Louise.

She moved the curser onto the file marked number two and clicked open the box.

The screen came to life and there were two young children, both around fourteen years of age who were both tied to a bed and a naked, gross, overweight man was hitting them both with a whip, similar to what someone riding a horse would use.

"I know that guy," McDermott said, "He is Madison Reid, the Senator for Ohio."

"Turn it off," Ward said.

Nicole-Louise leant over and closed the video box on the screen. She then moved the curser onto the file marked 'three' and then promptly turned and walked out of the room into the reception area.

Tackler turned and followed after her immediately. McDermott and his whole team looked at Ward; Buck shuffled on his feet nervously.

"Do you know who is going to be on that last video?" McDermott asked.

"Yes," Ward replied.

"But how?" How did you know what you were looking for in the first place?"

"I'll show you," Ward replied and he moved his hand and clicked file 'Three'. The video box appeared and the screen came to life.

Yana Podskalnaya appeared on the screen completely naked. The video was at least three years old when she would have been thirteen. She had cut marks on her chest and blood running down the inside of her legs. It was clear that she had been mutilated.

She was standing still, facing the camera, trembling.

The back of a naked man appeared on the screen. He was holding a hunting knife.

"I'm not watching him kill her, turn it off," Paul demanded.

"He won't kill her," Ward replied.

"How do you know?"

"Because she's sitting in my house in Santa Monica."

All of them looked at Ward in total disbelief.

They then turned back to the screen and saw the man approach the girl and run the tip of the blade down the outside of her right arm, she screamed as a thin line of blood appeared. The man then slapped her face hard and it knocked her onto her knees and she began to sob. The beast then pulled her up by her hair and threw her onto the bed. He threw the knife onto the floor and climbed onto the bed and began to carry out a vile sexual act. Ward paused the video, as the man's face came into view for the first time.

"That can't be right!" Buck exclaimed.

"You knew this?" McDermott asked.

Ward nodded.

"When? For how long?"

"From the night we hit the ship," Ward replied.

"And you have this girl somewhere safe? Right now?"

Ward nodded again.

The rest of them just stood there, open mouthed, saying nothing.

There wasn't anything that could be said.

Looking straight back at them on the screen, almost staring into their eyes was a man.

His name was Aaron Wilson.

He was the serving Vice President of the United States of America.

Hart Senate Office Building – Washington D.C.

Senator Madison Reid put the phone down and thumped his right fist hard on his desk.
He had just received a call from his men in Los Angeles that Andrea Yeschenko was dead; he had been brutally beaten to death.
His concern right now was no longer finding the evidence that he had been so desperately searching for; or indeed to protect his political and sick allies, it was simple self-preservation.
He dialled Centrepoint's number.
"Hang on a moment," Centrepoint answered, fully aware of how worried and stressed out Reid would be right now.
After what seemed like an age, Centrepoint's voice came back down the line,
"How can I help you Senator?"
"It seems I underestimated you," Reid said, "So well played McNair," he added, trying to sound as flippant and jovial as he could, while his stomach was doing summersaults.
"I have no idea what that is meant to mean Senator."
"Oh, I think you do," Reid said impatiently, "I think you know exactly what I am talking about."
"Perhaps you should explain to me so that we don't have any confusion?"

Reid cursed him under his breath, McNair was enjoying this and he was going to have to play along with him to get what he wanted.

"You hold all the aces. Your men have taken down Yeschenko and no doubt acquired the evidence that we were looking for and so we can end this now."

"I told you not to pick a fight with them. You should have left the hackers out of it," Centrepoint said with an 'I told you so' tone.

"We all make mistakes McNair. I apologise for the issues that might have caused you."

"So what are you proposing Senator?"

"You call your men off, return the evidence to me, with no other copies in existence and you get whatever you want in the future. I'm going to sanction whatever you throw at our committee. You will have unlimited power," Reid replied, trying to sound as sincere as a politician could sound.

Which wasn't very sincere.

"Surely I will need to keep my own copy as insurance?"

"There can't be any of them. This isn't just about me; it is about people more powerful than me. It will be safer if you don't have a copy. It's toxic."

"I want you to pass a notion that the department I run no longer needs Senate permission to function and that funding is set at unlimited. If you give me that, I will ensure that the evidence never sees the light of day and I will hand it over to you freely," Centrepoint declared.

"I can do that," Reid replied.

"And I want it done today. You can call an emergency meeting of your committee and pass it. I'm sure you have a few favours that you can call in."

"That's pushing it a bit"
"Then you had better push hard," Centrepoint replied, "Because I probably have one opportunity to call my men off and I need a very, very good reason to do it," he added.
"OK McNair, give me a few hours and I should have your demands signed, sealed and delivered to you."
"Thank you Senator," Centrepoint replied and the line went dead.
Reid hated McNair. He had always begrudged him the power that he knew that he held and more than that, he hated the fact that he knew so many more secrets than he did.
He picked up his phone and dialled Senator Calvinson.
"We have a big problem," Reid said as Calvinson answered.
"What?"
"McNair's men have got the evidence and there is nothing we can do about it, except give him what he wants."
"So give it to him," Calvinson replied.
"I will, we have no choice but I need your help in calling in a few favours for a notion I need passed in the next few hours."
"What notion?"
"Basically giving McNair the green light to do whatever the hell he wants to do in the future and we can't know a single thing about it."
"Then give it to him. And quickly," Calvinson said, complete panic ringing through his voice.
"I will," Reid replied and then he hung up the phone.

He sat back in his chair. The next call was the one that he really didn't want to make.

He picked up his phone and dialled the number.

The head of the Secret Service security detail for the Vice President answered.

"I know what happened. Tell me you will sort it and quickly," the guy said.

"I've already smoothed it over. The evidence should be with me by nightfall, tomorrow morning at the earliest," Reid said down the line.

"You had better be right Senator. You got him into this mess, you had better get him out of it and quickly," the guy demanded.

"I need your help with something," Reid said.

"What?"

"I need you to find out who McNair's men are, so that you can kill them. All of them," Reid spat down the phone.

"We've already tried. We got nowhere. We can't push too hard, McNair could run to the President and then we would be busted."

"Well I want them dead. They have caused all of this mess and they have to be held accountable to me for it," Reid said, his voice getting much louder.

"I don't know if you've noticed Senator," the guy replied, "But these guys are good, very good. Much better than we are; so I would suggest the safest thing you could do, would be to forget about them and walk away. Although that will still leave you with one possible and likely problem," he added.

"Which is?"

"If they have already decided to find you, then you are dead already," the guy replied and then hung up.

THIRTY

Marina Del Rey

Ward shut the door to the reception area of the warehouse so he could be alone. He took out his cell phone and dialled Centrepoint's number.
He answered immediately.
"Well done," he said.
"Good news travels fast," Ward replied.
"You've done brilliantly Ryan. You have all of the evidence?"
"Only some of it," he lied.
Centrepoint was quiet for a moment,
"So that's your way of saying that you've decided that this hasn't finished?" he eventually asked.
"No, it's my way of saying that we have half of the evidence and until we find the rest of it, we will carry on," he replied flippantly.
"Tell me what you know," Centrepoint asked.
"You tell me exactly who we are up against first."
"I thought we had this discussion already?"
"And I think you have a much better idea now."
"The mission is over Ryan. Yeschenko's dead."

"I'm coming to Washington," Ward replied.

"I strongly advise against that."

"Why?"

"Because Yeschenko has gone and there will be nothing to be gained by you chasing it any further," Centrepoint said firmly.

"They tried killing Nicole-Louise and Tackler. They got at two of your men, and they were assisting Yeschenko in bringing literally thousands of young children into our country to be abused. I'd say going to the top of the tree and avenging those poor kids has everything to be gained," Ward replied urgently.

"Do you know who these people are?"

"I know that two of them are Senators, I'm not sure if there are any others," he lied.

"Sometimes, it's better to let some things go for long term gain," Centrepoint said calmly.

"That seems to be a recurring theme with you lately. It almost sounds as though you are only interested in protecting those who can help you. Maybe you aren't much better?"

"I resent that," Centrepoint said angrily down the line, "You know damn well I have to balance your actions against the legal eagles in Washington, and I spend most of my day covering your ass when you are running around in the field, to stop those liberal vultures from ripping you to shreds, so don't you dare say I am one of them."

Ward realised that he had been too hard on him. He knew that The Old Man was fundamentally a good man and that he made his job extremely difficult at times.

"I'm sorry, I didn't mean that," he quickly said.

"You can't run around killing serving Senators, you know that."

"I'm coming to Washington. I need to find the last few pieces of the puzzle."

"So what exactly do you have so far?" Centrepoint asked.

Ward thought carefully. It wasn't that he didn't trust Centrepoint, in fact he trusted him with his life, but he figured that what he didn't know, the powers that be above him could not get out of him.

"I have a list. There are two serving Senators on the list and a host of celebrities. But I only have half of the list. I believe that one of the Senators has the other half. I won't kill them, I promise," he lied.

"OK," Centrepoint replied, completely disbelieving Ward's promise.

The lack of argument threw Ward slightly.

"Nicole-Louise and Tackler, you need to keep them safe until we know that this is over. Agreed?" Centrepoint asked.

"Don't worry; I have somewhere where they won't be found."

"And Ryan?"

"Yes?"

"Don't move on anyone when you get here without notifying me. This isn't one of our usual cat and mouse games where I let you have a free reign. Is that understood?"

"Completely! I won't move on any target until I have told you who and why," Ward lied again,

Centrepoint hung up the phone.

Now he had the task of explaining to Tackler where he and Nicole-Louise would be going.
It wasn't going to be well received.
But first he had to call Mike Lawson in London.

Ward trusted Lawson as much as he did McDermott and The Optician. He had worked with him a number of times in the UK and U.S and he was the person he trusted across the pond more than anyone. He had been instrumental in helping Ward make sense of things in New York last week. Ward's frustration with Lawson was that he could be the best if he wanted. He was lethal, smart and highly efficient.
If only he would use what was in his brain rather than his pants. Ward knew that he could trust Lawson with anything and he would never let him down.
Lawson was an intimidating guy to look at. He had excelled in the SAS for a number of years and Ward knew without a doubt, that Lawson was probably as efficient a killer as he was. He was in his mid-thirties and stood about six feet four and had an impressive physique. He had piercing blue eyes that every person who ever met him double checked and then checked again.

He was easily the most handsome looking man that Ward had ever seen in his life and there were very few women that could resist his charm.
Nicole-Louise had not been remotely impressed by him but Tackler saw Lawson as a major threat and took an immediate dislike to him.
Ward took out his phone and dialled Lawson's number.

"Missing me already?" Lawson answered.
"I'm amazed you answered, I assumed you would be having sex."
"Who says I'm not?" Lawson replied.
Ward laughed.
"What can I do for you? You can't even cope for a week without me?"
"I need your help with something," he said, "And it has to be entirely off the books. The Old Man can't ever know about it."
"I'm listening," Lawson said.
Ward spent three minutes explaining to Lawson all that had happened in crushing Yeschenko's empire and he finished by naming the three men who were on the video evidence that they had.
"You have got to be kidding. The Vice President?!" Lawson exclaimed when Ward had stopped talking, "Holding stuff like that is not a sensible, or a smart career move Ryan." he added.
"I know. That's why you are going to hold it for me," Ward replied.
Lawson started laughing.
"What's funny?"
"I just used your name and you didn't flinch, first time ever."
Ward's name was extremely well known to the dark ops people on both sides of the Atlantic and Lawson had always asked him for confirmation that he was indeed Ryan Ward, yet he had never confirmed it.
"I know you're dumb but I'm amazed it took you so long to work out it," he replied with a laugh of his own.

"So you want me to hold this video in an official capacity or somewhere no one would find it?" Lawson asked.

"Not official but whatever you decide. I trust you."

"I'm sure that I can manage to keep a little video file safe here in London."

"That's not all," Ward said, "There are some other things I need you to look after," he added.

"Always something else, isn't there? What is it?"

"It's not it. It's they"

"People?" Lawson queried.

"The girl that is on the video with the VP. Her name is Yana Podskalnaya and she is sixteen," Ward said softly.

"You have the girl?" Jesus, how do you do the shit you do?"

"Yes I do. And I want her out of The States and somewhere safe where no one knows her. Can you do that?"

"For how long?"

"For good. I want you to make her disappear on paper, and then have her set up in a nice foster family somewhere with a nice cover story. Can you do that?"

"I can do anything, you know that. Don't worry the video and the girl will be safe. You have my word," Lawson said reassuringly.

Ward knew that he would keep his word. He always did.

"That's not quite all," Ward replied.

"Jesus, you take the piss! What now?"

"Remember when I told you that if you ever tried turning Nicole-Louise's head, that I would kill you?"

"I thought that was code for I am allowed to work my magic on her" he innocently said, and then sent a long and excitable laugh down the phone.

"It was no code Mike," Ward said sternly, "I meant it."

"I'm only joking," Lawson said, sounding serious for a moment, "I did hear you," he added.

"Good. Because she is coming over as well and I want her kept safe until this is all cleared up."

"Alone? What about Mr Muscle?" Lawson asked, poking fun at Tackler's physique.

"Tackler too," Ward said, ignoring the name Lawson used, "And I want your word that they will both be kept safe and off the grid until I say it is safe for them to return," he continued.

"You have my word. I will keep them safe."

Ward knew that he would keep his word. He always did.

"One last thing" Ward said.

"Seriously?"

"Yes. It's Gilligan. He's alive."

Silence on the end of the line for a few moments.

"How?" Lawson asked.

Ward explained what Centrepoint had told him and how it seemed that he would recover.

"Great, great, great news!" Lawson exclaimed, genuinely happy with what he had just heard, "Keep me up to date on that. I want your word?" he added.

"You have my word," Ward replied.

Lawson knew that he would keep his word. He always did.

"I will talk to McDermott about delivering them to you and will keep you informed as soon as I know where and when they will arrive for you. OK?"

"Sure. I'll be waiting. I have three brunettes coming over shortly for a workout but will be ready as soon as they leave."
Ward didn't ask him to elaborate.
"Just keep them safe," he said.
"I will. And I know just where to put everything," Lawson replied.
Ward knew that he would. Mike Lawson always knew what to do without being told.
He hung up the phone.

He opened the door and walked back into the warehouse. "I need to talk to you two," he said to Tackler. He nodded at McDermott, and then nodded towards the reception area door to indicate that he wanted him to hear what the plan was too. It wasn't privacy he wanted so much; it was a closed environment, when Tackler was told what was going to happen.
Ward had never seen Tackler be close to being jealous in his life.
Until Mike Lawson had walked into their apartment.
Nicole-Louise's devotion to Tackler was unquestionable, but she had definitely enjoyed being in the company of a man that very few women in the world could resist.
Nicole-Louise walked into the reception area, closely followed by Tackler, with McDermott a few steps behind. Ward nodded at the door and McDermott closed it.
"This looks ominous," Tackler said, trying to lighten the mood.

"You two," Ward began, "You know how important you are to me, I have told you that many times. Yes?" he asked.

They both nodded.

"And keeping you safe is my main priority now. So I will do whatever I have to do to make sure that no harm comes to either of you. You understand that, yes?"

They both nodded again.

"The girl in the video with the VP. I need her kept safe too and so I am going to trust her into the care of you two. OK?"

"How can we look after her?" Tackler asked.

"McDermott is going to take you to England where you will be met by someone I trust and he will keep you all safe."

Nicole-Louise looked relaxed for the first time in days, "Can we go to London and see all of the sights?" she asked.

"I'm sure that can be arranged," Ward replied, not even looking at Tackler. Making eye contact and inviting any questions was not the route he wanted to take.

"And go to Carnaby Street?" Tackler asked.

"That too," Ward replied, "Anyway, so I want you to take the girl, the video evidence and the two of you over there as quickly as possible. When you get there, I will contact you because there is still a lot of work to do to finish this."

"OK," Tackler replied.

"Good, that's all sorted then" Ward said and headed towards the door back into the main warehouse.

"Who's the person that you trust to keep us safe?" Tackler asked, directly talking to Ward's back.

Here we go.

"Lawson," he replied.

"We aren't going," Tackler stubbornly said.

"You have to go. It isn't safe here."

"I don't like him. He tries to make me look stupid in front of Nicole-Louise."

Ward knew that Lawson, even with his inability to resist making every woman that he came into contact with desire him, would never deliberately make Tackler look stupid and he definitely hadn't. This was just a case of simple old-fashioned jealousy.

So Ward decided it was time to turn it back in Tackler's favour.

"What you did the other day, thinking on your feet, protecting Nicole-Louise, being brave and dragging Peacock and Murray outside for The Optician to take out, changed you," Ward said.

"What do you mean?" Tackler replied.

"Simple. You saved her life," he said, pointing at Nicole-Louise, "Lawson has never saved her life. The only hero she has, wants and needs is you. Tell him Nicole-Louise," he added, subtly passing responsibility to convince him over to her.

"I've told you silly, you are all I ever need. I love you. As stupid as that makes me, it's how it is. You are my hero, Always have been," she said and hugged him tightly.

Tackler's chest visibly grew bigger and he hugged her back.

"So we will go to England. Mike is just like these two, we both know that those kind of men are not for people like us," she said.

"What's wrong with us?" McDermott asked, genuine confusion showing on his face.

"My point exactly," Nicole-Louise replied.

A comment that left McDermott feeling even more confused and slightly insulted.

"I know," Tackler said, "I can take care of us both. I've changed, if he starts again, he will see a different animal this time," he added, staring at Ward.

Ward smiled. Not in agreement but at the vision in his mind of the one hundred and forty pound Tackler trying to take on the Adonis that was Lawson.

"OK. I'm in," Tackler said.

"Thank you." Ward replied.

"So what is wrong with us?" McDermott asked.

Nicole-Louise tutted, as if to indicate it was obvious. McDermott looked even more hurt.

Ward moved to step out of the reception area. As he moved, he heard a clearly insulted and hurt McDermott say to Tackler,

"You have to admit, Lawson is one hell of a looker."

THIRTY ONE

Washington D.C - Merrifield

Fourteen hours later, Ward was in Washington D.C. Everything was wrapped up in California, but he was a long way from being finished. He accepted that the V.P. was out of bounds, getting to him would be impossible through his security detail anyway. He had contemplated asking The Optician to take him out, but he knew that Centrepoint held more sway over him than he did and that he would never approve it. But Senators Calvinson and Reid had to pay for their sins, he was clear on that. It wasn't only the disgusting things that they had done to the children, or even the fact that they had tried to kill Nicole-Louise and Tackler that ate away at him. It was the fact that he had worked out that this was another politically driven act that was about power, blackmail and climbing the ladder on Capitol Hill. Ward hated politicians, as most people do. He had witnessed over and over again that they were the most dishonest people he knew and they generally did nothing but speak empty promises and use their position to benefit those who could afford to help their careers progress. Both of them were going to die; the V.P. would know Ward was in possession of the evidence against him, and for political stability, he would wait until his term was finished and reconsider the appropriate punishment for him then. Killing him now would start a war if the wrong people were blamed.

But Calvinson and Reid were fair game in his eyes. He knew that Nicole-Louise and Tackler would not be completely safe until both men were dead and that was good enough reason to justify it to The Old Man, after he had eliminated them.

McDermott, Wired and Fuller had gone with him to collect Yana Podskalnaya from his bungalow in Santa Monica. He had explained how Yeschenko was going to do a video interview with her about her abuse at the hands of VP Aaron Wilson, and then sell the interview to the highest bidding network. They had returned to the warehouse, and after Paul had secured the place, and collected Nicole-Louise and Tackler, they all drove to the airport. He insisted that Paul accompanied them on the flight to England with Fuller and Walsh. To his surprise, Wired then insisted that he went as well, without giving any reason. McDermott explained that he would be needed when they got to Washington, but he simply refused and said he was getting on that plane no matter what. Ward looked at McDermott, shrugged and then nodded, so it was agreed that Fuller would come with them to Washington instead.

And so would The Optician.

The Old Man had made sure there were two vehicles to pick them up when they landed at Dulles International

Airport and after a short drive; they arrived at McDermott's warehouse in Merrifield, Virginia. The warehouse was on an industrial park just off of Lee Highway where it joined Hilltop Road. They turned into the park and Ward saw the standard 'A & B Auto's sign fitted on the cladding above the reception entrance, and after they had parked the vehicles and stepped inside, Ward thought they could have been back in Marina Del Rey. It was laid out in an identical manner and had two black Range Rovers parked neatly inside.

"How many Range Rovers do you actually own?" he asked McDermott.

"Two in each warehouse, work it out," he replied.

He couldn't be bothered to ask how many warehouses but concluded that McDermott must have over three million dollars' worth of cars dotted around the U.S.

He then told McDermott, Fuller, Wallace and Fringe to get some rest and they instantly told Buck that he would be sleeping outside in one of the Range Rovers.

Buck tried protesting,

"It's the Californian air that made me snore," he claimed, but the team weren't buying it and so he was banished to the vehicle outside.

"I need a car," Ward said to McDermott.

"Where are you going?"

"I'm going to find where the Senators are."

"You aren't going alone," McDermott said firmly.

"I'm not going to make contact. Just to establish where they will be tomorrow."

"Truth?" McDermott said.

"Truth," he lied.

McDermott went into a drawer that was under the workbench nearest to him, pulled out a set of keys and tossed them to Ward,

"It's that one," he said, pointing to the Range Rover nearest the roller shutter doors.

Thirty seconds later, he was driving out of the industrial park on the thirty minute journey towards Capitol Hill. He took out his cell phone and dialled the first number that he had locked into his phone earlier that day.

"Offices of Senator Calvinson," a young woman's voice answered.

"I have a message for the Senator."

"It would be best to ring back tomorrow morning sir," she replied.

"You had best contact him immediately. Wake him up if you have to," he said casually.

"It would be best to ring back tomorrow morning sir," she repeated.

"By tomorrow morning he won't be a Senator and you will be out of a job if you don't get this message to him," he said firmly.

"What is the message sir?" she asked; no alteration in her tone of voice at all.

"I took care of Yeschenko and I have his secret safe. If he is not standing by the fountain in Upper Senate Park in 45 minutes, I'm going to the press."

He then hung up the phone.

He knew that Senator Clint Calvinson would not be there. But that wasn't who he wanted to turn up.

Upper Senate Park – Washington D.C.

He saw the two guys as soon as he walked into the park and headed towards the fountain. They made no attempt to hide the fact that they were some kind of protection duty. In fact, and much to Ward's amusement, they were advertising what they were.
The fountain sat inside a circular ornamental pool, and the park was pretty much empty. There were two guys, one on either side of the fountain and they were wearing long black coats and both standing still, looking out from the fountain. Oddly, they were both sranding with their legs apart slightly, turning their heads in an almost robotic fashion.
These guys would not die today he thought to himself, but they were willing to hide a vile secret for a politician and so they would be punished for that.
He walked towards the guy nearest to him and when he reached him, he said,
"Follow me please," and continued walking to the other side of the fountain where the other guy stood.
When he reached the other guy, he stopped three feet away from him and just stood there, looking him up and down. The other guy approached them and started mimicking him by looking Ward up and down.
Idiots.
They were both reasonably big guys, around six feet tall and their body size was hard to gauge as their long coats were hiding their physiques. He quickly established that the two of them attacking him together could be a problem but one at a time would be child's play. He just needed to work out who was the main man, so he continued looking the guy in front of him up and down, just waiting for the main man to talk.

Thirty seconds later, neither of them had spoken.
Idiots.
They both stood there, almost motionless, saying nothing, just looking at him. Worst of all was the fact that they were standing with their hands in their pockets, totally unprepared for any unarmed combat.
Idiots.
He shifted his weight subtly onto his left foot and then, with hardly any body adjustment and lightning speed, he shot his right leg forward and his foot connected, with the full force of his weight behind it, directly into the guy's groin. He doubled over instantly and made an odd screeching sound as he fell to the floor. He wouldn't be getting up.
He spun around to the next guy standing behind him and watched him comically trying to pull his hands out of his pockets, but they appeared to be stuck. He delivered a thunderous right hook that connected full on in the guy's nose and he started to fall backwards, his hands still stuck in his pockets. He hit the floor almost right next to the guy who was doubled over.
Idiots.
He pulled out his silenced Glock. The guy with the busted nose and the hands in his pockets, managed to free one of his hands and rather than put his hand up to his face, as instinct would tell you, he cowered down and put his free hand above his head.
"Like your hand would stop a bullet you idiot," he said as the guy cowered below him, "Who's in charge?"
"Him," the guy with the busted nose whimpered.
The other guy was still struggling to breathe, and he concluded that it would be some time until he could

speak properly, so he raised his right foot and kicked the guy hard in the right side of the temple. They guy was unconscious by the time his foot was back firmly on the ground.

"You've just been promoted to senior idiot," he said.

"We were just sent here to see what you want," the guy said, his other hand now free and attempting to stem the flow of blood from his busted nose.

"I want a cell phone. That's all."

The guy looked up at him, completely confused.

"I'm robbing you. Give me your cell phone."

The guy leant into his pocket and pulled out his phone and reached up and handed it to Ward, never once taking his eyes off the Glock that was pointing down at him.

"Now his," he said, pointing to the unconscious guy next to him.

The busted nose guy shuffled over to the unconscious guy on the floor and went into his coat pocket and pulled out a packet of gum.

Ward just shook his head in dismay. The guy dug further into the pocket and pulled out a cell phone, reached up and handed it to Ward.

"You don't know what you are doing," the nose guy said.

"Huh?" Ward grunted.

"We are meant to be meeting someone very important and robbing us will get you in a lot of trouble you can't handle," he said.

"I am the guy you are meant to be meeting," he said, almost in amazement, and he raised his Glock and smashed the handle down hard into the guys right temple. He fell forwards and his face smashed flat into the floor, his nose taking most of the impact. He was unconscious.

"Idiots," he muttered to himself, and he turned and walked away from the fountain.

Now he could go and grab some sleep. He would wait for the call, it would come tonight but he would make them wait. The guys on the floor would need a good few hours to come back around properly. He would turn the phones off until the morning and then he would call Nicole-Louise and ask her to block both phones, to prevent them from being traced, and also to make sure that she, Tackler and Yana had all arrived safely and the video evidence was secure.

And then he would do what he had to do.

He didn't want to go back to the warehouse. He wanted a bed and a shower. He found an Americana motel in Pentagon City, paid cash for a room and took a long shower, before settling down for the night.

He knew exactly how this was going to play out and he didn't like part of the outcome.

THIRTY TWO

Washington D.C - Merrifield

He turned up at the warehouse at 07:00am. He felt refreshed and clear about the events that were going to take place throughout the day.
He had spoken to Nicole-Louise and Tackler and they were both OK. Lawson had met them at the airport and much to Tackler's delight; he had arrived to pick them up with a stunning blonde woman attached to his arm. Lawson had told him that he had scrolled through the many contacts on his cell phone to find someone to accompany him so that there was no bad feeling between any of them. His friend had willingly obliged.
But he also felt the need to point out that he thought Nicole-Louise appeared jealous, a comment that made him laugh. Lawson then explained that he had another 'Friend' who worked for the social services department and she was making arrangements to help make Yana disappear and find her way into the foster care system as an unaccompanied child. Nicole-Louise had fixed the cell phones that he had taken from the two guys, and made them untraceable, and Tackler was excited because Lawson was taking them into London to visit the clubs where the Sex Pistols had once played. He said he would

be in touch with instructions for Nicole-Louise and Tackler once they had settled.

Paul, Wired and Walsh were already on their way back to Washington.

Back at the warehouse, Buck was sitting on the sofa drinking coffee and Fuller, Wallace and Fringe were sitting around the table by the kitchen area playing cards. McDermott was sitting in his big armchair. His team were used to doing a lot of waiting around.

"Plans for today?" McDermott asked, as he headed towards them.

"Just waiting for a phone call," he replied, as he removed the phones he had taken from the two idiots last night from his jacket pockets, turned them on, and put them on the table where everyone was sitting.

"Explain?" McDermott said.

He explained to all of them what had happened and what he intended to do.

"I have a pal who works in tech at Langley; you want me to find you Calvinson's home address?" Buck asked.

Ward nodded.

One of the phones rang.

He let it ring out.

He wanted to see how desperate Calvinson was.

Five seconds later, the other phone rang.

He was desperate.

Ward picked up the phone and pressed the answer button but didn't speak.

"Hello," the voice on the end of the phone said. The voice sounded young. Way too young to be a Senator and so he hung up immediately.

McDermott looked at him, he just shrugged.

The phone rang again.
"Hello," the same voice said.
"Calvinson only," he replied and hung up.
"You think he will ring himself?" McDermott asked.
"Guaranteed."
The phone rang again. He picked it up, pressed answer and put it to his ear.
"Hello," an older, irritated voice said.
It was Calvinson. Only a politician could sound so arrogant being in the position that he was in.
"You know what I have?" Ward said, faking an American accent.
"You might think you have something, but you won't be able to use it against me unless you are prepared to destroy our whole political structure," Calvinson said calmly.
"It's your actions that have done that. I was going to offer you one chance, but I will go straight to the news channels now," he said and then hung up the phone.
"You are so mean," McDermott said with a smile.
Ward laughed.
The phone rang again. He let it ring out.
And again.
In fact, it rang six more times, no more than five seconds apart.
On the seventh ring, he answered.
"OK," Calvinson said, "I'm listening."
"You like abusing little children and hurting them. I've got you on video doing it," Ward said calmly.
There was silence on the phone, so he continued.
"You have one way out of this and only one. And that is my way. Do you understand?"

"I'm listening," Calvinson said again.
"I want to know some things first."
"Such as?"
"Who controlled all of the people down in California? It wasn't you, you are too dumb," he asked.
"Senator Madison Reid."
Ward wasn't surprised that Calvinson gave up Reid so easily; all politicians were cowards and masters of self-preservation.
"He was the direct link to Yeschenko?"
"Yes he was. It was him who got me involved with it in the first place. He kept telling me about his preferences and he took me there the first time I visited," Calvinson replied, sounding almost as though he was recalling his first visit to a baseball match.
He felt a rage building up inside of him but he controlled it.
"Who else with any political power is involved?" he asked.
"What do you mean?"
"Apart from you two, what other political figure is involved?" he asked again.
"I don't understand the question. Someone else in the Senate is involved?"
Calvinson clearly had no idea what he was talking about. Another piece of the puzzle fell into place perfectly.
He decided to move on, he had found out what he needed to find out.
"You want me to make the video disappear?" he asked.
"Of course I do. But I assume that there is going to be a cost involved in that?" Calvinson replied, in a tone that

suggested that he was negotiating a trade deal rather than his career and life.

He was disgusted that Calvinson was confident that he would make this go away. He hated these spineless politicians.

"Four million dollars. I'm done with this game. I want to buy a house on a beach in a hot country and get away from this crap," Ward lied, "And I need a lot of money to do that."

"Do you work for McNair?"

"I did. But I saw what they did to two of my friends called Peacock and Murray; they just kill whoever they want and so I want out."

"Four million dollars is a lot," Calvinson replied, positioning himself to start negotiations.

"Not if I give you the video of Reid involved in acts too."

Ward could almost hear the cogs in Calvinson's brain turning. He could see a way to get the evidence he wanted, control of Reid and recoup the money he would pay out. Of course he would go for it.

"I need a few hours, maybe six to get the money together. Where shall we meet?" Calvinson said, almost sounding excited.

"I will come to your offices at 2:00pm to collect it," he replied.

"Not there. It will have to be somewhere else," Calvinson said.

"No, it will be there and if you try anything, you will be the star of the six o' clock news."

"OK. Calm down. What's your name?"

"It doesn't matter."

"My offices are in the Russell Senate building, you can't get in without a name or appointment that I have to authorise prior to you arriving," Calvinson said, sounding worried for the first time.
"Call me Andrea Yeschenko," Ward said and hung up the phone.

Washington D.C.

Centrepoint's phone rang for the first time that morning, just as he had just gotten comfortable at his desk.
"Hello?" he answered as he was emptying the folders from his briefcase.
"What the hell is going on?" Senator Madison Reid screamed down the phone.
"You created a mountain of a problem that I am trying to fix, that's what's going on," he replied calmly.
"I've just had Senator Calvinson on the phone screaming at me that your assassin guy wants to meet him at two o' clock today and is demanding eight million dollars for the video of him that he stole from Yeschenko. That means that your guy will come blackmailing me too," he said, continuing with his screaming.
"I doubt very much that the money is his priority," Centrepoint replied, "And if you continue to scream at me I will terminate this call. Right now Senator, I'm the only person in the world who can save your ass, so calm down."
"OK, I'm sorry but I want this sorted and call your men off immediately," Reid replied.
"You never should have gone after the hackers, I was really clear on that," Centrepoint reminded him, "But we

are where we are, so it's about moving forward from here."

"OK. I want this controlled," Reid demanded.

"Have the committee passed all of the items that I raised with you?"

"In principal, yes. I just need to call in a few more favours to get it signed, sealed and delivered today."

"Then as soon as I have that, I will stop it all," he replied and hung up the phone.

He then immediately dialled Ward's number.

"Hello?" Ward answered.

"What did I tell you about hunting Senators? This is Washington, you can't do that."

"I'm not hunting Senators, I'm hunting animals."

"This isn't open for discussion. It's a direct order."

"Do you know what and who was on those videos?"

"Not exactly but I can imagine. It was enough for you to pack Nicole-Louise and Tackler off into Lawson's care. Calvinson and Reid are animals, I understand and agree with you on that, but right now, they are passing legislation that will enable us to do what we need to do in the future without getting approval or justifying it. We can do so much more good," Centrepoint softly replied.

"What about right or wrong?"

"You've destroyed Yeschenko. We have Reid to call in enough favours that we no longer have to go begging to them, and your time will come in the future."

Ward realised that The Old Man had no idea that the Vice President was on the tapes. So he thought he would test the water.

"And what if they were not the only two on the videos?"

"What are you implying? Who else was on there?"

Ward ignored him.

"I can't let it go. I'm sorry."

"Ryan. I have had twenty years of this and I know as well as you do that all politicians are dishonest and have no moral compass. Reid will be retired in a few years, then you can punish him as you see fit, but until then we need him."

"There seems to be a pattern developing, of you protecting your powerful friends."

"That's unfair. My job is to look at the bigger picture so that we can crush all of the evil that affects innocent people, and we need Reid alive to make sure that we are given the legal support to do that. We have to remain unaccountable, you aren't called Deniables for nothing, and he will play a big part in that getting locked into the system. Your time will come," Centrepoint said.

"It's not right."

"Senator Reid is off limits."

"But Calvinson isn't," Ward replied and hung up the phone.

Centrepoint sat back in his chair and sighed. He did actually agree with pretty much all that Ward had just said, but every mission had to be played like a chess game, sometimes sacrificing things that you didn't want to. Then he suddenly sat up, almost in a startled state. He dialled Ward's number again.

"Yes," Ward said.

"I'm authorising you to administer whatever punishment you see fit to Calvinson," he said, "All I ask is that you tell me as soon as you have done whatever you are going to do, so that I can clear the mess up. Do we have an agreement?"

Ward was quiet for a moment.

"I know what your next question is going to be?" Ward replied.

"Then what is the answer?" Centrepoint asked.

"The Vice President."

"Is that definite? And authentic?"

"Yes."

"I need that evidence Ryan. You can't trust it to anyone but me. If there is the slightest risk that it could get out, I need it. Do you realise the ramifications of it being out there?"

"It won't get out," Ward replied.

"You can't take that chance."

"It's not a chance. It is a guarantee."

"How can you be so sure?"

"Because I have destroyed it," Ward lied.

"I doubt that, but I trust you. When this is over, you will hand it all over to me. No copies ever created. You will have your reasons for holding onto it right now and again, I trust your judgement, but that has to come back to me at the end. Give me your word on that Ryan?"

"You have my word."

"Now, there are a couple of things that you need to know"

"I'm listening."

"Both Calvinson and Read have security. Good security. Small teams of mercenaries who protect them and they will be looking for you."

"How good?"

"Not as good as you."

"Then they should have chosen who they worked for more carefully," Ward replied and then the line went dead.

Centrepoint leant back in his chair. He had been surprised to discover the Vice President had been involved in this whole mess but not staggered. Nothing in Washington surprised him anymore.

Madison Reid had put all of his resources into finding the evidence so that he could turn the screw on the VP, to no doubt gain political yardage. And he had lost. He had come up against Ryan Ward, his chief Deniable, and lost, comprehensively and emphatically. And now he was begging for his help and passing any motion that he suggested.

These politicians, he thought to himself, they have all tried over the years to beat him down and they had all lost. His plan was coming together perfectly and Ryan Ward was going to be the man to make it all happen.

THIRTY THREE

Russell Senate Building – 2:00pm

Senator Clint Calvinson had been born into a privileged lifestyle in Florida, the son of a wealthy businessman who had made a fortune in property development. He was earmarked for a political career by his father and the appropriate sponsors, who funded his rise to the Senate for their own greed. There were very few planning applications that were rejected throughout the State for his father's friends, and very few that were approved for his their competitors. His whole political career had been a show of sound bites and a trail of dishonesty. He was now fifty three years old and still bullied by his father and his associates. They all felt they owned a piece of him, and in essence, they did. They had paid for it with hard cash. He was your typical out of shape guy in his fifties. Too many fund raising dinners and a lack of dedication to exercise had resulted in him being way overweight. His once golden locks had been replaced by him desperately trying to hold on to the last remaining strands of hair that had not yet fallen out on top of his head.
He watched the giant clock on the wall of his office touch 2:00pm.

There were three guys in his office. He didn't like them much and he didn't think that they were as good as they had promised him they were. He had sent them over to California when he realised what was happening and they had not only returned empty handed, but they had no idea who had been leaving a trail of destruction behind them. By the time they got word of something happening and arrived there, the place would be swamped by cops, feds and social services employees. But they were all he had and he was confident that when the blackmailer stepped inside the office, they would take care of him.

"He will be here any minute now, so make sure there is no noise and that you take him out of the building down to the parking bays as discussed. Your passes will get you out of the building without question," he said.

"We've got it," one of the guys replied.

"What were you guys anyway?" Calvinson asked. He was feeling anxious; he needed a conversation to distract him.

"We were Marines," the guy replied, "The toughest and deadliest of them all," he added, staring deep into Calvinson's eyes as he spoke.

Calvinson was sure the Seals or Delta Force were tougher but he never said anything. He just smiled a toothy smile as if he was trying to win their votes.

By five past two he was getting nervous.

No one had turned up.

By half past two he was getting very anxious.

No one had turned up.

By 3:00pm, total panic had set in.

He phoned Senator Madison Reid.

"Yes?" Reid answered.

"He hasn't turned up. What shall I do?"

"Panic," Reid replied and then laughed down the phone.

"I'm being serious. I don't know what to do."

"Don't worry. I've just got McNair's motions signed and delivered and I've just put the phone down on him. He probably called his man off in anticipation of me delivering my promises."

"I just don't like it. He still has the videos."

"I'm positive McNair will have them in his possession by now. We are in the clear Clint, just relax."

"Well I can't just relax," Calvinson replied, "I have a family and career to think of. Who is this man who works for McNair?"

"No idea. I tried finding him in California, but he seems to be like a ghost."

"Well I'm going to try and find him and kill him. He can't threaten and blackmail a serving U.S. Senator for Christ's sake."

"Well good luck with that," Reid replied, "Just try and relax and enjoy being off the hook," he added and then he hung up the phone.

Calvinson looked at the three guys in his office.

"I want you to find this guy and kill him," he said to the Marine guy, "Do what I am paying you to do."

"We're on it," he replied and nodded at the other two guys and they all walked out of the office together.

Ward watched the three men walk out of the building and look up and down the street. He waited to see which direction they took and then moved the Range Rover one

hundred feet in front of them and pulled into a side street.
He turned to McDermott,
"What do you think? Ex-Seals?"
"No way, look at the way they walk. Marines at best," McDermott replied, "You three," he said to Fuller, Wallace and Fringe who were sitting patiently in the rear, "Follow them, take them down and then hand them over to Paul and he can take them back to the warehouse to find out what they know."
The three of them stepped out of the Range Rover and walked towards the three men. They passed Paul, Buck, and Wired sitting in the Range Rover behind them, and started joking and nudging each other like three close pals would do walking down the street.
The three guys barely paid any attention to them as they got closer. As they got level with them, Fringe unleashed a thunderous uppercut with his right hand that hit the biggest guy full under the chin, his head shot back and his legs buckled under his weight; he collapsed to the floor, unconscious, like a house of cards being knocked over. Before the other two guys could react, Wallace had elbowed the one nearest to him in the throat and the guy fell to the floor on his knees, while Fuller simply pulled out his gun and pointed it at the third guy. Paul pulled up the Range Rover and the two conscious guys were ushered into the back and Fringe and Fuller then picked up the other guy and threw him in the trunk.
It was all over in less than ten seconds.
Ward watched. He had seen the team do this a number of times and he found it more impressive each time they did it. It was a very well-rehearsed routine.

Now they would find out what these guys knew.

Washington D.C – Merrifield

Three chairs with three guys cable tied to them, laid out in a neat line in the main warehouse.
Three scared guys.
"What were you?" McDermott asked the big guy sitting in the middle, who was still not at full consciousness
"Marines."
McDermott laughed. In fact, everyone in the room laughed.
"All of you?"
All three of them nodded.
Buck walked over to them and started screaming in Russian. No one in the room understood what he was saying. Ward wasn't entirely convinced Buck knew either.
"I don't understand what he's saying?" the guy on the right said in panic.
"He's saying that he is going to cut parts of your body off and make you eat them," Ward interjected.
All three of them looked up at him. Not in fear, but in recognition of something else.
Buck continued to rant in Russian, using his fingers to demonstrate eating food.
McDermott was finding it difficult to stifle his laughter. They all continued to look at Ward. And then he realised what it was that had grabbed their attention.
"You got nowhere near us in California, did you?" he asked no one in particular, "You have one chance to tell me what you were sent to do."

The guy sitting on the left spoke for the first time, "We were told to find the British guy and to take him out."

"By who?"

"Senator Calvinson. We were told to find you and then follow you and when we knew where you were, kill you and steal some computer evidence from you."

"Was it only you?"

"Yes, we managed to find the other team of people, but we couldn't find you."

"The other team?" Ward enquired.

"The people that Senator Reid had sent before us."

"You know Reid?"

"We've not met him, but Senator Calvinson has told us all about him and why we needed to find the computer stuff before him."

"Why was that?"

"Because Reid was going to use it to blackmail the people who were on it."

"This other team, were they Marines too?" McDermott asked.

"No. These guys were heavy hitters, real bad guys."

"From the forces?"

"Yes. They were all Ex-Seals," the guy replied.

Ward looked at McDermott.

This wasn't good.

McDermott was a legend in the Seal world and his whole team comprised of the best that the Seals had produced over the past ten years, and asking them to fight their own was a situation that they would all rather avoid.

"You know these guys names?" Ward asked.

"No. We crossed their paths twice."

"Describe them?"

"They looked the same as us, as you, as all of them. Apart from one who was about six feet seven, he was a ginger haired guy."

Ward looked at McDermott, who nodded back to indicate that he had a good idea who the ginger haired guy was.

"Are you the only security that Calvinson has?" Ward asked.

"Yes," the guy in the middle replied.

"How much is he paying you?"

"Six hundred bucks a day each."

"Is that worth dying for?"

"No it isn't."

"Do you think we are big hitters?"

"You are the biggest. We saw the docks and two houses after you had been there. We aren't stupid. We aren't even mercenaries, we are just three ex jarheads trying to make some cash in the security business," the guy said, "We have realised that we are out of our depth," he added, looking at the floor as he finished, almost in shame.

"Who guards Calvinson when he is at home?" Ward asked.

"We do," the guy in the middle replied.

"How?"

"One spends time outside walking the grounds, the other guards the stairway inside and the other sleeps. We change every two hours."

"No one else at all?"

"No."

"Who were the two guys that Calvinson sent out to meet me in the Upper Senate Park?"

"They were off-duty cops."

"Do you want to die for six hundred dollars a day?" Ward asked.

"Definitely not," the middle guy said.

"Do you believe me if I tell you that I can hunt you down and kill you, anywhere in the world if I want to?" he asked calmly and slowly.

All three of them nodded.

"What do you think?" he asked McDermott.

"They aren't bad guys; they are hopeless but not bad. Calvinson is clearly mean with money and so paid the lowest rate that he could. That's why he ended up with these three clowns," he replied.

"So maybe we shouldn't kill them?"

"Definitely you shouldn't!" the guy on the right said urgently.

"But I want to kill them, I want to watch them eat their own fingers," Buck interrupted, bulging his eyes as he spoke for added effect.

The three guys looked petrified.

"We won't kill them," Ward said.

"Why?" Buck asked, looking as disappointed as he possibly could.

"Because they are going to help us, aren't you?"

"What do we have to do?" The middle guy asked.

"Nothing."

"How is that helping you?"

"Because when you take Calvinson home tonight, you will secure him indoors and then you will walk away.

You will do nothing, but simply walk away, all three of you," Ward replied, "Can you do that?"
All three of them said, "Yes!" at exactly the same time. He believed them.
No one would want to die for six hundred dollars a day.
"We will have eyes and a gun on you at all times, one wrong turn and you are dead. Is that clear?"
They all nodded.
"OK. Once I know you have left the house and you are long gone, you are free to live a normal life. I would suggest that the three of you try and find a different field to work in though."
"Thank you," the guy on the left said.
Ward felt sorry for them. It was so obvious that they were totally out of their depth; this wasn't meant to be what six hundred dollars a day brought to the table.
"We will take you back now. Remember, if you notify Calvinson of what happened today or what will happen this evening, then we will know, and you will be dead within two minutes," Ward said, "Do you believe me?"
They all nodded.
They believed him and they were not going to do anything but walk away.
"Cut them lose and take them back," McDermott said to Paul, "Can we have a minute?" he asked Ward.
They walked towards the reception area, walked in and closed the door.
"The tall ginger guy," McDermott started, "His name is Howley, he's good"
"If you want to step back from this I understand," he replied.

355

"No, He was into some bad shit and he got court martialled. He gave us a bad name; he raped a girl on one of our bases. But he's still good."
"As good as you lot?"
"No, don't be stupid. But there is a problem."
"Which is?"
"We worked with him twice, he was gung-ho, no brain. He used to tell a story, a story that everyone took as bullshit, but I had better mention it, just in case it is true," McDermott said.
"What was it?"
"He used to tell people that his brother was someone that everyone had heard of."
"Who?"
"The Optician."
Ward looked at him and smiled.
"I thought that might put you on edge a little, not make you smile," McDermott said.
"It's OK. Give me five minutes and I'll let you know."
McDermott nodded and left the room. Ward pulled out his cell phone and dialled the number.

In London, Tackler answered his cell phone.
"This place is amazing," he answered, "I've just been to Tom Salter's Café where The Sex Pistols played their first gig," he added.
"Is Nicole-Louise OK?" Ward asked.
"She's fine, she is well buddied up with Lawson's girlfriend. He is a nice guy, I had him wrong."
Ward smiled to himself; Lawson could charm anyone in the world.

"That job I asked you to do. Have you done it?" he asked.

"Yes I have. Do you want to know who and where?" Tackler asked.

"No. I made a promise never to find out. I will keep that promise, but tell me, have any of them ever been in the military?"

"No. One works as a carpenter, another……."

"That's all I need to know," he interrupted, "And you did everything I asked, including the messages?"

"Yes. Exactly as you asked."

"Thank you. Enjoy your vacation," he said and hung up the phone.

He walked out into the warehouse, just as the three marines were climbing into the back of the Range Rover. He knew that they would walk away and never look back. He also knew that they would never mention a word of what had happened.

He caught McDermott's eye.

"Well?" McDermott asked.

"Howley is a liar."

THIRTY FOUR

Washington D.C – Merrifield

Ryan Ward lived a life that was relentless and lonely. His only escape into a life of normality was the time that he spent with Eloisa. Recently, their time together had been restricted to stolen moments of passion in New York, and short phone conversations. He craved to live a normal life and he craved to live it with her. They had discussed the future in depth recently and concluded that in a few years' time they would walk away from the crazy world that they lived in and build a life and a future together. Eloisa always stressed to him that they were doing so much good in the world, and protecting so many innocent people, that they had an obligation to use their skills to good effect until the time was right for them to walk away. Eloisa not only gave his life balance, she was also a great source of information, drip-feeding him snippets of information that were fed to her.
He always found that when he was lost deep in a mission, he never gave her a thought. His strength of focus was one of the things that made him so exceptional. But during quieter moments, he thought of her, like he was doing now, he missed her and found his mind drifting off into daydreams of a simple future.

Right now, he was missing her a great deal. He walked out of the warehouse and into the bright sunshine.
He scrolled down to her name on his contacts and pressed dial.
"Hello you," she answered almost immediately, a fact that threw him a little, as she tended to answer her phone as infrequently as he did.
"Hey," he said, "You OK?"
"I'm fine Ryan, rushed off my feet as usual. I heard the news that Yeschenko was found beaten to death yesterday," she said, "Did he beg for mercy?"
"Yes he did. But he never got it."
"Where are you now?"
"I'm in Washington, just trying to tie up the loose ends of this thing."
"Washington?" she asked, "I don't like the sound of that. Washington normally means trouble."
"Just because a person works in a certain place, that should not give them an exemption ticket from the appropriate punishment, should it?"
"No. But I think you are into something very dangerous and probably beyond where you should go, and sometimes it's best to just walk away."
He didn't like this response. It made her sound like The Old Man and the last thing he needed in his world was someone else telling him about a bigger picture. Especially her.
"What makes you say that?" he asked bluntly.
"Because upon your request I dug around to find out who fed the information about Yeschenko to us and who effectively made sure that no one made waves for his evil little empire," she replied curtly, "And I don't

appreciate your tone with me. I worry because I love you and I am entitled to look out for you."

He felt angry with himself for reacting as he did. This wasn't The Old Man; it was the woman he loved.

"I'm sorry," he said softly, "It's just that this whole thing is a mess and the person that I answer to expects me to just walk away, and I can't."

"Well maybe on this one, you should."

"Why?"

"Because I think this is way too big for you to fix."

"Who protected him?"

"A powerful Senator," she replied.

He knew she was wrong; he had pieced it all together as soon as Yana Podskalnaya had told him who she was and why Yeschenko had been keeping her locked up in Russia, until the right opportunity arrived for her to make him lots of money. But right now, it seemed that only Yana, his team, Calvinson, Reid and the Vice President knew who was really involved and he wanted to keep it that way. If Eloisa didn't know, the secret could do her no harm.

"He's not the only one involved," he said

"More Senators?"

"Definitely two of them."

"Whatever and whoever, you have to be very careful. You aren't invincible Ryan. Perhaps you should just walk away and let the dust settle and re-visit things when the time is right. I know you can't let go easily and I know that your sense of retribution is one of your main strengths, but my job is to protect you. That's how love works," Eloisa said softly.

He knew that she was right, she always was.

"I'm tired of all the lies and protecting the powerful Eloisa. I feel like walking away from all of it right now and never looking back."

"So you let them win? I thought you always told me that you would never let them beat you. You have never quit anything in your life and if you do walk away, it will eat away at you forever, we both know that," she said firmly, "And how much of an impact will that have on our future in a few years when we start a normal life? You will constantly be feeling that there is something in your life that you never finished. No Ryan, you stay and you live to fight another day," she said assertively, her voice getting louder as she spoke.

Once again, he knew she was right.

"The whole thing is rotten to the core," he replied, "Why does everything always come back to money and power?"

"That will never change. It's how it is."

"I doubted The Old Man and I feel bad about that."

"Then maybe you should tell him. You've always spoken about him in a father-like way so don't alienate yourself from him, that will leave you feeling lost."

Yet again, she was right.

Eloisa was the only person, apart from his mother, who always knew what he was feeling and she could always bring a sense of calm and perspective to his personal demons, by simply helping him make sense of his feelings. For all the brutality and force he was capable of, he was as vulnerable as the next guy.

Everyone needs to feel loved and understood.

"I have something that will distract you and make it easier for you to focus elsewhere," she quickly said.

Ward knew what was coming. Outside of his directed missions, Eloisa fed Ward the names of people who abused the young and vulnerable; names that were on the radar of UNICEF, but they were powerless to act against. These names were fed down to Eloisa, by very powerful and nameless people and she would pass them onto him for resolution and action. He always delivered.
"Shoot?"
"There is a guy called Tom Bass who is in Denver and he is a bad one Ryan," she said,
"In what respect?"
"His people trawl the state of Colorado looking for drug addicted women, any age or race," she began, "They entice these people in by feeding them drugs and then move them into their farms."
"For what purpose?"
"To get them pregnant. Then when the children are born, they put them up for sale on the dark web. They sell them to paedophiles and abusers. He's the lowest of the low."
"How big an operation is it?" he asked.
"An operation that is producing over a hundred babies a year" she replied, her voice now sounding pained.
"You have a file on him and his operation?"
"Of course we do. They gave it to me yesterday. I said I would see what I could do."
"Then tell them you will fix it. E-mail it to me and I'll get my digital people working on it," he replied, "I love you, I really do."
"I love you too Ryan."
"I have listened to you and I will be careful," he said,
"Just promise me one thing?"

"Always," she replied.

"We have that week together after I have wrapped this up and taken care of this guy in Colorado. It is long overdue."

"I promise. I need it as much as you do. I need your touch, your kiss and your hugs, but most of all, I need to see your smile with my own eyes to reassure me that you are safe," she replied.

"I'll ring tomorrow."

"I am waiting already. I love you."

Before he could reply, the line went dead.

He instantly felt as though a weight had been lifted off of his shoulders. He had barely had any time to draw breath since New York and he felt completely relaxed for the first time in days. Eloisa always made him feel like that. One day he would ask her how.

He scrolled down his contacts and dialled Centrepoint's number.

"Progress?" The Old Man answered.

"Calvinson's guys weren't as good as you thought they were," he said.

"You've taken them out? What about the clean-up?"

"No. But they are gone, or rather they will be."

"Tell me you haven't moved in on Calvinson yet?"

"Why?"

"Why? Because I have spent all morning preparing a story and making sure the appropriate safeguards are in place to protect you and I told you that I needed to know as soon as you have done it, so that I can clean it up." Centrepoint replied, irritation running through his voice.

"No I haven't, and I promised I would let you know as soon as he has been dealt with."

"So where are we now?"

"I actually called you up to apologise for being such a pain in the ass and questioning your motives. I had no right to do that," Ward replied.

"So I assume that you have just spent some time with Eloisa?"

"We had a chat on the phone, yes."

"I should try and convince her to work for us, she seems to be the only one who is able to control you," Centrepoint replied, his voice much softer now.

"I shouldn't doubt you. You don't deserve that. I know you have to juggle what we do, with all of the political pressure that gets put on you and I know that you are in a no win situation at times. So I guess I'm saying I have never doubted you for real," Ward said with genuine sincerity in his voice.

"Ryan, if I had my way, I would let you eliminate them all, the problem is, there would be very few political figures left if you did that," The Old Man replied and followed it with a long laugh.

It was the first time that he had ever heard him laugh.

"If someone tried to kill you, what would you expect me to do?" he asked; the change of direction in the conversation throwing Centrepoint for a few moments, a fact confirmed by the long silence.

"Why do you ask that?" he asked after a few seconds.

"Humour me. Answer the question."

"I'm sure lots of people would like me out of the picture due to the things I know but they have more fear that I

might spill their secrets I imagine so I've always used that as my comfort."
"Don't give me a politician's answer. Tell me your initial reaction to the question?"
"Is someone trying to kill me?" Centrepoint asked without a hint of concern in his voice.
"Not that I know of but I would like your answer all the same."
Centrepoint paused and went quiet for ten seconds, clearly weighing up his reaction against why Ward would ask the question. He eventually spoke,
"The truth is Ryan, I would ask that another way. What would you do if someone was trying to kill me?"
"I would protect you and hunt them down."
"Then I could live with that."
"They should never have gone after Nicole-Louise and Tackler," Ward replied and hung up the phone.

He walked back into the warehouse and crossed straight over to Wired,
"I've spoken to Mike so thanks for getting Nicole-Louise and Tackler to London safely," he said, remembering how eager Wired was to get them both to safety.
Wired simply nodded.
He then walked across to McDermott, who was once again sitting in his armchair.
"We are going to move in a couple of hours. I'm going to need you and three of your team with me," he said.
"Inside or out?" McDermott asked.
"Outside. Just to make sure that the marines keep their word."
"Where is Calvinson's house?"

"It's in a gated community in Langley," Ward replied. "Where the real money is."

"Where the dead Senators live…"

"It will take us twenty minutes to get there. We will load up and get ready to leave now. The men are getting restless," McDermott replied, before turning away and walking toward the table where the rest of the team were playing cards.

Ward was ready. He picked up his Glock from the workbench where he had left it and screwed the silencer tightly into position. As he screwed it into place, he pictured how Calvinson would die. Simply shooting him would be too good for him, after the vile acts that he had committed, and so he decided to do what he always did when he felt people needed to understand their sins fully before they died.

He went over to the laptop that was running on the workbench and carried out a search on Senator Clint Calvinson. Five minutes later he had found everything he needed.

"We're ready," McDermott shouted, as he, Buck, Wired and Walsh climbed into the Range Rover.

Senator Clint Calvinson had two hours left to live.

THIRTY FIVE

Langley - Virginia

Calvinson's house in Langley was obscenely grand. Considering that he lived alone and that his family home in Florida was equally as big, it felt like a totally unnecessary and flamboyant statement to make. It reeked of someone who wanted to show the world how wealthy and important they were. It had a long driveway that led from the road in a straight line up to the front entrance. The front of the house was perfectly rectangle and Ward counted ten large sash windows on the ground floor and eleven on the floor above. In the middle of the ground floor was a giant double door which was made out of solid and strong wood, varnished immaculately without a single chip. The house was as long down the side as it was wide at the front. By the number of windows alone, Ward concluded that there must be at least forty rooms inside. The walls were painted brilliant white and the roof was covered in off-green, deep ridge tiles.

Getting into the gated area had been easy, in spite of the adequate security that the private security company provided. McDermott had simply driven around the perimeter of the estate and found a suitable spot where the Range Rover could be parked inconspicuously and pulled up two feet away from the perimeter wall and parked, Buck followed behind in the other Range Rover and pulled in behind them. They simply climbed out of the cars, climbed onto the roof and then stepped over the wall. The drop down was no more than eight feet and then they were in.

Buck and Fuller stayed in the Range Rovers with the engines running; they drew the short straws and got allocated the spotting duties. McDermott, Fringe and Wallace moved towards the house first and passed through the thick shrubbery. McDermott set himself up at the front of the house on the right hand side while Fringe covered the left. Wallace set himself up at the back. Most people use the front entrance to a house, particularly if they are totally unaware that two more than adequate snipers, under cover of the thick bushes, are watching them enter through their scopes. Wallace offered the security in case anyone ran out of the back door.

McDermott looked into his scope and through the windows of the house and stopped at the third window on the right on the ground floor. He spoke quietly into his radio microphone.

"We have a problem," his voice echoed into Ward's earpiece.
"How big a problem?" he asked.
"There is a woman in the house. Looks like a housekeeper. In her fifties, short and Hispanic."
"Can you see anyone else?"
""No. Wallace, what about you?"
"Definitely all clear at the back," Wallace replied over the radio.
"Fringe?" McDermott asked.
"All clear boss."
"You hear that?"
"Understood," Ward replied.
"Where are you?" McDermott enquired.
"I'm just walking onto the driveway now."
He walked on the centre of the driveway, which was easily big enough to fit two passing cars on, so that if anyone else was looking at him from inside the house, he would be clearly visible. If anyone tried taking a shot at him from a window, he was confident that McDermott, Fringe or Wallace would take them out before their finger ever got close to squeezing the trigger. He continued walking forward, reached the giant doors, and rang the intercom button that was positioned on the right hand side of the door.
"Hello?" a loud voice came through the speaker box, a heavy hint of a Spanish accent accompanying it.
"Police," he said into the intercom.
He waited a good thirty seconds and then the door opened.
A short, thick set Mexican woman stood in front of him.

"I need to see Senator Calvinson urgently," he said sternly.

"He won't be back for an hour. You have a card to leave?" she asked.

The last thing that he wanted was to frighten the woman and so he tried a softer approach.

"Are you the live-in housekeeper that he told me about earlier?" he said, putting the fact that he knew Calvinson and was not a threat into her sub-consciousness.

"Yes I am."

He now had a big problem. He wasn't going to rough up an old woman and lock her in a room and then leave her to find Calvinson after he had finished with him and provide the police with a witness. So he did the only thing he could do.

"OK, thank you for your time, I'll come back later when he is here," and he turned and walked back down the drive.

When he was out of sight of the house, he spoke into the microphone.

"We will have to change the plan. We'll have to hit his car when he gets here."

"Where?" McDermott asked.

"At the entrance to the drive, then we can drag him to the wall and take him back to the warehouse," Ward replied, "Buck?" he then said into the microphone.

"Here."

"I need you to move your car closer to the entrance to the estate and let us know when he gets here."

"What will he be driving?" Buck replied.

"How the hell should I know?" Ward said, "Be imaginative."

As it turned out, Calvinson's car was a silver Mercedes Benz S-Class, expensive, but not as pretentious as Ward had expected. Buck had seen the car roll up to the gated entrance to the estate and he recognised the driver as one of the Marines that they had interrogated at the warehouse earlier.
"Silver Mercedes," Buck's voice came over the radio, "It's on its way to you now."
"You all ready?" Ward said into the microphone.
"Always," McDermott replied.
He stepped out of the shrubbery that was concealing him at the end of Calvinson's drive and then jogged twenty feet up the driveway, stopped and turned around to face the entrance. He pulled out his Glock and stood in the middle of the drive and raised the gun. The six hundred dollar a day guys would see him, stop and just walk away. He knew it.
The car came around the corner slowly and turned into the drive. The driver instantly recognised him.
"Just stop slowly and walk away," Ward muttered to himself.
The guy's eyes met his and he started to slow the car gently. It was the quiet guy of the three who never said much.
And then the engine screamed and the car shot forward straight at him. He instinctively dropped his left shoulder as if he was going to move to the left and then switched all of his weight to his left foot and as the car was twenty feet away, he pushed hard and went to the right, like a running back evading a tackle, and the car missed him by no more than two feet, the drivers reactions were not

quick enough to move the car back completely in his direction. The car then sped up the drive to the house and stopped by the front doors.

"He must have given them a pay rise," he said into the microphone, as he started to walk up the drive slowly, "Over to you boys," he added.

The rear door opened first, and one of the Marines stepped out holding a handgun, moved six feet away from the car and pointed it at him. The guy was at least one hundred yards away. Ward wasn't concerned; he wouldn't hit him from there.

Then the front passenger door opened and another Marine stepped out and rested his arm on top of the car roof with his gun pointing him.

He continued walking up the drive.

A muffled shot rang out and the guy facing him dropped his gun immediately and gripped his thigh, before toppling over onto the gravel. Another shot rang out and he saw the guy's right foot explode. A third and final shot rang which hit the guy in the stomach and he was finally dead.

He continued walking up the drive.

"Who was that shooting?" he asked into the microphone.

"Me," Fringe's voice came over the radio.

"If The Optician saw you shooting like that then he would probably shoot you himself. You get that right?"

He heard McDermott laugh down the radio,

"I mean seriously Fringe that was bad," he added.

Fringe didn't bother responding.

He continued walking up the drive.

The Marine who was leaning on the car roof with his gun pointing at him was switching between looking at him and looking at his dead colleague.

All for six hundred dollars a day.

Another shot rang out and it hit the guy leaning on the car roof directly in the head. Only it wasn't the kind of headshot that was The Optician's trademark, the neat efficient shot that Ward had become used to witnessing. No, it skimmed the guys' head and just tore his ear off. The guy dropped his gun and started hopping around, with both hands clutched to his ear.

He continued walking up the drive.

A second shot rang out and hit the guy in the chest. He dropped to the floor immediately and was dead before he hit the ground.

"That was a little better. The headshot was terrible though," Ward said.

"I was playing with him," McDermott replied.

He was now about fifty feet away from the car. He felt disappointed for the Marines. Dying for just six hundred dollars a day was a stupid thing to do. He started to wonder if they ever were Marines, or just bumbled their way through things.

When he got close to the car, the rear door opened and Senator Clint Calvinson was bundled out. The big Marine was holding a gun to the back of Calvinson's head.

Ward shook his head. These guys were never Marines. Which pissed him off slightly, because it showed how arrogant Calvinson was by thinking employing Joe average off the street would protect him, but comforted him more because he had a lot of respect for the Marines and he knew they were much, much better than these three idiots.

The fact they were idiots was confirmed, as he got to within twenty feet of the guy holding Calvinson's hostage.

"Stop!" the big guy shouted, "Stop there or I will kill him."

"That's what we are here for dipshit. To kill him," Ward replied with dismay in his voice, rolling his eyes as he spoke.

Realisation hit the big guy, and he looked totally dejected when it sunk in that he was not bargaining from the position of strength that he thought he was.

McDermott's laugh cackled over the radio, unnerving the big guy even more.

"Please, please, don't," Calvinson whimpered.

He continued walking up the drive.

"You have three more steps to drop your gun or you are dead," Ward said.

The guy dropped the gun immediately but did not release his grip on Calvinson.

He reached the two of them.

"I can help, I have money, please don't hurt me," Calvinson begged.

As he reached them, he unleashed a thunderous right hook that caught Calvinson flush on the left temple, his knees gave way and he fell to the floor, unconscious by the time he landed on the right hand side of his face on the gravel.

The big guy now looked terrified.

Ward studied him for a few moments, looking him up and down, occasionally shaking his head in contempt.

"You weren't even in the services, were you?" he asked. The guy shook his head.
"Sorry? I didn't hear you."
"No, none of us were," the guy said, refusing to make eye contact with him, instead choosing to study the unconscious Senator on the floor.
"So what were you?"
"We were cadets at one time," the guy replied, saying it with such enthusiasm that Ward almost felt sorry for him.
"But you didn't make the cut?"
"I had a bad knee."
"And I would have pitched for the Mets if I didn't have to wear glasses," Ward said.
"It sucks, doesn't it," the guy replied.
"I was taking the piss."
"Oh, sorry."
"So how did you get into security? I mean, you are all hopeless, so how does a Senator end up with idiots like you protecting him?" Ward asked, genuinely interested to establish how they did it.
"We just made a load of crap up about our service history, found some files on the internet and advertised ourselves," the guy replied.
"As what?"
"First line of defence"
"That sounds like a flea deterrent to me."
The guy shrugged and started walking off down the drive.
"Where are you going?"
"I'm walking away like you told me to?" he replied.

Ward smiled. This was one of the funniest moments that he had encountered in a long time; he wasn't going to let it go.
"What about your friends?"
"We live by the sword, we die by the sword. It's how we roll," the guy said.
In Ward's line of work, there was very little to smile about and even less to lighten the mood, but this guy was priceless. He decided he had to be the most stupid guy he had ever met in his life.
"I thought I told you to walk away. And then you tried running me over and pointing guns at me?" Ward said.
"Instinct kicked in."
"Can I trust you to keep quiet about what just happened here?"
"Yes."
The guy continued to walk away. He could most definitely not trust him.
"Take him out," he said into his microphone quietly.
The guy walked another six feet and a muffled shot rang out, his head exploded and he fell to the floor like a rag doll.
"That's how you shoot," McDermott's voice came over the radio.
Ward looked at Calvinson. He was just starting to come around when the front door opened and the Mexican woman stood there looking at him.
But something was off.
Ward walked towards her, putting his gun in his pocket as he moved.
"I didn't want you to see any of that," he said softly.
"See any of what?" the woman asked.

"You haven't seen anything?"

"No," the woman replied, "Just like I never had to see what that animal did to some of the poor children they brought to the house."

"You have children?"

"Yes, and grandchildren," she replied.

"Will you be able to find another job?"

"Yes. Being a housekeeper for a Senator gets you good jobs."

"And you definitely didn't see anything?"

"Nothing. He came home and then I left."

"Thank you."

He bent down, hauled Calvinson up and pushed him into the back of the Mercedes. Wallace appeared and then climbed into the back of the car with Calvinson and Ward walked around to the driver's seat. As he was climbing in, the woman said,

"Wait!"

"What is it?" he asked.

"Do something for me," she said, "Make that evil bastard suffer as much as those poor girls they brought here did," she added.

He nodded, climbed in the car and drove down the gravel drive and disappeared.

THIRTY SIX

Washington D.C - Merrifield

"Tie him up," Ward said to Wallace as the roller shutter doors were closing, "I need to make a quick call."
He got out of the Mercedes and walked through to the reception area and closed the door.
He called Centrepoint's number.
"Hello?"
"There are three guys who need cleaning up at Calvinson's house."
"And him?" The Old Man asked.
"He's with me now. I need to talk to him first."
"And when you have finished with him?"
"We will leave him by the side of the road like the animal he is," he replied, his voice calm and factual.
"OK. Let me know where," Centrepoint said and hung up the phone.

Calvinson was now tied to the chair and wearing only his suit pants and shirt. He walked over to Calvinson's jacket, which had been thrown on the hood of the Mercedes and sifted through the pockets.
He found what he was looking for instantly.
"What's the code?" he said to Calvinson, waving the cell phone he had just taken from his jacket pocket in the air.
"One, two, one two" he replied nervously, while trying to take in the surroundings that he had found himself in.
"What is the significance of that number?" he asked.
"Nothing."
"Is that the age of the children you like?"
Calvinson said nothing.
"I think it is," he continued "Or maybe even younger?"
Calvinson just looked down at the floor.
He grabbed a chair from the table in the corner and walked it across to Calvinson and set it down three feet away from him. He sat down and studied him for a few moments. Buck, McDermott and his team all walked over to where they were sitting, folded their arms, and just stood there, staring at Calvinson, with pure hate in their eyes. It was enough to make him start to sob quietly.
"Can you see a way out of this Mr Politician?" he asked.
Calvinson said nothing.
He was fighting the urge to shoot him in the face right there and then, just to get it over and done with and get the animal out of his sight; but he had to ask him questions first, so he breathed in deeply and composed himself.
"Do you understand why you are sitting here, tied to a chair right now?"

"Of course I do. But I don't think you realise that it wasn't my fault," Calvinson replied.

"I have the video footage; we beat everyone to it and from what we saw, it looked very much like it was your fault."

Calvinson looked at the floor.

"So what I have to tell you now," he continued, "Is that you have two children back in Florida with your wife, and at this moment in time, they are one call away from being dead," he added.

Calvinson's head shot up,

"Please, I swear, not them, I will tell you anything," he begged.

"You want to protect them, right?"

"Yes, please, don't hurt them."

"You are probably feeling right now, how the parents of those poor children you and your disgusting friends violated, have felt."

"It wasn't my fault. You don't understand what is happening here," he proclaimed.

"So tell me, who knows, you might save the lives of your own wife and children."

"It was Reid. He instigated the whole thing."

"Why?"

"Because he wanted to blackmail us?"

"Us?" Ward asked.

Calvinson looked at him, he was starting to gain a little composure, and he was becoming the slimy politician once again.

"It wasn't just me that he got involved with it."

"Who else?"

Calvinson thought he had an ace to play, and like all politicians, he tried twisting the truth.

"There is someone else; I have the proof in my office, so you could take me to get it?"

"Who else? We already know about Reid," Ward replied.

"A bigger fish than Reid."

"How was what you did not your fault?"

"Reid got me drunk and then I woke up the next day with two young women naked in bed with me and he had filmed it," Calvinson replied, trying as hard as he possibly could to sound like a victim.

"They weren't young women, they were children," he corrected Calvinson, "So after that you thought that you may as well keep doing it off of your own back?"

"I'm not excusing what I did," Calvinson continued, "I was wrong and for that I will suffer the consequences, but Reid is the one. He set it all up for political gain."

"How? What could he gain?"

"He hit problems with his funding and so he started blackmailing me to get some of my contributors to support him. He kept threatening to expose me to the press if I didn't make it happen," Calvinson replied.

"But how could he. He was doing it too?"

"I didn't know that at the time."

"So when did you find out?" Ward asked.

"Just three weeks ago, when the Russian crook, Yeschenko, sent us both the same e-mail."

Ward felt there was real irony in Calvinson referring to anyone as a crook.

"What did the e-mail say?"

"It said that we either paid out ten million dollars each, or the news channels would know what we have both been doing," Calvinson replied.

"But why just you two? There are a lot more high profile people than you. Actors, sports stars and singers, so what made you two so special?" Ward asked.

"Two things. Firstly, we had the power to make sure that the women he……..."

"Children!" Ward interrupted.

"That the children that he brought into the country could get here without detection and that there would be no traceable documents that ever went back to him."

"And secondly?"

"We have a direct path to the other person involved. He was the big fish that he was going to take for fifty million."

"And did this other person, this secret big fish, know what was happening?" Ward asked.

"Yes he did. He provided some men to help."

"What type of men?"

"The best."

"They weren't better than us. Not only have we wiped out Yeschenko, all of his men and the Secret Service guys, we beat everyone to the evidence. We are the best," Ward replied and then leant back in his chair, "So Reid was as guilty as you but he manipulated and blackmailed you?"

"Yes. And not just with the sponsors; with committees too. Yesterday I had to pass some motions that I didn't want to but he insisted."

"What motions?"

"It's black ops stuff. A team of unknowns who work off the radar, they have now been given complete control, so no one knows what the hell they are doing. If you think you are bad, think again. Those guys are probably out here right now looking for me and they will probably be close," Calvinson declared.

"I doubt that," Ward said.

The penny dropped instantly with Calvinson.

"You are McNair's team?"

"I'm one tenth of it. These are my friends. Although credit where credit is due, these guys are better than anything that The Old Man has to offer, so really, we are your worst nightmare," he said with a smile, "Who is the big fish?"

"The Vice President."

"At least I know you have told the truth about one thing," he said, "We have everything. The video evidence, the money and the shipping documents. You have nothing to offer me."

"There's always something," Calvinson replied.

"There is one thing" Ward said, "There were some computer hackers, what do you know about them?"

"I know Reid was going crazy saying they had found stuff that compromised us."

"And who are they?"

"Some kids in New York."

"Who ordered them to be killed?"

"Reid did. Even though McNair warned him not to, he still wanted them taken care of," Calvinson replied.

Ward was happy. Centrepoint had done his part in warning Reid to keep way from Nicole-Louise and Tackler, and he now felt even worse for doubting him.

"How old are your kids?" he asked, even though he knew the answer.

"Twelve and fourteen," Calvinson replied, shame sweeping across his face.

"And you would do anything to save them?"

"Of course I would!"

"Cut him loose," he said to Buck.

"You are letting me go?" Calvinson asked eagerly.

"No. You are going to die shortly. I'm giving you one chance to save your kid's lives."

"I don't understand?"

He unlocked Calvinson's phone.

Buck cut the last cable tie that was holding Calvinson to the leg of the chair.

"You are going to confess your sins and you will implicate Senator Reid, but make no mention of the Vice President. You will say who you are and that Reid was the one who cut through all the red tape so that Yeschenko was able to become the biggest trafficker of children, solely for use in the sex trade, into the United States. You will also state that you and Senator Reid have both engaged in sexual activities with these minors."

"It will destroy me," Calvinson protested.

"You are already destroyed. This is your one chance to save your families lives," he replied.

"OK. I'll do it."

"Tidy yourself up, put your jacket back on and look like the liar you are."

"Are you ready?" Ward asked a few minutes later, after Calvinson had cleaned up and put his jacket and tie back on.

Calvinson nodded.

He held up Calvinson's cell phone, pressed the record button on the camera and nodded at him.

"I am Senator Clint Calvinson; elected with a resounding majority by the people of Florida, to sit on the United States Senate. I have failed the good people of Florida and my family, but I am now confessing my sins. I was introduced into a life of sin by Senator Madison Reid and these sins were having sex with children. I seek no forgiveness for my sins. Senator Reid also sinned against these poor children and was the key figure behind the trafficking of children into the U.S. from Albania and Russia by a criminal called Andrea Yeschenko. Yeschenko was the biggest trafficker of people into the States that we have ever known. Senator Reid blackmailed me into getting financial support for his continued political career and to illegally have certain motions passed by Senate committees.

To my wife, I am sorry. To my children, I love you and be better than the man I was, and to the good people of Florida, you are forever in my heart."

Calvinson finished his confession with a smile at the camera that only a politician could produce.

Ward stopped recording and sat on the chair and played the video back through the cell phone. It was perfect. Complete clarity and sound.

"Do you feel any remorse, truthfully?" he asked, as he slid Calvinson's phone into his pocket.

"Remorse I got caught, remorse I did wrong and remorse that I got caught up in this? Of course I do," he replied. Ward didn't believe him.

Senator Clint Calvinson of Florida did not live long enough to see his next birthday. He died in the most unimaginable pain. He was beaten to death by nine ruthless defenders of the innocent. It took twenty five minutes for him to die. Every time he passed out, he was woken with water thrown on his face. Almost every single bone in his body was broken. It was eventually a broken rib that killed him, the stamp from McDermott's boot forcing the bone to puncture his cold, evil heart.

"Put him in the trunk of his car," Ward said, as he took out his own cell phone and called Centrepoint.
"Calvinson is finished. He's in the trunk of his car. Where do you want him?"
"Drive him a mile up from where you are now and I'll have the car picked up," The Old Man replied, "It's over now Ryan. Do you understand that?"
Ward hung up the phone.
"Decision time Ryan," McDermott said to him.
"As in?"
"Do you walk away now or do we move forward?"
"What do you think? The Old Man is adamant that's it."
"You know as well as I do that the right thing to do is finish this," McDermott said.
"That is all I needed to hear," he replied.

THIRTY SEVEN

Washington D.C – 16th Street NW

Ward had decided that he needed a hotel room for the night so that he could freshen up and sleep. He found a mid-range hotel just off of 16th Street NW, called The Embassy Inn. He wanted to get away from the warehouse so that he could think clearly and without influence. As much as he trusted McDermott with his life, McDermott was a warrior who could only ever see one answer. Calvinson's revelation about Centrepoint telling Reid to back off made him more sympathetic to The Old Man's need to look at the bigger picture before acting. He promised himself that he would do that.

He showered and changed his clothes. He tried calling Eloisa, but her cell went straight to voicemail.

As much as he tried to relax and think calmly he couldn't. So he decided to make the call that would dictate what happened next, if he stopped now or he did the right thing.

He took out Calvinson's cell phone, unlocked it and scrolled down through the contacts until he reached 'M Reid'.

He dialled the number.

"I've been trying to get hold of you, where have you been?" the voice spat down the phone.

"Surprised?" he said.

Reid's voice went silent. So he waited him out and didn't speak.

"Who is this? Reid asked after fifteen seconds.

"Have a guess?"

Ward's English accent was confusing Reid, he knew that for sure.

"I don't know. Put Senator Calvinson on the line immediately."

"There is no Calvinson anymore."

"Who are you?"

"I'm the guy who was one step ahead of you all the time and now I'm five ahead of you," he replied, mocking Reid as best he could while remaining calm.

"McNair's guy?"

"I'm my own guy right now," he said, "And are you in trouble or what?"

"You don't intimidate or scare me," Reid said aggressively.

"Then you are more stupid than you look fatso."

"Where is Senator Calvinson?"

"He's dead. Beaten to death. I enjoyed it. I inserted long sharp objects into his body to cut and damage his insides. It's only fair. You fat boys like pain so much, I thought I would show you how those poor kids felt. He cried, do you know that? He cried more than those poor innocent children. My money says you will do the same and cry like a baby," he said and then laughed down the line.

"What do you want?" Reid asked.

"I have something that I think you should watch Reid. Want to see it?"

"What is it?"

"Not what you were looking for. I have that somewhere safe where you will never find it. This is something new that has come to light."

"What is it?"

"I'll send it now."

Ward hung up the phone and attached the video to a message and sent it to Reid.

He knew he would only have to wait a minute for Reid to ring back.

A minute later, the phone rang and Reid's name flashed on the screen.

"Good viewing?"

"What do you want?" he asked, his voice sounding shaken.

"You should never have gone after those hackers fatso. You were warned about it, but you thought you were above reprimand and so you did what you always do and did whatever the hell you wanted."

"I told McNair I would not go after them anymore."

"You can't touch them now, they've disappeared," Ward replied, "Oh, and before I forget, I have videos of you, Calvinson and the VP engaged in acts with children. Add Calvinson's testimony into the mix and there is nowhere for you to turn fatso."

"Let me explain something to you boy" Reid began, "I have been sanctioning McNair's activities for years and I call the shots here. The sanctions come through the Vice president to me, so effectively through the President, your President. So you don't dictate shit to me," he continued, his voice visibly shaking with anger.

"I'm not American so he isn't my President fatso."

"Prime Minister then boy, the Brits don't fart without asking first."

"I'm not British either. You actually have no idea what I am going to do to you, do you?"

Reid went quiet.

"Your inadequate protection, including Howley the liar, are so far out of their depth with us that no one can help you. Fatso is in a lot of trouble," he said, "Whoever you want to call me off can't influence me. I make my own choices; I'm not interested in that political crap. You hurt a lot of innocent and defenceless children. That's good enough reason for me to kill you and after that, publicise to the world what sort of animal you are."

"You are jumping the gun a bit here son" Reid said, his voice much calmer, "I'm sure that there is something that can be sorted out between us. I have just granted your boss a lot of concessions that mean you now have unlimited resources and no questions for whatever you do. I can be of use to you in the bigger picture."

There it was again.

The bigger picture.

Ward was sick of hearing about it. To him, the picture was small and simple. These animals had destroyed the lives of countless innocent children and someone had to make them pay for it. He had no interest in the bigger picture.

But he was smart enough to know that he would have to draw Reid out, get him to hunt him down, away from central D.C, so that he could justify going after him.

"And how can you put right what you have done wrong?"

"There is no more Yeschenko, so no more evidence," Reid replied, "If you pass that over to your boss, he will keep it safe and then everything has gone away."

Ward was staggered at Reid's arrogance. He didn't realise what he had meant by 'What you have done wrong', he genuinely believed getting filmed without him knowing in the most degrading way was all that he had done wrong. Not a thought for those poor, innocent children.

"Let me sleep on it," he said.

"You do that son. We can work this all out so that everyone gets what they want in the end."

"Goodbye fatso."

Ward hung up the phone.

He opened the back of Calvinson's phone and dropped the battery out. He would never be stupid enough to allow the phone to be traced.

He picked up his own phone and dialled The Optician.

"That motel is a little cheap," he answered.

"It's good enough for me. I need a shower and a sleep, no more than that. You know everything that has been going on?" Ward asked.

"What The Old Man has told me, but no doubt there are a number of parts that are missing because you haven't told him."

"What do you know about Senator Reid?"

"The Old Man doesn't want you to go after him, that's it."

"You know what he did?"

"Yes?"

"Do you think I should let him walk?"

"I'm not here to think."

"Then tell me as a friend?" Ward asked.

"If you go after him and all hell breaks loose, I will be there to protect you and you alone. The Old Man will probably throw a fit but he will smooth it over and calm down after a week or so," The Optician replied.

"You know that I promised you years ago to never find out your real identity?"

"I do. I have always respected you for that."

"I still haven't, never. No matter how curious I have got and how desperate I have been to learn more about you, I have never done it. And I never will. I just wanted you to know that."

"Why mention that now?"

"Because it's important to me. You knowing that I have always kept my word to you is more important than anything."

"I know," The Optician replied, "Get some sleep. I'm watching over you."

Ward hung up the phone.

He lay down on top of the bed and turned off the lights and had just gotten comfortable when his cell phone rang. He looked at the caller display and Centrepoint's name was flashing.

"I was just trying to grab a few hours' sleep," Ward answered.

"Turn on the TV to USBC News," he demanded.

Ward reached for the remote and turned on the TV and scrolled down to the news channel.

There was a reporter standing by a roadside with a silver Mercedes in full view behind her. Ward turned up the volume and listened.

The reporter was explaining how Florida's Senator, Clint Calvinson had committed suicide. She explained how he had secretly been battling mental illness for the past ten years and he had connected a pipe to his exhaust earlier and subsequently, he had died of carbon monoxide poisoning. At the bottom of the screen, a breaking news item was scrolling across. It read,

'BREAKING NEWS....... 100 ALBANIAN REFUGEES RESCUED FROM A BOAT IN THE PORT OF LOS ANGELES.... ALL REFUGEES NOW IN THE CARE OF SOCIAL SERVICES....'

"That's nice and tidy," Ward said.

"All part of the bigger picture."

"You enjoy being The Newsmaker, don't you?"

"I manage things to our advantage so that we can do more good than all of our governments combined. You know there is only one way to fight bad people in this world, and that way is our way," The Old Man replied defensively.

Ward had to remind himself not to keep being so hard on him.

"You're right. You've done a good job cleaning that up and all of the children we rescued are safe so we've done a lot of good."

"But it is over now."

"Are you sure about that? I think that Senator Reid is pretty pissed at me."

"What have you done?"

"I called him up and told him what I had on him," he replied.

"I thought I was crystal clear. Reid and the Vice President are completely off limits. Reid has just passed a number of motions that make our life a whole lot easier and we need him on our side," Centrepoint replied angrily.

"They went after Nicole-Louise and Tackler," he said defensively.

"You will have your time soon with Reid but in terms of this mission, it is over. You won again Ryan. The children are all safe, you have all the evidence stored wherever you have it, which incidentally, I need you to hand over to me as soon as possible, and we have basically been given control over everything we do from now. Maintaining the political structure and integrity of our country is vital," Centrepoint said, almost without pausing, a fact that made him wonder if he had the speech pre-prepared.

"I think belief in integrity is pretty much in the gutter anyway, but I get your point," he replied.

"I am going to ask you what I never ask you. Promise me, with your word, that you will stop this now and not go after either Reid or the VP?"

"I struggle with how wrong this all is," Ward said, "How do you live with all the covering up you have done for these people over the years?" he added, genuinely curious to know how The Old Man coped with the frustration, of letting someone vile get away with the things they have done.

"Our job is to keep the people in the street safe. The guy who works hard for his family and the kids who don't even know we exist. Sure, we have done a lot of bad things, but all for the right reasons. Have you ever wondered exactly how many lives you yourself have saved?"

He had never given it a thought. He wasn't entirely convinced that The Old Man had either, because all he ever seemed to mention was the number of people that he had killed and the problems that he had clearing up after him.

"Quite a lot I expect," he reluctantly replied.

"Well that's what gets me through each day. If saving all of those lives means we have to let some people live to use for our benefit in saving more lives in the future, it's a price I accepted a long time ago that we have an obligation to pay," Centrepoint said, "It's just how it is Ryan" he added, followed by a sigh.

"OK. I get it. You have my word. They are off limits."

"Thank you," Centrepoint replied and the line went dead. Ward turned off the TV, then the lights and lay back on the bed and closed his eyes.

But it wasn't done.

Not by a long way.

Because as he closed his eyes, Senator Madison Reid was preparing to bring the fight to Ryan Ward.

THIRTY EIGHT

Hart Senate Office Building – Washington D.C.

Reid threw his cell phone across the office and it landed hard into the soft leather sofa where the two guys were sitting. They didn't flinch, they just stared at him.
He picked up the landline on his desk and said, "Did you get it?"
He started scribbling something down on a piece of paper and then slammed the phone down.
Mark Howley stood next to Reid at the desk, trying to see what he was writing.
"If he thinks I am going to tolerate being spoken to like that by a snivelling upstart like him then he doesn't know who Senator Madison Reid really is," he said, to no one in particular.
"Have you any idea who this man could be?" he asked Howley. "You are supposed to be the Special Forces expert."
Mark Howley was an expert. He had served two years in the Seals before deciding that he could make more money through being a mercenary. Howley was tall. He

stood at almost six feet seven and he had bright ginger hair. Even cropped short, his hair was a bright colour. He wasn't overly well built and all the hours and hours in the gym on the weights had given him, was an average physique. They mocked him in the Seals a lot; they called him 'Matchstick' because of his long body and bright head. But he had made a good career as a mercenary. He had assembled a team of adequate men who were reasonably skilled in every aspect of warfare. He insisted that they called him 'Sir'; discipline was important, as he would always remind his team, emphasising that his brother, the legend known only as The Optician, had taught him that at an early age. He had a team of eight men. Two were sitting on the sofa right now and the other six were in and around the Harte Senate building, looking out for anyone that could be heading in Reid's direction. Reid was paying them well, twenty thousand dollars a day, the majority of which he kept for himself, to find this guy who was hunting evidence that Reid had been a naughty boy with kids. Howley didn't care what Reid had done, he paid well and that was all he needed to know.
But he was worried.
He had run around California, from one place to another and witnessed first-hand the trial of destruction that this guy had left in his wake. Howley knew that this man could not be working alone, no man was capable of creating that much carnage alone, and that meant that he had a very, very good, or very, very big, team supporting him.
Howley had watched Reid crumble over the past few days. He knew that whoever this guy was, he was under

the control of someone called McNair and that he had a secret group of operatives called The Deniables; but Reid knew no more than that. Howley had asked for this McNair's whereabouts and a description but Read had just shrugged and said, no one knows. A few days ago, Reid was buoyant and full of himself. Howley had convinced him that he and his team would fly over to California, find this video evidence that Reid wanted so bad and kill the Russian guy Yeschenko for him. With each report that Howley had sent back to Reid about someone else hitting a house before them, the ship at the docks and finally Yeschenko's demise he was losing control more and more.

Now he was livid.

"This guy, he has an English accent. You must know who he is?" Reid demanded.

Howley had no idea. He had only ever met one British guy during his time with the Seals and he was a PT instructor on a fact finding mission. But he entertained his demand nonetheless,

"I have a contact in the SAS," Howley began, "I ran a few missions with them five years back and saved a couple of their assess, so they owe me. I can make a few calls," he added.

Reid raised an eyebrow. Everyone in the world knows how good the SAS are. The fact that Howley had contacts within the unit calmed him down instantly. If Howley had friends there, then he really was as good as he kept telling him he was.

"I have an address where this man made the call from. It's a hotel on 16th Street North West," Reid said, "I want you to go and check it out."

"No point," Howley replied, "It's an old special forces trick. Call from one place, let them think you are there and reduce the enemies manpower when they are out chasing ghosts and then strike at the heart," he added. Reid instantly put his own self-preservation before all else,
"OK. You and your men stay here, I'll send four of the others to check it out," he quickly said.
"Wise move Senator," Howley replied.
He picked up his phone and issued instructions to the person on the other end of the line. He read out the address and then said to let him know what was happening,
"But do not kill him. If you find him, bring the weasel here so I can find out where he has taken my items," he shouted down the phone before hanging up.
"Wise move Senator," Howley said again.
"You have to find this man for me though, I need to get my hands on the evidence that he stole. It belongs to me," he declared, "I don't care how much it costs or how long it takes, you find it, is that clear?"
"Yes Senator."
"And then you can kill him in front of me."
Howley moved away from Reid's desk and approached the two guys who were sitting down,
"You two," he said firmly, "On your feet and focus."

Washington D.C – 16th Street NW

The Optician watched the dark blue Ford Taurus pull up in the hotel car park. He knew instantly that it was a government car because through his scope, he could clearly see the reflective watermark repeating the phrase, 'U.S. Government', a stamp all federal cars have on their vehicle plates. He watched as four guys climbed out of the car and stood in a group speaking. They all wore dark suits, white shirts and ties. Two of them wore long black Mackintosh coats, even though it was a warm night. The only thing missing was the shades to make them the complete stereotypes. He watched as one of the guys walked off in the direction of the reception area and came back a few minutes later appearing animated and excited. All four of them drew their handguns and then the guy who had gone into the reception started pointing towards the first floor room where The Optician knew Ward was sleeping.

He pulled out his cell phone and pressed the number one. Quick dial for Ward.

Ward was woken up from a deep sleep by his cell phone ringing. He turned over and looked at the caller display. It was The Optician.

"Do you honestly never sleep?" he answered.

"It's a good job I don't my friend. You have four visitors."

"They are coming my way?" he asked as he sprung to his feet.

"Not yet but they will be in a moment or two."

"Who are they?"

"Definitely Secret Service," The Optician replied, "They are starting to move now."

"All four of them?"

"Yes. Handguns drawn. Want me to take them out?" he asked, as casually as if he was offering Ward a doughnut.

"No. I need to see who sent them and what they want," he replied.

He picked up his Glock and was pleased to see that the silencer was still attached from earlier. He took the safety off and then stood next to the curtains on the left hand side of the door. Anyone busting into the room would instinctively look towards the bed on the right side of the room.

"Where are they now?" he whispered into the phone.

The Optician watched as two of the guys started to climb the stairs on the left hand side of Ward's room and two on the right.

"Two coming from either side," he said, "I'm going to have to take three of them and leave you one to interrogate if they don't stop moving," he added.

As it was, two of them stopped moving. Two of the guys stopped at the end of the landing as the other two guys slowly approached Ward's room.

"Problem solved," The Optician said down the line, "Two of them have stopped at the end of the landing."

"As soon as the other two bust into my room, take the landing guys out. OK?"

"Understood."

Ward ended the call, turned his phone off and slid it into his pocket.

There were a number of things that made The Optician the best; more than the standard things that people read about snipers, such as controlled breathing, stance, the pressure required on the trigger and the standard wind

and distance assessments. Being the target was for him, the most important thing. He closed his eyes and pictured being in the shoes of the guy who was stood on the left hand side of the landing. He felt him, he felt that they were his shoes and he knew that when he saw the guy at the other end of the landing have his head blown apart, he would duck, without doubt, he would duck. He smiled to himself as he lined up his partner. He was an easy shot. No assessment needed or feeling of being in his shoes, he would have no time to react.
The Optician glanced along the landing and the guys were now only four feet away from Ward's door and they were moving slowly, with their guns pointing at the window. They reached the door and moved back against the railings that ran along the landing.
He had slowed his breathing right down. For his own entertainment, he decided to kill the two guys with his eyes shut.
Just because he could.
He watched out of the corner of his eye, as one of the guys outside Ward's door lifted his boot to kick the door and then he closed his eyes before squeezing his trigger, then he moved his rifle to the right in a split second, dipping it eighteen inches in the process. He opened his eyes. Both guys were down.
He just needed to check that the shots had hit the guys in the dead centre of the forehead as he intended.
They had.

There was a loud crack and the door swung open, one guy stepped into the room four feet and the other guy came in tight behind him.

Ward had his gun raised.
They both looked right.
Straight at the empty bed.
The guy who was standing at the back started to turn his head to the left in Ward's direction, while the guy at the front started lifting his head in the direction of the bathroom.
As the guy at the back caught a glimpse of an object in the corner, Ward pulled the trigger and shot the guy in the centre of the face. His head exploded; a thick spray of blood covering the wall behind him and he started falling sideways, he was dead by the time he was in mid-fall. The guy at the front seemed to move in slow motion and he lowered his gun and shot the guy in the left arm. The guy dropped his gun immediately. He pumped another bullet into the guy at the back, just to make sure he wouldn't miraculously come back to life, and then kicked the front guy's gun away from his reach as he moved forward.
He closed the hotel room door.
The guy was on his side, screaming.
He turned the light on and stood over the guy, his Glock pointing down at him.
"Who sent you?" he asked.
The guy said nothing.
So he shot him in the right arm.
The guy screamed out in agony.
"I know the answer but want to hear it anyway," he said, "So last time, who sent you? Tell me and I'll let you live. I have no axe to grind with you."

"Senator Reid," the guy said through gritted teeth, and screamed again as the pain of the holes in his arms started to intensify.

"No. You are Secret Service, you don't work for Senators," he raised his gun and shot the guy in the leg. The guy screamed in agony. He was unable to move his arms to clutch his leg like instinct dictated.

"We are off duty. We are doing this as a favour."

"You came to kill me as a favour?"

"No. We were told that we have to bring you back to find out where you have hidden some evidence."

"To interrogate me?" he asked.

"We were just doing a favour," the guy replied, appearing to be struggling for breath now.

"Who was the favour for?"

"Lance Williams," the guy replied.

"Who's he?"

"Head of protection."

"For who?"

"The Vice President."

Ward pointed his gun at the guy and shot him three times in the chest and then took the guys phone from his pocket.

He grabbed his bag and walked out of the hotel room, closing the door behind him.

He turned left and walked along the landing and saw a dead guy laying on the floor staring up at him.

He had a perfect hole in the centre of his forehead.

He never misses

The Optician could probably do that with his eyes shut, Ward thought to himself.

The Optician watched Ward walk along the landing, and followed him down the stairs and watched him climb into one of McDermott's black Range Rovers and drive off. He packed his rifle away and started to move off of the roof of the drug store where he had set up. His phone vibrated in his pocket.
He pulled out his phone and looked at the caller display.
It was a cell number he didn't recognise.
He ignored it.
He climbed down from the roof, slung his bag onto his shoulder and climbed onto one of his trusted Kawasaki superbikes that transported him everywhere.
His phone rang again.
It was the same number.
He still didn't recognise it but he pressed answer.
He put the phone to his ear.
"Hello?" a female voice said.
It seemed familiar but he couldn't place it.
"Hello?" the voice said again.
When he heard it the second time, he recognised the voice instantly.
He hung up the phone immediately.
He felt a lump develop in his throat.
It was the first time in over ten years that he had heard that voice.
It was a voice he had missed every day, of every year, in those ten years.
It was his eldest sister's voice.

THIRTY NINE

Washington D.C. - Merrifield

The job of Vice President is a nothing job, similar to Deputy Prime Minister in the U.K. Officially, the Vice President is supposed to preside over the Senate and have the casting vote in a tie, but that never happens. The only other point of the Vice President is to take over from the President if he dies while in office, which is equally as unlikely. Cynics believe that is why all Vice Presidents and Deputy Prime Ministers are always carefully chosen, to be individuals who are incapable of carrying out the role effectively, therefore prompting an immediate election battle. It had generally become a position filled by idiots. The kind of idiots who were so self-centred, that they weren't even aware that the general population viewed their job as a joke role.
Vice President Aaron Wilson was a hopeless politician and a despicable man. He had coat-tailed a ride to the White House on the back of the President's campaign, in

exchange for giving his public support and the financial backing of all of his sponsors.

Ward pulled the Range Rover off of I-66 and stopped in a lay by. He now knew that Wilson was providing support for Reid and that he was as desperate to get his hands on the evidence that he had safely secured in England, as Reid was.

He scrolled through the contacts on the phone that he had taken from the guy in the hotel and found a number with the initials 'LW' above it and so he pressed the call button.

The other end started ringing.

"Status?" a voice answered.

"Not very good I'm afraid," he replied, "They won't be coming back."

"Who is this?"

"It doesn't matter. What does matter is that I know who you are Lance Williams, and that puts you in a very dangerous position."

"You are McNair's guy? Do you realise exactly how bad the position that the line you have stepped over has put you in?" Williams asked.

Ward laughed. It was a genuine laugh.

"You send four of your best men, four of your most loyal men, to kill me and I killed them in my sleep, literally. You think my position is bad?"

"Do you know who we are?" Williams asked, trying to sound as assertive as he could.

"Not yet. But right now my people are ripping your life apart, your parents, family, friends and even your old school teachers. When they have done that, we will decide who we go and kill first," he lied.

"I have the full power of the United States government behind me," Williams replied, managing to retain a calm tone to his voice, a fact which impressed Ward slightly.
"But you don't, do you?"
"I think we do."
He decided to take a gamble,
"You don't. I've just spoken to the President," he said.
Williams' voice was quiet for a lot longer than it should have been.
Far too long.
He knew exactly what was happening now; he could picture the scene clearly.
Williams eventually said,
"You have told the President about this?"
He decided to roll the dice.
"Is Wilson that stupid that he can't talk for himself?" Ward asked.
Another long pause.
"I'm the Vice President of the United States, please afford me the correct respect, and address me appropriately," a voice said. He recognised Wilson's voice immediately.
"You aren't my Vice President Wilson, and I am talking to you as you deserve to be spoken to you piece of shit," he said, "I have you on video, and if I had my way you would be looking down the barrel of my gun now."
"Back off with the threats," William's voice interrupted, "That's a federal offence."
"So is mutilating twelve year old children and violating them sexually, so shut your mouth Williams," he said firmly, "If you piss me off any more, your parents, siblings, wife, although it's unlikely you could find

someone dumb enough to marry you, kids and anyone else who is close to you will be dead before this call is finished. Is that clear?"

A long pause and Ward could hear slight mumbling over the line and then Williams eventually said,

"Clear."

"How about you come and see me yourself Williams?" Ward taunted him to gauge his reaction.

"Anytime you want. Name it?" Williams said.

He smiled to himself, he was rattled.

"Are you still there Wilson?"

"Yes."

"Want to know something?"

No answer.

"Don't piss me off scumbag. Do you want to know something?" he asked again.

"OK," Wilson replied.

"I love this country and I risk my life every day doing the right thing by it and sometimes, against my better judgement, I have to put my feelings aside for, let's call it the bigger picture," he said, "Do you find that admirable?"

"Yes, I suppose I do," Wilson replied.

"A few hours ago, my boss, told me to walk away from this and leave it alone. I reluctantly agreed."

There was silence on the end of the line.

"And a few hours later, you send four guys, four hopeless guys I might add, a fact which is even more insulting, to capture me, interrogate me and then kill me," he added.

"That wasn't me," Wilson said.

"You are the one I am talking to on the phone I took from one of the dead guys."

"No. What I mean is, it wasn't me who sent them. Senator Reid requested some help as he said he knew where you were, I just gave it to him."

"Reid is blackmailing you. Tell me what he wants from you?"

"What do they always want?" Wilson replied.

Ward thought about this. Everything always comes back to money, power and greed in the end.

"He needs you to convince some people to help him in some venture or other that is a money making scheme?"

"More than one, and……"

"Shut up scumbag," he interrupted, "You know, the truth is, I don't even care what it is. It's just always the same with you people, money and power, and you don't care who you hurt and tread over to get it," he added, genuinely becoming irritated now.

There was silence for a good ten seconds.

"And you, Williams," Ward said, "What sort of moral compass do you have, protecting an animal like that. It must make your skin crawl? You know what he has done because you would have been there protecting him. So actually, that makes you as guilty."

"My job is to protect the constitution of the….."

"Save it. Mum, Dad, wife or sibling," Ward said, "Who do you want to die first?"

"Why are you making this so personal to me?" Williams replied.

He could sense the fear, coming through as agitation, in Williams' voice.

"Because it was personal to those poor kids," he said softly.

He then decided to turn the screw a little more before getting to his end game.

"You are just a glorified doorman," he began, "You rarely see any action and you spend your life watching rooftops and doorways. Not very exciting, I get that, but you couldn't always have been so useless. Selection for your field is pretty rigid, I guess, so what were you. F.B.I. or services?" he asked.

"I was Delta Force for five years," Williams replied, convinced there was no point in lying, as the detail Ward had given about his family led him to believe that Ward had his whole career details in front of him.

He smiled to himself. Williams had just given him a perfect answer.

"Have you ever heard of The Optician?" he asked.

He could hear inaudible mumbling again and then Williams eventually said,

"Yes."

"Well he's on my team," he replied, "So you now understand how easily I can take out you, the scumbag next to you, or anyone associated with either of you that I choose?"

Before Williams could answer, Ward continued,

"Scumbag," he said, addressing the Vice President of the United States of America, "I know you are stupid but how can you let Reid blackmail you, I don't get it?"

"He knows how to acquire the video of me for God's sake, what am I supposed to do?" Wilson replied.

As soon as he said the words, everything fell into place. Ward smiled to himself.

"You really are dumb, aren't you?"
"I've made mistakes, yes. But……"
"No," he interrupted, "You really are dumb, aren't you?" he repeated.
"Yes. I guess I am," Wilson replied.
Ward rolled his eyes. How this idiot could seriously be the Vice President of the most powerful nation on earth, was beyond his comprehension.
"Two things," Ward said, "Firstly, none of you will ever find the evidence. Because I put the good of our country first, I have to accept the fact that it will never come out. I will keep it hidden for my own security," he added reluctantly.
"Thank you," Wilson replied.
"It's not for you scumbag. If I forced you to resign after two Senators have just died, people will start digging and I can't take that chance. So it's not for you, it's for the country. If what you and your vile little friends have done ever got out, what little faith is left in politics will be gone for good," he said angrily.
"Two Senators?" Wilson asked.
"Reid will die by the end of the day as well."
"But….."
"Just keep quiet idiot," he interrupted, "And secondly, you've been blackmailed by someone who is as much of a scumbag as you."
"Everyone has always known how devious Senator Reid is," Wilson replied.
This guy really is dumb; Ward thought to himself, he doesn't get it.
Thankfully, Williams did, because Ward was getting very close to losing his patience.

"Are you saying that Reid was involved in the same thing?" he asked.

"Finally," Ward replied, "Someone gets it. I have Reid on video too, committing an equally vile act."

There was a long silence on the end of the line.

"He was using your resources to assist him in covering his own ass, and at the same time, finding the evidence that he could use against you. He was using you to provide him with the evidence to blackmail you" Ward said, "You are one stupid scumbag."

"I gave him use of my men," Williams said angrily.

"Well you have become as stupid as the idiots you protect."

"He's despicable," Wilson replied.

He couldn't be bothered to respond to that comment, he was done with lecturing.

"Right, so we have to move forward. I want Reid. So here's what we will do."

"I'm listening," Williams interrupted.

"Are you listening scumbag?" he asked the Vice President of the United States of America.

"Yes I am," Wilson replied.

"Firstly, you will not let Reid know that you are aware that he is on video too."

"Got it."

"Secondly, you will champion a new initiative to make resources available to tackle the human trafficking crisis, and give new powers to seize assets and money of those proved to be involved. That will at least give you some purpose," Ward said wearily.

"OK," Wilson replied.

"Don't just pay lip service to it Wilson. If I haven't seen you on the TV screens within the next month promoting your new initiative then I will resurface. Is that clear?"

"I promise," Wilson replied; a promise that Ward wouldn't have believed, except that this was about Wilson's own self-preservation, so he knew that he would deliver.

"Next," he continued, "You call my boss and kiss his ass because the only reason you are alive and the video is not all over the news channels, is because of his commitment to our country. I would suggest that you move heaven and earth to give him whatever the hell he wants," he added.

"I will most definitely do that. I promise."

He had no doubt that Wilson would keep to his word; the relief in his voice was now rushing into his ear.

"Williams?" Ward said.

"Here."

"You call all of your men off. I will deal with Reid and end this. The evidence won't ever come out into the public domain; you have my word on that. I will keep it in case I ever need it to protect myself and for that reason alone. Do you believe me?"

"Yes I do," Williams replied.

"I'm sorry about your men."

"So am I. They were good guys with families."

"But you understand that I was just protecting your boss as much as you were, just in a different way?"

He now felt terrible for Williams. He knew the feeling of losing one of his team and he felt awful for what Williams was feeling right now. He would probably have to be the one who would have to make the house calls, to break the news to devastated families.

"I understand. Doesn't make it any easier though," Williams said softly.

"And I lied about your family. I know nothing about you, I was bluffing," Ward added.

"And you lied about The Optician too?"

"No. That part is true."

"Scumbag?" Ward said to get the Vice President's attention.

"Yes?"

The idiot was now even answering to an insulting name. Ward rolled his eyes again.

"You make sure that you compensate the families of those four guys that you sent to their deaths earlier. Not the standard compensation that the government provide, at least two million dollars each. If you don't do that, I'll be coming back," Ward threatened.

"I will. I promise," The Vice President replied.

"You happy with that Williams?" Ward asked.

"As happy as I can be in the circumstances," he replied, "I should have seen this."

"Don't blame yourself," he said, "Every time I am out in the field I too curse myself that I missed something, but the truth is, sometimes it takes a while for things to unravel. So don't beat yourself up too much."

Williams didn't reply.

"And I will ring you in a month. If he hasn't sorted out payment for the families, let me know."

"I promise. I will have it sorted by the end of today," Wilson replied.

"Last thing Scumbag?"

"Yes?"

"You ever go anywhere near a child again, I will hunt you down and kill you. Is that clear?" Ward spat down the phone.

"I promise I won't, thank you so much. I won't let you down. I'm sorry," replied the Vice President of The United States of America, the most powerful nation on earth.

"You had better not scumbag," Ward replied.

And he ended the call.

He then dropped the battery out of the phone, threw it out of the window and pulled away. He drove another three miles and then threw the phone out of the window as he passed a river.

He never wanted to talk to the scumbag again.

FORTY

Washington D.C.

Centrepoint was woken by his cell phone ringing. He looked at the caller display and it simply said 'White House'. All calls from the building were re-routed through their switchboard which showed no caller ID, but he had got one of his tech guys to set up a link to his phone so that he knew when he was receiving calls from the most powerful house in the world.
His first reaction when he saw the display was that Ward had gone against his wishes.
He pressed answer,
"Hello?" he said.
"Sorry to wake you Mr McNair, I have the Vice President on the line for you," a woman's voice said.
There was a click and then a voice said,
"Hello?"
"Good morning Mr Vice President," Centrepoint replied.
"I hope I didn't wake you?"
"No, I was up anyway," Centrepoint lied, "How can I help you?"

"I've just had a very interesting conversation with one of your men," he said, "The British guy."
Centrepoint waited for the complaint to begin.
"And what a remarkable man he is too," he added.
"He certainly is that."
"Anyway, I'm sure you know what he has been working on and where he is with it, so I won't beat about the bush," Wilson began, "I understand from talking to him, that you have been the main factor in dealing with the issue at hand discreetly, and your insistence that none of it comes back to me has led to him discovering that the whole thing was a straightforward blackmail plot against me."
"With all due respect sir, you were most definitely in the wrong here so I have spent most of this week cleaning up your mess," he replied, drawing a line in the sand immediately so that the Vice President remembered who was holding all of the aces.
"Of course, and your support and understanding for one slight mistake is much appreciated. With that in mind I have already spoken to a few colleagues and I understand that Senator Reid passed certain motions, affording you pretty much complete control of black ops and being accountable to no one. Is that correct?"
"Yes it is sir."
"Well I am calling firstly to thank you for your help, and also to let you know that I can see clearly now how important it is that your team have the flexibility to keep certain information to yourself and to not share, even with the President himself, so I have proposed some amendments to the bill that Reid prepared and have made you unaccountable from this day forward. No

more committees or funding requests need to be submitted. And all financial applications will be met, by law, without requiring a breakdown of expenditure and reason. You can continue to keep the identity of your operatives off the books too. I trust that you are happy with this arrangement?" the Vice President asked.
"Certainly sir, it will make keeping our country safe so much easier."
"There is one other thing McNair."
"Yes sir?"
"I believe that your man, the British man is going to visit Senator Reid?"
"He has agreed that Senator Read was off-limits sir."
"When was that?"
"Last night," Centrepoint replied.
"I think that has changed. There was an incident in the early hours of this morning, an unfortunate incident where your man encountered some hostility; hence him calling me. He and I have resolved that matter amicably, but unfortunately Senator Reid has caused way too many problems, so perhaps it would be better if your man is able to resolve this whole matter in the way that he sees fit?"
"As in Senator Reid?"
"Exactly," the Vice President replied.
Centrepoint smiled. His plan had fallen perfectly into place. He now had what he had always wanted, total control of The Deniables, and he could now progress with his long term plan.
"There is one thing I would like your help with sir" Centrepoint said.
"What is it?"

Centrepoint spent the next few minutes explaining in detail what he wanted and why. He requested that the Vice President moved on it immediately as he would need to know if it was possible.
"Of course it's possible. I'm the Vice President of the United States of America," Wilson replied.
"Thank you sir"
"No McNair, thank you. Good job"
And then the line went dead.

Washington D.C. - Merrifield

It was 06:00am when Ward arrived at the warehouse. He parked the Range Rover and went inside. Everyone was already up. McDermott was in his armchair, his entire team were sitting around the table drinking coffee and recalling stories of previous operations, and Buck was sitting on the sofa in a trance like state, looking like he had been dragged through a bush backwards.
"Christ Buck, you look like crap," he said.
"So would you if you had to spend every night sleeping in a car," he replied, "I mean seriously, who doesn't snore?"
"You don't snore Buck, you rattle," McDermott quipped, "You sound like a busted radiator," he added.
"Your wife doesn't complain," Buck replied.
They all laughed.
Ward liked Buck.
"How was your refreshing night in a comfortable hotel?" Buck asked sarcastically.

"Eventful," Ward replied, before giving the team a quick summary of the events that had passed.

"Scumbag?" McDermott asked with raised eyebrows.

"Yes, and I had no idea how stupid the guy is."

"So we've got the green light to take out Reid? Does The Old Man know this?" McDermott asked.

"I'll tell him after," Ward replied.

They all laughed.

"But first things first, I'm hungry. Is there a decent diner around here where we can get some breakfast?" he asked.

"There's one a couple of blocks away," Paul replied.

"Well let's go then. Breakfast is on me."

"But Buck, can you walk ten feet behind us please, because you stink."

They all laughed again

Ward walked over to the laptop that was running on the workbench and logged into his e-mail. He found the file that Eloisa had sent him and printed it out. It was a big file, over forty pages. He decided that he would read it when they were having breakfast and he would call her later.

He missed Eloisa.

Washington D.C.

Centrepoint's cell phone rang for the second time that morning. He didn't recognise the number.

"Yes?" he answered.

"What's going on?" Senator Madison Reid's voice shouted in his ear.

"Specifically?" he asked.
"The Vice President has shut me out. He's overruled the motions I spent days getting passed and made amendments to them that give you more power than any one man should have. He won't answer my calls and neither will his security detail acknowledge my requests to be put through to him. So tell me McNair, what's going on?" Reid spat down the phone.
"You made the wrong choices Senator."
"Meaning?"
"You never should have gone after the hackers."
"Get over that will you, it's getting boring," Reid shouted.
Centrepoint was losing patience fast with Reid. He no longer needed him, the Vice President would make sure that he had all that he needed to run The Deniables however he saw fit, but he wasn't going to give Reid too much of a heads up.
"You sent four men to find my guy last night. You know they were killed I take it?" Centrepoint asked.
Silence on the end of the line.
He didn't know.
Now the whole dynamic of their relationship had changed for good.
"You stupid little man," Centrepoint said. "That was actually the dumbest thing that you could have done. You are on your own completely now. I can't control him. You made it him against you. He does not lose." Centrepoint said, trying to sound as calm and as flippant as he could.
"Then call him off," Reid replied.
"I can't"

"What do you mean you can't for God's sake?"
"He won't listen to me."
"You can't control him? Perhaps it is about time I had you replaced with someone who can then? You've been left to do as you please for too long and now you have gone soft," Reid said.

As much as Centrepoint wanted to tell Reid that he had no need for him anymore; he had learnt over the years that politicians have a bad habit of bouncing back and so he did not want to make an enemy of him, even though he doubted that he would see many more sunrises.

"He's in Washington. I don't know where, but he's here somewhere," Centrepoint said.

"Does he have many men with him?" Read asked.

"Only two," Centrepoint lied, "He doesn't trust too many people."

"What does he look like?"

"He's about six feet tall, dark skinned, Mediterranean looking and he has bleached hair, almost white," Centrepoint lied.

"Anything else?"

"Yes," Centrepoint replied, "I know he's in the Merrifield area."

"Then I will find him myself."

The line went dead.

Washington D.C. – Merrifield

Everyone was in fine form as they all enjoyed their breakfast. McDermott and his team were rounding on

Buck relentlessly and Buck was taking it all in his stride. They had moved from teasing him about his sleeping habits, to his clothes and now they were mocking his inability to eat with his mouth closed.

Ward had now established that every fault Buck possessed was due to the fact that his mother had sold him to a group of travelling performers, for three magic beans that turned out to be pebbles.

Buck was good for the team; his humour was a great source of laughter and enabled the team to be able to relax.

He was reading the file that Eloisa had sent him with interest. The ringleader, Tom Bass, was a nasty piece of work and as soon as they had finished in Washington, he would put his energy into finding this guy and killing him.

His phone rang.

The Old Man's name appeared on the caller I.D. Ward answered immediately.

"I want your word that Nicole-Louise and Tackler are now one million per cent safe and that it is OK for them to come home."

"You have my word. They will no longer be bothered. The Secret Service and all government agencies are now fully aware that they are off bounds completely. Not just now but forever. You can bring them back," Centrepoint replied.

"I'll make the call shortly. Thank you."

"You seem to have made very powerful friends," Centrepoint said, completely ignoring Ward's gratitude.

"Certainly not my friend, but I did listen to you and out of respect for you; I took your advice on board. And then Reid sent some guys to kill me," he replied.

"I know all about it. I spoke to The Vice President this morning."

"You mean the scumbag?"

"One and the same no doubt."

"I'm going after Reid. Did he tell you that?"

"Yes he did but there is no need."

"There is every need."

"No, there really isn't"

"Why?"

"Because I'm sending him to you," Centrepoint replied.

"Meaning?"

Centrepoint explained the content of the conversation that he had just had with Read.

"Bleached hair?" Ward said in bemusement.

"I got carried away with the false description," The Old Man replied, "Anyway, the point is, I can't have you running around in the middle of D.C. close to the Senate buildings and so I thought it was much safer to send him your way."

"You know he has a team, of mercenaries working for him?"

"Yes I do, the Vice President told me. I doubt they're better than you and McDermott. For the money we pay him, I sincerely hope not."

"Of course they aren't, I just don't know how many."

"Eight of them in total I have been reliably informed," Centrepoint said, "I am sending two clean-up crews over to Merrifield now, The Optician is there with you already and he will call the crews in so we can clear the streets quickly."

"I won't say thank you, this could have been sorted days ago if you had trusted me and my judgement."

"I will next time Ryan."

"OK. We will take care of Reid and his men and then we are done. Agreed?"

"Agreed."

"And then I need some time for myself."

"Will you be requesting our resources?"

"Yes."

"While we are talking about Eloisa, I have something to tell you," Centrepoint said.

Ward never liked him using her name. He had always tried to keep Eloisa separate from their work.

"What is it?" he said aggressively.

"She has just been promoted to a senior position within the child protection arm of the U.N. By senior, I mean they have promoted her onto the Executive Committee."

"And why was that? What favours did you have to call in for that?"

"I can't influence that. I have no jurisdiction at all as far as the U.N is concerned."

"So how?"

"It was by recommendation."

"On whose recommendation?" Ward demanded.

"The President of the United States of America and the Prime Minister of Britain."

"And that is done to pacify me and keep me on board I take it? You were a little transparent with that one. Eloisa is totally separate from our work, I have always told you that," he said angrily.

"It can't be separate when you use our resources all of the time, without any dispute and question from me I might add, to tackle the requests that she puts to you. It's a good thing Ryan, don't over-analyse it."

"I'll deal with Reid and then we will discuss it again," he replied and he hung up the phone.

"Problem?" McDermott asked as the others continued to tease Buck, reverting back to his snoring as the point in question again.

"It's Reid. He's sending his team over to Merrifield to hunt us down."

"Howley and his men?"

"Yes. Do you have a problem with that?" Ward asked, "I understand if you don't want to go toe to toe with Ex-Seals."

"They aren't Ex-Seals," McDermott replied, "No real Seal would ever work for a guy like Reid knowing what he has done, and anyway, a couple of years doesn't make you a Seal. It's what you are that does."

"Good. We had best get back to the warehouse to plan to hit the street then, so we are ready for them when they arrive," he said with a smile.

"Are you going to tell The Optician that his brother is coming?" McDermott asked with a big smile.

"Let's keep that between us at the moment; family is a big issue for him right now."

Before McDermott could ask what Ward meant, he stood up and said,

"Time to go gentlemen."

As they walked back to the warehouse, Ward called Mike Lawson,
"Are they with you?" he asked as Lawson answered.
"You owe me big-time."
"Why?"
"I've had to go to at least fifteen clothes shops and then be dragged around London sightseeing for the past two days, and if Tackler says the words 'Sex Pistols' one more time I am going to shoot him."
"Apart from that?" Ward asked, smiling as he spoke.
"It's worse. To keep Tackler happy I had to call up an old flame to play my girlfriend and I've been stuck with her for four days. Do you know how hard it is to have sex with the same woman for four days?"
Ward laughed out loud.
"Give me some good news Ryan, I'm going crazy here," Lawson begged.
"You can bring them home. I want you to deliver them personally. Call The Old Man, he will arrange the transport."
"Let me tell them. I want to see the disappointment in their faces. At least give me that?" Lawson said. He sounded serious.
"See you tomorrow Mike," Ward replied and hung up.

FORTY ONE

Merrifield – Town Centre

Merrifield was a quiet place when you took into consideration it was so close to the nation's capital. It was a place where only a few high rise buildings had been erected, and if you stood in one spot anywhere in the town and turned three hundred and sixty degrees, you would be hard pushed not to be able to see miles into the distance. It was a small town with a population of no more than seventeen thousand people, with a suitably sized police department to serve the population and no more.
It was the perfect place to play hide and seek.
Even more perfect if you knew that the bad guys were coming and they were looking for a six foot Mediterranean guy with bleached blonde hair.
Centrepoint had done one thing right; Ward thought to himself.
They had discussed the plan for spotting Howley and his team back at the warehouse. Ward and Buck would be out in the open, in different places, just doing what

people with nothing to hide do, sipping a beer and drinking a coffee at one of the diners. Howley's men were bound to check these kinds of places out and ask the locals if they have seen anyone fitting the description that Centrepoint had given them. With that in mind, McDermott had broken the team up; with Paul taking the North entrance into the town, McDermott, Wallace and Wired the East, simply because that would be the direction they would be coming into town from D.C., Walsh the South and Fuller the West. Fringe would be positioned in the heart of the town, in the main centre, at an elevated point monitoring the vehicles.
They would communicate via the telecoms system that they always used, radios, small earpieces and miniature microphones, and once they had identified where Howley and all of his team were, they would draw them out to a place where the general public would be, as much as possible, out of harm's way.
The Optician would be wherever The Optician wanted to be and he would call Ward whenever he needed to communicate something of value.
It's what he did,
McDermott dropped Ward down in the town centre at a place called The Sweetwater Tavern. It was a busy place. It served good quality food and lots of different beers. It clearly had a good reputation, as the place was extremely busy. It had the feeling of being that place in the centre of the town that everyone gravitated towards. Ideally, it also had a few tables outside where Ward could sit and drink a cold beer and watch any vehicles approaching. He had a perfect view of all he needed to see.

Sometimes, being the decision maker had its perks; he thought to himself and smiled.
He ordered a cold Bud and went and sat at one of the tables outside in the glorious sunshine.
And waited.

Merrifield – Town Centre

Buck concluded that being the new boy on the team sometimes had its perks. He was sat in a coffee shop, looking out onto the main road through the town, drinking a piping hot Latte. It was hot inside, the midday sun building up temperature by the minute, but he knew he had the best spotting position by a mile. He had a perfect view of the main road in both directions and he fitted in with the locals perfectly.
He mopped yet another bead of sweat from his forehead and thought if only Ward could see him now, he definitely would have chosen the coffee shop.

Merrifield – Town Centre

Fringe was on top of a building in Penny Lane which was in the heart of the town. It was a new apartment building, built out of orange brick with sky blue cladding dotted throughout. He chose the building not only because it gave the best elevated view of the town from all sides, so all roads could be covered; but also because he loved The Beatles and Penny Lane was perfect for him. He sat on top of a meshed fence that protected the highest fan on the roof and peered through his binoculars, three seconds in one direction before turning to the next.

Merrifield – North

Paul McDermott sat in his Range Rover facing the road that led into the town. He could see everyone and everything. He was careful to have a baseball cap tilted down over his face, just in case Howley recognised the resemblance to his father. While he was sitting there, he discovered the ideal place to bring Howley and his men to. There was a large area of waste ground just off of Charing Cross Road, opposite some overflow parking spaces for people who used the adjacent industrial park, and it was quiet, no cars and no people about. Perfect. He informed every one of the place that he had found over the radio. Now they knew where they had to bring the fight to.

Merrifield – South

Walsh was standing on the street on the south side of the town, eating a burger and drinking a coke. He looked like your average construction guy taking a break from a day's hard labour. He sat on one of the benches that lined the street and just looked around aimlessly, like a construction worker would. But his eyes saw everything, every vehicle, every license plate, every driver. If they came into town this way, he would see them.

Merrifield – West

Fuller had eyes on the west side of the town. As luck would have it, he had sat down on a bench and an old guy, well into his seventies, had sat down next to him and started talking football with him. It was a decent conversation too. They looked like a couple of family members out for a walk or a visit, and they would not have invited a second glance from anyone. It was the perfect camouflage. But his eyes were constantly flickering; watching the road into the town, monitoring the drivers, assessing each passer-by on foot to see if they fitted the profile. None of them did. But he kept looking.

Merrifield – East

McDermott, Wallace and Wired had found the perfect place to wait on the east side of the town. Right at the start of the main road into town there was a house that was part way through renovation. As they had pulled up, they had watched the construction workers pack everything into their trucks, secure the property doors and drive off. They wouldn't be coming back. McDermott reversed the Range Rover onto the drive. It looked like it was the resident's vehicle; it was meant to be there and would not warrant a second look. They could see the road perfectly in both directions and the view from the road to the drive was partly concealed by a sign welcoming people to Merrifield. They sat and watched patiently. They had been there no more than twenty minutes when Wired said,

"This looks interesting."
McDermott and Wallace looked in the direction that Wired was looking.
Three Sedans were driving slowly along the road coming into town. They were no more than ten feet apart.
McDermott pulled his baseball cap down and studied the vehicles. When they were virtually opposite them, he strained to look inside the car.
Mark Howley, with his bright red head and pale skin, was sitting in the front of the car looking straight ahead, determination etched on his face. There were two other people in the car with him. In the second car there were three guys and in the third, three more.
A total of nine.
Their nine against our nine, plus The Optician,
Poor Mark Howley.

Merrifield – Town Centre

Ward heard McDermott's voice over the radio,
"Three grey Sedans, nine guys. They are here, coming in slowly from the east. Everyone monitor and report, slowly make your way in."
Ward took another sip of his ice cold beer.
He took out his phone and called The Optician.
"I know they are here," he answered.
"How?"
"Because I always tune into your radio frequency," he replied.
Ward smiled to himself.
"So you know we need to get them to the North side of the town. Any ideas how?"

"Sure, look behind you next to the fire exit," The Optician said and the phone went dead.
Ward slowly turned, so as not to arouse suspicion, and then stopped when he reached a table with two guys who were sitting down sharing a drink.
He could not believe what he was seeing.
One of the guys was short, had a shaved head and was wearing a bright orange vest.
The other guy was wearing a white shirt.
He was about six feet tall.
He was of Mediterranean origin.
He had bleached blonde hair.
"Paul," Ward said urgently into his microphone, using his hand in front of his mouth in an apparent attempt to stifle a cough as he spoke, "Come in and collect the boys and get them to the north side of the town. McDermott come to the Sweetwater now."
"Four minutes," McDermott replied over the airwaves.
Ward took another sip of his cold beer from the bottle and turned in his chair slightly so that he could face the guy who met Centrepoint's description perfectly. The likelihood of there being someone, sitting in the dead centre of the town, exactly at the time that Howley hit Merrifield, looking exactly how Ward was supposed to look, was almost impossible, and Ward afforded himself a discreet smile at the ridiculousness of it.
On one hand, it was a disaster, An innocent guy, out for a drink with a pal, who was about to be confronted by a team of Ex-Navy Seals, would most definitely end up dead simply because of the way he looked. On the other hand it was a blessing. Because if Ward could get him out in the street, just long enough for Howley to catch a

glimpse of the guy, and then get him out of harm's way, they could drag Howley's team over to the north side of the town.

"They are just coming into the town centre," Buck said over the radio.

"I have them too," Fringe confirmed from his elevated position.

"Three minutes," McDermott said.

It was time for Ward to make his move. He had no plan. How do you ask a stranger in a bar that you needed him to follow you down to the roadside to be visible to a bunch of mercenaries that are in town to kill him?

He took one more sip of his beer and placed the bottle on the table. He stood up and threw five bucks down to settle his tab and then casually walked across to where the two guys were sitting.

As he got closer, he realised that the two of them looked a lot younger than they did from a distance. To say they were both in their mid-twenties would be pushing it slightly too far.

"Hey," he said to the two guys.

They both nodded a friendly welcome at him.

"Are you two guys locals?" Ward asked, his British accent most definitely convincing them both that he was a tourist, and therefore warranted a friendly Merrifield welcome.

"All our lives," the guy with the bleached hair confirmed with a smile.

"Do you know where Charing Cross Road is?" Ward asked, "I have to visit it while I'm here. I actually live in Charing Cross Road in London. Can you believe that? I have to get a picture near the road sign."

The guy in the bright orange vest spoke,
"Walk down there and when you get to the end of that road, turn left and follow it to the end," he said, pointing to the main road and then moving his arm to the right to indicate the direction that Ward needed to go.
The guy was assertive and clear in what he was saying. He sounded like he was giving an order as opposed to instructions.
Ward suddenly realised that he had just gotten very lucky.
"You are in the services?" he asked.
"Yes sir, I am. United States Marine Corps," the guy replied proudly as he puffed out his chest.
"One and a half minutes," McDermott said.
"We are at the meet point now," Wallace's voice echoed immediately after.
"We are all mobile," Paul confirmed.
Ward studied the guy with the bleached hair. He was definitely not in the services.
"How long have you been a marine?" Ward asked the guy in the orange top.
"Three years sir," he replied.
"I need your help."
The guy looked at him quizzically, looking Ward up and down. The guy with the bleached hair did the same.
"Your friend," Ward said, "Can I borrow him for five minutes?" he asked.
The guy with the bleached hair interrupted,
"What are you, a freak?" he said, moving his chair slightly back as he spoke.

"Whatever your bag is pal, you are looking in the wrong place," the marine said, moving his chair back at the same time, ready to pounce if Ward made a move.

"You aren't understanding me," Ward said, "I need to borrow you both for five minutes, that's all. If you don't help me, there's a good chance that you will be dead within the next two minutes."

The marine stood up and turned to face Ward. He was only about five seven but he looked extremely solid and toned, as you would expect a marine to look. He clenched his fists.

"I'm giving you the opportunity here to tell your friends the most incredible story when you get back to base," Ward said.

"Beat it freak," the guy with the bleached hair said and stood up as well.

The marine looked into Ward's eyes. He then realised immediately that he was looking into the eyes of a killer, he had seen that look before on the faces of the senior marines.

"You won't be in any danger at any point. You simply stand next to me, jump in our car, head to Charing Cross Road and then you are done."

"Get lost or we will make you," the bleached haired guy said.

Ward played his trump card.

"Right now there are nine guys rolling into town hunting for me, all ex-special forces guys. Unfortunately, they think I look exactly like your friend. So the safest place you could be right now is with us."

"Us?" they both asked at the same time.

"There are eight of us and one very unique person that I am assuming you will have heard of. We need to get them out of the town and over to Charing Cross Road so that innocent people don't get caught up in the crossfire," Ward said, "You will be doing your country a great service and if you give me your name, I'll make sure that your superiors find out how you helped. A short journey, that's all."

"One minute," McDermott said.

"They are heading your way," Fringe said, "thirty seconds and they will be on top of you."

The guys looked at Ward putting his hand to his ear and they then saw the earpiece lodged inside.

"It's now or never guys," he said.

"How do I know we will be safe?" the bleached haired guy asked; clearly frightened by the whole experience.

"Because the other guy with us is called The Optician," Ward replied.

"For real?" the marine asked, his eyes widening as soon as Ward mentioned him by name.

"There's your story," Ward replied.

"Holy shit! OK, what do we need to do?"

"Just follow me," Ward said and turned to walk away.

"I'm not going with him," the bleached haired guy said.

"If you don't you will be dead in less than a minute from now."

They both followed, still in discussion. He pulled his Glock from his pocket, just in case.

Then he saw the three Sedans coming towards them, one hundred feet away.

"Twenty seconds," McDermott said into Ward's ear.

"We are all on the north side now," Paul's voice confirmed.
He hoped that they would not take a shot as soon as they saw them. He was well aware that right now, they were sitting ducks.

Mark Howley saw them first. Three guys, one in an orange top, the guy they were hunting for and another guy, who to his trained eye, looked different.
Being in control at all times and of everything, was crucial to Howley; impulsive decisions led to mistakes and he didn't make mistakes. Such was his need for control that even his men were referred to as a number rather than a name. He felt it kept order.
The other guy with them looked different. His senses told him that a proper assessment needed to be carried out before he made any rash decisions. It was too good to be true. Just as they rolled into town the three guys they were looking for appear? Luck is never that kind to anyone.
"The guy with the hair and the one in the orange top look very young sir, maybe too young?" Number three, who was driving the lead car, said.
"Drive past and then turn around by the lights and come back so we are on the same side of the road," Howley demanded.
They reached the lights and did a U-Turn, as they started heading back towards the three guys, a black Range Rover appeared from the other side of the road, screeching to a stop in front of the three guys who promptly jumped into the vehicle and it sped off in the direction of the north side of town.

"Go, go," Howley screamed, "Do not lose them," he added, as he picked up his Colt M4 machine gun from the foot well of the passenger seat.

FORTY TWO

Merrifield

McDermott sped onto Gatehouse Road at seventy miles per hour; it was risky driving taking into account the early afternoon traffic, but not as risky as confronting Howley's team in a public place. The three Sedans were in hot pursuit, no more than two hundred feet away and as Ward turned to look at the chasing vehicles, he could see Howley's red head in the lead car, even though he was too far away to make out a face.
"Everyone in position," McDermott said into the microphone.
"Just pulling up now," Paul replied over the airwaves, "Take them right to the end of Charing Cross Road, where it turns into Le Havre plaza, and we will take them from the side and behind," he added.
"When can we get out?" the guy with the bleached hair asked, panic rushing through his voice.
"You don't need to get out, you will just stay here in the car where you are safe," Ward replied.

"Give me a gun, I can help," the marine said, the total opposite tone in his voice to his friend, excitement and determination.

He wasn't going to involve a civilian in the confrontation with Howley, even a civilian who was in the marines and was more than likely able to help, so he declined the offer,

"You have no authority here so I am going to have to insist you stay in the car," he confirmed.

The guy grunted something and Ward noticed the guy with the bleached hair nudge him on the arm as if to tell him to stop talking.

McDermott jumped a red light as he shot through the crossroads with Gallows Road and just missed a white pick-up truck, which luckily braked at the last moment to avoid hitting him. The Sedans followed, getting closer, maybe only one hundred feet away now, the lead Sedan swerving around the pick-up at the last moment too.

"We're in position, bring them in," Paul's voice said in Ward's ear.

"Two minutes," McDermott replied.

Ward had his Glock ready,

"Stop at the end, swing around and let me out. And keep these two safe and out of harm's way," he said to McDermott.

"Any chance you can leave Howley to me?" McDermott asked, more in hope than in expectation.

"No chance. I'm hoping his brother turns up to the party," Ward replied and McDermott laughed.

The Range Rover turned off of Gatehouse Road and onto Charing Cross Road. By now, McDermott had increased his speed to eighty miles an hour, as much to try and

keep the distance from the chasing Sedans as to gain a few seconds of time to get Ward out of the vehicle.
McDermott pushed the Range Rover up to ninety as he sped up Charing Cross Road, past the Amway Distributor warehouses, and towards the end of the road where it turned into Le Havre Plaza.
The Sedans kept pace, and then some, as they were now only sixty feet behind.
When McDermott reached the end of the road where it turned, he hit the brakes and applied the handbrake. The Range Rover spun around and Ward opened the door while it was still sliding, and jumped out and over a small wall and into the cover of the wasteland, where he sprinted ten feet and crouched behind a thick shrub just as the three Sedans screeched to a standstill, all laid out in a neat little line.

And then Paul and the rest of the team well and truly took over.
An explosion echoed through the air and the rear Sedan instantly caught fire, three guys jumped out of the car and they were met with a prolonged burst of fire from three machine guns, each of the guys taking at least seven bullets, and their upper torsos exploded in a sea of red mist.
One Sedan down.
The next volley of noise ripped through the air and the second car took the full force of five machine guns. Windows shattered and metal ripped apart and the three guys inside never stood a chance. For good measure, Ward saw Wired throw a grenade into the car's window

out of the corner of his eye. The explosion followed almost immediately.

Two Sedans down.

Ward could see Howley from his position behind the shrub. He was not looking in Ward's direction; he was twisting himself around in panic. His Sedan could not move forward, as McDermott was blocking the route with the Range Rover between the wall and the parked cars, and behind him, two Sedans burned.

He was trapped.

And then he did what only a coward would do.

Without any protest or hint of a fight, he stepped out of the car, threw his M4 on the floor and held his hands high up in the air. The driver stepped out and a moment later, so did the guy who was riding in the back. Guns were thrown on the floor and hands were raised in the air.

McDermott looked at them with disgust from inside the Range Rover. They were a disgrace to the Seal name.

The whole thing had taken less than forty seconds.

Three Sedans down.

Ward pulled out his phone and dialled the number.

"You don't need me," The Optician answered.

"You see that guy with the red head?"

"It's hard not to."

"He's been spreading rumours about you?" he said.

"What sort of rumours?" The Optician asked.

"He's earned a lot of kudos claiming to be your brother. He's dined out on the claim for years."

"Let me take him out."

"I need to talk to him first."

"You have three minutes" The Optician replied and the line went dead.

Paul, Wired, Fuller, Wallace, Fringe, Walker and Buck appeared from the thick trees that were thirty feet from the road, machine guns pointing firmly at the three guys. Ward came out from behind the shrub, jogged forward and jumped over the wall.

"Take them back," Ward said to McDermott.

The two guys in the back of the Range Rover had now replaced any fear they had felt with curiosity and excitement. Ward could see the marine say something to McDermott as he started to slowly pull off.

"On your knees and hands above your heads," Ward demanded.

All three of them promptly did as they were instructed to do. As Wired moved in and picked up their guns, kicking the guy who was kneeling to Howley's left hard in the face as he did so.

Such was the brutality of Wired's kick, it totally unnerved Howley. This long, thin, bright red headed guy now looked pathetic kneeling before Ward, with fear etched all over his face.

"Are you still picking up our radio frequency my friend?" Ward asked into his microphone.

"Yep," The Optician's voice came back after a few seconds.

"That was my friend I was just talking to," Ward said, looking down at Howley, "I think you know him. Very well in fact."

Howley looked at Ward blankly.

"You've followed me all over the country to protect some sick, vile, politician's ass," he started, "What sort of person do you think that makes you?"

Howley didn't answer.

"You were a Seal, right?"

Howley nodded.

"You know who that guy there is?" Ward said, pointing to Paul.

Howley studied him for a few seconds. Ward noticed the look of familiarity creep across his face but not confirmation.

"Any of these?" he asked, pointing towards the others.

Howley looked at them, the same look on his face.

"You know why you sort of recognise them but you don't?"

Howley said nothing.

"Because they are all Ex-Seals," Ward continued. "The best ones actually, and the thing about being the best is that you don't need to shout about it, you just do it."

Howley sensed there was a get out here, after all, Seals stuck together, once a Seal, always a Seal was their belief.

"If I knew that you were Seals, I would never have taken the mission," Howley replied defensively.

"I'm not a Seal, never was," Ward replied, "I wasn't good enough."

"I was never a Seal either. I can't swim," Buck added.

Ward smiled.

"They should have a problem killing you right? But they don't, because you knew what Reid did to those children and it made no difference to you. Money is money, right?"

Howley didn't answer. He just knelt beneath Ward looking unsure of where the conversation was going.
"How many men does Reid have protecting him when he is in his house?" Ward asked.
"Just us," Howley replied.
"And you were meant to call him when you found me?"
"When we killed you, yes."
"Ring him now and tell him that you have found us but you will not be able to hit us until it gets dark, but you have me under your expert surveillance and there is no way we can move. If you see us move, you will have to kill us in public. And tell him that you need to avoid that to keep him well out of things. Is that clear?"
Howley nodded.
"Do it now," he demanded.
Howley took out his phone and made the call to Reid. He quoted almost word for word what Ward had told him to say. He clearly wasn't dumb, his only way out was to change sides immediately, and he knew that.
He was a coward.
"As soon as it's done, I'll ring," Howley said and he ended the call.
Ward flicked his microphone to open, and then he stepped back about ten feet from Howley.
"Do you want the right or left first?" Ward asked.
Howley looked at him blankly.
"It's a simple question. Pick one. Right or left first?" he repeated.
"Right I guess," Howley replied.
As the words left his lips, a 7.62mm bullet slammed into the dead centre of the forehead of the guy kneeling next to him to his right. There was very little blood, just a

perfect hole where the bullet had entered his brain. The guy slumped forward, landing face first into the tarmac. Howley scrambled back slightly and the guy to his left immediately jerked back, as an equally perfectly aimed 7.62mm bullet formed a precise hole on his left temple. The guy's body lunged to the right, and the spray from the entrance hole covered the left side of Howley's face. He froze and then positioned himself with one hand on the floor supporting his weight and the other protecting his face.

"You weren't a very good Seal, I see that," Ward started, "But you weren't a very good brother either, were you?" he added.

Howley looked at him with desperation on his face. He had no idea what Ward was talking about,

And then a voice echoed in Ward's ear,

"Let him run," The Optician said, "Drive away and leave him to me. Let him run."

He looked at Howley, he was a pathetic sight.

"Let's go," he said to Paul, Buck and the others. They nodded. They all understood exactly what was happening.

"You can go now," he said to Howley, "But first, I need to tell you something."

Howley looked confused.

"You only have a couple of minutes to live and the person who is going to kill you is someone who is very close to you, so you should know what he is capable of."

"Someone who is close to me? Who?" Howley asked; desperate to make a run for it as he watched Paul and the others walk away towards the Range Rover, as

McDermott came driving back into view in the other vehicle.

Ward noticed Howley's urge to run and smiled,

"He wants you to run," he said.

"Who? Who are you talking about?"

"The Optician," he replied, "You know, the one who you've been telling the world is your brother," he added as he turned and walked away.

Howley went white.

And then he scrambled to his feet and sprinted behind a blue pick-up that was parked fifteen feet away.

The Optician picked up his rifle and sprinted to his right twenty yards. He then slid down the bank until he reached the wall that surrounded the car parking area.

Howley lay flat on the floor and looked under the pick-up, craning his neck to try and catch a glimpse of movement.

Howley saw nothing.

The Optician watched as Howley lay flat and twisted his body, trying to catch a glimpse of him.

The Optician saw everything.

He raised his rifle, set his sights on Howley's right knee and squeezed the trigger.

A 7.62mm bullet hitting your kneecap is about the most painful, non-fatal shot that the human body can experience. The bullet smashed into Howley's knee and he instantly felt a pain that seemed to affect every nerve in his gangly frame. His kneecap shattered into a hundred pieces and he let out a scream that seemed excessively high-pitched. He rolled onto his back and clutched his knee.

He struggled to compose himself through the excruciating pain that was consuming him, as his instinct to survive kicked in, but he managed to turn his head to the left and search for a glimpse of his attacker.
But Howley saw nothing.
The Optician watched as Howley rolled onto his back and adjusted his head to look twenty yards to his left. Howley was blind, he could not see him.
But The Optician saw everything.
He ran a further twenty yards to his right, skipped over the car park wall and darted across the tarmac thirty feet, past three rows of parked cars, and then slowly moved forty feet to the left and stopped exactly three rows of cars directly behind Howley.
Howley was flat on his back, with his knee curled up and clutched in both of his hands, looking under the blue pick-up truck to the right of the bank.
The Optician laid flat on the floor, set his sights and fired a single shot into Howley's right arm.
He instantly let out another high-pitched scream, let go of his shattered knee and clutched his upper right arm with his left hand to try and ease the pain of the shattered bone and torn muscle.
The pain throughout his body was now so severe that he was struggling to remain conscious. He looked right and then left, his head moving in desperation and panic, trying to see someone, anything.
But Howley saw nothing.
The Optician stood up, walked slowly past the first row of cars and he could hear Howley's groans becoming louder and longer. He passed the second row of cars and Howley's desperate breathing was now the

overwhelming noise that he could hear; short, sharp, loud breaths. He walked past the third row of cars and stepped out into the gap between the parked cars six feet away from Howley, then stopped.

Howley tilted his head back and then twisted his body around so that he was lying flat on his stomach.

Howley saw everything.

He looked up at The Optician and despite the pain that was ripping through his entire body; he still felt the urge to study him. The Optician watched as Howley looked up at him, fear etched over his entire face but curiosity in his eyes.

But Howley did not recognise The Optician. He just saw a guy who was totally unnoticeable, nothing spectacular or memorable about him at all. Howley almost felt disappointed. But then reality set back in and he realised that he was going to die very soon.

"Do you have a family?" The Optician asked.

"I only said we were related once and that was just for a joke," Howley lied, desperation running through his voice.

"I lost my family a long time ago. Do you think that if I could choose my family again, I would pick someone like you?" The Optician quietly asked.

"I didn't mean any offence," Howley said through gritted teeth, the pain in his body intensifying with every passing second.

"You have no morals or principals. They were children. And you chose to work for that scumbag Senator and so you made the choice to die," The Optician said as he raised his rifle and pointed it at Howley's head.

"Please, don't," Howley begged.

The Optician squeezed the trigger. The bullet smashed into the exact centre of Howley's forehead and his head kicked back, as bone and brain matter spurted two feet forward, and then it fell to the front and smashed into the tarmac.

He turned to his left and saw two black vans speeding towards the end of Charing Cross Road where he was standing; the clean-up crew were here.

He dropped his rifle to his side and headed briskly in the direction of where he had parked his Kawasaki. He felt his cell phone vibrate in his pocket and pulled it out, expecting to see Ward's or Centrepoint's name appear on the screen, but all he saw was a new number that he didn't recognise. There were very few people in the world that had his number and he was curious how his sister had found him, so he pressed the answer but didn't speak.

"Hello?" a male voice said.

"How have you all got my number?" he asked.

It was the first time he had heard his brother's voice in over ten years.

FORTY THREE

Merrifield

Ward and the team arrived back at the warehouse. They had spent the journey back laughing at McDermott recalling the conversation that the Marine and his bleached haired friend were having in the Range Rover, when he was taking them back to The Sweetwater Tavern. The Marine had wanted to go back to assist the team and fight and the bleached haired guy had offered him two hundred bucks not to.

They all got out of the cars as the roller shutter doors were closing and Ward stepped into the reception area and closed the door.

He had to call Eloisa and tell her that she had been promoted simply to pacify him, and that there was so much corruption and dishonesty in the world they lived in that he just felt like walking away.

He took out his cell phone and dialled her number.

"Hello?" she answered. She sounded different, more vibrant and alert.

"Hey," Ward said.

"Oh my God Ryan, you will not believe what has happened," she excitedly said down the line, almost shouting, "I've been appointed to the executive committee!"

"Eloisa?" he began.

"Do you realise how amazing that is?" she asked.

Ward said nothing.

"All of the hard work I have put in over the last few years has finally paid off. I am so proud of myself and I love you so much because you have helped me so much!"

"Eloisa?" he said again, his voice sounding flat.

"I am so excited. I have never been so happy in my life. They called a meeting this morning and they said that they had been so impressed with me from the day that I started working for them, that they had anticipated that I would make the committee one day, but such has been the impact that I have made, they were bringing the promotion forward by three years. Can you believe that?" she said without pausing for breath.

There was something in her voice, a total sense of achievement and happiness that he had never heard before. She sounded younger and more energetic than she normally sounded. But most of all, she sounded happy.

She sounded happier than he had ever heard her sound.

"That's great news Eloisa, but…"

"Do you realise what this means?" she interrupted, "After the initial twelve months where I set up my team and consolidate my position on the committee, we can start to live a normal life. Do all of those things that we have always spoken about. We can live in New York and be like normal people. I am so excited. I am so happy and I love you so, so much. Your assistance in taking down so many bad people has influenced their decision, I know that and I love you so, so much for that. Thank you, thank you, thank you," she added, still not pausing for breath.

This was all wrong, all so very wrong, he thought to himself. She had been promoted simply because the Vice President wanted to pacify him and make sure that he would never reveal the things that he knew. He had all of the evidence secure and hidden, and only he, McDermott and Lawson would ever know where it was and what it was. He wanted to tell her. He knew the right thing to do was to tell her, in essence, they were manipulating her too.

But he couldn't.

She sounded so happy and alive and the promise of the normal future that he so desperately wanted with her now seemed to be a reality, within touching distance, more than a daily fantasy that he ran through his head. So in the end, he did what was the right thing to do by her.

"I am so happy and proud of you," he said, feigning excitement in his voice as well as he could, "I love you so much too. It is all your work; the things I have done are small compared to what you have done. You are amazing, inside and out and I am so proud of you," he added.

"I knew you would be as happy and excited as me," she replied, "We are a team, we have done this together. Initially, they called me to discuss the Tom Bass information that I gave you on the guy in Colorado but they just hit me out of the blue with it. God, I am so happy!"

Ward felt a wave of anger rush through his body.

How could he tell her after hearing how happy she was? He couldn't crush her dreams. They were a team, an exceptional team, he knew that, and he had no doubt that her merits alone deserved the promotion, but it was a tool simply to pacify him.

But only he knew it.

"I'm almost done here now, I can then put my efforts into this guy in Colorado," was all he could think of saying.

"And after that, we have our time together in New York. Promise me that Ryan? Whatever you are asked to do or where they want you to go, you make time for us. I am desperate to see you and I want to celebrate with you. I want to do everything with you, for a whole week. And I mean everything… I love you so much. You are my world."

Ward smiled for the first time during the conversation. He felt the love that she had for him flow down the line and he felt a calm wash all over him. He decided there and then, that rather than think negatively about her promotion, he would feel proud of her, and of his part in it to a degree; that the most powerful people in the world influenced events that would have a positive and long – term effect on both of their lives.

"I can't wait to see you. I should be finished with your guy in Colorado in a few days and then I will be with you," he replied.

"Good. And hurry up. I want you, I need you and I love you so much," she replied, "Ring me later; I have a meeting to attend. A committee meeting no less," she added, and then followed the comment with her sweet, perfect giggle down the line.

"I will. I love you," he said, still smiling to himself.

"I love you too Ryan. Thank you," she replied and then the line went dead.

He felt a mixture of emotions as he stood in the reception area, leaning against the desk, some of them frustrating, but mainly he felt happy. He would let it go. He had trained himself well in how to let things go, he would not be able to function as effectively on his missions if he carried things over.

He had one more visit to make, to end this and then he was done.

His phone rang. He looked at the caller I.D. and saw The Optician's name appear.

He pressed answer.

"Did Howley cry like a girl?" Ward asked.

"Don't they always?" The Optician replied and then went silent.

"We have one more person to see in a few hours," he said.

"OK"

Then there was silence.

"Everything OK?" he asked.

"How did you find them?" he asked.

Ward knew immediately what he meant.

"I didn't find them. I have no idea who they are and I have no intention of finding out. I gave you my word on that," he replied.

"Then how?"

"Tackler found them after I had asked him to. No one else knows, not even The Old Man. You have my word on that."

Silence on the line again.

"Have they contacted you?" Ward asked.

"My brother and big sister have."

"And? What did they say?"

"I'm not very good at this type of thing. And I'm not sure exactly what they were told."

"Shall I explain?"

"Yes."

"After our conversation the other day, I realised that you have sacrificed so much for so many people and no one knows. So many people sleep safely in their beds at night because of your actions and yet none of them know that you even exist. We live and work in a shitty world, don't we?" Ward asked.

Silence on the line.

"You've lost your family through no fault of your own, they were taken away from you and worse than that, they have no idea that you are one of the biggest heroes our country has ever had," Ward continued.

Silence on the line.

"So I asked Tackler to find them and to tell them what the country owes you and how proud they should be of you."

"And the money?" The Optician asked.

"We had four million dollars floating around that we took from The Bahia Shipping Company and I figured your four siblings deserved a million each after having been deprived of their brother for the past ten years or so."

"I'm an uncle seven times over," The Optician replied.
"You are a hero a thousand times over. But no one knows that. So maybe they can know who their uncle is, that is something you can share with the world," Ward replied.
"The money has changed all of their lives," The Optician said.
"Not as much as having their brother and uncle back will. You've looked after me so many times that I can't remember, and that is apart from the times that you have done it without me knowing. You saved Tackler and Nicole-Louise's life and McDermott and all of us think of you as family, you know that. So for once, I wanted to look after you and those close to you. If I was wrong, I was wrong, but families don't always get it right. Sometimes family members make the wrong choices for the right reasons. I wanted to do the right thing by my family; you and I made a choice. Just like you did by walking away from your family because you felt what happened was your fault. You were wrong. On this one, I don't think I am," Ward said, softly, slowly and calmly.
"You didn't tell them what I do?"
"No. I gave a simple message to Tackler to send to them and deposit the money in their accounts. It's all untraceable, he guaranteed me that."
"What was the message?"
"There has been one million dollars deposited in your current account courtesy of the U.S. government. The deposit has been made in recognition of outstanding and continued service by your brother and this payment reflects a small minority of the good that he has done for the United States of America," Ward replied, "It was that

short and simple. You can then give them whatever cover story you want."

"How did they get my cell number?"

"I told Tackler to attach it to whatever form he contacted them in."

Silence on the line.

"You have an opportunity here to start again," Ward said, "Just take it. You've more than earned it."

"I'm not good at this stuff," The Optician replied, "But thank you."

Ward felt a rush of happiness wash over him.

"So you aren't going to kill me, right?" Ward asked, and then laughed.

"No. Well not today at least," he replied.

"When are you planning on meeting up with them?"

"This weekend."

"Good. We have to pay Reid a visit now, then I could do with some help in Colorado," Ward replied.

"You're on. Send me the file when we are done with Reid."

"I'll send you his address."

"No need," The Optician replied, "I'm already there. The housekeeper has just left."

Ward smiled to himself.

Then the line went dead.

He walked back into the main warehouse and approached McDermott,

"The Optician is already at Reid's house and there won't be any resistance. I want to go there and get into his house and wait for him. Then I am going to make him suffer in ways that he couldn't imagine."

"Who do you want with you?" McDermott asked.
"I don't need anyone but I have noticed that this has affected quite a few of your guys more than usual."
"Not just them. Me too," McDermott replied.
"So, I think it is only right that you ask them who wants to come, do you agree?"
McDermott turned and looked at his team and Buck. They were all sitting at the table now drinking coffee, while Buck sat on the sofa drinking his alone, banished once again.
"We need to visit Reid now. Last port of call," Ward said, moving his eyes to make eye contact with all of them as he spoke, "I don't need support but if any of you want to come, you are welcome to join me."
Every single one of them raised their hand without speaking.
Ward looked at McDermott who raised his right arm too.
"Point taken," he said, "I guess that we can all take turns beating him to death."
"No. I have a much better idea than that," Buck replied, "I picked up some very good techniques during my time in Russia," he added.
"Such as?"
"I'll explain on the way. I just need some pliers, an adjustable spanner and a bottle of vodka," he replied, "And lots of salt," he added.
Ward smiled.

FORTY FOUR

Woodland Drive, NW Washington

It had only taken them twenty five minutes to drive from Merrifield to Reid's house on Woodland Drive. It was close to the United States Naval Observatory. His house was smaller than Calvinson's had been, but was still only affordable in the wildest dreams of most normal people. It was set back about fifty yards from the road and was built on top of a bank that rose steeply from the level of the road. In the garden, a thirty foot flagpole proudly flew the stars and stripes flag. The house itself was built out of red brick and it had four grand white pillars that held up a red tiled roof, creating a grand entrance through the front door. The front of the house had a five foot wrought iron fence running along the perimeter and there were two breaks in the fence. One where a gate was hung, which opened up onto a long path up to the front door, and to the left of it, a break that opened up to a long tarmac drive that led around the back of the house. McDermott drove past the house in the Range Rover, with Paul following in the car behind. The street was completely empty. It wasn't the kind of neighbourhood where people walked up and down the street. They would have their chauffeurs drive them. They drove down to the bottom of Woodland Drive and parked. Ward had noticed on the way down to the end of the road that there was only one house on the left hand side of Reid's place and the lush and full garden offered sufficient cover and protection for the team to creep through the garden, over the fence at the rear of the house and onto Reid's property.

They moved around the back of the house, covered by the thick shrubs and trees and the house was quiet. Ward was pretty sure that no one was in, but he remained hidden by the natural camouflage of the garden just in case.

They reached the wrought iron fence that marked the back of his property and climbed over. Ward knew that the house was empty. The Optician would have told him otherwise, but to make sure, he checked his phone. No missed calls.

They approached the back door and stopped. There were CCTV cameras that were positioned at four different points along the back of the house, and three that they could see down the side. There were two alarm boxes on the gable end of the house and Ward was pretty sure that the alarm system would be linked not only to a security company, but directly to the local police.

"You have a way around that?" he asked Wallace.

"Child's play," Wallace replied as he took off his rucksack and pulled out a small hand held device that looked like a mini laptop. He moved along the back of the house until he came to a panel on the wall which was locked. He took out a device that looked like a corkscrew to Ward, inserted it into the lock, turned it and the door opened.

He then leant inside, and connected an alligator clamp to a wire and started typing into his hand held device. Just under two minutes later, he said,

"It's disabled."

"All alarm systems?" Ward asked.

"All systems, CCTV and auto calls to the police and security company," he replied.

Wallace picked up his rucksack and put the mini laptop back inside, walked along to the back door of the house and then inserted the corkscrew looking object into the lock, and after struggling for a few seconds, turned it sharply and then pushed down on the door handle.

The door opened.

They all stepped inside, Buck being the last one, and he closed the door.

"Go and take care of the CCTV footage," McDermott said, "Make sure that no one will ever know we were here."

Wallace nodded and walked through the kitchen and through a door which led into the house; Fuller and Fringe followed him, with their guns out and pointing in front of them.

They were always prepared. Even in an empty house.

"Check the rest of the house," McDermott said to Paul.

He walked through the kitchen door with Buck, Walsh and Wired following him, leaving Ward and McDermott in the kitchen.

"You do realise that people are going to be asking a lot of questions as to how two Senators have died within a couple of days of each other. People will be investigating if there were any links between them and they will probably find that Calvinson was linked through committees to Reid," McDermott said.

"I don't care. The Old Man can sort it out. Once we are done here I will call him and tell him. That's his crap to deal with."

Paul came back into the kitchen and said,

"The house is all clear. You should see the rooms, how one person can live in all of this is ridiculous."

Paul turned and walked out of the kitchen and Ward and McDermott followed.

They walked into a grand foyer that had an open staircase leading up to the first floor, splaying out wider as it reached the top and there were nine doors leading into different rooms on the ground floor.

One of the doors was open and Ward could see Wallace knelt on the floor with his mini laptop connected to what looked like a computer hard drive, erasing any evidence that the team were ever there.

They walked up the stairs and reached the first floor. Buck was standing in the doorway of a room and Ward approached him.

"Do you think he carried out his sick acts on children in here to?" he asked.

Ward stepped around him and into the room. It was the main bedroom. Or more precisely, it looked like six bedrooms that had been turned into one giant bedroom. There was an eight foot opening on one side that led into a tiled area. He stepped across the floor and looked inside. There was a long walk-in shower with four separate heads pointing down and a ten foot long glass

shower screen that ran all the way along to the end wall, the only gap being at the nearest end for someone to walk through into the shower. It looked like it belonged in a sport changing room, rather than an exclusive house. Ward stepped back out into the bedroom.
There was another opening to the left and he walked across to it, it was a long walk-in dressing room. There were rows and rows of suits all hung up on hangers, nearly all of them black, and below them, at least twenty pairs of highly polished black shoes. On the opposite side, there were rows of white shirts and ties.
At the far end, a giant double mirror, where Reid no doubt told himself how great he looked every morning. He stepped out back into the bedroom. The bed was huge, at least twelve feet wide and fifteen feet long, a pale quilt adorned it and there were at least ten pillows at the end of the bed.
Wallace walked into the room and said,
"We were never here."
Ward looked at McDermott and said,
"All we have to do now is wait. The Optician will call as soon as he turns up. But be prepared, we could be waiting for a good few hours yet."

As it was, they only had to wait for an hour and twenty minutes. The Optician called Ward and simply said,
"He's here. He's got out of the car on his own and they have now driven off. He's all yours," and then the line went dead.
Ward, McDermott and the team had all converged on the spare room adjacent to the master bedroom. They were silent as they listened to Reid finishing a phone call with

someone and then heard him whistling as he walked into the master bedroom. A minute later, they heard the shower come on and thirty seconds after that, they heard Reid singing an out of tune rendition of 'My Way' as he stepped into the shower.

Ward opened the door to the spare room, stepped out into the hallway and then along to the master bedroom. The others followed.

Reid was under the middle two shower heads, with shampoo in his hair and his back to him, as Ward stepped into the bathroom. They all followed him into the bathroom. Reid appropriately sang the words, "And now, the end is near" for the fifth time as he turned around to face the glass wall and opened his eyes.

Then he stopped singing immediately.

And he jumped back in surprise.

Because on the other side of the glass, he saw nine men standing there.

All nine of them looked like killers and possessed that look that only real killers have.

Then the one in the middle smiled at him.

And he knew instantly that he was the British guy who had been the architect of his downfall, despite the fact that he did not have bleached blonde hair.

Fuller reached in behind the glass and turned off the shower and then stepped back out.

The noise of the water disappeared and Reid backed up against the shower wall, getting as far away from the glass as he could.

"You look even grosser in the flesh than you do in your videos," Ward said to him.

Reid said nothing, he was still pushed hard back against the tiles at the back of the shower.

"Your tough guys are all dead. It took no more than twenty seconds to eliminate them. I told you that we were untouchable."

Reid still said nothing, his face went crimson red, Ward was not sure if it was the heat of the water that had caused it or that Reid was on the verge of an impending heart attack. He didn't care which one.

"Get out of the shower now," he said, using his Glock to point Reid in the direction of the access point to the shower.

Reid stepped to the right and walked out of the shower.

"Why do all fat guys have small dicks?" Buck asked Reid innocently.

McDermott and his team all laughed.

Reid reached out to grab a towel to protect his modesty and Wired slapped him hard in the centre of his naked back with the flat of his hand. Reid jumped and Wired then pushed him hard, out into the master bedroom.

"Sit!" Ward said pointing to an expensive looking armchair.

Reid sat down.

"You never should have gone after my friends."

"I'm sorry," Reid replied, "I won't ever go after them again"

"No you won't. Tell me, why do you think it is acceptable to abuse children as you do?" he asked.

Reid looked at the floor.

"It's no good trying your politician crap with me. People don't believe you parasites anymore. The world has changed. Social media is king now, people talk to each

other. So forget trying to look remorseful and ashamed, I won't buy it. So tell me, do you think it is acceptable to abuse children in the way that you do?"
Reid studied Ward for a moment, trying to gauge what he had in store for him, but as soon as he looked into Ward's eyes, he looked away.
They frightened him.
"No I don't," Reid quietly said.
"Louder!" Ward demanded as he moved to within three feet of where Reid was sitting.
"No I don't," he repeated, much louder this time.
Ward unleashed a lightening quick jab to the bridge of Reid's nose with his right fist, forcing his head back hard against the back of the armchair. He immediately brought both of his hands up to his nose.
"I like inflicting pain on people like you. Does that make me like you?"
Reid said nothing.
Ward slapped him hard around the left side of the face.
"Answer me fatso?" he demanded.
Reid shook his head.
"That's right. We are nothing like each other," he replied, "You've got two minutes to convince me why I shouldn't kill you. Go!"
He looked up at Ward and saw a seven foot giant standing over him pointing a gun at him. But once a politician, always a politician, and so he began,
"My daddy was strict with me growing up and he used to beat me if I did something wrong or my grades slipped. I was abused myself and it clouded my judgement of what abuse is. I associated violence with a form of love and I don't know how to express myself any other way. I'm

sick, I realise that and I know I need help and I will get help," Reid replied, his voice growing in confidence and expression the longer he spoke.
And what he had just heard was every reason why Ward hated politicians. Asking for sympathy and forgiveness, none of it was his fault, he was sick. The same old story had been heard from every politician caught with his pants down throughout history.
"You know that I have been authorised to kill you by the Vice President. So he gets away with everything and here we are with you. Life's a bitch isn't it fatso?"
"I can pay money. Help you bring down the Vice President, please, don't kill me," Reid begged. And then he started crying. Not a few tears due to the realisation that he was in deep trouble, but sobbing, loudly.
Crying like the poor children had been sobbing in the videos that they had watched.
Ward had so much that he wanted to say to Reid but the sight of him was making him feel sick, he wanted him dead.

Senator Madison Reid did not live long enough to see his next birthday. He died in the most unimaginable and grotesque pain. Nine men took turns to break every bone in his body apart from his ribs. They didn't want his heart punctured. They kept reviving him when he drifted into unconsciousness by pouring vodka into his nostrils and down his throat. When he wanted to close his eyes, they poured salt into them. They used pliers to pull out all of his front teeth and his fingernails. When his body started to adjust to the pain and they were out of vodka, to revive him, they used an adjustable spanner to crush his testicles until he was alert again. The last act, the one that killed him, was the important and symbolic act to them. They cut off his genitals and ripped open his stomach, placing the severed genitals inside of him and then they watched him bleed to death.

Senator Madison Reid died in exactly the way that he deserved to die.

FORTY FIVE

Merrifield

They arrived back at the warehouse, and the first thing Ward saw was Lawson in the driver seat of a black Sedan. The back door of the Sedan opened as they drove into the warehouse and Nicole-Louise stepped out, a beaming smile on her face. The Range Rovers pulled to a stop inside and Ward stepped out, just as Lawson and Tackler were walking into the main warehouse.
"Hey Mike," he said, extending his hand out for Lawson to shake.
"You owe me big time," Lawson said, "Having to have sex with the same woman four nights on the trot…" he added, rolling his eyes in disgust as he said it.
Ward laughed, within five seconds he had remembered why he found Lawson so endearing.
Nicole-Louise walked over to him and gave him a big hug, she squeezed him tightly.
"Did you finish everything?" she asked.
"Everything is OK now and no one will ever try and hurt you again, I promise."
"I know. I trust you."

Lawson walked across to McDermott and his team and shook each of their hands individually. Within thirty seconds they were all laughing; no doubt Lawson was still complaining about his lack of different sexual partners.
Ward noticed Buck, sitting down on the sofa.
"Hey Mike," he shouted across to Lawson, "Come over here and meet Buck."
Lawson moved back over towards the sofa and Buck stood up and extended his hand. Lawson shook it firmly and Ward watched as Buck did a double check on Lawson's eyes.
"Buck is a good man and he has been a big help to us," Ward said, "I like him."
"Then I like you too," Lawson said and Buck laughed.
Tackler walked across to Ward.
"Can I talk to you a minute? In private?" he asked.
"Sure," Ward replied and headed towards the reception area, he stepped in, holding the door open for Tackler who followed him in and closed the door.
"Everything OK?" he asked.
"Firstly, I have all that stuff you wanted on Tom Bass and tomorrow afternoon I am meeting up with someone on the dark web who can arrange a meeting for you, so I have made good progress on that," Tackler said.
"Thanks Tackler, I'll get you back to New York this evening and I'll be at yours tomorrow afternoon."
"One other thing" Tackler said.
"What?"
"That other stuff I did for you," he said, "Does he know about it yet?"
"Yes he does, I have spoken to him about it."

"And he was OK with it?"
"Yes he was."
"So he won't try and kill me?"
Ward laughed. He could imagine Tackler being terrified that he had upset The Optician.
"He is very, very grateful to you," Ward said, "We all are. Not just for that but for everything you do. I've felt a little vulnerable myself not having your support through this mission."
"Honestly?" Tackler asked in surprise.
"Completely," Ward replied, "You and Nicole-Louise are the most important people on our team, I tell you that all the time."
Tackler's chest expanded and he grew at least another two inches.
"How did you get on with Lawson?" he asked, thinking back to Tackler's dislike of Lawson in New York.
"He's a great guy," Tackler replied, "I was so wrong about him. He's so in love with Laura, she never left his side. Honestly, I've never seen a guy so devoted to a woman."
Ward smiled.
Lawson was a total one-off.
"So everything is cool with him?" Tackler asked, seeking confirmation one more time that The Optician was in fact, not going to kill him.
"I guarantee it. Just don't ever mention it to anyone."
"I've deleted all history of searches and everything. But I know his real name if you want to …"
"No I don't Tackler, I made him a promise. Go and tell Nicole-Louise we will be heading back to New York in an hour and she is to call The Old Man to get him to

make arrangements for the flight," he said, as he opened the door to let Tackler out.

Tackler stepped out of the reception area and Ward shouted,

"McDermott, Mike, have you got a minute?"

They both nodded and walked towards him, McDermott walking away from loading the Range Rover and Lawson breaking away from McDermott's team, who were all laughing at his stories once again.

"Everything alright?" McDermott asked as he stepped through the door.

"Mike, close the door," he said to Lawson as he stepped in, "What did you do with Yana?" he asked.

"She is in a foster home in a little village about twenty miles from Brighton," Lawson replied.

"Her cover story?"

"No one will ever trace her. She was given an authentic Russian name that even I can't pronounce, and her paperwork has all been verified by the home office, so no one will ever find her."

"But you know where she is?" McDermott asked.

"Yes. I will make sure that she is checked regularly without her knowing," Lawson replied.

McDermott and Ward both nodded their approval at the same time.

"And the other stuff. The videos, did you look at them?" Ward asked.

"Of course I did," Lawson replied.

"And?"

"You killed the two Senators I hope?"

McDermott and Ward nodded.

"But the VP is of limits I assume?"

"Yes," Ward replied, "But he's given The Old Man special powers to pretty much authorise us to do whatever we want without permission."

"Awesome," Lawson replied, "So when can I move to The States?"

"Do you want to?"

"There has to be at least twenty million women between the ages of twenty five and thirty five here. What do you think?"

Ward laughed again.

"But I really do Ryan. I feel hopeless sitting three thousand miles away while you run around saving the world."

"I'll talk to The Old Man; see if he can arrange it. Deal?"

"Deal!" Lawson replied.

"One last thing?" Ward said.

"What?"

"Where is the evidence now?"

"Somewhere very, very safe."

"How safe?"

"Probably the safest place on the planet," Lawson replied.

"I'm no good at guessing Mike; help me out a bit here?"

"If you had to think of one place in England that you wouldn't want to break into, what would you say?" Lawson asked.

"Buckingham Palace, Downing Street, your wallet?" Ward replied.

McDermott laughed.

"What about you McDermott. You are a fighting man, where is the one place in England even you wouldn't risk taking your boys into?" Lawson asked.

"The suspense is killing me, just tell me?" Ward said sarcastically.

McDermott smiled.

"I could think of only one place that I wouldn't even consider going near, and I know that is where you have it. Clever Lawson," McDermott said.

Lawson smiled.

"I'm either extremely tired or extremely dumb. Where is it Mike?" Ward asked impatiently.

"I've secured it in the SAS barracks in Hereford. My Brother is keeping it safe there. As Ex-SAS, I have the right forever to use their safes and lockers," Lawson replied.

"Why do they have safes and lockers?" Ward asked.

"It's a safe place to hide all the secrets that we steal from foreign governments. It's our security."

Ward smiled.

He knew, without doubt, that the evidence was safe.

He walked back into the main warehouse.

"The jet is waiting at the airport, we can go as soon as we are ready," Tackler said, "There will be a car waiting to collect us."

Ward looked at Lawson,

"Fancy helping me off the books in Colorado for a day or two?" he asked.

"If it keeps me from seeing Laura's miserable face, definitely," Lawson replied.

Tackler gave him an odd look.

Ward turned and looked at McDermott.

"Have a few days off and spend some of your well earned money," he said to him, "Maybe buy another couple of Range Rovers or warehouses."

"I'm going to take the boys back to California and then maybe up to Las Vegas, let them have a blow out for a few days. No doubt you'll be back in touch soon," McDermott replied, and he leant in and hugged Ward.

Ward then walked around to all of McDermott's team individually and shook hands and hugged them. They were incredible human beings, he thought to himself. Lethal killers with decency ingrained in all of them.
He moved over to Buck and extended his hand,
"Thanks for everything Colin."
Buck shook his hand.
"I'll talk to The Old Man about you and your availability, I'd like you on the team more often," he said.
"I'm not sure his lot do," he said, pointing at McDermott, "And no way am I sleeping in the car," he added,
Everyone in the room laughed.
Everyone liked Buck.

Ward had one more call to make.
He dialled The Opticians number.
"We are heading back to New York now," he said as he answered.
"OK. I'll meet you there."
"Thanks for everything my friend and especially for protecting Nicole-Louise and Tackler."
"They are good kids."
"And Tackler has destroyed any trace of your family and the money so I am still completely unaware of who you are. As I said, I always keep my word," he added.

"I've never told anyone the things I told you," The Optician said.
"And I will never repeat a word of it. I promise."
The line went dead.

Twenty minutes later, Ward was in the car with Lawson, Tackler and Nicole-Louise, on their way to Dulles Airport, to catch the jet back to New York.
"How many other politicians do you think are involved in stuff like that?" Nicole-Louise asked.
"Way too many. But one is too many," Ward replied.
There was no great sense of achievement in this mission for anyone. The children had still suffered horrendous abuse, no matter what punishment had been handed out. Ward felt flat, his only comfort being witness to the pain and suffering that Calvinson and Reid had endured in the last moments of their vile lives.
They reached the airport and Lawson drove straight through the back entrance towards the aircraft hangers. The Old Man had arranged for the jet to be ready and Lawson drove straight up to it, stopping twenty feet short of the steps.
They all climbed out of the car and onto the jet, where they were greeted by a different young woman in her late twenties. She did a double check on Lawson's eyes and then smiled a flirtatious smile at him; he extended his hand and shook it softly. She blushed.
Tackler looked totally confused.
They sat down in the comfortable, leather chairs.
It was the first time that Ward had relaxed properly in days. He exhaled deeply, tilted his head back and closed his eyes.

Nicole-Louise and Tackler did the same.
Lawson caught the attention of the stewardess and then nodded towards the bathroom.
She smiled and winked at him.
Five minutes later, they were airborne.
Ward was glad to see the back of Washington. He hated the place and he hated the immoral, deceitful, self-important people who descended upon it.
He pictured Eloisa and started to think of a new life in twelve months' time.

The pilot swung around and looked across to his co-pilot and informed him that they would be landing in just over an hour.
The co-pilot nodded
The co-pilot couldn't even fly.
The Optician was doing what he always did.
He was staying close to Ryan Ward.
Keeping him safe.

Part Three

Invincible

Maggie Davenport had twenty nine minutes left to live. She put her eighteen month old son, Troy, down in his filthy cot. He had not stopped crying for the past five hours. Maggie was uneducated and lived in a dirty apartment block in Queens, which social services had provided her with to get her off the streets. She had been raped nine months ago by four men, and exactly nine months later, Troy had been born. She tried so hard to see him as the one good thing in her life, but with each day that passed, she felt more and more trapped by him because he acted as a constant reminder of how worthless her life was. Troy had now become her prison, and there was no escape for people like Maggie.

Until now.

The Columbian guy who regularly walked the halls of her apartment building had seen her looking exhausted and unkempt, and asked her if she wanted to escape from her tiredness and destitution for once, before telling her that he could offer her the feeling of joy and pleasure that everyone who was the target of her envy regularly felt. He explained to her that he had a pill that would take her to a place where she would be like them. He said it would make her feel alive and free, and she could run to wherever her fantasies wanted to take her. She had immediately invited him into her filthy apartment.

She asked what the pill was called. He replied with one word.

Invincible

She put the pill in her mouth and within four confusing minutes, her world changed. Warmth and joy rushed through her frail body. She saw sunshine and open fields, and then a moment later, she was in a big house with a grand swimming pool in the garden, and all of her old school friends were lined up, sitting on a garden wall, looking at her with envy. The one great love of her life, Aaron Wisley, was there too, looking at her with such desire that her whole body longed for his touch. She savoured the way her life could have been, engulfed by the dreams that she had always dared not to believe in, but longed for to come true. And right then, she genuinely felt that she was living that life. This vision, this reality, was heaven. It lasted for twenty five minutes.

And then everything changed.

All of a sudden, she couldn't breathe. She felt a searing pain shooting through her chest, and she pulled at the tee shirt covering her breasts, trying to get air to her body and her lungs. Then she fell to the floor and her visions changed. All of her old friends, who had looked at her with such envy, were now laughing at her. She saw Troy open his arms wide for her to pick him up. And then everything went dark.

The Columbian guy took out his cell phone and called Miami,

"Twenty nine minutes," he said into the phone and then hung up.

He stood up, looked at Troy crying in the cot, walked over to him, and smothered him with a dirty, stained blanket until he stopped crying. He didn't want the cops being called by the neighbours sick of hearing a child screaming.
He walked back across the dirty carpet, stepped over Maggie's lifeless body and walked out of the apartment.

In Miami, the guy who had received the phone call looked out over his vast, immaculate grounds and dialled a number on his cell phone. He exchanged no pleasantries with whoever answered, he simply said, "Everything had better be ready. I want them all there by tomorrow evening, all thirty one of them. If you fail me, your whole family will be dead by midnight tomorrow," he then hung up.

He was sure the guy would not fail him. Just as sure as he knew that he was going to unlock the secret to running the most powerful drug cartel the world had ever known.

Printed in Great Britain
by Amazon